The Irish Goodbye
A Novel

George J. Hawkins

Dedicated to
Don Rothman
R.I.P.

1

Johnny Russian

Saturday Morning. After breakfast with his mother, Rita, seventh-grader Brian Reilly raced down the stairs to the front porch, stopping briefly at the top step to tighten the laces of his new Converse All Star sneakers, a special birthday present from his father. Taken from the box they had been stored in out into the sunlight, the sneakers glowed shiny white. Spread out before him in the morning sun was an exciting new world of summer vacation on Partridge Street.

He looked across the street at a house similar in design and paint scheme to the home where he and his mother and father lived. The sweep of his blue eyes came to rest on a two-family home occupied by the Maguires on the lower level and the McNallys on the second floor. To the right of the Maguire/McNally residence was another two-family home occupied by childless older couples; therefore out of Brian's scope of interest. To the left was the single family home of the Gardner sisters, Samantha and Agatha, two sibling spinsters who were forever bursting from their front door to threaten, scold, and chastise youthful miscreants running across their anemic front lawn, or, worse yet, riding bicycles roughshod across the trampled greensward.

Pausing, he looked up and down the street for the Freihoffer bread wagon pulled by a brown horse that eagerly accepted handfuls of grass pulled from the Gardner sisters' ever diminishing lawn. Not seeing the horse and wagon, Brian leaped the several steps to the sidewalk, where he sprang into the air to propel an imaginary basketball into an imaginary hoop. He pulled down his frayed and faded Giants baseball cap, a souvenir from last summer's trip to the Polo Grounds with his father, then bolted across the street at full speed, a velocity matched only by those lucky few whose feet were propelled by Converse All Stars. He came to an abrupt stop on the front porch of the house where his best friend and classmate Bobby McNally lived. The boys were on the tantalizing precipice of a three-month hiatus from Saint John Catholic grade school. Perhaps of equal importance, they had a full calendar of Little League baseball ahead of them.

He pushed open the door that allowed him entrance to the staircase leading up to the McNally residence, where a brood of six boys kept their mother bustling throughout the day and most of the night. After a precautionary knock on the door, Brian strode eagerly down the hallway to the kitchen where a chorus of shouts and yells, laced with explosions of laughter, erupted. In the background could be heard the gentle, nurturing voice of Mrs. McNally feeding her small army of ravenous boys. Brian recalled his mother commenting on what a cruel act of nature it would be if perchance a baby girl were ever born into the McNally clan, a comment Brian had never comprehended.

The absence of Mr. McNally at these familiar morning gatherings was possibly due to an early work schedule or, more likely, a way of escaping the chaotic breakfast hour. Brian usually observed Mr. McNally on weekends, when his corpulent frame occupied a worn easy chair in the living room. In the morning hours, a cup of coffee was seen on a chair-side table. In the evening, the coffee cup was replaced by a large pilsner glass and quart bottle of Schafer beer. The elusive patriarch was always concealed behind the pages of either the morning or evening newspaper, from which a telltale ribbon of cigar smoke spiraled up to the ceiling.

Mrs. McNally noted Brian's appearance with a smile, while the boys did so with waves and shouts. Bobby dutifully moved his chair next to his older brother Greg so that Brian could squeeze into the narrow space at the table, where boxes of cereal stood open with trails of their contents meandering toward numerous cereal bowls. Of interest to Brian were three open boxes of *Wheaties*, the *breakfast of champions*, each with an illustration of the sports world's reigning celebrity.

"Morning Brian, how's your Ma?" Mrs. McNally asked, lips pursed, as she placed a bowl in front of him while cradling one-year-old Connor on a narrow hip.

"She said to tell you she'll stop by this afternoon," Brian said while reaching for the Willie Mays cereal box.

"Did she see Dr. McCann yet?"

"Gee, I don't know."

Bobby looked up from his cereal to playfully punch Brian in the arm. To his left, brother Greg, captain of the high school baseball team, was engrossed in the morning sports page. Across from him, twins Dylan and Dermot wrestled each other until the contents of a glass of milk was overturned, sending a white stream of liquid soaking into clumps and trails of spilled cereal. The baby, now incarcerated in his high chair, peered down at his siblings. Scowling vehemently at the two offenders, Mrs. McNally made the necessary repairs. With a fist planted deep in his gaping maw, Connor apparently intuited the forthcoming inequities and outrages he would suffer as the youngest member of this rowdy male tribe. His exuberant screech of alarm momentarily captured the undivided attention of those encircling the breakfast table.

The mess mopped up, a heaping plate of buttered toast no sooner hit the tabletop than five eager hands sprang forth like the supple arms of a giant squid to instantly reduce the mound of toast to a single piece, which Brian managed to secure. A minor skirmish ensued as the same hands attacked the lone jar of strawberry jam, which was seized, as usual, by Greg. Following some ancient, unspoken tribal pecking order, the jam jar was passed to Bobby, and so on, until the empty glass vessel came to rest on the table near Sean, the second youngest McNally.

Greg finally folded the sports page, passed it to Bobby, and began rising from his chair. Taking their cue, his brothers began pushing cereal bowls and crusts of toast away. All the fleeing boys managed a clean exit, save Dermot, who was collared by his mother and gently reminded that it was his turn to clear the table and stack dirty dishes in the sink. Always a volunteer to whatever punishment or adventure his twin brother was engaged in, brother Dylan pitched in to help.

Brian and Bobby made their way down the backporch steps to a yard that could be generously characterized as an eyesore, what with its dearth of grass, shrubs and flowers. The clumps and clods of dirt and holes of various depths and diameters met the jaundiced eye of the rent collector on his monthly visit. Regardless, this miniature village green had, over the years, born witness to a roster of youthful activities, to include: cowboys and Indians, football, baseball, wrestling, water balloon fights—these during the clement months. In winter, when snow piled high inside the backyard fences, full-scale snowball battles were punctuated with ice-skating and hockey—all this, in an improvised sports arena of no more than six hundred square feet!

Is it any wonder the backyard was less than pleasing to the eye? However earnestly one could critique its shoddy appearance, one could also argue, with much credibility, that it had provided endless hours of wholesome physical activity to a legion of growing, mischievous boys, who cared little for neatly trimmed lawns or eye-catching flower gardens.

If disputes arose or injuries occurred, Mrs. McNally could be counted on to fill the void of referee, coach, or nurse, and, if necessary, even expel transgressors from the venue.

Leaping down from the Maguire back porch railing to the mutilated sod, the boys pretended to parachute from an airship into enemy territory. They landed with a forward roll then sprang like circus acrobats to their feet. Running in a crouched, weaving stance, they came to a stop at the back fence, their stealthy maneuvering accomplished in silence. Bobby turned an anxious eye to the upper regions of his home to insure no inquiring adult eyes were observing him and his friend. Unknown to either commando, of course, one of the Gardner sisters, stationed in her second story bedroom, was cataloguing every detail of their secret mission into enemy territory and would report it forthwith to Mrs. McNally, who would just as quickly banish it from her mind.

The two boys scurried to the upper reaches of the solitary chestnut tree, whose spiked fruit yielded the threefold bounty of food, ammunition, and barter. Though scarred and defaced, the tree limbs had somehow survived the perennial onslaught of youthful gymnastics. Here among the branches and leaves, they made a thorough visual reconnaissance of the acreage beyond the fence with its prolific gardens, flowerbeds, pruned orchard, grapevines and vast unspoiled fields of grass upon which goats were tethered. In this land of milk and honey was a three-story wood-frame building (painted battleship grey with war surplus paint) with a spacious veranda making a semi-circle around the sagging structure known to local youths as the Jewish Rest Home, or, more colloquially, as the *Jews Yard*.

Both young fellows scanned the premises, scouting for the much maligned and misunderstood caretaker whom the boys called *Johnny Russian* or, less formally, *Squirrel*. Through innuendo, gossip, hearsay, and insinuation, the boys had cobbled together their archenemy's colorful dossier.

It was indeed a fact that Squirrel was a Russian émigré who had survived the World War II Battle of Berlin. A member of the Red army, he had fought Nazi SS soldiers in hand-to-hand combat in the Third Reich's Headquarters, reduced to rubble in the wake of repeated bombardments by Russian and U.S. Army artillery batteries. According to neighborhood folklore, amplified with every telling, Johnny Russian was the sole survivor of his infantry unit. Out of ammunition, he had been reduced to fighting for his life with a bayonet, which, according to the boys, became so soaked with Nazi blood it finally slipped from his hands and was lost. Hurling paving stones with bloody fists, he continued the battle. When allied forces finally marched into the bombed out city, a U.S. Army infantry squad had found what they thought was a shallow grave, but, upon investigation, discovered a Red Army soldier whose body had been stripped of most of its uniform and all of its identification. Despite the victim's multiple gunshot wounds and numerous knife slashes, from head to toe, a medic had detected a feeble pulse. Stretcher-bearers transported the Russian soldier to an aid station, where a small harried staff of doctors, calculating his chances of survival as minimal, performed basic first aid then evacuated him to a U.S. Army field hospital in Berlin's American sector. A team of surgeons performed extensive operations to include emergency brain surgery to remove bullet fragments lodged in the cerebral cortex. The improvised procedure left a grotesque scar running from ear to ear across his shaven scalp. Additionally, his left eye had been removed, the empty socket sutured closed with a length of silk thread liberated from a dress shop miraculously untouched by the bombing. Although their patient was still alive after multiple operations, the doctors had guessed, wrongly, that he would soon die.

To expedite paperwork, the clerical staff, lacking any personal identification for him, had listed the patient's name as John Russian. He had been made as comfortable as possible with multiple IV's of morphine and transported, along with dozens of wounded G.I.'s, to a hospital ship off the coast of Italy, eventually finding his circuitous way to Walter Reed Hospital in Washington, D.C.

Here he had received blood transfusions and been weaned off morphine. When the bandages had been removed after many months, Johnny Russian was hideously disfigured, but he was alive. When at last he was able to speak, it was in his native Russian language. Translators had been summoned but reported that the patient merely babbled incoherently. After a consultation with psychiatrists, John Russian had been diagnosed to be a total amnesiac and mentally unstable. Questions put to him in Russian as to his name and home had gone unanswered, so medical staff had continued to document him as Mr. John Russian. In addition to his head wound, missing left eye, and numerous scars on his body, it had been determined that most of his upper lip had to be surgically repaired, the procedure exposing a mangled set of yellowish teeth, mostly chipped and cracked, making a thoroughly unattractive face more menacing. To add insult to extreme injury, the Nazis had ripped out the poor creature's fingernails in a futile attempt to gain intelligence before leaving him for dead.

The reconstructive surgeries had transformed him into an exceptionally brutal-looking fellow whose appearance generally shocked the most thick-skinned nurses seeing him for the first time. Nonetheless, he had begun to recuperate.

The legend also credited the medical staff at a secluded upstate New York sanatorium with performing an experimental craniotomy to drain fluid from his swollen brain. Part of this procedure had reportedly included the installation of a steel plate in his skull where the bullet fragments had entered brain tissue. The plate, surgeons had speculated, could easily be removed if additional surgeries were either necessary or advisable. The neurosurgeons had determined this would reinforce the bone structure surrounding the wound that had not healed as well as they'd hoped. Having no known next of kin and remaining incommunicable, Johnny continued to be classified as "identity unknown."

If he did not survive the trial procedure, well, they'd done their utmost.

Once again Johnny Russian had beat the odds and pulled through, and, once again, a long and unpleasant period of recuperation had ensued. After a year and a half of rehabilitation, special diet, and physical therapy, his doctors determined that the time had come to discharge him. Somewhere in his thick file it was noted that he had never displayed any violent behavior during his many years of treatment and convalescence. The risk to others, they had calculated, was minimal to non-existent.

However, the hospital staff had questioned where he would go and what he would do for a livelihood. Their copious concerns included Johnny's minimal English language skills, mostly limited to requests for food and medications, his anonymity, and his complete lack of family and friends. His health, though good, was marginally sufficient to enable him to live independently. Their quandary was confounded further by the fact that he was an amnesiac. Technically he was both mentally and physically handicapped, but, to his credit, nursing staff observed over an extended period of time that Johnny Russian had two nurturing skills. When he was ambulatory, he labored in the various gardens about the grounds, yielding improvements in the less-than-appealing flora. They had also noticed that he had a keen interest in birdlife, especially that of pigeons. On many occasions, nurses and orderlies had observed him feeding the birds out of his mutilated hands.

Since nothing further could be done to fortify his health, Johnny was scheduled to be discharged. With the help of the Director of the Jewish-Russian Relief organization affiliated with the hospital, a caretaker position was secured for Johnny Russian at a Jewish Rest Home in Albany, New York. It was noted in his file that in-house staff there would monitor his physical and mental health.

Johnny quickly became a favorite of both staff and residents at the rest home. With little encouragement, he resuscitated long neglected flower and vegetable gardens, as well as a small orchard on the grounds. Soon, dining tables, windowsills, and all manner of vases were filled with colorful, aromatic flowers. Meals previously lackluster and boring were supplemented with fresh, nutritious produce. Johnny's labors in garden and orchard were responsible for a colorful cornucopia of vegetables and fruit.

In no time at all, Johnny Russian turned a shabby, nondescript rest home into a visual feast and source of pride to all who lived and worked there. With little encouragement or motivation, save his example and the edibles supplied to their dining table, the residents enthusiastically joined him in toiling in the gardens, which in no small way helped to improve their own health and well-being. Early on, Johnny took a special interest in the flock of pigeons roosting in the heights of an unused barn in back of the rest home. In the months that followed, all, especially the neighborhood boys, observed him training the pigeons to fly down to him from their aerie to receive treats out of his hand. As if by a miracle or dormant spiritual power, a few of the pigeons were seen in flight doing backward somersaults. Overnight, Johnny Russian had become characterized, by most observers, as either magician or devil's disciple.

Tidings of Johnny's special gift with the pigeons spread rapidly through the neighborhoods. Soon, squads of small boys gathered in concealment behind fences or on garage rooftops to witness the spectacle of the tumbling pigeons.

One of the older boys, from a distant city ward, who claimed a flock of pigeons of his own, surmised that the birds at the Jews Home were outcasts and renegades from various flocks around the city. Furthermore, he asserted that some of the pigeons had likely possessed the skill to do backward somersaults before immigrating to the Jews Yard. Then, too, he speculated, rollers were a special breed and must have required expert training. The only way to prove this conjecture was for a few brave souls to sneak into the barn and climb up to the coop where they could inspect the pigeons for ownership bands that would be secured on each pigeon's leg, if indeed they were renegades.

In attendance at this bold pronouncement, Brian and Bobby looked at each other with raised eyebrows.

"That's crazy, only a few guys have ever been up to the pigeon loft," Brian claimed.

"Not only that, if Johnny Russian caught you up there, you'd be trapped. There's no telling what he'd do," added Bobby.

One of the few words that issued from the mouth of Johnny Russian was *Squirrel*, this in a high-pitched hysterical scream that echoed from one end of the Jews Home to the other. He had a deep-seated, unnatural antipathy for the long-tailed rodents that wreaked havoc on his flourishing gardens and orchard. When a miscreant squirrel was spied plundering one of his gardens, he would retaliate by chasing after the interloper with a shovel or axe handle, all the while muttering and cursing incoherently.

Soon this behavior prompted the arrival of small squads of boys lying in wait at various hiding spots about the Jews Yard, eager to provoke Johnny into one of his maniacal seizures. From concealment they would call out *Squirrel* when spying the alienated creature.

Concealed behind fence slats, on garage rooftops, or behind thick tree trunks, the rogues took special care to remain undetected by what they saw as the rampaging "beast" in his pursuit of two-legged rodents.

What child would not run screaming to the protective skirts of its mother upon catching a mere glimpse of the savage? In addition to facial scars, a black patch over the left eye, fingers plucked of their nails, the mutilated upper lip exposing deformed teeth, it was considered gospel truth that a steel plate was embedded in his battered skull. Moreover, part of the folk legend made note of a green liquid that seeped from beneath the black patch concealing the empty eye socket when he was harassed.

Johnny Russian, or "Squirrel" as the youngsters called him, wore the same tattered, ill-fitting, greasy, wardrobe in fair weather or foul. A threadbare blue gabardine sport coat, sleeves riding well above wrists, drew additional attention to his abnormally large hands and missing fingernails. The garment was decorated with colorful stains, rumored to be the gore and bodily fluids of young victims lured into a chamber beneath the Jews Home and where, before flaying them alive and eating their flesh, he tortured them for days. A large safety pin, reputed to be one his many fiendish torture devices secured the suit jacket. A pair of bib overalls was worn in all seasons and weather conditions.

The scar that made a semicircle from ear to ear was covered during inclement weather with an olive drab Army forage cap with flaps that concealed his ears. It was said by our young troopers that his feet were shod in the same scuffed combat boots he had been wearing when American G.I.'s had pulled him, near death, from his makeshift grave in Berlin.

He was no fashion plate to be sure, but he was alive.

With alarming speed, rumors regarding this rampaging, malevolent fiend were created, embroidered, and circulated to neighborhood kids, who passed them on to schoolmates, cousins, and friends in outlying neighborhoods. Eventually, the bolder boys with a penchant for misadventure made pilgrimages to the Jews home to bait the monster with screams of, *Squirrel! Squirrel!* With Johnny in hot pursuit, they would barely escape over fences or onto garage roofs where they would pound each other's back and laugh uproariously.

But woe to the lad who did not escape!

From their observation post high in the chestnut tree, neither boy spied their nemesis, but it was Bobby who spoke first.

"Don't see him, but look at that pear tree, it's loaded with fruit."

"And look at all the pears on the ground. Come on, let's sneak over and get a few"

"Okay, but keep on the lookout," Bobby said.

Climbing stealthily over the back fence they lowered themselves noiselessly to the ground in the Jews yard. To their advantage they had the protection of an extensive vegetable garden that allowed them to crawl unobserved to the pear tree fifty yards distant.

At the base of the fruit tree they momentarily dispensed with their security precautions and began scooping up windfall pears littering the ground. Unable to contain his curiosity any longer, Bobby bit into one of the pieces of fruit, only to instantly spit it out.

"That's terrible," he said.

"Maybe they've gone bad or somethin'," Brian said while pulling pears from the pockets of his jeans.

"You sure these things are ripe? They don't taste ripe to me," said Bobby.

Never willing to admit any purloined fruit was anything but first rate, Brian looked into the upper reaches of the pear tree.

"I'll bet those pears way up there are ripe. Come on, let's climb up and pick a few of those."

"Yeah, they must be better than these," said Bobby.

Hastily, the boys shimmied up the tree trunk to the lower branches that doubled as a convenient ladder to ascend to the highest reaches of the tree where the toothsome fruit they'd spied from below dangled seductively. Slowly and with concentration, the boys began a perilous journey to an outer limb where pears were suspended from the tips of branches. As Brian inched his way precariously outward, the branch began shaking and dipping down, slowing his progress to a snail's pace. Curious about Bobby's progress, but afraid to look in back of him, he focused his attention on the limb he clung to.

While the limb sagged and swayed, Brian clasped the branch with his left hand and reached for a particularly attractive pear with his right. It was at that moment that Bobby chose to yell at the top of his lungs.

"Squirrel! Squirrel!"

With that surprise warning, Brian's entire body went rigid. He grasped the sagging, swaying limb with both hands, praying silently that it would not snap under his weight. Bobby had already achieved the safety of the tree trunk.

"Come on, Brian, he's coming. We gotta get out of here. Hurry."

Unable to turn around, Brian began a slow retreat to the main trunk where his friend waited to help him. Once off his unstable perch, Brian joined Bobby in a quick descent to the ground.

"Come on, come on, he's getting closer," Bobby warned as he dropped to the ground from the lowest tree limb, to be joined there seconds later by Brian.

No sooner had they clamored to their feet, prepared to race to the McNally back fence, than the ragged, panting shadow of Johnny Russian loomed over them. As a mangled hand reached out to grab Brian by the scruff of the neck, both boys leaped away and began sprinting toward Bobby's backyard fence. Perhaps a second or two passed before Squirrel, realizing his hand clutched nothing but air, plodded off in steadfast pursuit. Though he gained slightly on the boys, they reached the fence and vaulted to the top. Clutching the wooden boards, they sprang into the McNally backyard sanctuary. Exhausted and scared, they listened as Squirrel stomped about on the opposite side of the fence, grunting, and smashing the boards with his fist.

2

Mumblety Peg

Turning the corner of the house into the driveway, Brian stopped in his tracks. Before him in all its shiny black metal glory was a police car, a Buick with a large chrome-plated siren perched on the front fender.

Why is that here? Bobby and I didn't do anything wrong, Brian wondered.

He hurried past the prowl car, making his way quickly to the backstairs. Taking a big breath, he exhaled and began climbing the steps in an unusually slow, precise manner all the while juggling thoughts of illicit pears with Johnny Russian in pursuit.

Upon opening the back door leading into the kitchen he was immediately confronted by his parents and his dog Arrow, a 13-year old border collie named after one of his favorite radio show heroes, *Straight Arrow.* His father was seated at the kitchen table finishing a cup of coffee. Beside his cup was his gray fedora hat. His blue suit jacket swung open to reveal the leather straps that secured his snubnosed .38 in a shoulder holster. He was a detective on the city police force. In his blue suit and gray hat, Brian thought his father appeared twice as tall as his 6'2" frame. Though baptized George, his family and friends called him Chick, as he was the youngest in an Irish family of ten.

"Hi, Sport, come on sit down, have some lunch. What have you been up to this morning?"

Reassured Brian was home, Arrow's head dropped to his paws, eyes fixed on his master.

Brian looked cautiously at his father before he answered.

"Just playing some catch in Bobby's backyard."

Rita, standing beside the table, an apron covering her dress, put a hand on his shoulder as he slipped into a chair opposite his father. With a practiced maneuver she removed his baseball cap and hung it on the side of his chair.

"Here, honey, take this sandwich. I'll make another for myself. Go ahead," she said, pushing the small plate with a bologna sandwich in front of Brian, followed shortly by a glass of milk.

"Thanks, Ma."

"Hey, that's right, this is your first day of vacation, huh? I'll bet you and Bobby have been running wild," his father said with a smile.

Taking a huge bite from one half of the sandwich, Brian felt his father's eyes lingering on him. He swallowed quickly, gulped down some milk and looked up skeptically at his father.

"Just playing pitch and catch. We have little league practice tonight."

"That reminds me, I have a present for you," his father said, reaching beside him for a baseball bat propped against the wall.

"Sid Alomar, the manager of the Senators gave this to me. Told me it was one of the left fielder's bats, Jackie…"

Out of his chair and standing beside the bat, Brian blurted out, "Hart, the Senators' home run slugger."

Never one to be left out of Brian's enthusiasm, Arrow, limping slightly, moved quickly to his side and brushed his muzzle against Brian's leg.

Before Brian could snatch the bat from his father's grip, his mother escorted him back to his uneaten sandwich half. This accomplished, she retrieved the bat and placed it against the wall.

"Kind of heavy for you now, but you can use it in practice, get a feel for it," his father said rising from his seat and securing the fedora on his head.

"Say, you kids better stay away from the Jews yard. Old Mr. Rubenstein called the station house complaining again. Hope it's not that Parker kid and his pals. You stay away from them; they're a bunch of rotten apples."

Brian looked sheepishly at his father, who stooped to kiss his wife on the cheek.

"Sure. Thanks for the bat. I'll try it out at this afternoon's practice.

Buttoning his coat as he moved past his son, Chic ran a hand over Brian's recent brush cut, also noticing a few incipient hairs on his upper lip.

"Dad, turn the siren on when you leave, would you, please?"

"Sure just for a second, don't want to frighten the neighbors."

After stuffing the other half of his sandwich in his mouth, Brian ran to his bedroom, grabbing the bat from its resting place on the way. From the window looking down into the dirt and cinder driveway, he watched his father get behind the wheel of the prowl car. Soon the engine started and with that the growling siren reverberated briefly in the driveway.

Back in the kitchen, Brian knelt beside his dog and petted him.

"Honey, take Arrow out for his walk. He's been waiting on you all morning. Please."

"Sure, Ma." Brian said as he snatched his ball cap from the kitchen chair.

As if fluent in the English language or at least with certain words like walk, food, water, Arrow sprang up, tail wagging, tongue swishing back and forth in anticipation. The back door being pulled open by his master, the dog rushed out and down the back steps. Gone now was any evidence of that sluggish hindquarter. Watching them descend the backstairs, Rita Reilly's forehead wrinkled with concern. She hesitated briefly before closing the door.

At the bottom of the backstairs, Brian looked away when Arrow circled his favorite telephone pole, then shortly rejoined him to peer into the car garages that stretched across the back of the property. Giving the dog a quick pat on the head, Brian started down the wide driveway to the street. At the curb, he saw the familiar black and yellow Freihoffer Bakery wagon parked under an oak tree across the street. Waiting patiently between the traces, with blinders obstructing its peripheral vision, was the huge brown horse that pulled the wagon.

Brian started to jog slowly across the street with Arrow at his heels. Alongside the horse, Brian patted him heartily on the shoulder. Feeling momentarily abandoned, the dog curled up at the base of a nearby tree. While petting and fussing with the horse, he heard a door slam and looked up to see Bobby jumping down from the front porch. Bobby joined his friend at the delivery wagon.

"Hey, let's feed him some grass," Brian suggested.

"Yeah, but I don't think we better pull any from old lady Gardner's lawn. She'll get real mad," Bobby warned.

"Okay, how about the grass between your house and the Schermerhorn's?"

"Good idea. Let's go."

Arrow raised his head to watch the two boys run up a sloping lawn and disappear in the shadows between two houses, then gave a tentative look at the large animal nearby. Satisfied it was no longer encroaching on his rightful affections, Arrow laid his head on his outstretched paws and closed his eyes. No sooner were the eyelids closed than the two boys came gamboling back to the horse's side with handfuls of freshly plucked grass. Alerted, Arrow opened a heavy-lidded eye.

Watching Bobby raise a fist of grass to the horse's saliva-dripping mouth, Brian stared at the animal's large nostrils with lengthy hairs jutting from them. His attention was then attracted to the large white teeth that mashed the proffered grass into a greenish slime before disappearing into the horse's cavernous throat. Brian extended his hand, clutching his offering with trepidation. When Bobby stepped aside, he guided his fist to the horse's mouth slowly and with much care so as not to frighten the beast. As soon as the slimy teeth caught hold of the grass, Brian pulled his hand safely aside.

"What do you two jerks think you're doing?"

Both boys turned simultaneously to see Gordy Parker and Mickey Delaney standing behind them.

"Feeding the horse; what's it look like?" Bobby retorted.

Parker, a blond, curly-haired eighth grader with a reputation for roughhousing and vandalism, was both feared and respected by neighborhood kids because his father was the leader of the local Boy Scout troop. No one wanted to incur the Scout Master's displeasure, since he dispensed merit badges and took his troop on campouts to the mountains.

It was said that, if you saw Parker, Delaney was not far behind. Pete and repeat, Brian's father disparagingly called the pair. Both boys shared a talent for encouraging the wrath of teachers, parents, and not a few neighborhood residents. Though Gordy's father was a taskmaster with his scouts, he never found fault with his only son. Tall and physically fit, Gordy showed no interest in athletics, a deficiency that made him more of a rebel to neighborhood boys.

A freckled redhead, Delaney was the same age as his friend, Gordy. He showed great talent as a shortstop, but, because of nefarious activities—on the field and off, was restricted from playing regularly on a team. His parent, a single mother, with two other children, often threatened to put him in the Christian Brothers Boys Home on Western Avenue, an institution whose notorious reputation was used by parents to encourage good grades, clean dinner plates, and empty milk glasses.

Parker pulled a large jackknife from a dungaree pocket. With a flick of his wrist the large, shiny blade snapped in place. Seeing the pointed blade, Brian and Bobby took a step backward.

"Come on horse lovers, let's play some mumblety peg? Loser roots for the peg."

Brian looked at Bobby, to find him smiling and nodding his head. All four youngsters then trooped to the grassy area between the two houses. Sitting on the ground in a wide circle, the boys withdrew jackknives from their pockets and made practice throws, flipping their knives and watching the blades stick into the sod at their feet. The longest blade of his three-blade jackknife pulled open, Brian threw it into the air, flipping it high above his head.

Parker eyed Bobby and Brian, looking for flaws in their technique. Finding none, he threw his longest blade into the center of the circle.

"We're going to use my knife, so everything is 'even-Stephen,'" Parker said.

Since Brian and Bobby had passed many an uneventful afternoon refining their skills at mumblety peg under the watchful eye of Bobby's brother, Greg, neither boy was intimidated by Parker's bluster.

"Sure, let's throw fingers to see who goes first," said Bobby.

"I'm going first, Mickey is second, and you chumps can figure out who goes next," Parker commanded grabbing his knife, "and remember—loser roots."

With that, Gordy Parker pulled his jackknife from the ground. Standing now with his legs spread, he placed the knife on his right fist, resting on top of his closed fingers, blade pointing out. With a flick of the wrist the knife performed a semi-circle in the air, the blade tip barely penetrating the ground at an extreme angle.

"Two fingers," Bobby challenged.

Mickey Delaney quickly reached out, grabbed the knife and handed it to his friend.

"That was fair and square; you wanna' make something of it?"

"No two fingers could have squeezed under that blade," Bobby said.

"Yeah, that's right," added Brian.

Delaney rose to a standing position. "Who says?"

"I says," Bobby snapped, getting to his feet.

"Alright, girls, just lay off, lay off. Let's get this game going again," Parker spat, laying the knife on his left fist, then flipping the blade in a near perfect move. The blade plunged straight into the ground.

Smiling with satisfaction, Gordy retrieved the knife, held it between the thumb and index finger of his right hand, chest high, then flipped it so it made one complete turn in the air and again hit the earth blade tip first. He then proceeded to the next movement.

Brian and Bobby watched with increasing anxiety and diminishing hope as Parker executed trick after trick with speed and flawless technique. At last, Parker advanced to the twenty-third of twenty-four innings in the game. Kneeling on the ground with his back to the circle, he held the tip of the knife blade against his forehead, dropped his head slowly to his chest and snapped his head back, letting the knife loose at the same time. The jackknife spun in the air four times before coming to rest with the blade sticking in the ground at an angle. Bobby quickly jumped forward placing two fingers, one on top of the other, between the blade and the ground to insure it was a fair throw. Parker, grinning with confidence, proceeded with the final stunt.

"Come on, Gordy, plow the field, plow the field, show these squirts how it's done," Delaney said.

Parker slipped the palm of his hand under the angled knife, still stuck in the sod, then with a flick of the wrist sent the jackknife spinning in the air several times, coming to rest with the blade cutting the ground in a perfectly executed throw.

With a great show of bravado and bluster, Parker got to his feet and passed the knife to his eager companion.

With speed and polish, Mickey Delaney proceeded to run the twenty-four-step routine in record time without a single gaff. After a pat on the back from Parker, he passed the blade to Bobby.

"Beat that, kid. Not on your best day," Delaney challenged.

With his usual intensity and focus, Bobby also ran the routine. Handing the knife to Brian, he said, "Let's show them who the champs are, come on Brian."

With that, Brian picked up from where he had stumbled in the first round. His twenty-third inning ended with the blade angled slightly in the sod. He prepared to *plow the field*, perhaps the most difficult trick, but, as he reached for his knife, Parker pulled the blade from the earth.

"That ain't two-fingers, that's a foul, so you lose. Time to root for the peg."

Before he could object, Parker began to shout.

"Come on, come on, loser, time to root," Parker said, grabbing his knife and whittling a small piece of a branch pulled from the maple tree near the street.

Bobby stepped forward, his face filled with rage.

"Hey, Gordy, that was at least three fingers. You're not playing fair. Come on, Brian, let's go. They're just a couple of cheats."

As Brian made ready to walk beside his friend, Mickey Delaney stepped in front of him. Parker grabbed Brian with one hand, while shoving the tiny wooden peg in his face with the other.

"You're going to have to eat a lot a dirt to pull this out of the ground you gutless punk," Gordy said.

"I got more guts in my pinky than you do in your whole body."

"Yeah, you're so brave let's see you sneak up into the Jews yard pigeon coop."

"That's nothing."

"All right, tough guy, prove it. Yeah, bring back a pigeon as proof," Parker said.

"Okay, okay. Me and Bobby will do it. Then you have to root for the peg."

"That's a deal," Parker snorted, an index finger poking Brian's chest.

"Well now, what's going on here, toenail scratchers?" said Greg, Bobby's older brother.

Dressed in his American Legion baseball uniform, Greg had just returned from the first game of the summer season.

"He cheated at mumblety peg and wants to make Brian root for the peg," Bobby yelled.

Stepping close to Parker, Greg looked down on his blond curly hair as he placed an open palm on the boy's chest.

"I figured it had something to do with you. Why don't you and your pal head back over to Hudson Street where you belong? And stay there."

The arrogant smile on Parker's face was instantly replaced with one of disdain. Already, the wily Delaney had hurried to the sidewalk.

"Hey, wait for me," Parker called as he eased around Greg's muscular arm.

Brian and Bobby, relieved and re-energized, watched them retreat toward the corner of Partridge and Hudson Streets, where they momentarily stopped to look back at the threesome still standing in the McNally front yard.

"Don't forget about the pigeon coop," Parker taunted.

Fearing Greg's wrath, both Parker and Delaney sprinted down the street.

"Thanks for the help," Brian said.

"Yeah, well, those toenail scratchers better stay clear of Partridge Street. Last Halloween those two ripped out the Gardner's flowerbed and stuffed the dead flowers in her mailbox. Guess who got the blame for that? If it weren't for Mrs. Maguire keeping a sharp lookout at the front window, I'd a been in Dutch."

The three boys headed up the porch steps leading to the McNally front door. Pausing at the door, Bobby looked at his older brother.

"Did you and Charlie really sneak up into the pigeon coop in the Jews Yard?"

"Yeah, sure. We brought back a pigeon too, just ask her," Greg said pointing to the Gardner house front window. While all three boys raised their eyes to the window, a lace curtain suddenly dropped down, and a shadowy figure retreated.

3

Missing Bat

Hearing the familiar footsteps on the backstairs, Arrow rose from his bed on the porch to join the boys rushing into the kitchen. In addition to companionship, his instincts told him an edible treat would soon be available.

Rita turned from the sink to greet them.

"Honey, put more food in Arrow's dish and fill his water bowl before you two listen to the radio."

"Sure, Ma. Hey, Bobby, will ya put some water in his bowl while I fill the dog dish?"

Arrow wagged his tail enthusiastically as he observed his dish being replenished and water bowl filled. No sooner had Brian begun pouring dog food into the dish than Arrow's muzzle began an untidy exploration of the contents.

"Easy, boy, there's plenty," Brian reassured his pet.

While Rita swabbed the red and white checkered oilcloth with a wet dishrag, the lively music of Duke Ellington's band streamed from a small Philco radio. The table cleaned, she placed a quart of milk, two glasses and a plate of cookies down.

Removing his baseball cap, Brian pulled up a chair facing his friend across the table. Surrounded by salt and pepper shakers, a bowl of sugar, and an empty ashtray, the radio was tuned to a local station. The youngsters pinned Captain Midnight Secret Squadron badges on their shirts and waited in silence.

When the music stopped and station identification was announced, the sound of a bell tolling reverberated from the radio speaker. The boys stopped chewing their cookies and looked intently at the radio. Suddenly, the sound of an airplane engine drowned out the tolling bell, growing increasingly louder until it sounded like the plane would burst from the little Philco and strafe the tabletop.

"The makers of Ovaltine bring you… Captain… MIDNIGHT," the announcer boomed, "a program of adventure for all red-blooded American boys and girls, and people young at heart."

Before the program ended, the boys pulled on their baseball caps and prepared to depart for Little League practice. Brian ran quickly to his room to get the new bat, a Louisville Slugger, his father had recently given him. He joined Bobby in a noisy dash for the back door.

Puzzled by their abrupt departure before the fate of Captain Midnight had been decided for that week, Rita also noticed the discarded secret code badges, unprecedented behavior for both young men.

"Remember, you two are supposed to go to Colleen Maguire's birthday party tomorrow, and no excuses," she called.

The boys looked at each other with faces contorted in what seemed to be excruciating pain.

"I already bought a nice card and present for Colleen and I'm sure Bobby's mother has done the same, in fact I know she did, because I saw her with little Connor at the Five & Ten just yesterday," she added.

"But Mom, she's an eighth grader. We're just seventh graders. All her girlfriends will be there, too," Brian said.

"No excuses. You'll be going to dances and parties real soon. Don't fret; you'll have loads of fun. The party will help develop your social skills. Remember, there are other things besides baseball and basketball. Oh, before you leave, put Arrow out on the back porch."

Slapping the side of his dungarees, Brian summoned the dog from the kitchen corner. Once Arrow was in his bed under a cluttered table on the porch, the boys hurried down the stairs to their bikes, passing Brian's downstairs neighbor, Mr. Urtz, who was struggling up the stairs with an assemblage of metal tubes and poles, a wisp of tobacco smoke curling from his pipe.

"What's he doing with all that stuff?" Bobby asked.

"Something on the roof. He's been going up there all week with his tools and junk. If he's not on the roof, he's down in the basement sawing, drilling and soldering stuff on his workbench."

They seized their bikes from where they were laying haphazardly in the grassless wedge of yard between the back of the house and a string of garages. Mounting his Schwinn with the bat held across the handlebars and his baseball glove hooked on the bars, Brian pedaled forcefully to catch up with his friend.

"Hey Bobby, ya know we could be hitting infield grounders on Saturday instead of going to that birthday party."

"Yeah, but we just might get a chance to meet Colleen's older brother Charlie. He was on that CYO basketball team that made it all the way to the state championship. Greg knows him from high school."

"Still, I don't like it. A birthday party with girls."

When they wheeled into the ball diamond, bikes were dropped and mitts pulled from handlebars as they joined their teammates scattered around the playing field. Bobby headed for second base, his usual position, while Brian left his new bat near the backstop before sprinting to right field.

Soon the coaches got practice underway, with the head coach, Phil Borland, hitting grounders to the infield and his assistant, Sherm Polaski, batting fly balls to the outfielders. After a half hour of infield and outfield work by his team, Coach Borland called a timeout to talk with the Patroons.

Gathering about Coach Borland on the infield grass, they waited for his season-opening pep talk. From his position near the pitcher's mound, Brian looked up at the coach looming over the boys, then, out of the corner of his eye, he scanned beyond the coach to the backstop. There behind the screen stood Gordy Parker and his partner in crime, Mickey Delaney. Smiling contemptuously at Brian; both miscreants had their fingers hooked through the chain link backstop. His attention was redirected to the posturing coach, who, with ball cap in his left hand, swabbed his sweat-soaked forehead with a blue bandana.

"I know I've said this before every darn season, but this time I'm sure, I'm absolutely sure, we've got the makings of a championship team—that's right, CHAMPIONSHIP."

Smiling, he swiped the back of his neck with the bandana.

"We've got a strong infield, with Bobby McNally at second and Pete

Urban at short, and Jimmy "Stretch" Claflin at first. All these fellas are returning from last year's team, that, I remind you, finished in second place in our league. Plus we've got some strong batters coming back from last year's team, like center fielder Mike McGinn and right fielder Brian Reilly, who led the league in homers last year." Coach Borland then pointed at Brian, who felt all eyes on him.

"What we've got to work on is pitching. Got a young southpaw joining us this season, Marty Caputo, and, of course, our strongest pitcher, Blackie Rourke; he'll start the rotation. But, as all you returning players know full well, the league champs, Diamond Backs, have their ace pitcher, Sid Bloom, coming back for his final season. Thank God it's his last year. For you new guys, he had the lowest ERA and struck out the most batters in any league, even pitched two no hitters. I'm not trying to scare you, just want you to know what we're up against. So anyway, we've got a bunch of starters coming back from last year, but there's starting positions open. Sherm and me will be keeping our eyes peeled during practices, so let's see some hustle, keep your eye on the ball and play to win. Remember we've got our first game coming up in a couple of weeks, so let's look sharp. Now, you guys from last year, take first bats. The rest of you go to the position you're trying out for and rotate turns. Okay, let's go."

Jumping to their feet, the boys hustled to their positions. Brian, Bobby, and several other kids huddled near the backstop where they made practice swings with their bats. Gripping his special bat Brian took two healthy swings. Turning around he found himself looking into Gordy Parker's pimply face, a malicious smile slashed across it.

Blackie Rourke was already on the mound warming up slowly with practice throws to catcher, G. G. Wallace. Coach Borland yelled, "Batter up! Come on, Brian. Let's see what you can do."

Never needing encouragement to step up to the plate, Brian positioned himself and took a few practice swipes. As the first ball came whizzing to the plate, Parker and Delaney began heckling him from behind the backstop. After fouling off two balls, Brian turned to his tormentors. Before he could challenge them, Coach Borland stepped in.

"You two scram. Get up in the bleachers or on the hill in back of first if you want to watch practice, but don't you go bothering my players. Now get moving."

Only halfway through the dressing down, Parker and his pal pushed their hands in their pockets and moved out to the grassy hill overlooking first base.

Brian connected with the next pitch, sending it deep into left center, where two outfielders chased it. At the last minute it dropped between them. After two grounders to Caputo at short, Brian laced a ball out to deep center, bouncing it off the fence. Smiling with satisfaction at his new bat, he took a quick look beyond first base and saw Parker and Delaney smoking cigarettes. He caught a waist high fastball driving it clear over the left field fence into a grove of birch trees. With a feeling of pride and confidence he walked away from the plate with a broad grin.

After the first squad of batters got their raps, Coach Borland called in a mixed platoon of infielders and outfielders to take some practice swings. With that change, Brian and Bobby and the rest of the batters grabbed their mitts and ran to their respective positions.

When the practice came to a close, the coach gathered his players together in the bleachers behind the home team dugout.

"Okay, okay, listen up, just a few things before I turn you loose. First, you're all looking aggressive. Good hustle. Two, remember, you gotta' stick with fundamentals—keep your eye on the ball, on both sides of the plate. You infielders, look the ball into your glove and, if you get a bad hop, knock it down, don't let it get past you. You gotta play heads-up ball. Keep hustling, don't give up, look sharp, be sharp. We'll make the final cuts tomorrow. If you get cut, don't stop playing ball; get on a farm team, play sandlot ball, practice as much as you can, and we'll see you next year. I guarantee—you work at it, you'll make the team. You fellas that make the team get uniforms this Friday. Guys coming back already have theirs, but better check to make sure it's all there and it still fits. Looks like some of you are eating your folks out of house and home. If your mothers can't alter the uniforms to fit, let me know soon as you can so we can swap things out. Okay. Now, who's gunna win that championship trophy this year?"

Jumping to their feet, they yelled in unison at the top of their lungs, "Patroons, Patroons."

Coach Borland smiled broadly while shaking his head. "Now this ain't no peewee farm team is it? Come on, me and Sherm want to hear some excitement. Make them people all the way down at Yankee Stadium hear you. Come on, now!"

With that encouragement, over a dozen ballplayers screamed at the top of their lungs, "PATROONS!"

Following this boisterous war cry, the boys collapsed in delirious laughter.

In the chaos that followed the departing, yelling, horse-playing kids, Brian and Bobby made ready to mount their bikes. Before he could accomplish this Brian searched among the few ball bats stacked haphazardly against the backstop but couldn't find his prized Louisville Slugger. With Bobby's help he looked all around the backstop then around the two sets of wooden bleachers behind the backstop. Still, the prized Louisville Slugger was missing. Lastly, he caught up to Coach Borland, who was dragging a heavy canvas equipment bag to his Ford station wagon.

"Say, Mr. Borland, I can't find my new bat and I looked all over heck for it. Can you see if it's in the equipment bag? May be it got in there by mistake."

"Sure, hate for you to lose that Slugger. By the way, you got some good raps at the plate today. I noticed you're eyeballing the pitches much better than last year," he said as he opened the bag and started pulling out catcher's masks and shin guards and several bats, but no Louisville Slugger.

"You sure that's everything?"

"Sorry, Brian, that's all she wrote," Borland said shaking the bag upside down. "Don't you worry, we'll keep an eye out for it. It'll come home."

"Well, thanks anyway," Brian said, his shoulders slumping as he walked back to where Bobby was waiting with the bikes.

"No luck, huh?" McNally said.

"Nope. Boy-oh-boy I'd like to get my hands on the jerk who stole that bat. What am I going to tell my father?" Brian said, hooking his outfielder's mitt on the handlebars.

"Come on, let's go over to Stackie's. I'll buy you a soda pop." Bobby said.

"Sure, but keep on the lookout for my bat, just in case."

Stackie's was a purveyor of newspapers, magazines, candy, pop, cigarettes and cigars, and paperback books whose themes generally ran to westerns and detective mysteries. The paperbacks, magazines and newspapers were arranged on shelves to the left as customers entered the store. To the right were glass display cases with shelves crammed with candy, cigarettes, cigars, pipe tobacco, and books of matches. In the back of the store was one of the new telephone booths that had an accordion-like folding door and a dome light that came on when the door was closed. Mrs. Stack, the owner's wife, was seen behind the counter during the day, and her son, Billy, a fifth grader also at Saint John's grade school, helped his mother out after classes.

During the school year, the store was crowded, inside and out, mostly with high school boys and girls, but during summer vacation the store and the street corner at Madison and Ontario became a hangout for neighborhood kids.

In the back of the store was a full size bright red soda cooler filled with cakes of ice to cool dozens of bottles of pop dispersed within.

Brian followed at Bobby's heels, a grim cast to his normally cheerful face. At the red soda cooler he pulled an icy bottle of Royal Crown, dripping ice water, from the assortment of soft drinks. After removing a bottle for himself, Bobby closed the lid and waited as Brian used the bottle cap opener on the side of the cooler.

Mrs. Stack picked up the two nickels Bobby placed on the glass counter and pressed one of the many keys of the ornate silver-plated cash register before dropping the coins in a drawer that popped out with a clanging of bells and clicking of gears.

Brian stood in front of the magazine rack, where he eyed a copy of *Field & Stream* Magazine, the cover illustrated with a monstrous Northern Pike leaping out of the water with a lure hooked in its lower jaw. Moving alongside him, Bobby bent down to read the blurbs on the cover of a professional wrestling magazine. After a few more minutes of scrutiny, they were distracted by Mrs. Stack's insistent gaze. Shortly, she would query them as to their intention of purchasing the magazines they were perusing so painstakingly, knowing full well they had no interest in buying anything besides the bottles of pop.

To amplify the intensity of her presence, she moved down the glass display cases until she was directly in back of them. In this position, she began tapping a fingernail on the glass counter top, at first slowly, then with increasing rapidity and volume. The boys, of course, failed to hear her persistent warnings.

Finally, clearing her throat, she inquired again about the purchase of magazines, prompting the boys to drain their pop bottles and return them to the half-filled wooden case beside the cooler. Outside, sitting on the step at the front door, Bobby tried to console his friend.

"Come on, we'll find the bat if we have to go to every ball diamond in the city."

"Yeah, sure, that's just not any old Louisville Slugger, that's a Mickey Mantle signature bat, and a present, too. I sure hope my Dad isn't mad when I tell him I lost it."

"Well, I'll bet someone stole it—maybe one of the new kids who saw you hitting all those fly balls."

"Maybe," Brian said.

"Come on, let's go around the corner and look at that new soda shop."

With that, they jumped on their bikes and pedaled around the corner to the new store across from the three-story brick façade of Saint John's High School.

Large windows, just cleaned by a man with a rag and squeegee, covered all but a small section at the front of the soda shop. A glass and chrome entrance door separated the two front windows. Peering in one of the windows, scripted with the hand-painted words *Dipsy Doodle* in bold red letters, Brian could see, to his left, a counter lined with brightly upholstered stools set on chrome pedestals. On one such stool a teenage girl spun in slow revolutions, a smile of joy or glee parting her rouged lips. In her hands she clutched a fluted glass containing a soft drink from which a straw projected. Her upper torso was clothed in a pinkish, tight-fitting garment with a closed neckline. Short sleeves revealed freckled, plump arms. Brian couldn't help but stare at her chest, from which two lumps protruded. Flustered, he ran a jittering hand across his own chest, before turning to his friend.

"What are those… those things?" He said pointing at the girl.

"I heard Greg call them 'tits' when he was talking to one of his friends. He said they actually study them in biology class."

"Tits?"

"Yeah, but in the textbook they call'em breasts or teats, or something. Mothers use them to feed milk to their babies. Haven't you ever seen puppies sucking at the teats of their mother?"

Brian shook his head. A quizzical look slowly painted his face.

"Really… they study that kind of stuff over there," Brian said pointing to the high school across the street.

"And that ain't all. Get this, Greg said that human babies actually come out of an opening between their mother's legs and there's an awful lot of blood and a doctor cuts this cable thing that's attached to the baby's belly button."

Aghast, Brian narrowed his eyes at his friend.

"Nah, I don't believe it."

"Swear on my Topps Rizzuto baseball card. 'Sides, Greg said so."

"That sounds like a sin, like a triple mortal sin where you'd rot in hell forever and ever."

Though momentarily confused and disoriented, Brian continued his visual fixation on the girl's chest.

"What's-her-name," Bobby began, "Gina DeMelia, she has those things, too, not that big, but I noticed them when she walked by us in the school hallway."

"Gina DeMelia? You mean all girls get those things?"

"Well, I think most of them do. Didn't you ever notice your mother has them?"

"No, I never did, but I'll take a look when I get home. Jeez, Gina DeMelia, too?"

"Yeah, wait and see. She'll be at Colleen's birthday party."

"I wonder if Colleen has them?"

"Probably, but Greg says some girls, like that one at the jukebox, wear a kind of strap across their chest to make them stand out."

"Boy, Greg sure knows a lot, doesn't he?" Brian said.

"Well, my mother says he knows too much for his own good. How can you know too much?"

The topic seemingly exhausted, Brian watched the girl walk to a brightly lighted machine at the back wall of the shop, the source of the music they heard from outside. Colored lights of various hues flashed intermittently as the girl stood swaying from side-to-side.

Completely captivated by this new contraption, the boys pushed their way into the soda shop, stopping at the counter with its array of chrome-plated swivel stools. Hearing the door close, the girl turned sideways, enabling the boys to appraise her profile. They stared unabashed as she turned and dropped coins into a slot, then studiously punched ivory keys on the front of the device. When she stepped away and moved over to a booth, they read the name *Seeburg 100* on the record selection device. Rotating translucent cylinders on each side of the jukebox flashed and gyrated with red and blue lights. Awestruck, the boys watched while a mechanism inside the clear plastic jukebox face moved slowly sideways, eventually stopping to pluck a single 45 RPM record from a batch of one hundred. Suddenly, music gushed forth like a gigantic radio, but without commercials and station breaks. In stunned silence they heard Bill Haley and the Comets' rendition of their hit—*Rock Around the Clock*. It was Brian and Bobby's first experience assimilating the sounds of *Rock and Roll*.

Mesmerized, the boys ran their fingers over the numbered and lettered keys and read the small typewritten titles of records installed inside the music appliance.

Back at the counter they each mounted a swivel stool and looked up at the signage on the wall above the preparation counter and freezers containing gallons ice cream. Bobby pointed to one of the hand-lettered signs with an illustration of a jumbo milkshake. Brian's eyes swelled when his eyes stopped on the word, "FREE."

He elbowed Bobby.

Then in smaller print Brian read, "If you can drink a whole Awful-Awful, it's "FREE."

The counter girl, perhaps sixteen or seventeen, outfitted in a white uniform jacket and cap appeared in front of the boys. The name *Joanie* was embroidered on her waist length jacket.

"Can I help you?"

"Well, I was wondering how much that Awful-Awful milkshake cost," Brian asked.

"It's fifty cents."

With that the boys began extricating coins from their dungaree pockets.

"One person has to drink the whole shake to get it free," she cautioned.

They looked up at her disgruntled.

"Shoot, we don't even have fifty cents between us. Guess I'll just have a small Coke," said Brian.

"Me too," Bobby chimed in.

When their soft drinks were placed in front of them, Bobby looked up at the counter girl.

"Has anyone ever finished a whole Awful-Awful?" Brian asked.

"The only kid I've seen do it was G. G. Wallace. And he's done it twice."

Bobby looked at Brian. "Yeah, he's our catcher. I think he lives on the same block as Gordy Parker."

"Yeah."

"Well, someday I'm going to try one, even if I get sick to my stomach. Just think, a whole chocolate Awful-Awful."

"Bet ya can't," Bobby challenged.

Hearing the jukebox begin its noisy mechanical routine of selecting a record, Brian spun on his stool to see colored lights flash as the playback device whirred and clicked and finally pulled another black vinyl 45 RPM from the uniform row at the back of the machine. Suddenly, the air was charged with the unique electric guitar styling of Les Paul, accompanied by his wife, Mary Ford, singing *The World is Waiting for the Sunrise.*

Slurping the dregs of his soda, Bobby was preparing to push it away from him when he felt the grip of a strong hand on his shoulder. Spinning around, he was both surprised and relieved to see his older brother Greg.

"Hey, what are you toenail scratchers doing in the Dipsy?" A broad smile added playfulness to his question.

Two boys and a girl walked past Greg and out the door, waving at Joanie as they exited.

"Me and Brian just wanted to see what it was like inside. We heard that record machine playing and wanted to see it close up."

"Come on over to my booth. I want to introduce you to my girlfriend, Angie."

Trooping behind Greg, the boys slid into the booth. Greg pushed into the seat across from them. When Brian finally worked up the nerve to look across the table his eyes widened and his lower jaw dropped. Barely two and a half feet across the table was the girl in the tight-fitting pink sweater. At that very moment she was looking into a small compact mirror and smearing red lipstick on her puffy lips. As though drawn by powerful magnets, his blue eyes fixated on the girl's swelling breasts. The sound of her compact snapping shut cued Brian to lower his eyes to his fidgeting hands on the tabletop.

"Angie, this is my little brother Bobby and his pal, Brian."

She smiled broadly, exposing perfect white teeth. Stupefied, Brian watched as she ran her tongue slowly over newly glossed lips.

"Hey fellas, come on, say hello," Greg grinned.

The next thing Brian knew, Angie clasped his hand in hers, shook it gently, then proceeded to grasp Bobby's hand. Looking at his open palm, he half-expected to see smoke wafting from it. He snapped his hand closed and withdrew it from the tabletop. Moving a bit sideways so he could surreptitiously look at Angie, he suddenly felt a bit faint, but ecstatic at the same time, thinking that perhaps he may have consumed too much soda and candy. He felt his heart beating violently, accompanied by loud drumbeats in his ears. The strangest feeling he'd ever felt in his life encompassed his whole body. Beneath the dungaree material at his crotch he felt swollen for the first time. Next, he was aware of Greg asking him something. Looking up, embarrassed, he realized that vast quantities of blood had rushed to his face, turning it beet red.

"Hey, Brian, snap out of it, kid."

"Ah, don't mind him. We think someone swiped his Louisville Slugger. A surprise present from his father," Bobby explained.

"So, missing, huh?"

"Yeah. I think so," Brian mumbled.

Snickering, Greg winked, while looking slyly at his girlfriend.

"You think so. You either found it or you didn't. What gives?"

"We didn't find it," Bobby came to the rescue. "I still say those two creeps Parker and Delaney took it. You wait and see."

Brian started pushing at his friend.

"I just remembered I have to stop at Franco's market to get some potatoes for my mother," he said, encouraging Bobby to leave with another shove.

Once outside, Brian began to regain his composure. He plucked his bike from the sidewalk.

"What's this potato business?" Bobby queried.

"Nothing. I just had to get out of there. Every time I looked at Angie I felt like I was going to be sick or something. I got this… this swelling down here," said Brian.

Bobby began laughing uproariously.

"It ain't funny!" Brian snarled.

"I'm not laughing at you. First time that happened to me I asked Greg about it, 'cause he knows all about those things from Biology class. Anyway, he says it happens when boys and girls get together, something like a natural reaction, like when a baseball hits a bat. Bang, like that. I think he said it was an *erection*."

"So I don't have scarlet fever or polio?"

"Nah, you're not sick."

"Should I tell my mother what happened?"

"Are you nuts? Don't ever tell your mother or any of the nuns at school," Bobby said.

"How about the priest in confession?"

"Well, Greg says, technically it's not a sin, so stick with the usual stuff, swear words, disobeying parents, maybe a couple of mortal sins to balance things out. Hey, get this, Greg says it even happens to animals."

"Will it affect my swing or timing?"

"I don't think so, but I'll ask Greg, just to be sure. OK?"

"Yeah, come on, let's go home."

4

Pigeons

From the security of a garage roof overlooking the back of the Jewish Rest Home, two neophyte spies took turns in their reconnaissance of Johnny Russian as he fussed with and fed his growing flock of pigeons. Following a sharp whistle from Johnny, one airborne bird swooped down to peck small kernels of seed from his hand.

His face smeared with black shoe polish, baseball cap pulled low over hooded eyes, Brian watched as Johnny Russian gently raised his upturned palm forcing the pigeon to spread and flex its wings thus hurtling itself into flight. He poked Bobby in the arm.

Looking down from their redoubt the commandos observed the pigeon rise to the height of the barn that housed its nesting coop. At the sound of Johnny's whistle the circling bird, in the blinking an eye, performed a graceful backward somersault, recovered, then soared down to the ground at the caretaker's feet, where it pecked at scattered seed.

The boys looked on astonished.

At his feet was a small wooden cage made out of slats of wood, from which Johnny scooped up another pigeon and tossed it in the air, whistling to it as he performed these tasks. After circling the barn twice, the bird did a smooth backward somersault. The task accomplished, Johnny clapped his hands together, signaling the bird to return to him for his morning ration of seed. Shortly, the bird was released again, but this time it flew directly up to the loft, where it landed on a ledge affixed to the entrance holes, and then quickly disappeared inside.

Fascinated, both youngsters watched in complete silence as Johnny coaxed the other pigeons into flight. Suddenly, they froze at the noise produced by the caretaker's hand clapping. Gaining their wits while once again pulling their heads below the parapet that ringed the garage roof, they looked at each other in sheer delight. To have witnessed this aerial display by mere pigeons was more than they could have hoped for. More amazing was the fact that Johnny had orchestrated the aerial gymnastics.

When they worked up the nerve to peek over the garage wall, Johnny Russian, the pigeons, and the small cage were gone.

Inside the barn, Johnny pulled a knotted rope attached to a trap door in the ceiling above him, opening a multi-section extension ladder that enabled him to gain access to the pigeon coop some twenty feet above the barn floor. Clutching the empty cage under his right arm, the big man began a slow but steady climb up the ladder, wobbling slightly, until he gained the small wooden platform where a door allowed entry to the coop and prevented wayward pigeons from roosting in other areas of the barn. Dropping to his knees, he pushed the small cage before him as he moved awkwardly through the small opening into the loft. He tilted his head to the left enabling him to more easily scan the cramped interior.

Daylight streamed through the slits between warped boards of the barn siding and the small portals the pigeons used to enter the loft after flight. The cramped interior forced Johnny into a crab-like stance to avoid striking his head on the thick beam supporting the peaked roof. Once situated, he began the tedious, but necessary, process of segregating his tumblers-in-training from less talented birds. The rejected birds culled from his growing flock would soon be released to nature. The pungent odors of pigeon feces and the saturated straw of birds' nests did not affect the man, who had grown immune to the stench of the coop.

Squeaking noises coming from his right side prompted Johnny to turn awkwardly. Below him, in an enclosure, was a collection of recently hatched chicks that, if his breeding skills succeeded, would emerge as highly talented members of his kit of rollers. Of some concern to him when first taking over the care and feeding of the pigeons from its former custodian, Sol Horowitz, was the extensive variety of birds constituting the flock. Now confined to a wheelchair, Horowitz had built the flock over many years from stragglers and migrant pigeons that sought out the security of the barn loft. Horowitz had no experience with tumblers, so over the years the tumblers in the flock grew fat and lazy from excessive feed and total lack of discipline and exercise. Fortunately for Johnny Russian there remained a few promising tumblers that he was now retraining and breeding to take advantage of their superior tumbling abilities. His prize roller was a Romanian Galati cock sporting a white chest and white-tipped, blue tail feathers.

With the assistance of a nurse's aide, Horowitz would navigate his wheelchair onto the back porch of the Jews Home to watch, in amazement, as his protégé put the birds through their paces. Smoking a cigar, Sol would call out praise and encouragement as Johnny whistled and clapped his signals to the pigeons that, singly or in small kits of three to five birds, performed their tumbling routines.

Protesting to the white-smocked nurse's aide who ventured onto the porch to retrieve him for his medications, he would throw his cigar butt in the gravel drive, point at Johnny and declare in his high-pitched, scratchy voice, "He's a good boy. Such a good boy."

Assured that his fledgling tumbler stock was fed and watered, Johnny turned his attention to those mature birds that, for one reason or another, were underperforming. Selecting the worst of the three birds he had marked for removal, he clamped his hands about its wings and coaxed it into a small wire cage near the loft door. Without the slightest show of resistance the pigeon nestled in its new confines and resumed its muted cooing. Never mustering the nerve or gumption to destroy a pigeon, regardless of its lack of athleticism, he would entrust the bird to the man who delivered ice to the rest home. A swarthy Italian, Mario would smile gleefully, promising to dispatch the bird to a diverse flock of pigeons that had established itself at the ice plant where he worked. Though not understanding all of Mario's highly emotional declarations, a mixture of Italian and English, Johnny was reassured by the Mario's broad smile and compliant nature. Thus, by slow but careful attrition, the least promising of the flock were gradually culled.

Amidst the cooing of the birds could be heard the intermittent whistling of Johnny Russian. Though disfigured and handicapped in numerous ways, he possessed an unquestionably fine aptitude for whistling, a talent he had nurtured since childhood. Oblivious to the stench, the heat, the cramped quarters of the loft, Johnny plucked a tattered notebook, held together with a thick rubber band that also secured a stubby pencil, from the chest pocket of his bib overalls. Still on his knees, he removed the rubber band, moistened the tip of the pencil stub on his tongue and began to print notations in Cyrillic letters on the small, cramped pages.

Following his session of note taking, he stopped to ponder the cock and hen he had segregated in a breeding pen. His favorite hen, a Birmingham Roller—blue chest with blue-black wings, white-tipped tail feathers, and slim neck—looked up at him with a pinkish eye. Its head jerked slightly in various directions. Clicking his tongue loudly, Johnny peered down at the cock unmoving in the back corner of the breeding cage. Although the bird had showed promise as a tumbler, as well as a member of the kit, it appeared not in the least interested in mating with the hen he had chosen for it. Ruminating as he observed the bird, it suddenly came to him from the depths of his subconscious that a diet of wild dandelions, of which there were many on the grounds, might stimulate the pigeon's libido.

Johnny made a note of the cock's reluctance to mate and a reminder to remove it from the breeding pen in a day or two if the dandelions proved ineffective. Notes completed, he refastened the rubber band to the tattered notebook, a gift from Sol Horowitz, secured the pencil, and slipped the small pad back into its customary pocket.

His chores in the loft completed, he began a slow retreat from the coop, making sure to fasten the door latch lest a few of the more adventurous pigeons escape into the barn. Gripping the small cage with the culled bird in his left hand, he proceeded in a slow, careful descent down the wooden ladder one step at a time. On the ground, he closed the trap door with its telescoping ladder. Selecting a few tools from a neat, orderly row on the barn wall, he made his way to one of the vegetable gardens. Before leaving the barn, Johnny placed the wire cage with its feathered occupant on a workbench to wait until the horse-drawn ice wagon crunched to a halt at the back of the Jews home. Though his vision was compromised, he could easily hear the ice wagon rattle loudly up the gravel drive and stop at the back porch. Later that afternoon, alerted by the grinding of wagon brakes, he hurried to the barn for the caged bird.

After shouldering the blocks of ice into the kitchen coolers, Mario paused at the side of the wagon, lighted a small crooked cigar and conversed garrulously with Johnny. Understanding only a few words, Johnny held up the caged bird for Mario's inspection. In his musical native tongue, Mario, with operatic posturing, delivered a loud, verbose declaration of gratitude for the bird, accompanied by animated gesticulations. Up again on the seat of the wagon he regaled Johnny with a booming Italian monologue. Listening, but understanding little, Johnny unhooked the cement stop tethered to the horse's bridle, handing the rope and weight up to Mario, who would yell out as though singing an aria.

"Bravisimo, my great friend, my fellow socialista. Bon giorno, bon giorno. Ciao, ciao, my good friend."

A mere twitch of the long, thick leather reins and the two draft horses began lumbering their way around the back of the circular drive.

Watching their departure, Johnny's face, not given to or readily capable of expressing emotion, showed what might be perceived by the alert observer as a smile. Johnny's single eye followed the ice wagon as it rounded the Jews Home and disappeared with the grating noise of wagon wheels on gravel. In its wake, a single muffled word tumbled from Johnny's lips.

"Ciao."

When the yard was deserted of people and pigeons, the secret agents in their aerie sought each other's counsel before departing.

"How do we get in the barn without being seen and then climb up to the coop? It's nearly impossible."

"If Charlie and Greg did it, so can we. Of course, that was before Johnny Russian was here. Tonight, I'll ask Greg the best way to get up to the pigeon loft," Bobby said.

"Yeah, we can't let Gordy and Mickey give us the needle. We have to show them we have guts. Shut'em up once and for all," said Brian.

"I'll talk to Greg tonight."

"Good."

~

Alone in the driveway, Johnny looked up to see Mr. Rubenstein, the rest home administrator, step down from the back porch. Smiling, he approached Johnny.

"It's time to go. They're expecting you."

Johnny nodded his head. "Please," he said while hurrying into the rest home, down to his basement room where he put his notebook in the cigar box on his desk. While there, he changed his scarred boots for shoes and pulled on his sport coat. Soon he was back in the driveway, where Rubenstein waited in his car, the engine running.

He sat quietly in the chair on the stage. When his eyes strayed to his hands, he crumpled the fingers into fists. A doctor in a white smock stood at his side. Using a telescopic pointer he indicated the scar on Johnny's head running from ear to ear. Dr. Ishmael Reed, noted neurosurgeon and fellow at the Albany Medical College, looked up to receive the attention of hundreds of eyes peering down from the amphitheater seats. Medical students, professors, staff, and interns from area hospitals filled the galleries to overflowing.

During his residency, Reed had gained distinction far beyond the local medical college he was associated with and the procedure he'd pioneered on Johnny Russian. Recently, he'd been honored by the Societe de Medecine de Paris for his ground-breaking work. Medical journals worldwide featured articles about him, especially his craniotomy procedures. At best, Johnny's had been a radical operation, a unique and successful one, orchestrated by Dr. Reed, but experimental nonetheless. The truth of the matter was that Johnny's chances of survival, had not Reed initiated the radical surgery when and where he did, would have been minimal.

Johnny Russian looked away from his mutilated hands to a chart illustrating the structure of a human brain with all of its complex organs, sinews, veins and nerves. He followed the doctor's pointer as it referenced the chart. Not comprehending the doctor's commentary, his eyes swept away from the illustration down to his feet. He wore the late Mr. Cohen's cordovan wingtips with pride, even though the footwear was in stark contrast to his workaday denim overalls—a contrast noticed by many people in front row seats. To this inconsequential detail, among a myriad of others, Johnny was oblivious.

While Johnny admired the shine of his leather shoes, Dr. Reed continued a review of his case history and the successful prognosis, despite the high risk of the multiple surgeries performed. In conclusion, he admonished his audience to exercise extreme caution when attempting these radical procedures and also to bear in mind the unpredictability, the high risk involved. Ethical considerations aside, he was satisfied his decision to operate had given the man a reprieve from sure death. In this same pioneering spirit, he urged his audience to continue expanding the boundaries of medical science.

Placing his slim, manicured fingers on the shoulder of Johnny's blue suit coat, Reed reminded his listeners that, in terms of current surgical standards, his efforts had been clumsy baby steps compared to present-day procedures.

"After all," he said in conclusion, "that was over ten years ago."

Instantly, enthusiastic colleagues engulfed Dr. Reed. Unnoticed, an assistant escorted Johnny Russian from the noisy auditorium to a room where Mr. Rubenstein waited to escort him back to the rest home.

<u>5</u>

Birthday Party

Standing before the bathroom mirror, Brian pulled his father's hairbrush through his crew cut. Not seeing the slightest difference, he returned the brush to its place on the shelf. His hope had been that it would in some magical way transform his short brown bristles into the blonde locks that adorned the scalp of his baseball hero, Mickey Mantle. No matter the effort applied, the short brown hairs populating Brian's scalp remained unchanged. With a bit of stealth, he grasped his father's tube of Brylcreem from its place on the shelf above the commode. A squeeze of the tube released a few drops of hair dressing, which he energetically rubbed into his scalp, but to little or no effect. Wrinkling his nose, Brian turned to matters of more importance.

Smiling widely, he confirmed that his teeth, after several brushings were free from any contaminants that would otherwise mar their presentation to one girl in particular at Colleen's birthday party. He thanked God and all the saints in heaven that a chipped front tooth so hideous a few months ago, when it spouted a torrent of blood that soaked the front of his sweatshirt and sent his mother to her bedroom in tears, was no longer so conspicuous.

Never one to abandon a project no matter how futile, Brian once again swiped the hairbrush across his head in hopes the increased muscular effort would achieve the results he fancied. Resigned that his brush cut would not transform itself into golden curls, he now turned his attention to his new short-sleeved T shirt with horizontal stripes that he thought made his chest look more muscular. Smiling his ridiculously wide smile, he balled his fist and flexed his right arm so the bicep contracted into a protuberance the size of a golf ball.

"Honey, what's taking you so long?"

"Just brushing my teeth," he replied, curtailing his posturing before the mirror. He then turned his attention to his newly washed Converse All Stars.

All of these adolescent mannerisms were observed with the jaundiced eye of Arrow, who, from his vantage point near the tub noted it was not that far in the past when he was the chief recipient of his master's attention.

Turning from the mirror, Brian was surprised to see his mother blocking the doorway, one shoulder leaning against the door jam, arms crossed over her apron-clad chest, black hair spilling to the shoulders of a dark purple dress with renderings of red hyacinths and pink bougainvillea.

"Well, my little man, this is a first. Your face and hands are spotless, you're wearing a clean shirt and you even have clean dungarees on. And look at those sneakers."

His first reaction was to counsel his mother on the use of the phrase *little man*, but, not wanting to displease her in any way, he accepted her outstretched hand and accompanied her to the kitchen table where an elegantly wrapped birthday present awaited.

"Oh, Ma, thanks for getting the present 'n all."

"If I left that to you, I'm sure you'd get Colleen a basketball or a catcher's mitt."

"Nah, I wouldn't have done that. I was thinking of getting her some comic books."

Observing this familiar dialogue from the bathroom doorway, Arrow plodded back to his bed in the kitchen corner.

The glint of a belt buckle caught Rita's brown eyes. She patted Brian's shoulder.

"That's the first time I've seen you wear a belt with your dungarees. Sure you don't want to put on your dress pants?"

"None of the guys will. They'll all be wearing dungarees."

"And shoes—remember you have those new shoes you got last Easter and hardly ever wear."

"Ma, they're just for Sundays. Nobody wears shoes to birthday parties… do they?"

"Oh, yes they do, but I don't imagine that will happen to you for a few more years. Before you leave, take Arrow out for a little walk, please."

Ears alerted at the sound of his name, the dog transformed instantly into his affable, gushing self with wagging tongue and swishing tail.

While walking Arrow in the driveway between the two houses, Brian waved to Mr. Urtz, who continued to build some strange apparatus on the rooftop. Taking in the sight with questioning eyes, Brian's attention was diverted when Arrow began a tepid pursuit after a neighbor's cat.

Brian climbed the McNally's backstairs in order to rendezvous with his best friend and avoid any pre-party contact with Colleen's girlfriends. Bobby was found alone in the bedroom he shared with the twins. He was sprawled out on his single bed immersed in a Captain Midnight comic book. Upon seeing Brian enter, he put the comic down and threw his legs over the side of the bed.

His eyes roving over Brian's outfit, he felt reassured they both wore identical items of clothing, save for the footwear. Bobby still wore scuffed oxfords. Also cultivating a head of hair clipped short in a crewcut, Bobby let an appraising eye finally come to rest on Brian's spotless Converse All Stars, the sight sparking a flame of jealousy that would only be extinguished when he, too, had acquired a pair; a purchase that would soon be transacted with paper route profits and tips.

"Hey, what did you get Colleen?"

Bobby pointed to the gift-wrapped package on his dresser. "I think my mother got her some socks or stockings, I don't know. Does it matter?"

"Nah, just make sure you sign the birthday card; that'll make it look like you shopped for the present," Brian said as he sat down on the bottom bunk opposite Bobby. He set his present and card on the Hopalong Cassidy bedspread.

Brian rubbed his hands together. "Say, what do we do before Colleen blows out the candles on the cake and we get some cake and ice cream?"

"Well, Greg says they usually play pin the tail on the donkey, you know, and sometimes they have guessing games or you pull a number out of a hat and you have to pretend you're an animal or vegetable and everyone has to guess what you are."

"Maybe we could bring a baseball and play some pitch and catch."

"Nope, my mother said no mitts, baseballs or bats go downstairs."

"I know what, we could Indian wrestle."

"Ma says *absolutely* no roughhousing. Colleen's mother took a day off from her job at the Jews home so she'll be in charge and tell us what games to play."

"Anyway, at least I'll be able to look at Gina DeMelia. She sat next to me in class last year. She smelled kind of funny… good funny."

"Yeah, I suppose all the girls at the party will have that strange smell. I don't get it?"

"Me neither."

A silence followed while both boys secretly tried to resuscitate memories of those musky odors.

In the bedroom doorway, Greg's smiling face appeared. "Hey toenail scratchers, I don't want to hear about you guys kissing those lovely young ladies and trying to feel them up, you hear?"

Both boys looked at each other with contorted faces when Greg uttered the word *kissing*.

"Come on, men, let's show a little excitement, huh."

Bobby threw a baseball at Greg, whose hand instantly clasped the ball, flipped it behind his back, catching it with his left hand, then placed the ball on the dresser next to the birthday present.

"Hey Brian, that missing bat ever come home?"

Wincing, he looked up at Greg. "No, guess I'll never see it again."

"Too bad."

Turning to leave, he called over his shoulder, "Remember, no kissing or feeling up."

When Greg's footsteps could no longer be heard hurrying down the back steps, Brian looked across at his friend.

"What's he mean by *feeling up*?"

"I think it's like when the cops search a criminal and they feel them up for guns, something like that."

Brian let this sink in for a minute, then said, "I'll ask my father, he probably knows all about this *feeling up* business."

"Yeah."

Bobby was preparing to knock on Colleen's front door when it was abruptly pulled open by a smiling, freckle-faced redhead whose green eyes instantly spied the brightly wrapped package clutched in his arm. Behind her, the boys could see the giggling heads of several young girls.

"Come in, come in. Hi Brian. Let me take those presents," Colleen gushed as she agilely plucked the gifts from the boys' arms. "Follow me."

The gaggle of girls parted, allowing the two boys to navigate their ranks in a crude version of the Indian custom of forcing captives to run the gauntlet. In the center of the living room was a large table spread with festive party favors and napkins, all adorned with cartoon characters familiar to the youngsters. From the chandelier and various light fixtures hung bunches of red, pink and yellow balloons and twisted strips of red and white crepe paper.

Once the girls gathered around Colleen at a side table heaped with birthday presents, the two boys were set adrift. Spying their corpulent friend and teammate, G. G. Wallace of *awful-awful* notoriety, they made haste to the folding chairs beside him. Although only one school grade ahead of Brian and Bobby, Wallace dwarfed both youngsters at a height of five feet ten inches and overly generous girth made even more unsightly by a tight belt cinching layers of protruding fat. He tipped the scales in the school nurse's office at 220 pounds. His ability to consume sizable amounts of food was quickly established in school cafeteria lore. During more than one memorable lunch period, Wallace had devoured several platters of spaghetti, a favorite repast. Dumbfounded, classmates seated around him were awed by his lunchtime binges. To his credit, Wallace never had cause to rush to the boy's room to discharge his noontime feasts.

When Brian and Bobby took seats next to Wallace, the three boys nearby, all one or two grades behind them, were completely ignored. It was quickly ascertained by Brian that the party invitees were in some unwritten code of youth, divided into groups of boys on one side of the room and girls on the other.

"Drink any awful-awfuls lately?" Bobby asked.

Stifling a yawn, G. G. looked down at his teammate and scout troop friend.

"They won't let me have any more. Guess they figured I'd get a free one every time."

With no encouragement, Wallace launched into a gasconade of his gastronomic accomplishments, to include the number of watermelons he could ingest on a hot summer afternoon (15), the record number of gallons of ice cream (3), pizzas (13), Three Musketeer Bars (27), popsicles (49). He rambled on, citing likes and dislikes, his favorite eating holidays—Thanksgiving, Christmas and the Fourth of July, but was silenced when the front door suddenly opened, admitting two young girls. Gina DeMelia and her constant companion, Eileen Hansen, entered. Immediately, they joined the cluster of girls surrounding Colleen.

Brian's blue eyes followed Gina's every step. Thus preoccupied, he let a sigh escape his slack jaw as Gina seated herself across the room with Eileen next to her.

"God, she's beautiful," he sighed.

"Yeah, too bad her best friend is Eileen Hansen. I can't figure that out. She's the ugliest girl in school and older than Gina by two years."

Contrasting with the other girls, both Gina and Eileen wore dresses and pumps, while their girlfriends sported poodle skirts, short sleeve sweaters, saddle shoes, penny loafers and bobby socks.

Eileen, through no fault of her own, can be described as homely, a generous characterization in the opinion of her male classmates. These pubescent boys with the hunting instincts of a falcon and manners of a vulture were always on the alert for imperfections, however slight, in members of the student body or teaching staff, especially those of the opposite sex.

Eileen had been born and raised, for the most part, in London bomb shelters during World War II. She'd survived repeated bombardments of Luftwaffe planes that had dropped tons of ordnance on London. Her earliest memories were of life in dark, damp, crowded bomb shelters, the deafening explosions accompanied by teeth rattling concussions, never mind her constant companions: hunger and alienation. A babe in arms, she was suckled by strangers; few ever knew the little girl's name snuggling at their lactating breast.

No pink nursery for this little lady. While most children cast nostalgic looks back on their childhood, filled with smothering maternal love, a fluffy Teddy bear or perhaps being dandled and bounced on Papa's *horsey* knee, Eileen had enjoyed none of those. Her parents, both civilian workers at an aircraft factory that had produced hundreds of Bristol

Blenheim bombers for the RAF, had been killed when the Luftwaffe blitzkrieged the factory during late summer of 1940.

In addition to the trauma sustained by an impressionable, formative mind and body in the shelters, her subsequent years, growing up in the care of an Aunt whose husband had been killed in North Africa, were filled with dismal memories of food shortages, unheated, overcrowded flats and a city diminished of human population and depleted of resources. With foresight, the widowed Aunt had secured the necessary papers to immigrate, with Eileen, to Canada and subsequently to the United States, where they had relatives. When Eileen and her guardian got settled, it was decided that she should resume her schooling, but it was clear, early on, that Eileen was scholastically behind students her own age. She was held back two grades, which only served to make the beanpole-of-a-girl more conspicuous among her new classmates. Her British accent, her height, large green eyes always in a state of surprise or fear, made her the target of the boys' mischief, the primary object of their pranks and dirty tricks.

Of course, not knowing, nor caring, how or why the new girl came to be in such a state, they were unrelenting in their cruelty. In particular, loud noises such as the backfire of an automobile, the slamming of a door would transform the girl into a crouching, sniveling wretch. Class hooligans were constantly sneaking up behind her and popping paper bags or balloons behind her back, tossing the odd firecracker near her as she plodded alone down the school steps or trudged down crowded hallways trying with all her willpower to ignore their malevolence. Add to this archive of harassment a premature, excessive menstrual cycle and you would be hard pressed not to sympathize with the outcast.

For all the religious doctrine taught them, beaten into them by the nuns, they showed Eileen not one iota of pity, friendship, or camaraderie. Credit stubbornness or innocence, she had survived trials exceedingly worse at the behest of Adolph Hitler. Though she did not take her peers badgering and baiting in stride, she endured.

The taunting, the insults laid at her table, did not go unnoticed. The nuns did their part to shield her as best they could, but, when their backs were turned, classroom bullies unleashed their venom. Once the class bell rang at end of day, it was open season on Eileen Hansen.

A disastrous ending to the baiting and pranks would surely have occurred, but for the intervention of a single person. No exasperated school principal, no enraged teacher came forward to challenge the tormentors. Her savior materialized in the person of a classmate, Gina De-Melia. She was the solitary lifeboat of deliverance to navigate Eileen's storm tossed sea. Gina befriended the gawking, slender girl with the heavy British accent not out of pity, but because of some innate, incipient gift of humanity or human kindness that had begun to blossom. Its first object of nurture was Eileen.

If not a paragon of intellect, Gina did her lessons, passed her tests, and made her grades. Generally considered above average in her classes, it was acknowledged by all, especially the boys, that she excelled in physical beauty, a genetic gift from her Italian ancestors. Her maturing body was both a gift and a burden. The classical Roman beauty made her easy to look at and approach, but also made her increasingly the object of lust not only by her male classmates, who were in the excruciating throes of puberty, but by all males above the age of fourteen with a roving eye and libidinous nature. Gradually, Gina's life evolved to one of solitude and isolation because of her beauty, in much the same manner as Eileen's because of her lack of it.

Once Gina began to shower her new friend with the milk of human kindness, talk with her at recess, even share a table with her at lunchtime, the boys began to reassess their cruel behavior toward Eileen. If Gina the beautiful, Gina with the thought provoking body encouraged Eileen's friendship, they must have missed something, some inexplicable, redeeming trait. Not one of the boys in her class wanted to incur the least displeasure on Gina's part. If anything, they would submit to her slightest whim, her most unflattering wish, be it ever so humiliating. After all, anything to do with Gina was sacrosanct.

Over the course of the school year, the two girls became known as *beauty and the beast*, but nary a disparaging word was uttered that could, in any diabolical way, lead back to Gina. The pranks, practical jokes, insults, scathing remarks came to an end. Using her newfound friendship as a springboard, Eileen began to improve in her classes, even receiving an occasional compliment from a teacher. Under Gina's tutelage, after classes, Eileen was coached in the art and science of femininity. Gina styled her hair, showed her how to apply makeup, and tutored her in her choice of clothing. Over the months of this crash course in personal enrichment the beast was slowly transformed into an attractive, confident young woman. No raving beauty compared to her mentor, but a fetching young lass nonetheless.

While Brian stared uninterrupted across the room at Gina, his comrade made mental notes of Eileen's freshly minted qualities.

"Ya know, it was those big slimy teeth I couldn't stand, but get a load of them now, pearl white."

Bobby rattled on about Eileen's newly acquired refinements, while Brian continued his steadfast observation of Gina.

Suddenly, he was aware of Colleen standing in the center of the living room with all the smiling girls surrounding her.

"…and Brian will be our first Postman," she announced.

Hearing his name, Brian suddenly realized he was the center of attention. A poke in the arm from Bobby yanked him from his daydream.

Colleen lead him, complacently, to a door at the side of the living room.

"Remember, you have to knock twice and announce that you have a letter to deliver," she tutored.

Next thing he knew, he was alone. Rolling his eyes, he knocked on the door.

"Got a letter to deliver here. Anyone home?"

"Are any stamps needed," a feminine voice asked.

Befuddled, he looked at his hand thinking perhaps a letter would materialize.

Again the question came through the door.

"How many stamps?"

"I guess, just one stamp."

"Please deliver the letter."

Opening the door to a chorus of girlish twitters, he entered the darkened room. He could hear the door being pulled closed behind him. Advancing tentatively, he was able to see someone seated on the side of a bed. Drawing nearer, he recognized the person as the one and only Gina DeMelia. Frozen in his tracks, he would have stayed there, like Lot's wife slowly turning into a pillar of salt, but for a hand that reached out to grasp his.

He was seated next to Gina on the bed with not a word spoken, her long fingers still embracing his. A pleasant, intoxicating smell invaded and titillated his nostrils, while his eyes adjusted to the darkness. He noticed rouged lips contrasting with her almond skin. The lips beckoned. Black shiny hair fell to her shoulders; a few stray locks partially covered one eyebrow. His head moving slowly towards her, Brian noticed she was wearing a pink angora sweater, with short sleeves exposing supple forearms dotted with tiny black hairs. Around her neck was a gold chain with a small gold cross attached to it.

Drawing ever closer to the captivating fragrance, he felt a hand on his upper arm pull him closer. The intoxicating odor of her perfume assaulted his senses. Slowly, he became aware of a swelling in his crotch, which, although straining the inside of his jeans, felt oddly pleasurable. Their eyes were mere inches from each other. He could feel warm exhalations coming from her nostrils as her red lips pressed eagerly against his. As he moved his legs slightly to allow more comfort, his lips parted and her insistent tongue entered his mouth, exploring the interior and caressing his tongue with a pleasant, slippery stroke.

Feeling her arm embrace his waist, he let his right arm slither across her shoulder, his hand coming to rest on her neck and ear. Eyes bulging, he felt her hand slide gently over his leg and come to rest on his crotch. While she rubbed it gently, he let his tongue move into her mouth. His other hand found its way to her angora sweater, feeling the softness of flesh trapped within the silk brassiere. His eyelids crinkled as Gina's hand clasped his pant leg. Suddenly, they fell back on the bed; his hand reaching downward came to rest on her belly, while her hot breath pumped into his ear.

A persistent knock at the bedroom door startled Brian and Gina.

"Hey, Mr. Postman, times up, come on Brian," Colleen called, with a hint of impatience, from the hallway.

During all this time with Gina, neither had uttered a word. Their breathing slowed. He heaved a sigh of relief, at the same time feeling looseness in the crotch. Neither smiling nor frowning, Gina looked at him with her deep, dark eyes, a slight petulant smirk playing on her lips.

His head pulsating with freshly spawned hormones, Brian remembered nothing for ten or fifteen minutes, save that he'd pulled the bedroom door open to a group of snickering, giggling girls. At last coming to his senses, he was aware that he was sitting at the large rectangular dining room table, covered with colorful table cloth, party favors, plates, forks, and glasses. At the far end of the table stood Colleen poised over a large chocolate cake with a dozen or so candles all lighted and waiting for her to blow them out. Beside Colleen stood Mrs. Maguire with a protective hand on the girl's shoulder. Off to Colleen's left was a side table piled high with open presents, while the rug below the table was littered with wrapping paper and curly ribbons. For the life of him, he could not remember Colleen opening her presents.

Brian was aware of Gina, seated across the table; her face looked slightly angry and her dark eyes had what was commonly described as that *come hither look*. Feeling a slight tap on his left arm, he turned to his best friend with a disparaging look on his face.

"How come you were in the bedroom so long?"

"Long? It couldn't a been more than a minute or two."

"Minute or two! Jeez, it was at least fifteen minutes. The girls were giggling and making smacking noises with their lips. The jerks."

"Did you get to be a postman or what?"

Bobby frowned and raked his hand across his face.

"Yeah."

"Well, what happened, did you get to kiss a girl?"

"Yeah, guess who I got stuck with—good 'ole Eileen Hansen."

Brian wrinkled his nose while cutting a look down the table at Hansen.

"Did you kiss her?"

"That's the funny part. Once I figured out how to do it, it wasn't as bad as I thought. 'Course I won't ever do it again; it's probably not good for your teeth. How about you? You figure out how to kiss Gina?"

"Yeah, I got the hang of it, but I don't think I'll do it again either."

Glancing across at Gina, he watched as she wet her lips with a pink tongue. Once again a flood of hormones kindled his circulatory system. Secretly, he could hardly wait to kiss her again.

Of added significance to the boys, especially Brian and Bobby, was the fact that Gina's father, Franco, owned and operated a popular neighborhood grocery store a few blocks from Partridge Street. The store was a treasure-trove appealing to the sweet tooth of boys and girls. Coolers held cases of cold soft drinks. Candy bars and cookies packed the shelves along the front counter where Mr. DeMelia, a swarthy man, short of stature but wide of frame, tended to the cash register. The white apron hanging from his neck was always tattooed with a variety of colored splotches where his meaty hands frequently cleansed themselves. On a thick black leather belt encircling his protruding stomach, hung a pouch containing an ink stamper that enabled him to expeditiously mark canned goods with a date and price. Also encased in leather on the belt was a box cutter used to slash off the lids of cardboard containers with the speed and skill of an accomplished swordsmen.

Beside him, his wife Cecelia, threadbare sleeves of a gray sweater poking from her white apron, busied herself filling paper bags with canned foods, neatly wrapped packages of cold cuts, chicken breasts, lamb chops, clear plastic bags of pasta, a loaf of bread, one or two quarts of beer, a pack of cigarettes, a dozen eggs, an evening newspaper. While Franco's sausage fingers jabbed the adding machine keys with the dexterity of a concert pianist, Mrs. DeMelia would engage the customer across the counter in neighborhood gossip, weather predictions, reviews of radio shows—what a card that Jack Benny is, and Fibber McGee and Molly, did you ever? And say, Mrs. Carneglia was telling me about a radio that has moving pictures. Now ain't that somethin'.

Forever working and saving, within five years following marriage they had opened their first corner grocery store, eventually taking over a prime corner spot vacated by a prosperous Jewish grocer who retired to Florida. There they were ten years later side-by-side at the counter, Franco chomping a cigar, Cecelia gossiping with one of their loyal customers. The cash register overflowed with currency, books were balanced, bills paid.

Somewhere during that span of years a little girl was born to Franco and Cecelia. Sadly and with much reluctance, Mrs. DeMelia had relinquished her spot behind the counter to accommodate the birth of a girl. Franco's sister, Rosemary, filled the opening, but her proclivity for longwinded monologues and suggestive behavior to male customers soon produced a pink slip in her weekly pay envelope. The next substitute, Gertrude, was a war widow who lived in the neighborhood. She performed adequately, but she kept increasing the frequency and length of restroom breaks until Franco found her passed out in the stockroom toilet with three empty bottles of Schafer beer lying beside her.

"Mama mia!" exclaimed Franco.

After Franco revived her, Gertrude was let go on the spot.

Shortly thereafter, the familiar figure in the grey long-sleeved sweater now patched at the elbows, swathed in a clean white apron, was seen beside Franco. Cecelia, the proud mother of a giggling little girl, Gina, made sure all her regulars viewed the heir apparent, but then quickly placed the little princess in a nearby bassinette, and resumed filling the paper bags with cans, bottles, packages, cartons, and newspapers, all the while peppering her conversation with reminders of store specials on cans of pork and beans, creamed corn, pickled beets—three for a quarter. Except for the occasional diaper change, bottle, breastfeeding, Cecelia and Gina were fixtures at the counter.

Husband and wife had originally envisioned a sprightly mother's helper for Cecelia, but did a complete change of mind when Gina entered school and her figure began to hint of her emerging ethereal beauty. Both parents soon realized the extraordinary gift that was so apparent that even regular customers no longer bussed Gina's cheek or patted her head. In silence and with proper reserve they stood back, nodded their heads as if to say: this is a lady, a young lady of regal bearing, behold her that she may bestow a favorable glance upon your unworthy brow. Though pampered and coddled, Gina did not become the spoiled minx that many predicted. If anything, as she grew, she became seductive, otherworldly, ordained for celebrity.

Men and boys rushed to open doors for her. Scores of male classmates clamored to carry her books. She was a royal personage. All others were peasants: there to do her bidding, cater to her every whim, her slightest wish. Naturally, her near saintliness incurred the wrath and jealousy of female classmates and neighborhood girls. Nothing overt or confrontational, but things were whispered behind her back. When she left the room heads immediately swiveled; when she entered a classroom heads stared down at textbooks, at fingernails, at shoe tops. If Gina ever noticed this subtle campaign to discredit her, she never acknowledged it or gave it a second thought. After all, those were petty things of the common folk, far, far beneath her.

After the obligatory "Happy Birthday" and cutting of the cake, Bobby's mother appeared at the end of the table to help serve ice cream, while Mrs. Maguire sliced the cake. The slices having been placed on paper plates, were passed along until the first piece ended at the far end of the table, where G. G. Wallace sat in regal splendor. In front of him were several paper plates with scraps of macaroni salad, the tag end of a hot dog, bits and pieces of celery, carrots and pickles.

A loud belch caused Brian to look down the table at Wallace, who, in the fraction of a second, had consumed the cake set in front of him.

"Hey, pass me another piece of cake, will ya," Wallace bellowed.

Following this forceful request, Wallace emptied the contents of his ice cream bowl in one magnificent gulp. Having been forewarned of Wallace's prodigious capacity for desserts, Brian and Bobby shuttled additional rations down the table to the salivating leviathan.

After each girl and boy had been served a piece of cake and a dish of ice cream, Mrs. Maguire and her upstairs neighbor, Mrs. McNally, retired to the kitchen to light their cigarettes and enjoy a quiet glass of beer together before submitting to the inevitable cleanup chores.

A third slice of cake in transit to Wallace went airborne, landing with a plop on the table in front of him. Interpreting this as hostile enemy fire, he grabbed the cake with his fist and heaved it down the table like a hand grenade. When it exploded against the side of Colleen's face, the troops at the table engaged in spontaneous combat.

While fusillades of ice cream and cake filled the airspace above the table, like so much exploding flak from enemy gun emplacements, Brian looked across to discover Gina smiling enigmatically at him.

A ceasefire, initiated by the sudden appearance of Mrs. Maguire and Mrs. McNally, saw the combatants put aside their weapons. Upon seeing the carnage and destruction, the two mothers unleashed a counter attack that sent boys and girls scurrying to exits, front and rear. Though Brian was one of the first to escape, Bobby was captured and pressed into service cleaning up the battlefield.

6

Down Below

Morning sunlight poured through the back porch window highlighting a young man, clad in sweatshirt and dungarees, seated at the kitchen table. A spoon slowly stirred a dollop of *Wheaties* breakfast cereal floating languidly in the bottom of his bowl. If his head had been raised and tilted slightly to the right, those golden rays would have illuminated the boys piercing blue eyes, a rounded cheek dotted with freckles and full lips above a strong jaw line. But his head was set at an odd angle. Blue eyes peered into the cereal bowl, his brow wrinkled, his mind seethed with unfathomable mysteries.

At the kitchen sink, Rita plunged her hands into a basin of soapsuds and hot water. Across the room, Brian played with the station dial on the Philco radio next to the sugar bowl and ashtray. Rita's shoulders stiffening in an atypical gesture of annoyance, she turned from her sink of breakfast dishes, wiped her hands and looked over at her son.

"Honey, don't play with the radio. Find a station and let it stay there."

"Sure, Ma," he said oblivious to the screech and squelch of the radio.

"Oh, honey, why so glum? You're not still brooding on that old baseball bat, are you?"

Even, Arrow, could feel the electricity arcing from his master's furrowed brow. Ears twitching like two radar antennas, it waited with anticipation for the slightest command or request.

Rita poured coffee into her green coffee mug. Returning the pot to the gas stove above the pilot light, she pulled her chair up to the table across from her son.

Jealous, Arrow crept slowly across the linoleum floor, coming to rest protectively at his master's feet. The maneuver was accomplished without hostility to Rita, for in some inscrutable way the dog surmised that the food finding its way to his bowl, along with an occasional bone, was provided by the same woman now lavishing affection on his master.

After sipping her coffee and waiting several minutes, she reached across the table and placed her hand on his.

"Now then, what can be so important you're not listening to the baseball scores?"

"I dunno, it's not the same anymore."

"Did something happen at Colleen's birthday party?"

Flinching, Brian pushed his bowl away and reached down to pet Arrow, who responded with a slobbering lick.

"Well, see, I kissed a girl. It was strange, like riding a roller coaster for the first time. Other things happened too."

At this unburdening, Rita's cup smacked the oilcloth sharply, causing Brian to look questioningly at his mother. Her hand shot to her pack of Pall Malls. After lighting a cigarette with a shaking hand, she pulled the ashtray closer.

A look of torment and fear distorting his face, Brian looked up at his mother.

"Did I really come out between your legs?"

A bolt of electricity filled the space between mother and son, followed by an ominous silence. While Brian sat with jaw perched on his right hand, Rita exhaled a torrent of smoke from mouth and nostrils.

On high alert, Arrow's ears twitched.

Stabbing out half her cigarette and draining the dregs of her cup, Rita looked over at her son with a nervous smile.

"Well, yes, that's how you were born. All boys are born that way."

"Are girls born that way, too?"

"Oh. Yes, all kids, children, come into the world that way. Remember the time I pointed out the hospital you were born in. It's not that far from your school. In fact, your cousins Raymond and Michael were born there, too." Feeling an uncontrollable compulsion to prattle on, she added, "I'm pretty sure the McNally's boys were born there, as well, too, all of them, well, except the twins. Maureen couldn't make it to Brady Hospital, so they were born at home." While verbally stumbling along, she raked a hand through her hair.

"Was Gina DeMelia born at the hospital?"

Rita looked down at the chipping red lacquer on her tapering finger-nails.

"Well, I'm not sure of that, maybe. Probably."

"If I came out between your legs…"

"That's called being BORN, honey, or birthing. Yes, birthing. It's a medical term… I think."

"Well…"

Realizing that the crack in the dam was about to burst, thereby fore-shadowing a deluge, she quickly plugged the gap.

"Your father, your Dad, I think he wanted to talk to you about all that… that type of *thing*. So, if it can wait, just a little bit, why not ask him? He's a man and you are, ah, young man and it just makes all the sense in the world for him, your Dad, to attend to these matters. Sort of man-to-man, you see. Okay?"

Relieved of his burden, if only temporarily, Brian shrugged his shoulders. Not wanting to display his eagerness to escape to his bed-room for his baseball glove, then to Bobby's house, he toyed with his spoon and patted Arrow's head. The dog, sensing the passing of an electrical storm, closed its eyes while one hind leg scratched a haunch.

"Guess I'll take Arrow out for his walk," Brian said. Pushing away from the table, he made a beeline for the back door with the dog at his heels.

~

Five a.m. the next morning, Chick pushed open Brian's bedroom door and padded to the side of the boy's bed.

"Hey son, come on, time to get up, fishing *Down Below*," he whispered.

Smiling slightly, Chick waited a bit before shaking the boy's shoulder again. Brian turned his head, one eye opened tentatively. The other would have followed suit, but for the crusted eye mucus sealing it closed. Brian's right hand swiped away the blockage and squinted up at his father.

Realizing the motivational fires had been stoked, Chick, in bathrobe and slippers, moved noiselessly down the hall to the bathroom, leaving the latter-day Izaak Walton to his own devices.

Forcing both eyes wide and simultaneously contorting his mouth in a gaping yawn, Brian energetically cast off the bed covers to reveal the neophyte angler fully dressed and ready for the pleasures of lake or stream. Up he jumped, ready, save for the Converse All Stars that were hastily pulled on to complete his wardrobe.

Flicking on the bedroom light, he disappeared into his closet, emerging in short order with his Shakespeare rod to which was attached a highly prized Mitchell Cap spinning reel, set and strung up so he could instantly attach the new white and green speckled Flatfish lure secured in the pocket of his sweatshirt. Near the closet door was a dresser upon which segregated stacks of magazines titled *Field and Stream* and *Sports Afield* increased in monthly increments. A small upper drawer was dedicated to the burgeoning collection of Topps baseball cards and Captain Midnight decoder badges. With pole and tackle box, he hurried from the bedroom, stopping only to pluck his baseball cap from the bedstead and fix it to his head before switching off the light.

He and his comrade-in-arms were ready to carry out their secret, predawn mission to the posted county reservoir where fish of mythic proportions roamed the depths. A myriad of these finned and gilled monsters displayed the ravages of past battles; a hook or perhaps two snagged a lower lip or a dorsal fin. Numerous scars etched the scales of their prodigious bodies.

The code name of this clandestine mission was *Down Below*. Brian swore a secret oath that he would never reveal the name or location of their mission objective, for only a select handful of sportsmen, like himself, were privileged to penetrate its cloistered, guarded perimeters.

Caution!

Armed guards wielding sawed-off shotguns patrolled shores and woods. Mirror-like sunglasses shielded probing eyes, camouflaged caps pulled low over brows, toothpicks poked from glistening, canine-like teeth.

Turn back now you fool!

It was rumored these modern Centurions were the remnants of Rommel's *Afrika Korps*. Their jeeps navigated a labyrinth of dirt roads surrounding the reservoir where thousands of *Posted* signs warned trespassers of outrageous fines, jail sentences, floggings, the rack and wheel—the guards' stock and trade. Ho, ho. True depraved Nazis eager to break a boy's spinning rod over a knee, then drag the sniveling wretch behind their jeep on a tow chain, all the while guffawing sadistically.

Fee Fi.

More asleep than awake, Brian's gyrating mind conjured a storyline suspiciously like a Captain Midnight episode replete with covert military operations filled with heroes and villains, and increasingly with a young, impressionable damsel in distress.

Fo Fum.

Regardless of the prolific meanderings of his adolescent mind, Brian had the consolation that his father was a detective with badge and gun. Past encounters with the jeep driving Nazis had been defused with a flash of the badge prompting the stone-faced guards to wave them through. At moments like that Brian was grateful his father was a detective and carried a snubnose .38 on his hip. The badge and gun were their passport to Shangri-La.

I smell the blood of an Englishman.

More than once he had overheard his father tell some bush league angler about the Northern Pike and Muskies his buddies on the Jeep patrol had seen and heard breaking the glassy surface of the reservoir with ever-expanding circles.

"Like throwing logs in a pond, kerrrplash, regular monsters, hungry as refugees and meaner than a wino on Monday morning."

No sir, no Sunday morning idyll munching bologna sandwiches and dangling worms over the side of a leaky rowboat; *Down Below* was an epic adventure – faces smeared with camouflage paint, death stalking their every step, hand signals and whispered code words, synchronizing luminous-dial wristwatches by moonlight. Death before dishonor.

Be he alive, or be he dead,
I'll grind his bones to make my bread.

In the kitchen darkness, save for the soft glow pulsating from the gas stove pilot light, Brian set his fishing gear next to the backdoor where his father's equipment was already stacked. Once there, it dawned on him that Arrow had not been at the side of his bed when his father had wakened him. Seeing the aging pet slumbering contentedly in his corner basket, Brian went to him. Bending on one knee he ran a hand over the dog's black and white brow producing a licking tongue and a groan.

He turned at the creaking sound of linoleum to see his father enter the kitchen. Eschewing verbal communication, the two anglers gathered their tackle as quietly as possible and began descending the back stairs. Their secretive departure produced a mere one-eye observation from Arrow, who remained snug in his warm basket, secure in the knowledge that the mistress of the house would attend to his morning feeding—a morning chore overlooked of late by the young master.

Aware the Ford coupe had come to a stop, Brian roused himself from visions of bass and pike, to see before him the black trunk of a Cadillac bathed in the blinking neon reflections of the CAFE sign mounted on top of the all night diner. Years past, the establishment had been converted from a Pullman dining car. The café was located in the bowels of the city's oldest section, near the riverfront, the railroad yard, and a brewery. It catered to the working class and to policemen and detectives pulling a graveyard shift. The narrow, deserted cobblestone street was slick with the remnants of last night's rain.

Rubbing his eyes and squinting at the automobile in front of the Ford, Brian remembered his father telling him that his boyhood friend, Benny, bought a brand new Cadillac or Chrysler every year—an unheard of purchase to Brian, who assumed Benny was a millionaire. The glistening Cadillac meant that Benny, a regular on these secret missions to the reservoir, was seated inside at the counter hunched over a racing form, sipping coffee. Over time, Brian learned that Benny owned a number of restaurants and nightclubs throughout the city, but that his "bankroll" issued from wagers on horse races and card games or the roll of the dice. A wad of bills of various denominations, secured by a gold clip, was kept handy in his pants pocket where it could be quickly plucked to pay for food, beverage, gasoline, or in some instances, a "gratuity" to one of the city's police force.

With a wry smile, Brian recalled his mother referring to his father's chum as *Benny the Dip*. Making a mental note to solicit an explanation from her, it also occurred to him that his father was supposed to explain things, especially inscrutable items like childbirth, swollen penises and such. Benny's presence cast doubt as to how this delicate matter would play out. Encouraged with the knowledge that fathers always had answers to complex questions, under any and all circumstances, he turned his mind to thoughts of fishing and baseball.

His father held the door for him as they entered the steamy warmth of the diner redolent with the smells of brewing coffee, frying bacon, hashed brown potatoes and toast.

Chick sat on a swivel stool beside Benny, placed a silver thermos on the counter, then lit a Chesterfield cigarette. Benny looked up from his racing form to pass down the sports section of the local paper to Brian, seated next to his father.

"Hey, Brian, check out how the great Mantle's doing."

Retrieving the newspaper, Brian immersed himself in the box scores. Nodding his head at Hermie the cook in a nonverbal gesture, his father ordered the customary predawn fishing breakfast. Seconds later, Madge, Hermie's buxom wife and head waitress, placed steaming platters of grilled sugar buns garnished with mounds of ham and eggs in front of them. Shortly, three coffee cups were filled. Adding copious portions of sugar and cream to his coffee, Brian pushed the sports page aside to dig into the ham and eggs. Wolfing down the raisin bun, he listened to Benny regale Chick with reports of his gambling conquests and his "irons in the fire."

Once during a fishing trip to a lake swarming with perch, bullheads and other nondescript fish his father had deciphered the mystery of his boyhood friend Benjamin Mizelli. A young lad in the old neighborhood, a mixture of Irish and Italian Catholics, all of the Democratic persuasion, Benny Mizelli had fallen victim to Muscular Dystrophy, a disease that had kept him inactive and home-bound during most of his youth. Since the Mizellis were downstairs neighbors and he and Benny were the same age, Chick had found it incumbent upon himself to visit, share news of the schoolyard and block, or engage Benny in a friendly game of cards. Though Benny had sisters and brothers, all older, he had been left to his own devices. Chick's reward for his neighborly visits were generous platters of spaghetti slathered with red tomato sauce reeking of garlic and exotic spices, and, occasionally, a nip of homemade vino, all compliments of Mama Mizelli.

Unable to play ball or sell newspapers like his older brothers, Benny had begun passing the time with a deck of cards. At first it had been to fill up hours of loneliness, learn a few card tricks that might entertain the occasional visitor, but later, after thousands of hands of blackjack and poker, it had become a substitute for the sports and street games denied him. Slowly and inexorably, the hobby had emerged into a part-time job, and, much later, to a way of life. At age thirteen and no longer bedridden, he would hobble with the aid of wooden crutches to a public park a few blocks from his house. With his worn deck of cards, he would set up shop and deal cards to retired sanitation department workers, slothful delinquents, unemployed iron workers and troubled war veterans.

At four p.m. he would gather up his cards, winnings and crutches and make his way home for a glass of wine and plate of spaghetti with his boisterous family. In his late teens, the disease in remission, he was able to put aside the crutches, though there remained a slight limp. In his secondhand Cadillac he would drive to various bars, athletic clubs and road houses in and around the city where he turned a card or two and rolled dice, usually to his advantage. Instead of patched dungarees and down-at-the-heels sneakers, he would garb himself in pegged gabardine slacks, camel hair coat, gray fedora and suede shoes. His brothers, on the other hand, were taking the bus or trolley to work at grocery stores and meat markets. From his nineteenth birthday on, Benny began the annual purchase of a new Cadillac or Chrysler; the choice being left up to his aged father, whom he chauffeured to various functions at the Italian-American Club where he was a regular in bocce ball contests.

The boyhood friends followed each other's careers. While Benny was perfecting his gaming skills, accumulating money, even investing in bars or "joints," Chick attained local fame in swimming and diving competitions. Before Pearl Harbor and enlistment in the Navy, he'd made a brief debut in Hollywood as Tarzan's understudy. After his discharge from service, he'd returned to the old neighborhood to marry his girlfriend, Rita.

Occasionally, Benny would reach over to tousle Brian's hair and ask, "Hey Brian, 'gonna catch a big one today, huh?"

Never waiting for or expecting an answer, Benny would continue lamenting the risks and rewards of his perilous profession. His small bowl of oatmeal emptied, he would produce a fat cigar that soon filled the diner with a pungent wreath of smoke accompanied by smoke from Chick's fresh Chesterfield.

Glancing across his father's chest, half petrified, Brian nodded his head while sipping tongue-scalding coffee that produced a fleeting thought of his mother and what she would say if she could see him drinking *coffee*, regardless of the cream and sugar. Looking up with a tinge of guilt, his vision shifted to the voluptuous figure of Madge. Brian tried to look away, but his eyes remained glued to Madge's fleshy cleavage confined in a tight pink uniform. Even at 6 a.m. her lips were smeared with bright red lipstick, finger nails sparkling with matching polish. Overabundant red hair was piled on her head and topped off with a frilly cap. Noting the young man's roving eye, Madge bent over to adjust her nylons, exposing a substantial portion of her backside.

His eyes returning to the morning sports page, Brian had second thoughts about the *chat* with his father and the possibility that Benny would bear witness to it. He surmised that his father would most likely wait until they were alone on the shore, their poles cast out and bail set, allowing ample time to ask all the sexually charged questions that stimulated his imagination and threatened his innocence.

After his second cup of coffee, Chick snuffed out his cigarette, grabbed the filled thermos and motioned to Benny it was time to leave. A nudge in the shoulder dislodged Brian's further observations of Madge's cleavage as she wiped down the countertop in front of him. Holding up the check, he called to Hermie behind the grille. Looking up the cook shook his head and crowed.

"Next time, Chicky. Fix a parking ticket maybe, okay?"

Saluting Hermie, he pulled the door open to allow Benny and Brian to exit.

Clearing away the newspapers from Benny's place, Madge was surprised and elated to find a crisp twenty-dollar bill. With sleight of hand, perfected over a period of twenty years, Madge slipped the bill into the depths of her brassiere.

Outside, Brian could feel the chill morning air. After his father opened the trunk of the Ford, they transferred their poles and tackle to Benny's car. Although he longed for the spaciousness and comfort of the back seat, capable of accommodating a team of youthful woodsmen, Brian was snug in his usual place between the two men up front. Dreading the *talk* on the way to the reservoir, amongst mixed company, Brian planned to drift off into a pleasant nap as soon as the Cadillac crossed the river heading south. A none too difficult an assignment with a full belly, the hum of the tires on wet pavement and soft swing music drifting from the radio speaker directly in front of him. He pulled his ball cap down over drooping eyelids, the sleek automobile swooshed through narrow streets like a naval destroyer. While leaden eyelids grew heavier, snippets of conversation pierced his consciousness.

Wet tracks… rackets… muscle… handicaps... everything legit.

A Technicolor dream of a thrashing big mouth bass chomping down on his new green and white Flatfish plug was interrupted when the car came to a screeching halt. Suddenly awake, Brian looked up to observe the front entrance of a bait store, where a half dozen other cars stood idling at the curb, bluish-white exhaust puffing from tailpipes. He followed his father, clutching the tin bait pail, down the steps.

Before entering, Chick turned to his son.

"Remember, not a word about where we're going."

Brian nodded his head with grim determination. Silently, he assured himself not even the Nazi security guards could club that information out of him. The specter of Fang, Captain Midnight's archenemy, a maniacal laugh erupting from a cavernous mouth dripping saliva, stirred his imagination. Over his shoulder he glimpsed Benny at the wheel of the idling vehicle, head nearly obscured by the pages of the racing form.

While the bait pail was being filled with silver minnows, Brian gazed around the basement store in awe. All the accouterments of his boyhood dreams and fantasies clamored for his undivided attention. Every piece of hunting and fishing gear ever made was crammed into glass display cases or hung haphazardly from the ceiling and walls, this in a space no bigger than a two-car garage. Hunting knives, casting rods, reels, hip boots, lures, spinners, lead weights, hooks, flies, decoys, shotguns, wool socks with red stripes, .22 rifles, fish plugs and lures of every size, shape and color, shotgun shells and bullets of every caliber—all spewed from this cornucopia of sporting paraphernalia.

With Brian at his heels, Chick marched to the front counter, the dripping bait pail in one hand, and a ten-dollar bill in the other. Brian watched Mel, the storeowner, wink at his father.

"No Chicky, take care of my next speeding ticket. Okay?"

Chick smiled, pocketed the bill and turned toward the stairs leading up to the street.

Speeding from the curb, the black sedan was soon clipping along the river road at 75 mph, its driver safe in the knowledge that he was immune to moving violations with his friend the detective seated beside him. Recurring images of ravenous northern pike and starving bass filled Brian's head the closer they got to the fabled body of water. The fish grew in length and breadth with each passing mile.

He was startled awake when the Cadillac bottomed out on a tunnel-like dirt road that cut its way precariously through arching chestnut, birch and elm trees. Benny spat out a litany of expletives, some English, some Italian, as the muffler scraped a boulder, but continued to drive at break neck speeds more suited to a highway than the meandering dirt track he was piloting.

A few precarious miles up the gullied road the automobile breached a cavern of trees. There before the trio the first rays of sunlight kissed the glassy expanse of the reservoir, the surface marred slightly, Brian thought, with the zigzag patterns carved out by leviathan in search of prey. Brian trembled with anticipation as Benny braked to a stop. Unconsciously, his hand slipped into his sweatshirt pocket to caress the boxed Flatfish lure.

While his father and Benny baited hooks with wriggling minnows, Brian withdrew the small box, still sealed in clear plastic, containing the green and white speckled Flatfish. Ever on the alert for the whining transmission of the Jeep patrol, he attached the lure to his leader.

"Come on, Brian, try the shiners. Gotta go deep for the big fish," Benny advised from a cloud of cigar smoke.

Ignoring the entreaty, Brian began his sojourn down the shoreline in search of the ideal spot to make his first cast. Shuffling along with the spinning pole held high above the rocky shore, he half expected a hand on his shoulder, his father clearing his throat in preparation for the *talk*.

Distracted by an explosion in the water, he looked out to see an Osprey rise from the surface with a fish dangling from its talons. In a small cove he stopped, pulled back the bale on the spinning reel, hooked the tip of his index finger on the monofilament line, cocked his right arm and wrist, then cast out long and smooth. The lure splashed down a respectable distance from shore, small circles forming around its entry. He began to reel in assiduously.

An hour later, the sun sizzling behind a web of haze, he reeled in for the hundredth time without the anticipated gut-numbing strike. Later, with a lack of enthusiasm, he retreated to the campfire where his father and Benny drank coffee and smoked. Getting closer he could see a stringer in shallow water stirring with a half-dozen Northern Pike. Their poles were propped in the crook of V-shaped branches stuck in the sand.

"Hey, Brian, what I tell ya? Give the shiners a try fer chrissake. Chick, tell'em, go ahead—tell'em," Benny said..

But no advice was forthcoming.

Brian searched his father's face for a clue or a sign, but was confronted with the usual clam-like lips and eyes squinting through cigarette smoke. With a wink of an eye, Chick turned to attend to his pole, bobbing and weaving with the weight of yet another Pike or Muskie. As he reeled in, Brian began a lonesome trek down the shoreline listening to a whooping crane belt out its abuse at the pathetic lad below with the new Flatfish dangling from his fish pole.

Stopping momentarily, Brian spit in the water and swore that if he had his father's snubnose .38 he'd blast the eyes out of that scoffing bird and all the fraudulent Big Mouth Bass pictured in magazine ads.

He stopped at a broad cove as far from his father and Benny as he could get. The water was calm and choked with Pickerelweed, a good sign, perhaps an omen, he speculated. Brooding by a weather-beaten tree stump, he stepped up to the shoreline, his teeth set, his nostrils flared. Brian drew his spinning rod back lazily and, with a jot of disgust mixed with a dash of hope, cast out, sending the Flatfish on its longest journey of the morning. Halfway in on the second cast, while he watched a lone Mallard on a surface-skimming flight, the reel exploded. Line stripped off like a rifle shot. In shock and confusion he groped for the reel's handle while even more line peeled off. The faster he reeled the faster the line played out, until he adjusted the bail to insure a steady measured retrieval. Alternately cursing and praying, he worked the fish closer and closer into the muddy shallows in which his prized All Star sneakers were submerged. Closer yet, he could make out the bulging eyes of the biggest bass he'd ever seen. He screamed for a net or a gaff. Five feet… four feet. Closer and closer it came. He reeled in as though his life depended on the perfect execution of every movement. The fish's thrashing and maneuvering never diminished. When it was within spitting distance, Brian waded farther out into the chilly water until his calves were as numb as his brain. Coaxing the fish ever closer, the spinning rod held high and bent double, he knelt in the frigid water to slip two fingers into the fish's gill. Breathing heavily, he dragged his captive up on shore like a chest of Spanish gold, cursing the fish for its every flop and twitch.

Covered with weeds and mud, the bass clutched to his chest like a sacred icon, the spinning rod dragging in the sand behind, he hurried up the shore to his father and Benny.

Chick silently, but proudly, measured and weighed the fish. Fourteen inches, six pounds. Possibly a record, his father mused. Deserving of a picture in the sports pages, a little blurb about the skillful angler responsible, but damn, can't go bragging on a fish caught here, he cautioned.

"I guess we could always say you hooked it up at Warner's Lake at Grandpa's camp."

Already conforming to the charade, Brian formulated his story. "Yeah, Warner's Lake on a flatfish. Put up a heckuva fight."

No matter that his friends and the sports writer would see instantly through the sham; he was a veteran of *Down Below* sworn to secrecy. He thought briefly of sending a picture of himself and his catch to *Sports Afield* magazine with a brief note that they were welcome to publish the enclosed photo but that under no circumstances could he reveal the location of the catch.

On the drive back to the city, Benny let him hold the pearl-like steering wheel as the speedometer needle bent past the eighty mph mark.

Back at Hermie's Café, father and son transferred their gear and the bass, wrapped in layers of newspaper, to the trunk of the Ford. Brian watched Benny speed away into the early afternoon. With dungarees bristling with stickers and crusted with dried mud, he climbed into the back seat. Before falling into a deep sleep, he vaguely remembered his father patting his shoulder and saying they would have their special *talk* sometime in the near future.

7

Arrow

Opening sleep-swollen eyes, the first thing Brian saw that morning was the wall calendar above his desk. Displayed in all its graphic beauty was this month's image of a large mouth bass, its tail skating across the surface of a lake, a lure dangling from its lower jaw. Brian's lips bowed into a smile as he contemplated his recent battle with a similar fish caught on an outing to the city reservoir. Abruptly, the smile disappeared when he remembered his father teaching him how to clean the bass on the back porch. Although the blood and intestines had been quickly removed and wrapped in several layers of newspaper, there lingered a grim memory. His nostrils twitched at the thought of the fetid slime coating the internal organs before they were dispatched to the garbage pail. Eating the fish wasn't a pleasant experience either because of numerous bones that accumulated between his teeth.

He would have preferred that his trophy fish be mounted, like the ones at the bait store, so he could show it off to friends, but his father had, in no uncertain terms, lectured him on the rules of fish and game. Fish were for eating, not wall decorations. A true outdoorsman does not waste nature's bounty; neither does he gloat over his kill. If you didn't intend to eat your catch, which included the unpleasant chore of gutting it and disposing of the entrails, then you must put aside your pole and tackle. This woodsmen's code also applied to hunting. When old enough to have a .22 rifle and a shotgun, he would be expected to honor this unwritten law. If you killed an animal, be it rabbit, pheasant or deer, it was your obligation to clean it and consume the meat. Killing wildlife was not a cause for celebration. If this wasn't to your liking, and not everyone was cut out to be a hunter or fisherman, you shouldn't have a rifle, shotgun, or fishing pole. Besides, Chick explained further, after you clean a few fish and skin a rabbit, pluck a pheasant, you forget about the mess and enjoy the meal that much more because you're the one responsible, in a small way, for it. That's what you have to remember—responsibility.

He dutifully acknowledged his father's words, but would have preferred that fish were available without bones or skin festooned with slimy scales.

Pushing back the covers, exposing pajamas printed with a multitude of bats and balls, Brian stepped into his slippers and padded to the bathroom. With teeth brushed and face doused with cold water, he made a cursory investigation of the kitchen. His mother was busy at the stove, surrounded by pots and pans, the smell of onions, basil, and rosemary permeating the air. He lingered briefly at her side as she pecked his cheek, then off he shuffled to the back door. Opening the door slightly, he whistled and waited for Arrow to come slithering through the opening, tail wagging, tongue dangling from his mouth. To his dismay, the dog did not materialize. Opening the door wider did not produce his faithful pet either. Perturbed by its tardiness, he ventured impatiently onto the back porch and over to the dog's cushioned bed.

Appeased at the familiar black and white head propped on matching paws, Brian whistled and called out to the dog as he approached, but without success. Kneeling beside his pet, with jaw twisted, brow wrinkled, he reached down and pushed at Arrow's shoulder. Surprised at the coldness of the animal's coat, he pulled his hand back as though stung. Deeply concerned, he hurried into the kitchen.

"Ma, I can't wake Arrow up. I think he's sick."

Putting aside the bowl she was stirring, Rita turned to face Brian. The smile that usually saluted him was not in evidence. Mother and son hurried to the back porch to confront the day's first conundrum.

Rita examined the dog, also noting the lack of body heat. Brian stared at her hand as it swept slowly over the dog's head and down its side, then returned to the forehead where a thumb pulled back one of its eyelids. Her hand balled into a fist that found refuge in an apron pocket.

"How comes he won't wake up, Ma?"

No answer was forthcoming.

"Should I wake up Dad, maybe he knows something about this?"

"Your father's working an early shift today. Let's go into the kitchen."

There at the kitchen table, he watched with concern as her hands clasped and unclasped.

"Aw, Ma, I'll go and try to wake Arrow up again. He's just getting old, is all."

Her arm shot across the table and patted his shoulder, encouraging him to stay put.

"No, wait a minute, honey. Arrow isn't going to wake up. He died during the night," she said, adding quickly so there was no doubt about the finality of it, "He's dead."

"But Arrow's just a dog. I know people die, like all those soldiers in the war, but…"

"All things die, remember when your grandmother was real sick, well, she died."

"But Arrow is my only pet, my only dog. Maybe if we called the doctor."

"He won't wake up, honey. He has died."

Silent now, his hand rushed to his mouth. Hurrying to his mother's side, he felt her arm encircle his waist.

~

The blue Ford coupe moved slowly through the late afternoon sun. Brian looked out the passenger door window at a trolley car they passed. Chick was at the steering wheel, he reached up to adjust the rearview mirror, then he tapped Brian's shoulder.

"How you doin' son?"

"Okay."

"We can get you another dog if you want."

"Nah."

Chick glanced quickly at his son then back at the road. The exhaust purred loudly. Brian stared at the broken clock in the center of the dashboard, the hands frozen on twelve. Warm, humid air streamed through the open windows.

His eyes wandered down to his sneakers, no longer shiny white like they were last summer. The canvas material was now scuffed and dull, the soles worn down from the punishment of hundreds of ball games.

The automobile pulled off the main thoroughfare onto a narrow dirt road that ran alongside railroad tracks elevated above the road. Clusters of gaunt pine trees covered rolling hills punctuated with flat scrubland spreading out from the west side of the railroad tracks. Brian knew that on the other side of the railroad embankment was the Six Mile Water-works, a small municipal reservoir where city dwellers came to swim, fish, and row wooden boats painted with war surplus paint.

He remembered stopping on the railroad tracks when he and his two cousins were picnicking with his mother, father and uncle. He and his cousins placed pennies on the steel rails, hoping a train would speed by and squash the coins into flat disks. They waited nearby, alert for the roar of a locomotive or a whistle, but a train never passed by that afternoon. After a swim and a meal of roasted hot dogs they forgot about the pennies perched on the seemingly endless miles of steel rail that their Uncle Joe said ran all the way to the West Coast of America.

The Ford turned right, proceeded up a bifurcating dirt road and crossed the railroad tracks, allowing Brian and his father to see the deserted reservoir below them. Passing the boat dock and small cabin that housed a snack bar, the blue coupe continued down the rutted road, stopping finally in a field dotted with slender pines. Opening their doors at the same time, father and son stepped onto the sandy soil and walked to the back of the car. Chick grasped the handle of the trunk and flung it open revealing the carcass of the black and white dog stretched out on a burlap sack. Brian thought the dead animal appeared to be running or perhaps chasing a rabbit in his dreams, a phenomenon he had observed in the past. He shrugged his shoulders, realizing his pet of many years would never dream again.

Chick reached into the trunk and withdrew a long-handled shovel. Father and son walked into the field a short distance from the car. Chick speared the ground with the blade of the shovel, pushing it deeper into the loamy earth with his heel. Grasping the wooden handle of the shovel, he pitched the dirt aside. When the dirt had accumulated sufficiently, he handed the shovel to Brian while stepping away from the shallow hole.

Pulling a pack of cigarettes from the pocket of his polo shirt, he shook out a smoke and lighted it. Watching Brian expand the hole, he exhaled smoke from his nostrils.

"Hot enough for you?"

Brian paused for a second. "How deep should we go?"

Chick stepped closer to the hole where Brian now stood up to his calves.

"A few more feet will do it. You okay with this?"

The shovel plunged into the hardpan now making its presence known in the bottom of the hole.

"Yeah."

"Let me take a few more puffs and I'll spell you."

Brian continued shoveling for a few minutes then stopped to look up at his father.

"He was the best dog."

Chick took the shovel and resumed the work. Brian watched his father pitch dirt and rocks up onto the pile.

"You ever kill anyone with your gun?"

Chick stopped and turned. He looked directly at his son.

"Nope. Hope I never have to."

Satisfied, Brian sat down in the sand and wrapped his arms around his knees.

Standing beside the trunk, Brian watched his father lift the dead animal from within and carry it to the grave, placing it gently at the side of the oblong hole. After stepping into the void, he pulled the dog to him and, with Brian's help, lowered it to the earth. He looked up to see Brian offering his hand. Smiling, he took the outstretched hand to help gain purchase on the sand. Pulling the shovel from the dirt pile, he handed it to Brian, who began to upend soil onto the carcass at the bottom of the grave.

"He sure was a good dog, wasn't he?" Chick said.

"He was. I should have taken better care of him."

"You did fine. Think some day you'll maybe want another pet?"

"I don't think so."

"Tell you what. We finish up here, we'll go get a coke at the snack bar near the boat dock. What say?"

"I'd like that."

With the hole now completely filled and mounded over, Brian threw the shovel down and hurried to the car.

Nodding his head at the boy's back, Chick picked up the spade and tamped down the mounded sand.

~

That afternoon, Brian sat with his friend Bobby on a crate in the cellar of Gordy Parker's house watching a movie on a white sheet draped over a pipe running across the floor stringers. All the members of Scout Troop 4 were staring up at the screen mesmerized by the horsemanship and no-nonsense dialogue of Hoot Gibson and his trail partner, Bob Steel. A glaring cone of the high intensity light from the 16 mm projector turned the huddled scouts into silhouettes. Into the funnel-shaped light came the unmistakable bulk of G. G. Wallace in search of a seat that would accommodate his ungainly body. Nearly completing his navigation with only a few smashed toes, he at last reached an unoccupied wooden box. Lowering his heavy frame onto the crate, he settled down to watch the western and enjoy a Hershey bar at the same time. Suddenly, the box collapsed, spilling Wallace and his half-eaten candy bar onto the cement floor. During the fall his right arm shot out to seek support. His hand clasped the top of a storage bin, pulling it over and spilling the contents onto the floor in front of the improvised movie screen. Amidst the commotion, the cellar light was flicked on.

There before Scout Troop 4 was a collection of golf clubs, tennis rackets and Brian's missing Louisville Slugger. In the pandemonium that ensued, both verbal and nonverbal, the movie projector ground to a halt. Brian and Gordy were poised over the baseball bat, each ready to claim ownership. Parker, realizing his thefts were exposed not only to the scout troop but also to his father, the troop master and movie projector operator, fixed his attention on Brian. Before Mr. Parker could seize his felonious son, Gordy's fist came up to meet Brian's stomach and would have rendered him breathless and in pain had not Brian blocked the punch while wrestling Gordy to the floor, amidst a cheering, jeering group of scouts. Experienced at separating pugnacious boys, Mr. Parker succeeded in grasping his son by the shirt collar and dragging him out of harm's way. After sending Gordy upstairs to his room, he called his scouts to attention.

"Now settle down, just settle on down so's we can git to the bottom of this," he cautioned in a drawl. "Just what in the …devil's going on here?"

The bat now in possession of its rightful owner, Brian looked up at the Scout Master.

"This is my bat for sure, Mr. Parker. Gordy must have stolen it during one of the Patroon's practice sessions.

"You sure of that?"

"Well, it's my bat, just ask Bobby. He was with me when it came up missing."

Inured to his son's past iniquities, the Scout Master shook his head in resignation.

"You go ahead, take the bat. I'll talk to Gordy about this. For now, we'll call it a day. I'll see you boys next week. Remember, I want those of you concerned to finish up on your merit badge projects so's I can get everything into the council."

While the boys hurried up the cellar stairs, Mr. Parker pulled Brian aside.

"Son, go ahead take the bat. If you say it's yours, that's good enough for me. My-oh-my, that boy of mine can be a tribulation, a godawful tribulation."

The last scout to make his exit, one in which he attempted to draw as little scrutiny as possible, G. G. Wallace lumbered up the cellar steps, his face and fingers smeared with chocolate.

<u>8</u>

Pigeon Coop

From the heights of the chestnut tree overlooking the Jews yard, Bobby McNally looked down at his comrade straddling a lower limb and gave him the all clear sign. Descending from his lofty perch, he followed Brian across the limb from which they silently dropped, with the aid of imaginary parachutes, into enemy territory on the other side of the fence.

Any challenge, particularly one from Gordy Parker, could not go unanswered, especially if the liberation of a single pigeon from the barn loft would initiate them forever into neighborhood folklore. Only a handful of elite, audacious boys had ever returned from the loft with a captured bird. Heading that short list were Charlie Maguire and Bobby's older brother Greg, both of whom had achieved the near impossible mission of climbing into the pigeon coop at the Jews Home and capturing a pigeon that was later released after a day or two of gloating. Many a boy, having bragged of his courage and bravery before attempting the mission, but failing miserably, was forever shrouded in ignominy. Brian and Bobby swore that would not be their fate.

Braggarts who failed the pigeon coop mission became outcasts when exposed for their lack of backbone, a dearth of courage under fire. While licking their wounds, they became infrequent visitors to ball diamonds, football scrimmages, and street corners where *regular* boys congregated and communed. Embracing self-imposed exile, they transferred to schools outside the neighborhood or moved with their parents to far-flung regions of the city, or, worse still, to distant cities in the hinterland.

The two comrades bore those consequences in mind as they made their circuitous route to the barn that housed their mission objective. The malevolent image of Johnny Russian was also readily available. They made their way to the barn, perhaps with a tad too much histrionics, crawling on their stomachs, alert for the slightest threat. Silently they crept past a garden bursting with its bounty of vegetables. There they hunkered down when the ice wagon maneuvered noisily around the back of the Jews Home and came to a stop. The teamster, setting aside the thick leather reins controlling the two draft horses, stood up to end a solo Italian aria with theatrical flourish, then bowed to the dozen or more fans he fancied were seated or slumbered behind the windows of the rest home overlooking his ice wagon.

The boys watched with trepidation as the barn door opened exposing their archenemy. After hesitating briefly, Johnny Russian lurched into the backyard.

"Mister Johnny, mi amico, come, come, enjoy an excellent piece of ice, compliments of Antonio Mario Puccinelli, at your service," the teamster said with a bow while handing the chunk of ice to Johnny Russian. Johnny's single eye sparkled and his misshapen mouth formed what Puccinelli intuited as the ghost of a smile. Bowing his head in thanks, Johnny pointed to the skies above the barn. Antonio hooked his ice tongs onto the tailgate of the wagon, then cocking his head watched as a kit of Johnny's pigeons strafed the barn roof, then simultaneously executed synchronized backward somersaults.

Slapping his forehead, Antonio exclaimed, "Mama mia, mama mia, these pigeons have magic, Mister Johnny, bellissimo."

At the sound of Johnny's loud whistling and hand clapping, the birds circled above the two men before landing at his feet, where they were rewarded with a handful of seed. Antonio took his tongs and clamped them onto a block of ice at the tailgate. Hefting it onto a thick leather pad on his right shoulder, he hurried into the kitchen as melting ice dribbled down his back.

The commandos observed these activities wide-eyed from concealment in the garden. Their surveillance continued until the ice wagon pulled away from the back of the rest home, completing a circuit around the ramshackle structure and exiting onto Western Avenue.

When once again the area near the barn was deserted, the boys continued slithering from the garden to a string of garages butting up to the Rest Home property line. Once there, they jumped to their feet. Running around the building, they came to a wood fence that allowed them to climb onto the roof of the garages. Moving swiftly to the far end of these structures, they at last found themselves out of sight from anyone in the rear of the rest home, but, to their displeasure, they discovered that their position on the garage rooftop forced them to jump across a four-foot space to the adjoining rooftop attached to the back of the barn housing the pigeon coop.

Though the distance of a mere four feet would not normally intimidate the daredevils, who had bounded across greater distances on level ground, looking down from the parapet to the earth below gave them pause for thought. Not wanting to appear indecisive or jeopardize his gumption, Brian backed up several feet before making a running leap across the gulf onto the shed rooftop. Shortly, Bobby also vaulted across the chasm.

From their position on the sloping rooftop they were able to push open a window allowing them entry to a second story gallery of planks and beams where hay had been stored for the livestock that once occupied the stalls on the first level. Brushing aside cobwebs and spider webs, they stood shoulder to shoulder, alert for signs of danger—a tripwire, a snare, a trapdoor, the ogre. Peering up into the shadows, they were able to see the pigeon loft at the apex of the barn roof. A small platform was attached to the entrance door of the coop. Brian estimated the distance between themselves and the loft above at fifteen feet.

Except for the subdued cooing of the pigeons above them and the scuttling of mice below, the barn interior was cloaked in the silence of a tomb. With few windows and no openings for ventilation, the dusky interior was filled with fetid, stagnant air common to farm structures housing animals. Somewhere in the shadows they could hear goats milling about chewing hay. Minimal illumination was supplied by shafts of light, replete with motes of dust, invading the warped barn siding and by numerous holes in the ancient shingled roof. With the exception of the window they had just entered, the other windows, many with broken panes of glass, were boarded over.

Silent and motionless, the boys waited until their eyes adjusted to the dim light, their nostrils to the smells of beast and bird.

Hesitantly, Brian began to shin up a steel pipe supporting the thick wood beam that would allow them access to the pigeon coop. Swiftly achieving the support beam, Brian straddled it and waited for his friend to join him in the heights. From their position on the beam the boys looked down briefly at the floor below, then quickly focused on the entrance door of the pigeon coop located at the far end of the beam, a distance Brian calculated at twenty feet.

Not wanting to dwell on either the height of his perch or the distance across the beam to the loft, he lowered himself, belly first, onto the beam and began a slow but steady hand-over-hand crawl, mindful to keep his eyes straight ahead. Halfway across the beam, with Bobby close behind, he stopped abruptly. Closing his eyes and wrapping his arms tightly around the thick beam, he wrinkled his nose before sneezing loudly. The noise shattered the silence. Fighting off another voluminous sneeze, he felt Bobby's hand on his right foot.

"Shhh, I heard something."

Attempting to turn his head to report his condition, Brian heard the squeal of rusty hinges on the barn door. Fearful of looking down, the boys clung immobile to the beam like lizards while listening attentively to the sound of footfalls, the clink and clank of tools either being taken up or returned to storage. The billing and cooing of pigeons housed in the loft, a mere fifteen feet in front of them, intruded on the foreboding silence.

Sensing the ever-present danger of Johnny Russian, they faltered. Was their mission compromised?

Feeling nauseous, Brian managed to whisper back to his companion to begin a retreat. With a similar unpleasantness in his belly, McNally started the difficult and thoroughly unmanly maneuver of crawling backwards. The retreat accomplished, the boys slid down the pipe, exiting speedily out the back window. On the shed roof, they rested with their backs against the rough plank wall while they regained their composure.

"Come on, let's get out of here. That was too close for comfort."

"Did you see Squirrel?"

"Nah, but I heard him go in the tool crib."

"Yeah, it had to be him."

"Who else?"

"You get dizzy up there?"

"A little, how 'bout you?"

"A bit. Ya know, Gordy said he walked across that beam to the coop."

Bobby spit. "He's a liar, no one can tightrope walk across that beam."

"Yeah, I don't believe him either."

The thick rubber soles of their sneakers scraped against the asphalt shingles as they scrambled down the slanted shed roof. At roof's edge they climbed onto an overhanging tree branch that allowed them to drop to the ground. Sprinting through the narrow, tunnel-like space between garages, they were halfway through when they came to an abrupt halt. In the shadows ahead, two silhouettes appeared. They stopped abruptly, thinking Parker and Delaney had covertly observed their failure. Alerted to a possible confrontation, the boys prepared themselves for a scathing chastisement. Waiting cautiously, they finally recognized the two boys approaching. They were Brian's cousins Ray and Mike.

"Where you guys going?" Ray inquired.

"Nowhere," they replied simultaneously.

"Where you headed?" Brian asked.

Ray patted the pocket of his jeans, "There's a meeting of the Partridge Street smoking club in Sherwood Forest. Come on with us."

"Sure," both Brian and Bobby echoed.

Following Ray, who was the oldest among them and, therefore, undisputed leader, the two boys followed behind him and his younger brother. Along the way, Brian cautioned Bobby not to divulge anything about their failed attempt to achieve the pigeon coop. The foursome followed a path behind the barn next to a high wood fence. The path soon ended at another long line of garages, now used for storage, at the back corner of the rest home property. Using an abandoned wagon, its high spoke wheels warped and sunk into the dirt and weeds, the boys gingerly climbed to the top of the garages. Crossing the roof they came to a halt overlooking a section of land owned by the Jews Home. Abandoned for years, the area was choked with birch, elm, and sumac trees all growing in incestuous fecundity. The neighborhood boys called this derelict piece of real estate, Sherwood Forest.

It had all started at the Madison Theatre at a Saturday matinee that had included two or three cartoons, a world events newsreel, and a main feature, generally a western, a swashbuckler or a movie about Robin Hood and his band of merry men. Rushing from the movie theatre after the show, they would invade Sherwood Forest with cunning and stealth. And act out with much athleticism and boisterousness the battle scenes, sword fights, and barroom brawls recently observed.

One by one, the boys climbed down the most accessible tree to the ground. Ever on the alert for an authority figure or the ubiquitous Johnny Russian, they surveyed the shadowy glade before moving in single file through the woods. Ray stopped abruptly and assumed a kneeling position when the shed came into sight. The other boys followed suit. They waited in silence as Ray made an imitation bird call that was soon answered in a similar manner by Mouse, the sentry and youngest member of the gang, posted on the roof of the shed.

The squad moved quickly and silently to the open doorway of a shack, long abandoned, in a far corner of Sherwood Forest. Inside were three other neighborhood denizens, their spokesman being Jimmy "Stretch" Claflin, the Patroons' first basemen. Though known to all from their earliest childhood, he was set apart by his attendance at a public school.

Following jovial greetings fraught with cryptic handshake rituals, the boys began displaying cigarettes recently pilfered from open packs left casually on kitchen tables, dresser tops, and window ledges. Ray pulled a red package of Pall Malls from his dungarees to discover the cigarettes severely crushed. Plucking them, one-by-one, from the pack, he passed them out to Brian, Bobby and Mike. Neophytes to this adult pastime, Brian and Bobby looked around the shed to observe the smoking techniques of the other boys. Though new to this type of behavior, they had, from their earliest years, observed parents and relatives either singly or in groups stick the cigarettes between their lips and strike a match to ignite them, producing thick ribbons of smoke. None the wiser, the boys assumed that the benefits of this adult habit would in some mysterious way enrich their lives.

They watched Stretch Claflin strike a match to the cigarette in the corner of his mouth. Smoke soon wafted into his eye, causing him to squint, his eyes to water. One after another, cigarettes were lighted, puffed, looked at, and speculated about. Soon smoke was billowing from every crack and crevice of the woodshed, filling shafts of sunlight with its swirling, aromatic vapors.

Ray looked over at Brian and asked, "Say, when are you and Bobby going to sneak up to the pigeon loft?"

"Ah, real soon, real soon."

"Just wondering what you two were doing in back of the barn."

"On a scouting mission, you know, getting the lay of the land."

"Sure, you gotta dope out these things real good, nail down all the details, right?"

"Yeah," Brian said, as he and Bobby nodded vigorously.

Mike was puffing his cigarette with such concentration and energy that it appeared he was attempting to start a fire by coaxing the glowing embers to flames. Satisfied that he could perform, albeit awkwardly, this hitherto adults-only ritual, Brian inhaled a lungful of tobacco smoke, which was just as quickly expelled through his gaping, gagging mouth, this to the accompaniment of uncontrolled laughter from gang members. Before the laughter died away, there was a loud thumping on the roof of the shed, followed by a warning yell from Mouse.

"Here comes Squirrel, better amscray," he called.

Hurling their cigarettes away, the boys scattered in all compass directions. Within seconds the shed was empty of everything but the lingering smoke of their cigarettes and spent matches used to ignite them. Crawling under fences, escaping to garage roofs, the boys vanished.

Sherwood Forest quickly returned to the leafy, tranquil arboretum it had been, except for the singular presence of a man in bib overalls, blue sport coat, and army forage cap partially covering a hideous face that looked out at the world from a solitary eye. The intruder made his way slowly and cautiously to the woodshed so recently abandoned by the cigarette smokers. There he inspected the remains of their experimentation. After a few minutes of contemplation, or perhaps empathy, he departed as slowly and quietly as he had come.

~

Stopping at the top of the back stairs, Brian, for barely a second, expected his old pet Arrow to come bounding in from the porch to leap up and press his front paws on his chest, but, to his regret, the outpouring of canine affection had come to an end. With eyes cast down, he entered the kitchen door.

Seeing his parents seated across from each other at the kitchen table, he cocked his head in surprise. Not only was this an unusual event for a weekday afternoon, but, moreover, they were dressed in the clothes usually reserved for Sunday dinners or church.

Stepping close to receive the obligatory hug from his mother, he saw a curious mark on her upper left arm that to him looked every bit like a cattle brand he'd seen in dozens of cowboy movies at the Madison Theatre. Noticing his puzzled look, Rita pulled Brian close to her.

"Nothing gets past those blue eyes of yours, does it?"

"Well, it kind of looks like a circle X," he said while rendering the figure on the oilcloth with his index finger.

"It's just a little surgery Dr. McCann did in his office. He wanted to remove a mole, but I might have to go to Brady Hospital for an operation. Dr. McCann will take the stitches out next week. In another week you probably won't even notice it."

Looking at his father, who had just stubbed out a cigarette in the ashtray, Brian watched with more than casual interest as he exhaled the last of the smoke.

Rita patted Brian's rear, before realizing that he had informed her not too long ago that he was getting too big for that kind of affectionate caress, even going so far as to suggest that from here on out it might be best to shake hands.

"Honey, why don't you go into your room for a bit so we can finish our conversation, okay hon?"

Always anxious to be left out of adult conversations, Brian hurried to his room, where he plucked his baseball mitt and ball from his desk and began to pantomime Mickey Mantle racing back to the center field wall of Yankee Stadium, turning at the last second to rob a rival of a home run. Suddenly realizing that, if he dawdled any longer, he would be late for an important practice, he pulled on his baseball cap and grabbed his bat.

After making his announcement about the baseball practice for a playoff game the very next day, he turned to leave, but felt his father's hand on his arm.

Chick looked him in the eye while his hand toyed with the gray fedora hat on the table in front of him.

"You know I owe you an apology about that bat. Just like you said, it was stolen. I should have known you were right. Say, can I give you a ride to practice before I go back to work?"

"Nah, Bobby and I are going to ride our bikes over, probably stop for a coke on the way home. Okay?"

"Yeah, hit one for the Mick, okay."

"I'll hit one for you."

After a speedy embrace, Rita smiled at him.

"Now don't be late for supper, it's Friday and your father and I are going to a party at the VFW tonight. Now don't forget."

"Sure," he said escaping her grasp.

Unintentionally slamming the back door, he raced down the stairs.

9

Movies

Saturday. With Brian helping Bobby throw his paper route, the two boys had accumulated enough change to go to the matinee at the Madison Theatre several blocks from Partridge Street. As fate would have it, their walk up Madison Avenue took them past their school, a none too subtle reminder that another summer was drawing to a close. They stopped momentarily by a three-story Victorian house, once the lone beacon of life on this broad tree-shaded boulevard, also the terminus of the United Traction trolley line, among rolling hills, vast fields of corn, tomatoes-in-season, a copse of birch trees; a visual dessert served gratis to the keen observer.

Back in the 1800's, the Dutchman who had owned the house, with its handcrafted stained glass windows, shingles, copper drainpipes, and cupola had been also the proprietor of the county's largest flower garden, greenhouse and mushroom farm. His marinated mushrooms gained regional fame for their exquisite taste. As always, time had marched on.

Being the political center and capitol of the state of New York, the city prospered, the population burgeoned, in no small part due to the Catholic Church's policy on birth control having resulted in proliferating hordes of Irish, Italians and Poles. Of course, the genetic fecundity of these ethnic groups was not to be discounted either, birth control or no. Eventually, numerous dwellings were built in the area, soon encircling the Dutchmen's thriving greenhouse and mushroom farm. Not far behind the new homes came grocery stores, churches and schools, followed soon by the establishment of the city's legal boundaries. When the bucolic enclave was annexed and incorporated into the local municipality, with all the legal humbug and baggage that came with that, the encroachment included certain ordinances and codes that affected commercial mushroom farming within the city limits. These legal codes, along with leverage applied by high-ranking officials of the Catholic Diocese forced the multigenerational proprietors of the greenhouse-mushroom enterprise to literally uproot and find a location less offensive to the sensibilities of the residents. Unfortunately, stench and swarms of flies go hand in glove with the farming of mushrooms, an industry that relies principally on two things: darkness and substantial quantities of manure.

To no one's surprise, shortly after the greenhouse-mushroom establishment relocated far from the city, a Catholic elementary school was under construction on the site. A local newspaper columnist, with Protestant leanings, suggested that, really, things hadn't changed much, save that now, instead of mushrooms, it was impressionable young minds that were kept in the dark and subjected to prodigious doses of horse manure.

For some reason known only to the Bishop of the diocese, the Victorian house was preserved. Presently, it was a venue for PTA and Knights of Columbus meetings, and monthly meetings of Scout Troop 4, Brian and Bobby being members in good standing.

Brian looked out across a rolling green lawn that ended at the front door of a glass green house converted from enclosed flowerbeds to kindergarten classrooms.

"Remember going to kindergarten?"

"What I remember is wearing short pants with suspenders and having to wear those dumb sunglasses."

Brian laughed at the image, but quickly agreed. "I guess 'cause kindergarten was in the glass greenhouse we had to wear the sunglasses all the time. I don't remember much else, except it was always warm in there. We were lucky we didn't have to go to school in the summer."

"Yeah," Bobby said.

"Kindergarten was the first time I skipped school. Don't know why, but I sat under that tree over there all morning 'til class was out. Sister Monica and my mother found me under the tree. My mother took me home, but never spanked me," Brian confessed.

Brian's eyes roamed to the gray cinder block edifice of the grade school, now a decade old, where he and his friends would soon be eighth graders. Dejected at the thought of the forthcoming school year, the two friends resumed their walk in silence to the movie theatre a block and a half away. The only solace they had in acknowledging the end of summer, coincidentally the end of the Little League baseball season, was the fast approaching World Series. They would be allowed to listen to one or two of the baseball games on a radio in their classroom *if* they maintained something the nuns called *deportment*. The sisters used this technicality as their principal bargaining chip to insure the discipline of boys fresh from three months of unrestricted fun and adventure. Of course there were a handful of boys more interested in Morse code and arithmetic than World Series baseball, never mind all the girls in class who would rather draw angels or diagram complex sentences on the blackboard. Hooray! For once their bizarre proclivities would not be accommodated.

At the Madison Theatre, Brian and Bobby took their place in an unwieldy, unruly queue of youngsters waiting for the bored teen, in her glass kiosk, to pull back the small wood block from the opening in the glass partition, signaling that ticket sales had commenced. To insure orderly conduct, an usher, the center on the high school football team, paced back and forth in his blue uniform with brass buttons, red piping and ostentatious gold epaulettes nesting on his broad shoulders. A blue pillbox hat was secured at the chin with a gold elastic band. Not long ago, before the presence of this brawny usher, the ticket kiosk had been the scene of chaos, under siege by a horde of Lilliputians.

Surveying the kids in back of them, Brian and Bobby nodded to G. G. Wallace, already into his second box of popcorn. Nearly blocked from view because of Wallace's bulk, they saw Brian's cousins Ray and Mike. Also in attendance was Jimmy "Stretch" Claflin, their first basemen, standing a head taller than all the kids in line. To Brian's displeasure, his eyes came to rest on the crooked smile of Gordy Parker, who stared back at him with venom-filled eyes. Parker pantomimed aiming and pulling the trigger of a handgun. It was all too apparent that he had not forgotten the stolen bat incident that had led to his father's scorn and expulsion from Scout Troop 4.

"You'll get yours, Reilly," he managed to yell before eye contact was broken and the usher, in all his sartorial splendor, ejected Parker and his partner in crime, Mickey Delaney, from the line for cutting in. They were escorted under protest to the end of the block-long queue.

Reading the marquee beside the ticket booth, Brian elbowed his friend to get his attention.

"Hey look, a new Captain Midnight serial."

"Yeah, this is a new one where Ivan Shark steals a top secret bomb-sight."

"You know, it's kind of funny *seeing* Captain Midnight. He doesn't sound like he does on the radio. I wonder if it's the same guy."

"Hard to tell 'cause he always wears that black leather flying cap with the aviator goggles. Besides, since they made it into a movie serial, it's just not the same. It's like Captain Midnight was replaced with a third stringer."

"Guess I'd rather listen to a Yankees game any day than see a Captain Midnight movie."

Distracted, Brian looked back over his shoulder.

"I hope Gordy doesn't start anything. Heck, his father already kicked him out of the Scout troop."

"He deserved it. You see all the other stuff he stole, besides your bat?"

Suddenly the line pushed forward as shouts and laughter burst from the pushing, shoving youngsters as the ticket window finally opened and a multitude of raised hands, clutching shiny quarters, mobbed the kiosk.

Once inside, the boys elbowed their way to the candy counter, where Brian bought a piece of black licorice and a box of Jujyfruits. Bobby settled for a Three Musketeers bar.

Moving away from the counter to the door leading to the seats, Brian's cousin Ray called out to save seats for him and Mike.

In the dimly lighted theatre, with its two broad rows of worn purple seats sloping down to a stage, its massive velvet curtains climbing to the ceiling, the four boys wasted no time digging into their confections and at the same time calling out to friends and teammates seated nearby.

The protests of a few girls seated several rows behind them had the boys standing and looking for the source of the commotion. Brian instantly recognized Parker's blonde curly hair in the midst of four or five girls a few rows behind them. Both Parker and Delaney were attempting to force the girls to move from their seats. Their voices raised in protest, the girls unanimously asserted they had no intention of moving. As the exchange heated up, the uniformed usher, who had been keeping an eye on Parker and his cohort, hurried to the trouble spot. Securing the rowdies by the collar, he forcefully escorted them to the opposite side of the auditorium where they were seated and warned against roughhousing or they would be ejected from the theatre.

Just as his words of warning, accompanied by a threatening index finger, ended, the house lights dimmed and the velvet curtains slowly parted, revealing the floor-to- ceiling screen. To screams of delight, the familiar musical sound track that introduced Looney Tunes cartoons piped from the speakers. A fragile silence settled in as images of Porky Pig, Daffy Duck, and colleagues filled the screen with mayhem and slapstick played out to the applause and laughter of the audience.

An enormous frying pan battered a head, accompanied by a loud, echoing Boing! Followed in quick succession by a slip on a banana peel, a pie in the face, a pedestrian flattened like a pancake by a steamroller. Various musical instruments accentuated the comedic capers—the Wa-Wa-Wa of a trombone, a horselaugh produced by a French horn, the snap and roll of a snare drum.

The newsreel that followed showed an underground bomb shelter accommodating a family of four. Canned food, water, and medicine had already been stored in compartments dug into earthen walls. A father was pictured sitting in a rocker, smoking a pipe and reading a newspaper, while his wife in dress, apron and high heels was busy fixing a meal on a hot plate. In the background, the audience saw a little girl playing jacks, while her older brother constructed a model airplane. The images were accompanied by a baritone voice extolling the virtues of these shelters if an atomic bomb were dropped on the United States.

"Where do they go to the bathroom," Mike piped up.

The segment concluded with a wave and wink from Dad, who put his newspaper down and removed the pipe from his mouth, while smiling Mother hugged son and daughter to her skirts.

The sleek image of a space-age automobile displayed on a revolving platform cut to a pilot in white flight suit and helmet. A large backpack with a propeller on a shaft extending above his head was strapped to his back. Twin blades began rotating while the announcer described how the contraption worked. Magically, the pilot ascended to a height of three feet, where he hovered for several seconds before returning to the ground. The announcer concluded the scene with a bold prediction that people in the not too distant future would go to work, shop for groceries—perhaps entire families would go on vacations with these marvelous new devices providing airborne mobility. "And don't forget man's best friend," the baritone voice crooned as the image of a frisky Basset hound, equipped with a scaled down model of the portable helicopter harness, barked at the camera, ending the newsreel.

For a few seconds the screen went dark, followed by the high-pitched sound of an airplane engine growing louder and louder and segueing to a tolling bell. The audience responded with tense silence. Overlapping the ear-shattering engine noise and the tolling bell's descending volume, a deep male voice announced *Captainnnnnn Midnight*. Cheers and shouts of approval roared from the audience as a goggled, leather-clad aviator in the cockpit of his fighter plane raced across the screen while the announcer brought the audience up to date on the day's episode involving the theft of a top secret Government bombsight and the kidnapping of its inventor, Professor Millard Edwards. Captain Midnight's adversary, Ivan Shark, and his gang of thugs were suspected of being at the bottom of these treasonous acts. Credits rolled, to the tolling of the bell, while, in the background, the hands on a Gothic clock tower synchronized over the Roman numeral twelve on the clock face, this to the accompaniment of dramatic orchestral music.

"Captain Midnight, one of aviation's greatest heroes, a one-man war against crime and corruption. Through fog, sleet and snow, he daily risks his life in the cause of justice and the American way."

As the announcer recapped events to date, the text of his review was displayed on the screen. Not wanting to miss a single titillating detail, the audience read the subtitles aloud.

Abruptly, the movie serial cut to a fight scene in a remote cabin where Ivan Shark's gang was holding the bombsight inventor captive. Gang members were all dressed fashionably in suits and ties, fedoras cocked stylishly on their foreheads.

Captain Midnight, clad head-to-toe in his black leather pilot's suit, including goggles and cap, grappled athletically with the thugs while the inventor, Millard Edwards, made an escape in the gang's Packard convertible town car. Kapow! Blam! Smack! Punches flew, bodies crashed onto tables laden with liquor bottles only to collapse onto a littered floor.

The orchestra music increased in volume and pace to a barrage of fisticuffs until Captain Midnight was struck on the back of the head with the butt of a pistol wielded by Blackie, the gang leader. Silence followed as an exploding bomb shook the gang's hideout. With Captain Midnight lying unconscious on the floor, the gang leader advised his cohorts to *vamoose* before another bomb blew the *joint* to kingdom come.

Regaining consciousness, while the music took on a hectic pace, Captain Midnight staggered to his feet, groggy but coming to his senses. Cut to an image of an evil pilot, a Shark flunky, pulling a lever that sent a bomb plummeting onto the roof of the cabin, the identity of which was easily seen by the pilot because of a large bullseye conveniently painted on the cabin roof. Captain Midnight was now on his feet, staggering, alert to the imminent danger. Cut to the bomb falling. Closer and closer to the cabin it speeds. At the last minute, Captain Midnight dives through an open window… then an earsplitting explosion somewhere in the theatre triggered an outburst of screams and yells. Boys and girls jumped to their feet. Gunfire in the theatre? What the?

Instantly, the house lights came up; the screen went dark. The audience was on its feet gazing toward the rear of the theatre, the source of the detonation. Standing on his seat Brian could see the usher hovering over someone or something. The high-pitched screams of girls filled the air and were especially loud closer to the row where the usher examined an inert body. Trying to grasp what was taking place, Brian wasn't sure if this commotion had something to do with the serial or was something altogether different. Confused, he stepped down from his seat. Youngsters jammed the aisles, pushing and shoving at each other to get away from whatever mischief had occurred and out into daylight where things were safe and understandable.

Two blue uniformed police officers waded through the stampeding kids and stopped in the aisle by the usher. The boys trailed behind Ray as he pushed his way up the main aisle to the exit. While passing the scene of excitement and confusion, Brian saw one of the policemen clamping handcuffs on Gordy Parker's out-stretched wrists. He elbowed Bobby and nodded his head toward the manacled Parker.

The other policeman was bent over the seat where Brian thought he saw the body of Jimmy Claflin. Before he could acquire more information, the boys found themselves out in the glaring sunlight in front of the movie theatre where they joined a crowd looking back at the entrance.

A black Buick with chrome-plated siren on the front fender screeched to a halt at the curb. Doors were flung open in haste to disgorge two plain-clothes detectives, Chick and his partner Ed McEvoy. Chick's look of alarm was softened to one of concern when he saw Brian safe on the sidewalk with his best friend Bobby and cousins Ray and Mike.

"I want you kids to get on home right away and stay there."

"What all happened, Dad? Something bad?"

"Just do as I tell you."

Obediently, the boys began their trek homeward, pausing only briefly to watch two white-smocked attendants pull a stretcher from an ambulance and hurry into the movie house.

~

The bedroom door opened slowly, exposing his father, still in a pinstriped suit, holding a gray fedora in his hand. Seated on his bed, baseball glove at his side, a comic book in his hands, Brian looked up and waited for his father to enter the room.

"Hi kiddo, come on into the kitchen."

Relinquishing the comic, Brian jumped up and followed his father.

Seated at the kitchen table across from Brian, Chick hooked his fedora on the chair back. Pulling an ashtray toward him, he lighted a cigarette. The clatter of plates and glasses in the kitchen sink filled the silence. Rita stood with her hands submerged in soapy water; the recent surgical scar all but vanished from her left arm.

"Okay, your friend Jimmy, well, he's dead. What happened, that damned fool Parker kid, for some crazy reason, snuck his father's old Army .45 automatic into the theatre. He took it with him to the movies and was playing with it, showing off to the Delaney kid, I imagine, when it accidentally went off. Claims he never checked to see if it had live ammo. The bullet went clear through the seat in front of him into Claflin. Killed him instantly."

Brian was aware of a silence in the kitchen. He looked up to see his mother standing beside her seated husband, a hand on his shoulder. Brian's eyes wandered to the tabletop where smoke from the cigarette in the ashtray curled up in a long silent ribbon toward the ceiling light. A long gray ash dipped from the white paper and fell silently into the ashtray. Slowly, the cigarette extinguished itself.

"Honey…" Rita began.

"Let me finish. Well, there's no question Parker had a loaded pistol and a bullet from the pistol accidentally killed Jimmy. It gets tricky here. Say, listen, if you want to go to your room that's okay, this is tough sledding, I just want you to know what happened exactly so there's no mystery or questions that don't get answered. Okay?"

Brian nodded his head. His mother stood behind him now. She placed her hands on his shoulders.

"Technically, it's involuntary manslaughter with circumstances, but what will probably happen, since he's not eighteen, the judge will most likely remand him to a reform school. Ah, the dumb bastard."

"Honey, please don't get upset."

"Hell of it is, you hate to see things like this happen, it's so, so un-called for. Listen, I have to get over to Parker's house. His father's pretty shook up. I want to make sure he doesn't do anything stupid. Listen, son, if you have any questions or want to talk with me or your mother, we'll be here for you."

Reaching across the table, he placed his hand on top of Brian's clenched fists, which relaxed upon feeling the warm flesh of his father's fingers.

Chick rose from his chair, grabbed his hat and looked at Rita.

"Didn't know it, but Claflin's parents are divorced. Father moved down south. Mrs. Claflin has been raising the boy on her own. I had to break the news to her. She took it hard."

"I'll stop by to check on her a little later."

Pausing at the back door, Chick turned to his wife.

"Don't count on me for dinner."

Rita continued rubbing Brian's shoulders. It suddenly occurred to him that even boys just like him died.

10

Digging Worms

September. The boys stopped at the corner of Partridge and Madison to wait for the bus that would take them to the end of the line at Six Mile Waterworks for a day of fishing. This outing was a way of celebrating one of their last free days before returning to school. Another summer had passed so quickly it wasn't yet a bittersweet memory, to be relived disconsolately while staring grimly at blackboards and pages of textbooks. On Saturdays, the buses didn't run as regularly as they did during the week. So they waited. In back of them was the green expanse of grass where they would play hundreds of games of football during the next few months. North of the tract of grass was the LaSalle Boys Home where neighborhood kids sneaked into the gymnasium to shoot baskets, always on the alert for a black-cassocked priest who just might ferret out their trespass. The penalty for this transgression, rumor had it, was incarceration in a cell teeming with poisonous spiders, carnivorous cockroaches, and a breed of rat that feasted exclusively on succulent Catholic boys.

Though neighborhood basketball devotees, with Brian and his friends foremost, had succeeded in this clandestine maneuver many times, not a single boy had ever been taken prisoner. Just the hint of becoming an inmate at this institution, as many a mother throughout the city knew, was enough to insure beds were made, teeth brushed, hands scrubbed until glowing red, and all manner of exemplary behavior achieved—achieved without protest or argument.

In Brian's recollection the only denizen of the Boys Home he'd ever come in contact with was also a member of their Boy Scout troop. Nicknamed *Frog*, this undersized urchin was a dictionary of profanity and thesaurus of roguery. He was released monthly from the iron-gated, brownstone fortress to attend Troop 4 meetings at the Victorian house near the grade school. A hunchback, with short muscular arms and bow-legs, Frog was a study in asymmetry. His oversize head had an uncanny resemblance and similar skin texture to that of the leaping amphibian he was nicknamed for. Often, he would go AWOL on scout troop camping trips, but, because of his unique physical appearance was expeditiously captured and repatriated. On one troop camp out, Brian watched confounded as Frog ate a whole loaf of Freihoffer white bread at one sitting. He and his fellow scouts learned quickly to guard their caches of candy bars when Frog was in camp.

Brian was staying with his cousins, Ray and Mike, at their home around the corner on Hudson Avenue while his mother was in Brady Hospital for an operation on her arm. It would only be overnight, his father assured him, so no need for a hospital visit. His sleepover allowed for endless activities with Ray, his oldest sibling cousin, the doyen, who was a freshman at St. John's High School across from the Dipsy Doodle soda shop. Cousin Mike, a year younger than Brian, was always an eager companion in any sport or adventure Ray organized. Many an evening would find the boys poring over Ray's extensive collection of *Sports Afield* and *Field and Stream* magazines.

Sitting on the curb at the bus stop, they leaned their fishing rods against a nearby tree. In short order, Brian plucked the Flatfish lure from his tackle box to show off. Attempting to maintain his position of authority, Ray opened his tackle box to withdraw a newly purchased plug with two sets of treble hooks called a Hula Dancer, because of the plastic skirt dangling from the bottom of the plug.

"This little baby is guaranteed to catch a huge pickerel. Your father told me there's some monsters out at Six-Mile."

Replacing the plug in the box, Ray picked up a whetstone and began a cursory sharpening of his jackknife blade.

Following suit, Brian put the Flatfish back in its compartment in his tackle box. He nodded his head in agreement with Ray's comment on monster pickerel, but secretly acknowledged that his father was undoubtedly referring to the pristine, clandestine waters of *Down Below*. Feeling magnanimous, he almost let slip a promise to take his cousins there on a fishing expedition, with all of its early morning coffee-drinking camaraderie, but checked himself when the memory of his solemn oath never to discuss the subject in public thumbed its nose at him. Loose lips sink ships, warned the outdated posters at the National Guard Armory where he and his cousins went to see local college basketball games. He took his role as conspirator seriously.

Pacing back and forth in his Converse sneakers, Ray kept looking impatiently down the street for the orange and yellow hulk of the bus. Brian looked with envy at Ray's blue satin windbreaker with white piping running down the sleeves, knowing full well it was a garment worn exclusively by St. John's high school boys. His only solace was that in not too many years he would walk those hallowed halls outfitted in an identical garment.

Disgruntled, Ray glanced at the wristwatch he had received upon graduating from eighth grade. The watch would insure their return home at the appointed supper hour, thus avoiding confinement in separate bedrooms, never mind the requisite penalty of short rations and extra chores.

"That bus isn't ever going to get here and those fish won't wait for us all day so let's try hitching a ride," Ray asserted.

His suggestions were always interpreted as orders to be carried out promptly and with little or no discussion. Yet Brian recollected his mother's disapproval of boys hitchhiking. Already, their leader was positioned a few feet from the curb with his thumb extended. Brian and Mike quickly assumed a similar stance alongside him.

A maroon Chevrolet sedan finally pulled over.

"You guys wait here," Ray cautioned as he jogged to the passenger door and opened it.

Minutes later they had their fishing gear stowed in the back seat of the automobile, where Brian and Mike installed themselves. Fittingly, Ray occupied the passenger seat. Separating him from the driver was a large curved gearshift, poking up from the floorboard. The driver manipulated the bent steel shaft from gear to gear as the car made its way out Western Avenue toward the waterworks.

The skinny man driving, perhaps in his forties, with black-framed glasses looked into the rearview mirror. A tense silence was broken by the whine of shifting transmission gears until a comfortable cruising speed was reached. The silence was interrupted again when the man's right hand reached up to turn the knob of the dashboard radio that piped the lyrics of the Mills Brothers' *You Always Hurt the One You Love*. The driver was dressed in green work slacks and soiled blue windbreaker. His hands were encased in leather gloves. It appeared that he might be going to or returning from work. Once again, his hand went to the dashboard turning the radio off.

"So you fellers are headed to the waterworks for a bit of fishing, eh?"

"Yeah, that's our favorite spot," Ray said.

"Don't say. Do a bit of fishing there myself," he said resting his gloved hand on the pearlescent gearshift knob.

After a quick look in the rearview mirror, the driver pulled the glove from his right hand with his teeth, letting it fall to his lap. With his gloved left hand on the steering wheel, he pulled a cigarette from a shirt pocket and inserted it in his lips. Ray followed the boney hand to a cigarette lighter on the dash. Watching the man push in the lighter, Ray noticed most of his pinky finger was missing. Even from the back seat the boys could hear the lighter pop out of the dashboard. The interior of the automobile quickly filled with tobacco smoke.

"Here's an idea," the driver said while exhaling, "why don't I rent one of them rowboats? We can all go out fishing in the boat, do some trolling."

Ray shook his head. "We mainly like to cast from shore."

"Well, there you go, we'll stop somewhere and dig us some worms. That's one of the best fish baits, doncha know."

"Nah, we got our own lures. Thanks anyway."

Brian was on red alert when he heard the man suggest *digging worms*. His mother had warned him of this ruse, cautioning him against hitchhiking altogether. And definitely don't go digging worms with anyone, she'd admonished in a tone of voice bristling with innuendo that eluded him.

"So you're going fishing too?" Ray added.

"You betcha. Got the afternoon off. Yessir, perfect day for a little fishing."

"Where's your pole and tackle?"

The hand with the severed finger clumsily crushed out the cigarette in the dashboard ashtray.

"In the trunk, of course; keep it there all the time. Sometimes of an evening I'll go down to the river, near where I work, dig some worms and do a little river fishing. Sturgeon down on the river," he said, his voice slightly agitated.

Soon the four-door sedan passed signs signaling the perimeter of the waterworks.

"You can just let us off near the snack shop. We want to get a soda first," Ray suggested in his authoritative voice.

"Now, I'll do you one better, son. I got a cooler with cold drinks in the trunk with my tackle. What say we stop at the first cove beyond the boat dock? Have our cold drinks and dig some worms, like I said."

In the silence, all three boys looked with misgivings out the side windows as the car passed the rowboats tied up at the small dock beside the snack bar.

Ray was about to protest, when the sedan pulled onto a dirt road that took them away from the lake into an area of sand hills and scrub pine. Brian and Mike looked at each other with eyes wide, but were afraid to speak up. Brian was depressed further when he realized they were in the area where he and his father had buried Arrow.

The driver shifted down into low gear as the sedan bumped and swayed over the serpentine track. Ray noticed out of his peripheral vision that the man had managed to pull on the leather glove. Also noted were little beads of sweat forming on the man's forehead.

Alerted to the situation, Brian and Mike readied their poles and tackle boxes for an expeditious escape, but waited for a sign from Ray. At last the Chevrolet came to a stop at the base of a sand hill. The driver shifted the transmission into neutral and left the engine running. As if on cue, the boys had their doors open, fishing gear in hand, out onto the sand where they came to a stop behind Ray who watched the driver make his way to the back of the car. Brian could see Ray had his open jackknife clenched in his hand.

"Say, don't you fellas want a cold drink?"

Brian's right hand gripped his spinning rod, his left the tackle box ready to bolt when Ray said the word. At his side, he could see that Mike was prepared to run as well.

The humid air was filled with a stench of smoldering rubber, decaying garbage—this from the nearby dumpsite.

When Ray saw the trunk lid go up, he made a single motion with his arm, like a quarterback, that sent all three boys running up over the sand hill and down a path through the pines, the sounds of the contents of their metal tackle boxes shattering the silence. In their wake they could hear the man's high-pitched voice calling after them.

"Come have a soda pop, there's nothing to be afraid of. You hear?"

Nearly out of the scrub pines, Brian noticed the smell of the dump getting stronger. Looking off to his left he could see thin plumes of smoke rising above the tree line. As he made a tight turn around a pine tree, fast on the heels of Ray, his foot caught on an exposed tree root in the path, sending him head-over-heels. His tackle box hit the ground, spilling its contents onto the sandy soil. Ray stood over him shouting at him to gather up his tackle and keep running. With that directive fresh in his mind, he watched his cousins move quickly down the path, leaving him to scoop his lures, sinkers, floats and assorted tackle, along with the sand that accompanied them, back into the tackle box. Within seconds, the box was shut and latched. He took one quick look behind him before sprinting down the path, calling to his cousins to wait up.

He rejoined them at the edge of a clearing on the outskirts of the dump in a patch of wild grape vines where Ray and Mike had stopped to catch their breath and reconnoiter. Brian looked across the clearing to see a woman, mostly skin and bone, seated at a cobbled-together trestle table in front of a faded blue and white house trailer set up on cement blocks.

Ray motioned for him to kneel down and keep quiet.

The boys watched as the white-haired woman worked at a small machine on the raw planks before her, but could not see what she was fabricating, only that her hands kept repetitiously operating the contraption. Occasionally, she would pluck up a fly swatter, make a swipe at an annoying insect, and then resume her work. Toward one end of the house trailer, a young boy about their age, dressed only in shorts, a deep tan covering sinewy muscles, was sorting pieces of clothing and assorted pans and pots, placing some of the items in a push cart, setting others aside.

They watched as the boy said something to the woman, who they surmised was his mother. Her answer prompted the boy to bring an object over to her and place it on the table. After a quick inspection of the item, her hand groped a quart bottle, pouring the contents into a nearby glass.

Brian tapped Ray's shoulder.

"Hey, that's Joey Layton," he whispered.

Ray looked back at him.

"He was in my fourth and fifth grade classes. I heard he's going to public school now."

"Let's get on over there. I don't think we have to worry about that guy in the Chevy anymore. Don't say nothin' about this to your mother. Mothers are awful skittish about things like that."

The boys made their way slowly across the clearing. As they got closer, the woman stopped working the apparatus before her and eyed the three approaching youngsters. The boy at the cart also stopped what he was doing and went to her side, not alarmed at their presence, but surprised at having company.

Getting closer to the woman and boy, Brian held up his hand in greeting. He noticed how tan Joey was. His hair was cropped short in a ragged crew cut, perhaps the work of his mother.

"Hey Joey, how you been?"

"Hi, Brian. Looks like you're headed over to the waterworks."

Brian watched the woman gather up the dozen or so cigarettes she had rolled. Opening an empty cigar box next to the machine, she placed the cigarettes inside, and then closed the cover of the box. Her thumb, the nail chewed to the quick, pushed down a tiny latch that secured the lid.

The woman spoke up. "Now, you introduce me to your friends, honey," she encouraged, her tanned face wrinkled like a walnut.

She picked up a single cigarette left beside the small mechanism that mated strips of paper to bulk tobacco. Striking a kitchen match, she lighted the slender cigarette in her mouth. Even from the other side of the table Brian could see saliva soaking into the end of the cigarette.

"That's Brian Reilly and his cousin Mike. Brian and I were in Sister

Josephine's class. Mike there was a year behind us. I don't know the other fellow," Joey said.

"That's my cousin, Ray. He started high school this year," Brian beamed.

"Well, this here's my mother," said Joey.

The boys said hello and watched as she took a puff on her smoke. When she exhaled, they could see that some of her teeth were missing.

"How do you like the public school?" Brian inquired.

"It's okay, just that I miss my friends at St. John's."

Mrs. Layton took a quick drink from her glass.

"Whatcha going to do with all that stuff in the cart?" asked Mike.

Joey looked over at the cart. "I'll sell it around the neighborhoods."

Ray elbowed his younger brother.

"You kids are a long ways from the waterworks," Mrs. Layton said pointing a thin index finger at the fishing poles and tackle at their feet.

Ray spoke up. "The guy who gave us a ride, he wanted us to dig worms with him. I didn't trust him, so we ran down a path that came out here."

"Ain't that somethin'? Remember what I told you?" she said looking over at her son, Joey. "What did this fella look like?"

"He was kind of thin and had one of them skinny mustaches, was wearing leather gloves when we first got in the car. It was a maroon Chevy with big spare tires in the front fenders," Ray answered,

"Don't say. A maroon Chevy, huh?"

"Yup, four-door job. When he took off one of his gloves, the right hand one, I think, I noticed part of his pinky was sliced off. Say, you might keep an eye out for him just in case."

Her mouth opened in a smile revealing spaces between her teeth. Dropping the last bit of cigarette in the dirt at her feet, she hooked a thumb up pointing in back of her where a single-barrel J. C. Higgins shotgun rested against the side of the trailer.

"Oh, don't think I don't know how to use that. Keep it handy when Mr. Layton is off looking for work." She nodded at Joey. "This here boy of mine has got him a single shot .22 rifle, don't ya, hon'?"

Smiling proudly, Joey looked across at the three boys.

"And I'm real good with it, too."

"Son, why don't you see if your friends would like some Kool-Aid?"

Checking his watch, Ray piped up.

"We better be getting over to the waterworks, get some fishing in."

"Well then, why don't Joey guide you over there, okay hon'? You get your pole and git. And be sure to come back with a mess of fish. We'll have us a little fish fry tonight."

Joey retrieved his pole from the backside of the trailer. Signaling for the three boys to follow, he started walking smartly across the clearing toward an opening in the trees.

On the shore, Brian opened his tackle box to be confronted by sand scattered over and under his fishing gear. Worse, he discovered his prize Flatfish was missing.

"Crap, I must a lost it back where I fell," he cursed while removing most of the sand collected in the small slots where his lures were billeted.

Untangling a DareDevil from a Gordian knot of hooks, lures and fish line, he hooked it onto the bill of his baseball cap while stringing up his spinning rod. Carefully, he removed the lure from the cap and connected it via a swivel to the end of the line.

Walking to the shoreline after rigging his spinning rod, he was the last one to cast out. Down the shore, Joey sat on a stump, watching a red and white float bob in the water. Up the shoreline, Brian saw Ray standing on a rock in shallow water, casting out his Hula Dancer. Mike was still farther away, making his casts and retrieving his lure in a slow, precise manner.

In no time, Joey Layton had two bullheads on a stringer in the water near the stump.

"Got some grasshoppers if you want to try them," Joey suggested.

"Thanks, but I've always had good luck with DareDevils. Wish to heck I had my Flatfish though. Caught a huge bass on it about a month ago."

"Don't have any lures, but I always get fish with the hoppers or even night crawlers," he said pointing to his stringer of fish.

"You going to come back to Catholic school?"

"Nah, since my Dad's been out of work, my mother says we're too short of cash, what with books, uniforms and tuition."

"Yeah, guess that stuff is expensive."

"Ma says I can learn just as much in a public school that don't cost nothin'."

"Well, why don't you come over to the Boys Home and play football with us. We'll be starting games right after the World Series ends."

"Sure, that's not too far from P.S. 24. I can stop by on my way home. My bus stops there."

Their conversation ended when Layton's float disappeared below the surface of the water.

Feeling a bit inadequate, Brian moved down the shoreline to try his luck elsewhere as Joey unhooked a perch and added it to his stringer.

Thirty minutes later, Brian heard Ray whistle. He looked up from reeling in his lure to see him waving his arm.

Reaching his cousins on the sandy beach close to where Joey was fishing he looked at Ray for orders.

"Look. I got a pickerel after all," Ray said holding his catch aloft.

"I got skunked," Brian said.

"We better be getting on home," Ray said holding his wrist up to indicate the watch.

"Gunna take your fish home?" Brian asked.

"Nope." Ray said walking to the shore, where he knelt down to clean the fish in the shallow water. Setting it on a nearby log, he slit the stomach of the fish and skillfully pulled the entrails out. After discarding the offal in nearby bushes, he again washed the gutted fish off then walked over to Joey.

"Go ahead take this. I don't think the bus driver will let me on the bus with it."

Joey looked up from his stringer of fish, now cleaned and gutted.

"Thanks. You fellas can come over for a fish fry if you want."

"We'd like to, but if we don't get home on time we won't be able to come out fishing for a while. Hey, maybe next time, okay?"

Smiling, Joey hefted his stringer. "Long as there's fish to fry, you're welcome."

The three boys hurried down the well-worn shoreline path toward the snack shop and bus stop.

"Hey Joey," Brian called over his shoulder. "Keep an eye out for that guy in the Chevy."

Joey nodded and waved as he disappeared in the dense tree line.

Hurrying down the trail as it dipped over a hill, the boys could see the last bus of the day idling at the pickup spot beside the snack bar. Waving at the driver standing beside the vehicle, they shouted for him to wait up.

Seated at the back of the bus, Ray cautioned his fishing partners. "Remember, don't say nothin' about hitching a ride or we'll be in Dutch."

Intuiting the possible consequences, Brian and Mike nodded their heads.

~

Seeing his father's blue coupe parked in front of his cousins' house, Brian hurried ahead of them to the back door. Leaving his tackle box and pole outside, he rushed into the kitchen where his father was seated across from his Aunt Peggy. Watching Brian enter the room, Chick set his coffee cup down.

The kitchen was particularly warm from the heat of numerous pots and pans bubbling and simmering on the stove.

Peggy rose to her feet as her boys came in the backdoor.

"The great fishermen," Chick smiled.

"Not so great, got skunked." Brian lamented. Then added quickly, "Well, I didn't have my Flatfish. I lost it."

"Don't tell me, another big mouth bass snapped your line and took it with him?"

"Yup, lost him and the lure," Brian mumbled, embarrassed by the fabrication.

Ray and Mike yelled a greeting to their mother, then said hello to their Uncle Chick, who winked at them.

"Looks like we don't eat fish tonight, hey Peg?"

She turned from the gas stove, a wooden spoon in one hand.

"Got a nice roast in the oven. Who wants boney old fish anyway?"

She turned to her boys. "Go and put those fish poles in the cellar and clean up. Just look at all the stickers you boys have on those pants. My heavens."

"Well, sport, let's get on home. Your mother's anxious to see you. I brought her home from the hospital earlier this afternoon."

Suddenly, the cooking noises of pot lids being lifted, contents being stirred, were silenced. Turning from the stove to look at Brian, Peggy quickly turned back to her cooking.

Chick carried the tackle box while Brian walked beside him down the driveway to the Ford, the spinning rod clutched in his right hand.

Pulling into the drive between the houses, Brian turned to his father.

"I have to tell you something, Dad."

Chick turned the ignition key, silencing the engine. His left hand pulled back on the emergency brake.

"Go ahead."

"This is between you and me," Brian said with all the adult seriousness he could muster.

"Okay, between us," Chick assured him with a hand on his shoulder.

"Well, we hitched a ride."

Chick smiled. "You don't say."

"Thing is, the guy who gave us the ride, he… well, he acted kind of funny. And he wanted us to dig worms with him."

Chick's smile vanished. "He did, huh.

"Yeah, but we got away from him."

"Tell you what, after dinner we'll finish our talk, just you and me. Better not mention this to your mother, especially now; you know how she feels about hitchhiking. I want to know what this guy looked like, what color and make of car he was driving. Think you can remember things like that?"

Brian nodded his head.

Chick opened his door. "Better go up, say hello to your mother, she's anxious to see you."

After putting his rod and tackle box on the porch, he followed his father through the back door, excited to see his mother. For some reason the kitchen was empty, even the little Philco radio, normally on all day long, was silent.

His father motioned to follow him. They turned in the doorway to his parents' bedroom. Surprised and a bit confused, Brian saw his mother sitting up in bed, a pillow behind her back, her pink housecoat draped over her shoulders.

This wasn't right, he thought.

Turning to get clarification, he was doubly confused by not seeing his father.

His mother's long black hair fell to her shoulders and glistened like it did when she washed and brushed it. And she had lipstick on. In bed with lipstick?

Something is wrong here.

Her brown eyes looked directly at him as she slipped the housecoat from her shoulders. The left sleeve of her nightgown was empty. The whole arm was missing. The one with the brand on it. Gone.

"Mom?"

He went to the bed, tears dropping from his eyes. He put his head down on her stomach, like he used to do… when he was a child.

11

Tumblers

From a covert rooftop observation post, the commandos carried out their mission with stealth and silence. Unbeknownst to brother Greg, Bobby had *borrowed* his binoculars to aid in the reconnaissance of Johnny Russian and his pigeons. Concealed on the rooftop they surreptitiously zeroed in on the birds and the ogre's handling of them.

From previous missions they knew that he was in the habit of tending to the tumblers on Saturday mornings. Now that school had started, the training sessions fit in perfectly with their weekend activities. Also noted by the spy duo was the awe-inspiring aerial display the pigeons executed on weekend mornings—a performance they did not want to miss.

Pressing the binoculars to his eyes, Brian watched as the barn door slid aside. The caretaker, in overalls, emerged with a small cart and portable cage containing his kit of tumblers. Members of the kit had been selected, through trial and error, over the summer. Although their tumbling abilities were a paramount consideration, Johnny considered other traits, such as their ability to maintain formation when airborne, as well as the intelligence to respond to his commands and signals. Laziness and tendencies toward individualism were grounds for expulsion from the kit.

The cart came to a halt in the middle of the gravel drive. Constructed of widely spaced wood slats, more than enough light and air entered the cage to the pigeons' greatest advantage. The semi-darkness calmed the enclosed birds.

The boys watched as Johnny carefully released the pigeons from the cage; in an instant the birds were airborne. With the aide of the binoculars, Bobby watched as they circled above the barn. Once in formation, the pigeons disappeared with amazing speed over the roof of the rest home. The boys' attention now swiveled back to Johnny Russian, who held a pole with a piece of bright yellow cloth attached over his head and waved it vigorously. When the kit flew over the barn they did a synchronized backward somersault. Brian and Bobby clamped hands over their mouths to suppress stifled whoops of delight. The sight of tumbling pigeons had the same effect on the boys as Fourth of July fireworks.

Mr. Horowitz, Johnny's regular Saturday morning audience, waved and clapped his arthritic hands while seated in a rickety wheelchair, all the while puffing energetically on a cigar while anticipating the approach of a nurse who would whisk him away for his medications.

Following that display, the kit disappeared. Again, Johnny began swinging the yellow flag back and forth. Brian swept the skies with the binoculars without success. Beside him, Bobby pointed in the direction of his house, visible over the back fence, where the kit came winging over the trees and executed a synchronized backward somersault, then regrouped and landed at Johnny's feet, where they received small quantities of seed as a reward for their performance. With all the tumblers accounted for, Johnny clapped several times, sending the birds up to the loft entrance at the peak of the barn where they squeezed through the entrance portals.

Still unmolested by the overly efficient nurse, Sol Horowitz waved a hand at the retreating man and cart.

"Johnny, you're a maestro," he called. Turning in his wheelchair to address an invisible audience, he proclaimed, "He's a maestro!"

Feverishly, he searched his sweater pockets for another cigar, but, hearing the screen door open, accompanied by the heavy tread of the nurse, Sol raised his cloudy eyes to the heavens and moaned, "Oy vey."

The boys repaired to Bobby's bedroom, where, with the door closed, the shade pulled, they conducted a top-secret debriefing. Before the meeting began, Bobby had returned the borrowed binoculars to their case on Greg's dresser.

"We can't put this off any longer. I mean, school started and we've got our first CYO basketball practice in a few weeks. We have to climb up to the coop and capture a pigeon."

"So what's the rush? Why can't we wait until next summer?" Bobby reasoned.

Brian rubbed his chin with the knuckle of an index finger. "Nah, kids in school keep asking if we made it to the pigeon coop yet. We don't want to be called a couple of bullshitters, ya know. It'll be a long year if we don't get to the loft soon."

"Yeah, Greg's been riding me too, him and Charlie Maguire. He says, 'Put up or shut up. Put your money where your mouth is,' stuff like that," Bobby said.

"Yeah, let's sneak up to the pigeon coop next Saturday, come hell or high water."

"Sure, why not, we were only ten or fifteen feet away last time. Yeah, we got it all doped out," Bobby agreed.

"I think maybe the trick to getting across the beam is not to look down."

"That's what Greg says. He says to practice by tightrope walking the banister in front of the apartment house where Jimmy Claflin used to live."

Brian's eyes sparkled. "Sure, sure, why didn't I think of that? Okay, so next Saturday we climb up to the loft and get a pigeon. Shake on it."

The boys locked their right hands together and made a solemn oath to complete their mission, or else.

Upon their completing the pledge the bedroom door opened. Greg peered into the darkened room.

"You guys mind?"

"No, come on in," Bobby said.

"What's up, you plotting the overthrow of the Commies?"

"Nah, just another mission up to the coop," Bobby said, watching his older brother rummage in their cluttered closet, finally emerging with a half-inflated basketball.

Sitting on his bed, he began pumping air into the ball with the aid of a hand pump, which he worked back and forth vigorously.

"Say, you guys want to shoot some hoops over at the boys' home? Come on, Ray and Mike are going and Charlie Maguire, too. Come on," Greg said.

Simultaneously, the boys blurted their assent, always amenable to a pre-season practice session, especially with the likes of Greg and Charlie.

Putting the pump aside, Greg began a series of test dribbles on the floor, but came to an abrupt stop upon hearing his mother call out from her sanctuary in the kitchen. "No basketball in the house!"

Winking and smiling at Brian and Bobby, Greg got to his feet with the ball clutched under his arm.

"Let's go, troopers."

With the boys following at his heels, he announced over his shoulder, "By the way, I know you used my binoculars. No big deal, but next time, just ask. Okay?"

"Sure," Bobby replied sheepishly.

The six boys were eager to invade the sanctity of the LaSalle Boys Home gym, especially now when it was empty, the residents engaged in various chores about the extensive buildings and grounds. Entering a rear door unobserved, they stopped. In silence, they surveyed the gymnasium and its full-sized basketball court. The boys coveted the wood floor and the two regulation baskets, with corded string nets, at opposite ends of the court. A far cry from the backyard dirt courts they were accustomed to.

Brian's eyes sparkled with anticipation that only a boy schooled on outdoor basketball courts with dirt surfaces and steel rims lacking nets could appreciate.

Assured they were alone, the boys bolted to the nearest basket while Greg dribbled the ball twice and jumped in the air for a one-hand shot at the hoop. Bouncing once against the backboard, it dropped through the net into Ray's hands. Producing a second basketball, Mike stood at the foul line, a regulation fifteen feet from the backboard to make a two-handed set shot that circled the rim twice before dropping in. Brian watched with particular interest as Charlie, the All State CYO champ, dribbled across the floor to the corner boundary line, where he executed a one-hand jump shot that swished cleanly through the hoop.

When enough practice shots had been taken, the boys split up into two teams for a scrimmage. Brian and Bobby teamed up with Charlie, leaving Greg, Ray, and Mike forming the opposition. After a match that went back and forth, one basket up, one down, the boys sprawled on the gym floor to catch their breath after Charlie's team had finally won.

Smiling at his best friend, Brian nodded in Greg's direction. Both knew what was coming next: a game of free throws in which Greg would be the referee, scorekeeper and gym heckler. The shooter stood at the foul line for free throws, one basket counting two points. The shooter kept the ball until he missed. If he missed, he got to make a lay-up, earning one point if it sank. Each player attempted to make as many baskets as he could, for up to twenty-one points. First shooter to reach twenty-one points won the game. For Brian, Bobby and Mike the distance from the foul line to the basket was more of a challenge than for Charlie and Greg, but the acid test was to survive Greg's insults and acrimony as he rebounded balls and fed them back to the shooter at the foul line.

"Come on girlie, shoot that ball. You going to marry it or shoot it? Let's go you sad-sack toenail scratcher, watch the line, watch that foul line, toenail scratcher!" Greg's repertoire of ridicule and harassment unreeled, punctuated by laughter from the boys waiting their turn to subject themselves to his unique verbal abuse.

When Brian had first been initiated into this singular brand of degradation he had become infuriated, nervous, had lost his focus and missed most of his shots, but after adjusting to Greg's good-natured vitriol, his skill at shooting fouls in CYO league games had improved measurably. Toeing the foul line in a CYO game, his first thought of Greg usually brought a sly smile to his face and a surge in confidence.

Missing a shot after six consecutive baskets, Brian handed the ball off to Bobby, who was tied with him at 16 points. Charlie, the master foul shooter, having shot ten straight swish shots, started shooting with his left hand, giving his pals an even break. After a few preparatory dribbles, Bobby launched a two-handed shot that hit the steel rim and bounced over the backboard into a small gallery above and behind the basket. Knowing the protocol, Bobby ran to the side staircase where he gained entrance to the balcony. Quickly retrieving the ball, he launched it down to his brother Greg, who handed it off to Ray, the next shooter.

Wanting to hurry down to the court as well as show off his athleticism in the process, he stepped over the balcony rail onto a steel pipe that anchored the lower half of the backboard to the balcony projecting it a few feet over the court. Balancing on the pipe, he lowered himself until he was hanging full-length from the support. As he swung out from the pipe, his hands slipped, sending him plummeting to the gym floor. Attempting to cushion the fall, Bobby thrust his arms forward, allowing most of the impact to be absorbed by his forearms.

Immediately Greg was there to assess the damage. Bobby's screams of pain sent the boys into a time-tested escape and evasion drill that left the gym in complete and utter silence in a matter of seconds.

With Greg on his left side and Brian on the right, Bobby held his throbbing arms up in front of him, crying out in pain all the way to the McNally household. Once there, Mrs. McNally, a veteran of numerous scrapes, cuts, fractures, and bloodlettings, took charge of the situation. Greg was assigned to guard the home front, while she rushed Bobby off to Doctor McCann around the corner on Western Avenue.

Later that afternoon, Mrs. McNally escorted her son home from Doctor McCann's, both his forearms encased in thick white plaster.

<u>12</u>

Solo

Brian Reilly stood with his back against the clean blackboard. He was happy, if somewhat nervous. He and Mary Marcy were the only two pupils remaining in the religion contest. Brian looked beseechingly at Sister Eugene as she read the next question to Mary. The whole class was looking at the slender girl. All but a few thought she would answer correctly and be the winner. Mary consistently got A's on tests and was usually the first in class to raise her hand when Sister Eugene asked a question. Brian rubbed his hands together and scanned the ceiling, then cut a look at Bobby's seat, empty now for two weeks while he convalesced at home with both arms in casts.

"How many persons are there in the Holy Trinity and what are their names?" Sister Eugene asked.

"There are, ah, three…" Mary faltered, her voice trailing off in a low murmur. The seconds ticked off slowly.

Finally, Sister Eugene looked up from her desk. "I'm sorry; your time is up."

Mary walked silently to her front row seat in a rare moment of defeat.

Brian stood rigid against the edge of the chalk tray; he was the only one left, but would have to answer the next question in order to win. He wanted the prize more than anything he'd ever dreamed of. He looked across at the pigeon in its confining wire cage. It was pure white, except for a few black-tipped tail feathers. The pigeon's beady eyes were pink with small black pupils. Its rough, flesh-colored claws were unmoving; its head jerked sideways, tilting up slightly.

Brian's eyes moved cautiously to the Nun as she prepared to read the question.

"How many persons are there in the Holy Trinity and what are their names?"

After a moment of hesitation, Brian spoke confidently. "There are three persons in the Holy Trinity: the Father, the Son, and the Holy Ghost."

His mouth clamped shut and he fell silent.

Sister Eugene looked up from her desk. Brian stared at the face trapped in the starched white forehead linen and black veil.

"First prize goes to Brian Reilly. Come over and get the pigeon, Brian."

When he was halfway to the desk and his coveted prize, the door opened and in stalked Monsignor McGinty in his red-trimmed cassock and hat. There was instantaneous silence in the classroom. All hands were folded genteelly on desks, all feet planted motionless on the floor. The monsignor peered down first at Brian, then at the caged bird, then at Sister Eugene who was now standing at attention next to her desk.

"Well, well, and what do we have here, Sister?"

"We just concluded our annual religion contest, your Eminence, and Brian has won first prize, the white pigeon."

Brian longed to escape to his seat where he could join his classmates, but, as he turned, he felt a claw-like hand clamp his shoulder.

"Now, the winner of the religion contest is it? Might just be a sign, yes indeed, a sign from above. Perhaps there's a vocation here; picture yourself as a missionary on the Dark Continent, serving the heathens, the lepers, the pagans. What do you think of that, Mr. Reilly?"

Before Brian could verbally outline his career plans of playing baseball for the New York Yankees or basketball for the Boson Celtics, the monsignor gripped his other shoulder.

"A fine thing it is to answer the calling, oh yes, yes indeed. And don't I know. I can see it now. Another St. Francis, eh?" he said peering down at Brian and sneaking a look at his watch. Releasing his thick-boned hand from Brian's shoulder, he turned to Sister Eugene.

"What a pleasure it's been looking in on your class, Sister, but I'd better be moving along or I'll be late for saying a special mass for vocations right after the last class. I'm sure I'll see all of you boys and girls there," he said scanning the room.

All faces smiled, all heads nodded a bit too eagerly.

Abruptly departing while their half-hearted pledges to attend the mass lingered in the air, Brian at last picked up his prize and returned to his seat.

It seemed like forever until school let out that day. Slipping away from the monsignor's vocations mass, he ran all the way home with the caged pigeon clutched tightly in his arms. Reaching Partridge Street, he slowed to a fast walk while looking about for his neighborhood friends, anxious to tell them of his accomplishment, as well as exhibit his prize. Remembering his best friend, he ran the remaining half block to Bobby's house, foolishly traversing Mrs. Gardner's front lawn, thus eliciting a loud rap on her front window for his miscue; then up the steps he hurried to greet Mrs. McNally at a stove jammed with pots and pans and skillets, all pumping steam and smoke into the air. While simultaneously cooking a meal for her troops and tending to the screaming Connor in a nearby highchair, she smothered Brian with verbal praise and a pat on the back for capturing the coveted religion class prize. Turning back to the stove, she advised over a shoulder, "Bobby's in the living room."

Before he could take a step, she seized him by the arm. Pulling him close, she whispered, "How's your mother doing?" Not waiting for an answer, she added, "You tell her to come over for a little visit, anytime."

She turned back to the stove.

"I will," Brian said, again turning, but again Mrs. Reilly latched on to an arm.

Looking into his freckled face she said, "You help your mother now. She's depending on you."

Her voice had become so stern and rigid that little Connor's cries for attention ceased, and his hands began a gentle massage of the Jell-O he had meticulously emptied onto the tray of his highchair.

With her back to him again, Brian turned quickly and rushed down the hallway unimpeded.

Entering the living room, sunlight burst through the windows overlooking the front lawn, where Brian could see the twins engaged in a wrestling contest. Bobby was seated in his father's overstuffed easy chair, both arms encased in thick plaster casts from wrists to elbows.

Brian set the caged pigeon on the table beside the chair, allowing Bobby an eye-to-eye examination of his prize.

"So Little Miss Perfect didn't win?"

"Time ran out. Guess what, now I don't have to make up the homework I missed last week."

A cast weighing down his right arm, Bobby pointed an index finger at the stack of books and papers on the table beside him.

"I thought I'd be able to get out of schoolwork since I've been home, but my mother got together with Sister Eugene so I wouldn't fall behind. I bet I'm ahead of everyone in class for a change."

Brian sat down on the hassock in front of Bobby's chair.

"How're your arms doing?"

"Better, but they still ache at night. Can't sleep sometimes."

"When will Doctor McCann take the casts off?"

"A week or two, I guess."

Brian was silent for a minute.

"Listen, I'm going up to the pigeon coop by myself."

Bobby sighed and looked out the bay window.

"I got to. I made a promise. Some of the kids in school keep asking if we've been up there and captured a pigeon. Can't put it off or they'll be calling me a coward."

"I just wish I could go with you," Bobby said holding up his plaster-covered arms.

"We'll do it again, don't worry. Next summer."

Bobby looked skeptically at his pal.

"I know it sounds like a long way off, but summer will be here before you know it," Brian said trying to placate his friend.

Silent, Bobby peered at the casts then slammed them down on the frayed arms of the chair, sending currents of pain through forearms surgically repaired with steel pins.

Crossing the street cautiously, Brian ran up the driveway around the back of the two-story house. The green and yellow paint was beginning to chip and crack. Mrs. Silverstein, the landlord, would send her rent collector and jack-of-all-trades around next summer to slap on a new coat of paint before raising the rent that fall.

Brian hurried around to the back of the house and up the stairs, taking two at a time. The back porch was crowded with discarded furniture, boxes, and freshly washed clothes hanging from a clothesline affixed to a telephone pole. He pushed Arrow's unused bed out of the way before setting the cage down on an old thick-legged table. Staring into one of the pigeon's pink eyes, Brian accused himself of not being a good student. He remembered a recent scolding from Sister Eugene for repeatedly looking out the window at the new brick houses across from the school. But a week earlier when she announced that the white pigeon would be first prize in the contest, Brian had vowed he would somehow win. With his prize, he planned on having his own coop of tumblers and teaching them to do the fancy aerial maneuvers like those executed by Johnny Russian's kit. He would be the envy of every boy for miles around. It just might surpass the notoriety of his trophy bass.

The pigeon was his now, the beginnings of a tumbler dynasty, he conjectured. Standing beside the cage on the table, examining his new pet, he smiled with satisfaction. Feeling proud of himself, he thought he might just stand there on the porch for a long time observing his pigeon.

Hearing the kitchen door open, he looked up to see his mother approaching.

"Well young man, what have you got there?" Rita said, smiling at Brian with her hand tucked into the side pocket of her leather waistcoat. Since her operation she had begun wearing sweaters and coats to camouflage the loss of her missing left arm.

"I won it, Ma. I won first prize in the contest. Isn't it great?"

"So this is what you were talking about all week. It's a pretty little thing, almost pure white, too. Go in the house now and change."

"Okay, Ma," he said as he hurried inside, and then stopped in the doorway. "I'm going to make a nice new home for it. He'll like that, won't he?"

He decided against confiding to her, just yet, his plans for a coop of champion tumblers.

"Yes, yes dear, now go and change."

Rita remained on the porch while Brian went inside. As she looked at the caged bird, her face went slack. She thought of her own childhood, of the times when her mother and father would argue and wouldn't speak to each other. She shook her head and looked away. Then she remembered that her husband, Chick, would be home early. He always worked an early shift on Fridays. She thought of the nice time they would have at the VFW dinner-dance that night. They didn't go out often since her operation, so they would have a special time, and in the morning they would sleep late. She cherished those moments lying next to him in the morning. Instinctively, her right hand reached up to her left arm, but realizing she was grasping an empty coat sleeve, she bit her lower lip. The backdoor slammed, and Brian came bounding onto the porch.

"Ma, where are the wooden crates I was saving?"

"They're down in the cellar next to the coal bin. Take a flashlight when you go down to get them."

When Brian returned with the flashlight, his mother was gone. There was a chill in the air, even though the porch was partially enclosed. He squeezed shut the last snap on the neck of his frayed corduroy jacket. Within a matter of minutes he'd found the crates in the cellar and dragged them noisily up to the back porch. After finding a hammer in his father's toolbox under the table he began pulling nails from the crates. Soon, he had constructed a four-sided, closed-bottomed wooden cage more than twice the size of the wire cage. He'd even made a cover out of an old window screen his mother had discarded at the end of summer. He opened the small cage the pigeon was in. Slowly and carefully, he slipped his hands over the wings as he'd seen Johnny Russian do. Extracting the bird from the cage, he rubbed its soft feathers against his cheek. The trembling warmth beneath the feathers pleased him. After he'd placed the pigeon in its new home, he decided to ask his mother for a piece of bread crust to feed it.

He remembered watching Johnny Russian feed his tumblers some type of grain or seed that he would be able to examine first-hand when he completed his solitary quest to the loft tomorrow.

Early Saturday morning, Rita Reilly shook Brian as he slept peacefully in his bed with one arm hooked through the bars of the bed frame. After a few gentle pleadings from his mother, he climbed out of bed and began to get dressed. Still sleepy, he shuffled into the kitchen. His mother looked up nervously from her cup of coffee. Brian hurried to her side.

"Mom, did something happen to the pigeon, did it get hurt?"

"No, no honey, I'm sure it's fine."

Brian looked at his mother, then at the empty chair where his father usually sat.

"Where's Dad?"

"He's down in the car. Before you have your cereal I want you to go down and get him, please."

"Why is he in the car? How come he's not in bed or reading the paper like he usually does on Saturday morning?"

"He got sick last night and was too tired to come upstairs. Now hurry down and wake him up, hurry now," she coaxed.

"Okay, I'll be right back." Brian said while tying his sneakers.

He ran down the front stairs to the first floor, jumping every other step. At the bottom of the stairs a faded yellow curtain blurred what was on the other side of the mullioned glass and wood door. Rushing onto the front porch, Brian came to a halt. A few of the neighborhood kids were sitting on the porch railing in stony silence. Billy Urtz, who lived downstairs, joined two other boys viewing something in the street.

He wanted to tell them about his pigeon, but hesitated when he saw their tight, mean smiles. Then he recognized Mickey Delaney. Changing his mind, he raced down the porch steps to the sidewalk and over to his father's blue Ford parked at an odd angle at the curb. He pulled down on the chrome door handle opening the door. A foul smell rushed from the inside of the car.

His father was half-sitting and half-lying across the front seat. A coat was rolled up under his head. There were traces of dried yellow at the corners of his mouth. Brian shook his father, but he only mumbled a few words and pushed Brian away.

The boys on the porch jumped down to the sidewalk and gathered around the open car door.

"Free show, free show, see the drunk, see the drunken cop," they chanted.

Their voices grew louder and louder, echoing and reverberating in Brian's head.

"Come on, pigeon boy, something wrong with your old man?" Delaney taunted. All three tormentors flapped their arms pretending to fly.

Brian pressed his hands against his ears and thought of being holy and pure. Was he not the winner of the religion contest? He could not be affiliated with this, could he? Finally, shrieking like a wild animal, he ran through the alley gate to the backyard. With tears streaming from his eyes, he climbed the steps to the back porch. Grabbing the hammer that lay nearby, he threw off the top of the cage. With hot, cloudy eyes he beat and thrashed at the whiteness until his tears turned crimson. Finally, the hammer slipped from his hand as he doubled over gagging and sobbing.

"Easy now, that's a good boy, everything is all right," his mother whispered, holding Brian protectively in her arm. He looked up into her face for a long time, while she stroked his brown hair.

"Mama, mama, I'm sorry I did it…I didn't mean to, honest I didn't."

"Shush now, everything will be okay."

"But they called Dad a drunk and made fun of him. I couldn't listen, I couldn't. I told God I hated him. I was best in religion class. I proved I was."

"It's all right now," she said pulling Brian close to her. "It wasn't God's fault, believe me, it wasn't."

She stood up. With her arm around Brian's shoulder they walked through the kitchen door to her bedroom. His father was sitting on the edge of the bed with his head cupped in his hands. She sat down next to him. Brian slipped his arm slowly around his father's neck and hugged him. He clenched his jaw. He had to prove himself. The only way to do that was to climb up to the loft in the barn and capture one of Johnny Russian's pigeons.

Saturday afternoon found him on the garage roof next to the barn in the Jew's yard. From concealment he scanned the backyard with its gardens and orchards, but saw no one, not even the ubiquitous Johnny Russian. Suddenly, the screeching of the rest home back door made him flinch. He scanned the porch and watched while a cook outfitted in a white uniform and floppy hat pulled a pack of cigarettes from a stained shirt pocket and quickly lit a cigarette.

Brian guessed the residents and staff were inside enjoying their dinner, giving him ample time and opportunity to carry out his secret mission. Backing up ten feet from the edge of the garage roof, he broke into a run and leapt across the breach to the slanted roof at the back of the barn. Landing with a thump on the asphalt shingles, he knelt to catch his breath and steady himself before moving to the window that would allow him entry to the barn's interior. Attempting to push up on the window, and finding it stuck, he was momentarily deflated. Successive attempts were equally futile. Upon close inspection of one of the lowest panes of glass, he could see that a nail had been driven into the bottom of the window frame insuring the window's impregnability.

Gritting his teeth, he sat down with his back to the barn siding. Should he abandon the mission? Admit defeat again?

After a few minutes of contemplation, he jumped to his feet, rummaged in the pocket of his dungarees and pulled a jackknife from his pocket. Engaging the long blade, he began digging at the cracked putty holding the small piece of glass in its frame. In no more than ten minutes, he had removed the small panes of glass for an opening that enabled him to reach in and bend the nails back that held the window in place. Once this was accomplished, he pushed the lower window up far enough to allow him to squeeze through the opening. Kneeling amidst scattered hay, he listened to goats on the ground level busy chomping on a split hay bale, their hooves striking the wood plank floor. Satisfied that Johnny Russian was not present, he dashed over to the pipe, shimmied up quickly and was soon on top of the beam that would be his pathway to the pigeon coop.

He paused to catch his breath and regain his composure.

So far, so good, he thought.

Shafts of sunlight, swirling with motes of dust, splashed down from the gabled roof, like so many spotlights, illuminating the upper reaches of the barn.

Sitting astride the beam for a few minutes and conscious of the time he'd lost when stymied by the window, he got to his feet. His nostrils filled with the aroma of hay and clover, his ears with the bleat of a goat, the scuffling of hooves. With arms stretched out from his side for balance, he stood on the narrow beam, holding his breath and staring straight ahead. Concentrating, he began to tightrope walk across the beam, placing each foot precisely and carefully ahead of the other, his eyes fixed on the loft door. He shifted his weight with short, quick movements to maintain balance. With each breath he could feel his stomach muscles tighten, his entire body a machine of muscle and sinew. Midway across the beam, he stopped to poke at a speck dust irritating his eye.

Judging his distance from the coop at only ten feet, he resumed his quest with the careful placement of each footstep, but only two steps were achieved when the door of the pigeon coop flew open. Brian froze. The hulking body of Johnny Russian was framed in the dim, dusty light of the loft doorway.

Gasping, Brian took one awkward step backward before slipping and falling from the beam. Johnny Russian watched the boy plunge downward through shafts of light, then suddenly crash onto a hay bale, sending up clouds of dust and scattering the goats in noisy flight.

Johnny peered down at the boy while a thick-boned hand went to his mouth in alarm. Closing the loft door behind him, he hurried, as fast as his crippled body allowed, to the trapdoor ladder that enabled him to descend to the second level, then down by extension ladder to the ground floor. Once there, he rushed to the unconscious boy and knelt beside him.

For a fraction of a second, Johnny Russian saw himself in a shallow, earthen grave, his limbs battered, his vision compromised, his mental faculties devastated. His last fleeting memory from that time of near death was of a thing called spirit or soul attempting to disengage itself from his shattered body, but not quite succeeding. He would not let it forsake him.

From her second story bedroom window, Samantha Gardiner, observed the brute slip through the McNally back fence with the Reilly boy in his arms. He stopped and peered around in bewilderment. Suspecting mischief on Brian's part, she ran downstairs. Sizing up the situation immediately, she gripped the beast's arm and propelled him like a child down the alley and across the street to the Reilly backstairs. Later, safe in her own home, she confided to her sister, Agatha, that she had forecast this type of misadventure every time she had observed those two rowdy lads. "It was only a matter of time," she huffed.

Rita Reilly opened the back door and looked in terror at the sight before her. A brute of a man, with one eye, stood before her with her son held protectively in his arms. Johnny Russian peered at the woman through his good eye, a black patch covering the missing one. Observing the void where her left arm had been, he then looked her in the face. Immediately, silently, Rita motioned for the man to follow her. With Brian placed in his bed and wrapped in a blanket, she checked his pulse; finding it strong, she tested his forehead with her hand.

"Thank God," she whispered.

Turning to thank the man—whoever, whatever he was—for helping her son, she was disconcerted to see that he was gone. No time to waste, she turned back to Brian pressing her hand to his forehead.

Preparing to call out to her husband, she was surprised and comforted to see him in the doorway. While she tended to her son, Chick went to the telephone to call Dr. McCann.

Upon hearing a car pull to a stop in the drive below the bedroom window, Chick looked down to see the doctor's Packard. Instantly, the driver's door opened and the doctor scurried, with black bag in hand, to the front steps. While they climbed the stairs Chick told him what little he could of Brian's condition.

Making way for the Doctor, Rita moved to her husband's side while Dr. McCann examined the boy. Satisfied his vital signs were in order, he snapped an ammonia capsule and waved it slowly under Brian's nose. Seeing the boy flinch, he withdrew the capsule. To his parents' delight, Brian at last opened his eyes. Blinking, he looked around in confusion. Only then was he aware of the pain in his legs.

"We have to get him over to Brady Hospital. We'll take my car. Don't you worry, he'll be fine," Dr. McCann advised while packing his stethoscope and thermometer into his black leather bag.

Lastly, he patted Brian on the shoulder. "Now this is going to hurt some, but we've got to get you to the hospital."

Brian winced as his father gathered him up in his arms.

~

Two days later, Bobby McNally, with his mother beside him, made his way slowly across Partridge Street. Mrs. McNally waved at the Freihoffer man as he exited his bread wagon in front of the Gardner house, where both sisters observed the comings and goings from half-drawn window curtains. Bobby had a jacket pulled over his shoulders, his plaster casts too large for the jacket sleeves to accommodate them.

Dinny Healy, the itinerant knife sharpener, looked up from his revolving sharpening stone, manipulated with his right foot, to watch mother and son mount the stairs to the front porch. Seconds after the buzzer gained them entry to the Reilly household, Mrs. Urtz opened her door and walked onto the front porch with purse in hand to pay for her newly sharpened kitchen knives.

The smell of freshly brewed coffee tickled Mrs. McNally's nose as Rita escorted her into the kitchen.

With his mother engaged, Bobby entered Brian's bedroom. Directly in front of him was his best friend, ensconced in a wheel chair with both legs thoroughly swathed in plaster casts. Smiles appeared, simultaneously, on their faces.

13

Television

Sitting on the side of his bed, Brian looked wistfully at the baseball trophy on his desk. Fumbling and fuming, his mother was attempting to button his shirt with one hand. He finally realized the source of her frustration and quickly completed the task himself.

Beside him was a pair of wooden crutches. The only remaining cast, an abbreviated one on his lower right leg, allowed him to navigate upright on his own for the first time since he had plummeted from the beam.

"So, Johnny Russian really brought me home?"

"Sure did. I met him at the back door with you in his arms."

"Hope Dad isn't mad at me for trying to sneak into the pigeon coop." Rita chuckled.

"Mad? He was scared stiff you were… you know."

"Huh, the last thing I remember is seeing Johnny Russian in the doorway of the loft. He looked so mean and ugly. He scared the heck out of me."

"That's not all he scared out of you. You wet your dungarees."

"Ah, Ma!"

"You did."

"Geez. Don't tell anyone, will ya? Promise?"

Rita pressed her thumb and index finger to her lips twisting an imaginary key.

"Honey, don't ever call people names like ugly, especially him. I think he saved your life. Some people are sensitive about how they look."

"But…"

"But nothing. Oh hon, looks aren't always what they seem. Sometimes the prettiest and handsomest people in the world can be the meanest. Now you take that Hansen girl you and Bobby are always making fun of, well Gina and Eileen visited you in the hospital."

"Well, they're best friends for some reason," Brian said, before being quickly sidetracked by an image of Gina in her pink angora sweater standing at the side of his hospital bed.

"Okay, now let's get you on those crutches, get you moving around on your own. You ready?"

"I'll say."

Grasping his mother's outstretched hand, he pulled himself to his feet then grabbed a crutch in each hand, plunging the padded supports into his armpits.

"Got a surprise to show you. Think you can make your way to the back porch?"

A frown appeared for a few seconds as he recalled the recent debacle with his religion class prize.

"I guess," he managed, while putting most of his weight on the crutches and stepping out with his left leg. Slowly, he hobbled from the bedroom down the hallway to the kitchen. There, he stopped and looked at his mother.

"Not as bad as I thought it would be."

Looking over at the radio on the kitchen table, then to the clock on the wall he announced, "Hey, it's almost time for the Yankee-Braves World Series game. Bobby will be here real soon."

"Just come with me. This will only take a few minutes," Rita said with a smile, while pulling the back door open.

Together they walked onto the back porch where Brian had kept his prize pigeon from religion class. They stopped in front of the table looking down at the cage he had built. He grimaced, remembering his act of desperation. While Rita's hand massaged his shoulder, he realized there was a new pigeon in the cage. He stooped over for a closer look.

"Wow, Ma, look! That's a Birmingham Roller, a real tumbler. Bobby and me looked that up in the encyclopedia. I've seen that kind of pigeon in Johnny Russian's flock."

They continued their inspection of the bird in silence. The roller strutted about the confines of the cage with its head held high, a puffed up chest of bluish-white feathers, and short white and blue tail feathers bobbing slightly as it moved to a small cup of water.

Hearing rapid footsteps on the stairs, mother and son turned to see Bobby McNally bound onto the porch. His forearms now free of plaster had lost their muscular tone and were paler than the upper arms projecting from a short-sleeved T-shirt.

"Hey, come here and look at this," Brian said.

Bobby knelt down in front of the cage.

"Say, that's a tumbler ain't it?"

"Sure is. Go ahead, get him out of the cage, will ya?"

Pulling the window screen aside, Bobby carefully maneuvered his hands until he had the bird firmly secured. Slowly, he transferred the tumbler to Brian's outstretched hands. Balancing on the padded crutches, he held the bird to his cheek feeling the smoothness of its feathers and the pounding of its heart.

"Your father give it to you?" Bobby asked.

Brian looked to his mother.

"I heard it making that pigeon sound when I came out to put an empty milk bottle on the porch. I guess it just appeared like magic," she teased.

The boys glanced at each other with quizzical looks.

Simultaneously they looked at the bird.

"I think I know where it came from," Brian exclaimed.

"Yeah, me too. You want to see if it will tumble for us?" Bobby speculated.

"You boys will miss the World Series…"

With that, Bobby returned the Birmingham roller to its cage and adjourned to the kitchen where the Philco radio was already tuned to the correct station. Before Brian could get seated comfortably at the table, the voice of the announcer, Mel Allen, promoting White Owl cigars and the World Series piped from the radio.

During the seventh inning stretch, Brian looked over at his friend.

"That was one of his prize rollers. We watched it with our own eyes, remember?"

"Sure did. Heck, I'd never give away a tumbler like that. Maybe we should stop heckling him?"

"Yeah. I think you're right. My mother said I have to thank him for the present. When I do I'm going to see if he'll show me how to train tumblers."

Bobby looked at his friend dubiously, "Hey, come on, the game got started again."

~

Later that day, while practicing walking with his crutches, Brian was maneuvering back and forth in the kitchen when someone knocked on the back door.

"Come on in," he said, opening the door to see Mrs. Urtz from downstairs.

She leaned in. A bright blue dress and red lipstick enhanced her large front teeth.

"Get you mother and come downstairs and see Reggie's new invention."

Before he could say a word, visions of Mr. Urtz's utopian inventions of years past emerged in his mind: a miniature sun dial worn on the wrist like a watch was the first of several strange gizmos to issue from the basement workshop.

"Oh, hi, Millie, won't you come in?" Rita said.

Her face lit up. "Can't. Just want to invite you down to see the latest creation Reggie has been working on at the plant. Hurry down," she encouraged, then disappeared down the staircase.

His mother retreated to the hall closet to pull a leather waistcoat over her shoulders, soon reappearing at Brian's side.

"Honey, button that button for me. I just can't manage it."

With this small task accomplished, she preceded Brian down to the Urtz's first floor apartment.

Slowly, Brian made his way down the semi-circular staircase. At the bottom of the stairwell, he pushed his way into the Urtz kitchen, an exact duplicate of the Reilly floor plan and furnishings, except for an elegant kitchen set.

In apron and high heels, Mrs. Urtz escorted them to the living room where a small group was gathered around her engineer husband.

In the Urtz living room, Brian confronted the backs of a half dozen neighbors. Reginald Urtz was in the midst of explaining what it was he and the *boys* at GE had been working on for the past four years. He tapped the top of a wooden armoire with the stem of his pipe.

"Mark my words—radio is dead. This little baby will be in every living room in America. That's right, throw those radios out and make room for *Television*," he chortled as his hand gently slapped the walnut cabinet beside him. Two open console doors exposed a glass screen five inches by five inches.

Pushing closer, Brian examined the polished wood console with skepticism.

"Thousands of hours of testing and experimentation…" Urtz prattled on with an overly enthusiastic endorsement of the piece of furniture he kept referring to as a *television*.

He flicked a knob, and the diminutive screen began to glow. The guests murmured and gasped.

"Here you see what, in engineering circles, we refer to as a *test pattern*," said Urtz adjusting his red bowtie and refitting the pipe in his mouth. He proudly tapped the glass tube encased in wood with a pencil tip.

"The test pattern is used mainly by studio engineers to calibrate their cameras and a myriad of broadcast equipment. When the image appears on the television screen, what we see is an optimized black and white picture, though, I will admit, at least in present company, that there are numerous other technical and non-technical factors that may or may not affect the quality of the broadcast image, for example, the angle of the reception antenna that I've affixed on the roof of this house. This particular antenna, my brainchild, if you will, was constructed to optimize the television signal originating at the New York City studio. If, per chance, the wind blows the antenna off kilter, the picture may become distorted and fill the picture tube with what we refer to as *snow*. Not so with my baby. I have connected a small motor, built in my home workshop, capable of remotely adjusting the rooftop antenna to perfect calibration and performance. On rare occasions, the picture tube's horizontal or vertical holds will start skipping, but I won't get into that now," he droned while raising a hand to discourage the deluge of technical questions he foolishly anticipated.

Brian kept looking from the screen to Mr. Urtz wondering when something was going to happen. Other than a miniscule black and white image of an Indian chief outfitted in an elaborate bonnet of eagle feathers, the *test pattern* was composed of a grid of closely spaced lines and a series of graduated bars. Blinking his eyes, he turned back to Mr. Urtz.

"Now here's the most exciting part, the test pattern we are seeing here in my living room is in fact a graphic card in the NBC television studios in New York City. That's right, this image is not, I repeat, *is not*, inside this attractive piece of furniture. The NBC studio, located in downtown New York City, has a television camera that is pointed at the *test pattern* card. Picture, if you will, pointing your little Kodak box camera at a similar card. That's exactly what the studio television camera is doing *right now* in downtown New York City, some one hundred and fifty miles away. Astounding, isn't it?"

His eager smile dissolved into a grimace. The anticipated cheers and accolades were not forthcoming. His initial presentation, the previous day, before colleagues and company executives, had garnered thunderous applause.

Well, what can one expect from the public, he thought before proceeding.

He was about to launch into other technical aspects of the device, when he noticed Brian's raised hand. He jerked the pipe from his mouth.

"Yes, go ahead," he encouraged.

Sneaking another look at Mrs. Urtz, Brian was startled by the size and shape of her front teeth, which closely resembled those of her husband.

"Well, does it do anything?" Brian asked.

"Does it *DO* anything? The question is, *does it do anything*? It is *doing* something at this very moment. That image before your eyes on that screen is being broadcast, just like a radio signal, from New York City to my living room, and, I might add, to your living rooms in the not too distant future."

"But it hasn't moved an inch," Brian blurted out, pointing to the stationary test pattern.

Hoping to divert his attention and evade the question, Urtz knelt before the television set and placed his hand on a knob.

Brian wrinkled his nose.

"When I turn this knob, similar to a radio knob, you will hear, for the first time, the *sound* of television," Urtz said with authority.

With a flick of his wrist, a steady audio monotone suffused the room. People looked from the television to their neighbor then back to Urtz, whose hand went nervously to his red bowtie. He was losing them, losing his captive audience, he thought, while sneaking another quick look at his wristwatch.

"That, my dear friends, is called a reference tone. It is being broadcast, simultaneously with the *test pattern*, I might add, at 1000 Hertz, zero decibels. Truly an extraordinary feat, don't you agree?"

Looking around, he was met again with faces twisted with suspicion, rolling eyeballs, hands scratching heads, fingers pulling at earlobes.

Immediately deciding to jettison his scientific explanation of how sound and images were bound together with electrons and neutrons and shot into the air, he rose to his feet, checked his watch one more time, and announced, with the pride of a new father presenting a cigar to a colleague, "I now direct your undivided attention to the *television*," he encouraged with a tap of his mechanical pencil on the small glass screen.

As if by sleight of hand, a continuous series of moving images appeared on the screen, accompanied by orchestral music.

Startled, his audience chirped their surprise and eyed one another with trepidation. One or two backpedaled.

The television screen was filled with a cuckoo clock, its hands gone haywire, the picture then segued to the image of a freckle-faced puppet named Howdy Doody, all in black and white. While Urtz adjusted several knobs and dials on the TV set, two of his audience slipped unobserved out the backdoor.

"Hey kids, what time is it?" Howdy, the puppet, chortled.

Needing little encouragement, a group of youngsters in the New York City studio, known affectionately as the "Peanut Gallery," burst into song.

"It's Howdy Doody time, it's Howdy Doody time…"

A voice somewhere in the depths of the television set proclaimed, "It's Howdy Doody Time. Starring Howdy Doody and Buffalo Bob."

Urtz stood before the television, his head bobbing in time with the music, expecting all the while to hear gasps of surprise and bold exclamations embroidered with words like "simply amazing," "technologically brilliant," "a pioneering breakthrough." With none forthcoming, he slowly turned around. Abject disappointment slashed his face. Half the audience gathered to view the first television on the block, possibly *the* first television in the city, had fled.

Gripping the pipe angrily between his protruding teeth, he looked down at young Connor McNally seated in his stroller, little sausage fingers beating time to the chorus of children singing Howdy's praises.

Urtz nodded conspiratorially to Mrs. McNally, "Smart as a whip, that lad," he said, pointing the pipe stem at the youngest McNally now jumping up and down spouting unintelligible baby talk.

Feeling magnanimous, he added, "You're more than welcome to stay for the *Kukla, Fran and Ollie Show*, coming right up."

She skewered him with an icy look. "Where's the color?"

~

A week later, crutches abandoned, Brian burst into the kitchen, his mother pulling, as best she could, wet articles of clothing from a washer.

"Mom. I have to learn to dance."

She looked up with a smile.

"Well, if you can wait until we get these clothes on the line, I'll do my best. Where will the dance be?"

"At the high school gym. We play our CYO basketball games there. Just us seventh and eighth graders."

"Why that will be your first dance. That's exciting. It will be fun, I'm sure."

"I thought you'd know how to dance. Come on, let me take care of that," he said putting the remainder of the laundry into a wheeled cart, then quickly pushing it out onto the back porch where a clothesline looped out to a telephone pole at the corner of the garage.

Watching Brian push the cart loaded with wet laundry onto the back porch, Rita ran her hand slowly over the pinned up sleeve of her sweater.

Finishing with the laundry, he checked on his tumbler pigeon to insure it had enough to eat and drink. That accomplished, he rushed inside.

In his absence, his mother had tuned the Philco radio to a station playing songs from *Your Hit Parade*. She had slipped off her sweater to better move her unbalanced torso. Brian returned to the kitchen. He stood beside the table not knowing what to do and waiting for a cue from his mother.

From her position in the middle of the kitchen, Rita looked pensively at her son. He's growing too fast, she thought.

"Alright, come here and I'll show you how to hold your dance partner," she said beckoning him with her hand.

"You mean I have to hold the girl I dance with?"

"Just give it a try; this isn't a baseball game after all. We'll do a waltz, a nice slow dance with just a few steps to learn."

Brian stood in front of his mother. Suddenly, he realized that he was as tall as she was. His eyes were even with hers. How could this be? Rita reached out, drew him close to her, draping her arm on his shoulder. His nostrils filled with the scent of the lavender soap she used in her bath.

"Does Dad know how to dance, too?"

She laughed. "He's an excellent dancer. We used to go dancing all the time before we got married and before the war. The war changed a lot of things. You were a baby then."

"How come you don't go dancing anymore?"

Her right arm grasped his left arm, hanging limp at his side. Lifting it above his shoulder, she encouraged, "Now put your right arm around my waist.'

Brian's mouth screwed up. Rita could feel his body go rigid.

"I wish you had your arm back, Mom."

"Well, you might not believe this, but right now it feels like my left arm is resting on your shoulder. I can even feel a tingling in the tips of my fingers, but, when I look, there aren't any fingers or arm. It's the strangest thing. Dr. McCann called it a phantom arm."

"Still, I want you to come and see me play ball when you feel like going out again. You've never seen me play. I'm really good."

"Just relax, hon'. You can't possibly dance when you're all tense and stiff. Try to relax."

"Do I have to put my arms around all the girls I dance with?"

"Yes, you do and you'll learn to love it. Silly."

"Well, okay, but I don't see why you have to hold each other so close."

"Just pay attention. This is a one-two-three slow waltz step. Like this, just follow me."

With his right arm encircling her waist, they moved only a few awkward steps before Rita prompted, "Honey, first thing to learn is not to step on my toes."

Brian looked sheepishly at his mother.

"I'm leading you, but in a real dance the man leads the woman. You lead and I follow. But for now, just follow me until you get the feel of it. This shouldn't be too hard; you're athletic. You'll pick it up in a jiffy."

To his surprise, he began moving in ever expanding circles in time with the music. Now, with a bit of confidence, he took the lead.

"Now don't get in a hurry; remember, this is a *slow* waltz, kind of a dreamy romantic dance.

"Ah, Ma."

She hurried over to the radio and turned a knob, doubling the volume.

"Oh, now listen to this music; it's a good waltz tune. And concentrate."

With Brian's right hand fixed firmly on his mother's back, they began moving gracefully about the kitchen while the Platters sang their hit tune, *The Great Pretender*.

Effortlessly, they circled the kitchen. Rita pressed her cheek against Brian's cheek. He felt her arm tighten on his shoulder as they waltzed, almost floating in time to the music. He even felt a slight throbbing in her chest, perhaps a cough or an attempt to catch her breath. They danced more slowly. Something cascaded onto his neck, hot and wet. Looking at her, he saw tears trickling from her eyes. As she pulled him closer, he was surprised at the strength of her grip. The sobbing in her body ran up to her mouth and into his ear. Suddenly, they were motionless. She held him tight, while shaking slightly. He was afraid to move.

Rita gently pushed him away and hurried to her bedroom.

He found his mother face down on her bed. Rita's body quaked with potent sobs. Slowly, he sat down beside his mother. Hesitantly, he pressed his left hand to her back.

"Mom, did I do something wrong?"

When her crying subsided, she released the pillow and turned over. Shaking her head, she said, "No honey, you were fine, you'll be a terrific dancer…just like your father."

"So why are you crying if I didn't do anything wrong?"

She stared into his blue eyes for what seemed like hours. Sitting at the side of the bed, she grabbed a Kleenex from the bedside table and dried her eyes.

"I've got to go away for another operation. To a hospital in Buffalo. They didn't stop the cancer when they amputated my arm. The doctors want to do another… another thing."

She shrugged her shoulders and continued.

"They said the cancer could move to other parts of my body if they don't operate."

"Does Dad know about the operation?"

She smiled. "Of course. He'll be taking me to the hospital. Auntie will come and stay with you for a few days while I'm gone."

"Mom? Will the operation hurt?"

She hesitated for a moment.

"They all hurt, honey."

"Are you afraid?"

Suddenly, her face turned to stone.

"I will fear no evil. For you are with me."

"Can I go with you and Dad? Can I? I don't want to stay here alone."

"You won't be alone. Auntie will be here. She'll have her bag of goodies for you. Besides, what about school and the big dance?"

He looked from his mother's face to the sleeve of her dress hanging empty, then back at her, directly into her eyes.

"Yeah, the dance. My first dance. I don't think I want to dance."

Perking up, she got to her feet and reached her hand out.

"Come on, let's work on that waltz, get you ready for all those girls who can't wait to get their hands on you."

"Ahhh, Ma."

Pulling him by the hand she led him back into the kitchen.

As they waltzed to a Duke Ellington hit, the music stopped suddenly, replaced by the harsh voice of an announcer.

"Ladies and gentlemen, we interrupt our regular broadcast to bring you this special bulletin. A young boy, reported missing, is suspected of being kidnapped while fishing on the Hudson River, in the North Albany ward of the city. Sources at police headquarters suspect this to be the work of a kidnapper who may be linked to three other missing children. Police officials ask parents to take precautions to insure the safety and welfare of their children. Anyone with information regarding the whereabouts of the missing youngster is encouraged to call police headquarters. Now back to today's scheduled programming."

When the music came on, Brian slipped his hand around his mother's waist to resume a slow, tentative waltz.

14

Detectives

Two police detectives were escorted down the first floor staircase leading to a lower level where the enormous printing presses were installed. With each step down the metal staircase they could feel the intense vibration created by dozens of printing presses running full throttle. At last, a door was opened to them and closed as soon as they passed the threshold. The presses, with their monstrous rolls of paper, spinning rollers, clattering gears, colored inks, all manner of mechanical and electrical devices were deployed in rows like so many platoons of soldiers at a regimental review. A press would stop its maniacal gyrations for a split second, belch a nerve shattering noise, then resume feeding miles of paper into its insatiable maw at nauseating speeds.

Chick turned to his partner, McEvoy. His lips moved, but not even he could hear the words that exited his mouth. McEvoy pointed to a figure approaching between two rows of printing presses. The aisle was so long, the man appeared to grow in height and width as he approached.

Clipboard in hand, the man stopped in front of the two detectives dressed in their lightweight suits and straw hats, cordovan shoes polished to a high shine, gold shields held before them. The man's dark blue work uniform was deeply stained with inks and oils. His shirt pocket was crammed with pencils, gauges, a metal ruler, a tiny screwdriver, even a crumpled pack of cigarettes managed to squeeze into the bulging pocket.

In back of the clipboard man, the detectives watched fascinated as an overhead crane, suspended on massive steel girders resembling railroad tracks and running the length of the building, slowly maneuvered a roll of paper the size of a city bus into position above one of the presses and hung there, swaying slightly, as a team of men below prepared the press to receive the roll. Both detectives were ready to turn and run if the roll came tumbling down from the chains that secured it. For all they knew, that happened on a daily basis, perhaps hourly? They eyed each other nervously.

The noise of the presses seemed to increase in both volume and pitch with every passing minute. The vibrations worked their way up from the concrete floor through their thin-soled shoes to the very top of their heads. Both detectives cut looks at each other, eyes bulging with anxiety. The man with the clipboard was either oblivious to the cacophony or reveling in it. His face, they noted, was a portrait of serenity. An opium addict? A functional alcoholic?

He stopped in front of the detectives, pulled a pencil from his right ear and pointed it at them, then at a glassed-in room in back of them. Not waiting for an answer or even an acknowledgement, he made a beeline for the room. Upon reaching it, he glanced over his shoulder to insure the two men were behind him. He flung the door wide, the pencil motioning them to enter. Once the door was closed, the detectives could hear again. Gone was the nerve-wracking vibration in the pressroom. Within the confines of the windowless, cramped room the detectives began to relax, regain their equilibrium and breathe easier.

"Jesus," McEvoy whispered, massaging his temples. "Reminds me of the troop ship that took my outfit over for the Normandy invasion. Pumpa-pumpa with the engines, the vibration from the steel bulkheads up the ass."

"Yeah," the man said, "tough sledding. But we kicked their cans. Pushed'em back to Berlin."

"Sure, sure. Wasn't no picnic either."

Chick's eyes fixed on a small plaque on the cluttered desk. The name *Albert Palazski* was inscribed with white letters in black plastic.

Setting the clipboard on a pile of papers, the man removed two earplugs, then quickly reached out to shake hands with his guests.

"Name's Al." Omitting his last name, he merely pointed at the nameplate on the desk. "Gets to ya, the noise, doesn't it? Biggest press operation on the east coast. *Time, Life, Collier's, Atlantic Monthly*, we print'em all. Those babies out there," he pointed out a thick plate glass window, "going all day, all night."

"Kee-rist," McEvoy cursed again.

"Listen," Chick began, "your guy in personnel said you might be able to help us."

"Oh yeah? Shoot." Realizing his gaff, Al held his hands up in mock surrender.

"Looking for a guy possibly worked or works in a printing plant."

With the only chair in the office behind his desk, Al perched on the edge of the desk.

He chuckled. "Needle in a haystack, huh?"

Chick nodded his head.

"Well, yeah, we got hundreds of guys," Al began, "press men, mechanics, what have you."

"This particular guy had an accident," said Chick.

Al chuckled, cracked his knuckles. "Got accidents, one-thing-or-another all the time, 'specially Monday mornings," he said with a wink.

"This guy lost a finger, a pinky, right hand."

"Don't say, don't say," Al glanced quickly at his right hand reassuring himself all his digits were accounted for.

"Yeah, pinky, right hand," McEvoy reiterated needlessly.

"Ha, lucky he only lost a finger. Those presses will swallow you up in one end and spit you out the other flat as a pancake, hold the maple syrup."

Chuckling, he replaced the pencil behind his ear and folded his arms across his chest. Abruptly, he snatched the crumpled pack of Luckys from his shirt pocket. The detectives watched as he angrily withdrew a half-dozen broken cigarettes from the pack.

"Shee-it."

"Think you can help us on this?"

Dispatching the damaged smokes to the tabletop, he looked from one detective to the other, lips curled in a playful smile.

"Got a lot a guys here, three shifts most of the year. Guys they come, they go. Lemme think, but still'n all, seems to me we had a guy here, maybe a year or two back, lost a hand or finger in a press." The pencil pointed out toward the clattering printing presses, "A roll change it was. I think?"

"Got a name?" Chick asked.

Shaking his head, Al peered into the damaged cigarette pack, frowned, and extracted a single broken smoke. He tore part of it away and put the remainder in the corner of his mouth, shreds of tobacco dangling from the torn end.

"A name he says. Nah. But hey, Personnel should be able to help you there. They keep records of all industrial accidents, ya know, in case some smart aleck tries to sue, all that baloney. Anyway, a guy loses a finger, gets a toe smashed, we send him down to the County Hospital." A sadistic smile forming on his lips, he added, "The pancakes get hauled off to the morgue. Va-voom."

"Hold the maple syrup," McEvoy deadpanned.

Chick looked at McEvoy, then back to Al.

"Thanks for the help."

McEvoy pulled a pack of cigarettes from his suit coat and held it out to Palazski, who tossed the broken cigarette away before reaching out for the fresh one. "Say, what's this all about?"

"A kid was fishing down on the river, not far from here. They suspect foul play."

"Jeez, that right? On the river, you say."

The detectives turned to leave.

"Say, I hope you catch the louse," Al said, as the flame of a match touched the tip of his cigarette.

~

They were waiting in the front parlor, Brian and Mike on the green sofa, Ray in the upholstered rocker near the window looking out at the front porch. The boys looked at each other then down at their hands or feet. No one spoke. Ray rocked back-and-forth slowly.

Chick walked into the room carrying a straight back chair that Brian recognized as one from the dining room set. He placed the chair in the center of the parlor. He sat down on it with his hands draped down, elbows resting on his legs. A white shirt and striped tie contrasted with blue dress pants held up with suspenders. A shoulder holster with a snubnose .38 was partially hidden in his left armpit.

The boys watched him anxiously, expecting to be lectured, possibly reprimanded.

He looked around at all of them with a broad knowing smile.

"You guys relax, okay? Just got a few questions about that fellow who gave you the ride out to Six-Mile, the guy missing the pinky. This is all between us, got it?"

They looked at each other again, before nodding their heads.

"You already told me this guy was a white male, maybe five six or seven, wore black glasses, a mustache, a pinky missing on the right hand. It was the right hand, wasn't it?"

They nodded.

"He was driving a maroon Chevrolet, a four-door?"

They nodded again.

"Anything else you remember about him or the car? Think hard now. Anything come to mind? Anything?"

Brian and Mike looked at Ray.

"Well, I remember it smelled funny, like paint or oil or something. Oh, and the car had two spare tires, one in each front fender," Ray said.

"Remember a license plate maybe?"

"No."

Chick turned to Brian and Mike on the couch. "How about you two, remember anything we didn't go over before? Small stuff, scars, tattoos? An accent, a stutter, anything?"

"I don't remember any stuff like that, just the missing pinky." Brian said.

"Me too," Mike chimed in.

Chick ran a hand over his face.

"If you do come up with anything, no matter what, let me know. Okay?"

"Well, he did have black leather gloves." Mike added.

"Is something wrong?" Ray asked.

"Well, a young kid out fishing on the river is missing," Chick shrugged his shoulders. "Could have something to do with this guy in the Chevy. Maybe, maybe not. I gotta get back to work, so thanks for the help."

There was a moment of silence after Chick left. Ray spoke up.

"Show us your pigeon, okay?"

"Sure, come on. Bobby and me built a coop on the garage roof. He can fly and tumble real good. Johnny Russian showed us some things. Like feeding and rewarding it with extra food, stuff like that. I'm not afraid of him anymore."

Bursting with repressed energy, the boys hurried out of the parlor to the back of the house and down the stairs, their minds bubbling with everything but severed pinkies, maroon Chevrolets.

~

A black wrought-iron weathervane with the iconic crowing rooster above the four compass points stood sentinel on the sloped roof of the rest home barn. Below, the gravel drive was occupied by a solitary figure. Dressed in frayed, patched denim overalls, his hands clenched the metal handles of pails containing warm goats' milk. Exiting the barn with the sliding door left open just wide enough to accommodate him and his burden, a squad of cats slinked through the door opening. Checking to insure the retreating man continued on his path, they hurry into the barn where several ewes graze hay after being released from milking stalls. The cats gambol across the hay-strewn floor barely out of reach of goat hooves that might attempt to injure them if they lose focus and wander within range. Suddenly, they pounce on a pie tin of surplus goat's milk that has been set aside.

Johnny Russian entered the open kitchen door at the back of the rest home where a negro cook, clothed in solid white from head to foot, even sporting a white moustache and white eyebrows, welcomed the man and, perhaps more importantly, the goats' milk he carried. The cook rationed the milk to numerous residents plagued with allergies, ulcers, and various gastric maladies. This select group of geriatrics paid the cook a small gratuity to insure they received a share of the precious, medicinal liquid.

For all the squabbling, quibbling and intrigue over the milk, of which Johnny Russian has been informed by his mentor, Sol Horowitz, he remains indifferent. His job is to milk the goats, which he does with alacrity, and to carry the milk pails to the kitchen, which he does with a sense of pastoral pride. Has he done this chore in a past life, he wonders: the young goatherd walking carefully with fresh milk to the village square where peasants ruffle his hair, drop coins into his jerkin pocket?

His singular reward and gratification comes from the smiles on those shriveled, toothless mouths that indulge in the fruits of his labor, be it fresh goats' milk, a carrot or green bean from the garden, or a tart apple or succulent pear from the orchard.

Financial remuneration, be it in the form of a pay envelope or gratuity, is secreted in a coffee can under his cot in the basement. He has no need for money—or *spondulicks*, as Sol Horowitz fondly calls them—for all his *needs* are supplied by the rest home and his *wants* are nonexistent. Although his physical health has vastly improved with his tending to gardens and orchards—never mind with his proven husbandry of goats, chickens, and pigeons, he is haunted by ghosts from the past. Communication skills are elementary, his preferred method consisting principally of hand signals and basic words: *yes* or *no*. In the case of his pigeons, melodious whistling is the lingua franca. Regardless of twisted mental cogitations and a repellent physical appearance, his ability to bring happiness and joy, perhaps even love, to those around him is universally recognized and, to some degree, reciprocated.

His sole passion or preoccupation is his kit of tumbling pigeons; the lineage he has illustrated on a genealogical chart on the wall across from his cot. It is constantly reviewed and updated, with marginalia scrawled in Cyrillic letters. On this chart he has recently crossed out the name of the Birmingham Roller gifted to the youngster injured in the barn. Here also, he has substituted the name and age of a Galati Roller, enlisted in the tumbler kit, replacing the Birmingham Roller. The new recruit has caught his attention with its ability to do consecutive backward somersaults—a sight to behold even for a man with only one eye.

Johnny Russian has taken special care to mentor the new custodian in the proper feeding and handling of the tumbler pigeon, lest it wax fat and grow lazy. Using an eyedropper from a discarded medicine bottle, he has demonstrated how to inject the disagreeable contents of the eyedropper down the throat of a sickly chick. In addition, he had revealed the proper use of reward and censure with varying amounts of feed, or, in extreme cases, the isolation of a rebellious bird from the kit, perhaps even banishing the offender from the loft altogether. During these tutorials he has intuited a quality in the boy that assures him the mature Birmingham Roller is safe and will prosper.

And too, something has risen from the depths of his subconscious, like a bubble of oxygen belched from the ocean floor, wending its way slowly to the surface. Is it a memory or a dream? He cares not; it is palpable; it is cathartic. Long ago, a hand is on his shoulder. Words in his native tongue tease his ear. Spicy aromas of cheese, garlic and cumin pester his nose. He even hears the wailing of tribal forefathers, all of this briefly, fleetingly, from somewhere, someplace, deeply.

Pausing on his way to the barn, Johnny stops before a mirror in the rest home hallway. He inspects the patch covering his missing eye. He touches it tentatively with a finger. He wishes with all his willpower that his face was not so hideous. Abruptly turning from the mirror, he strides down the hall, but he stops abruptly. A hand goes to the solitary eye where an arrow of pain has lodged itself. The increasing ferocity forces him to his knee where he remains inert until the spasm dissipates. Like all things personal with Johnny these occasional attacks remain private. Recovering, he gets to his feet. Alone and unobserved, he continues down the hall and out the back door. There is the boy with the Birmingham Roller. Waiting.

15

First Dance

They stood with their backs to the gymnasium wall with the other boys. Across the oak flooring stood clusters of girls engaged in animated conversations or chewing gum or inspecting fingernails, manicured for the first time.

If Brian's mother had looked closely (possibly she did), she would have seen the raw beginnings of a part in his hair; gone now was that sheathing of crewcut bristles poking from his scalp. The emerging part had been massaged with a generous dollop of ointment from his father's tube of Brylcreem. He stood side-by-side with Bobby. A long-sleeved orange shirt with a three-button neck fell to the waist of his blue pegged slacks. Ankle-high cordovan shoes sparkled from repeated buffing with brush and rag. Fully one-half of the pubescent peacocks milling about wore the same style cordovan shoes; the other half sported blue suede footwear. All wore pegged pants. Mickey Delaney's hair was coiffed in the latest teen fashion that combined a crew cut on top with long sidewalls plastered down with Vitalis hair oil. Those not so accoutered and embellished were considered hopelessly *square*.

Resplendent in identical garb was his compatriot, Bobby, as were most of the boys shifting uneasily against the gym wall. This display of conformity was adulterated by a single young man not so garishly attired. G. G. Wallace's wrinkled white shirt was stained with sundry food and drink, a button missing at the navel, a shirttail escaped a cinched waist belt. As usual, a full head of brown hair obscured his eyes.

At both ends of the basketball court, blue and white strings of intertwining crepe paper formed arches from backboards to walls. Close to the bevy of girls in poodle skirts and bobby socks was a console HiFi record player. Two chaperones patrolled the gym insuring deportment was maintained. Attending the girls, Mrs. Merkel, a tall, thin woman with high cheekbones and pouty lips, scurried amongst her charges, adjusting hairdos, ribbons, scarves, collars and generally preparing her clutch of girls to fraternize, perhaps for the first time, with their male classmates.

On the boys' side of the gym, Mrs. O'Mera, presiding in all her shortness and roundness, looked over the milling pack of boys with a cynical eye, poised to unleash a broadside or, in extreme cases, corporeal punishment. The boys, in particular, knew of her fabled background. On the eve of WW II, she had married a Goliath of a paratrooper who was held prisoner by the Germans for three years before his repatriation. The offspring of this union was a squad of seven boys, all of whom challenged their father in size and weight. It was said that, in rare cases, Mrs. O'Mera would have to stand on a kitchen chair to slap the face of a rebellious son or wash out a mouth that spewed profanity. All of her *lads*, as she called them, played football for Saint John's High School, where, for five years in a row, they were champions of their conference. Four of the seven boys on the same defensive team were tagged by local sports writers as the Cliffs of Moher, or, more colloquially, the Cliffs of O'Mera, in honor of their Celtic background and impenetrability. Generally, the name of O'Mera would strike a note of both pride and fear in the heart of any schoolboy.

Clothed in a loose-fitting black dress, hair pulled back and braided in a bun of monstrous proportions, she could easily have been confused as the distaff model of the boogeyman. The boys noted with displeasure that she was forever pacing back and forth before them during this evening of youthful exuberance punching a fist into an open palm, her eyes mere slits of black, her lips clamped tight like the jaws of a bear trap.

"There she is," Brian whispered to Bobby.

Surreptitiously, they looked across the gym floor at Gina DeMelia, jet black hair brushing her shoulders, vermillion lips glowing, olive skin glossed like Carrera marble and attired in a short-sleeved pink angora sweater, a pink silk scarf cinched around her slender neck.

"I just hope I can get a dance with her. Jeez, I still remember kissing her at Colleen's birthday party," Brian told his friend, omitting the additional titillating details.

"What I remember was the food fight," Bobby said with a smile, then quickly looked around to make sure Mrs. O hadn't noted his levity, knowing the back of her hand would fly if she detected a hint of frivolity.

"I don't care about that, just look at Gina's chest. I bet if the nuns were here they'd send her home."

"Yeah well, what I see is good 'ole Eileen Hansen right next to her."

Before Brian could say another word, the sound of hands clapping captured everyone's attention. One and all fell silent and glanced at the gym entrance.

The dance instructor, Arturo Galucci, swished silently across the dance floor in knee high, black leather boots. His raven-colored wardrobe included a wide-brimmed slouch hat, a silk cape fastened at the neck with drawstring, and trousers that looked uncomfortably tight, especially in the rear. A black silk bag was clutched in his right hand. With a flourish, he removed hat and cape, setting them in a neat bundle on a folding chair. A white brocade shirt revealed a sculpted V-shaped patch of black chest hair, matching the hair decorating his chin and upper lip. Curly hair, heavily oiled, cinched in a ponytail, fell down his neck to his shirt collar. Sitting on an adjacent chair he removed his boots, replacing them with paper-thin patent leather dancing shoes pulled from the black bag.

After patting down the oiled locks with his right hand, he sauntered to the center of the gym floor, where he raised both hands, motioning to the opposing groups of young people to gather around. In fits and starts, a bit of pubescent shoving and capering, he was surrounded. Following an explanation of the waltz movements, he executed the dance step. To the youngsters looking on, some with trepidation, some with puzzlement, a few with glee, the dance looked like a sketch from the Milton Berle show. Scattered titters were instantly stifled by a penetrating look from Mrs. O. Galucci stamped his foot twice and raised his hands for silence. While the group whispered and murmured, Galucci flitted to the Hi-Fi set where he lowered the arm onto the spinning edge of a 78-rpm record. Instantly, the opening notes of a Viennese waltz echoed throughout the gym.

Galucci signaled to the hovering Mrs. Merkel to join him. Blushing slightly, she swooped down on the bantam dance instructor and pulled him roughly to her voluptuous body. With his right hand clasped at her waist, their hands joined and raised to shoulder level, he found his goatee penetrating the cleavage of her bosom. They whirled in time with the music while the kibitzing teens looked on in various degrees of awe, boredom, and bewilderment.

While the music played and the couple waltzed, Mrs. O kept a beady eye on young Delaney praying for some inconsequential infraction or breach of decorum that would give her cause to cuff his red oily head.

The couple ended their dance with a graceful flourish just as the music ended. While Mrs. Merkel retreated, flushed and quaking, to her charges, Galucci removed the needle from the record. Stroking his black goatee, he glanced about at the youngsters encircling him, then pointed to Bobby.

"Yes, you, young man, come hither."

Bobby looked around, not sure he was the object of Galucci's attention. But the beckoning index finger made it clear he had been chosen for some undisclosed form of punishment or reward. Stepping forth, hesitantly, would be the only way to solve the conundrum.

The boys surrounding him smiled, scoffed or heckled their friend and classmate, provoking hostile body language from Mrs. O'Mera.

Brian nudged G. G. Wallace in the arm. "This should be good."

Amidst this undercurrent of subtle abuse from the boys' side, Galucci stroked his goatee a second time while looking over the tittering, giggling girls. At last, his finely tapered index finger found its target. Eileen Hansen's palm went to her face in disbelief. She was speechless. This was the first time she'd ever been chosen ahead of her classmates for anything. While Gina DeMelia gently pushed her forward, the girls nearby snapped their gum or covered sneers with hankies clutched with polished fingernails.

"This is getting better all the time," Brian scoffed.

Regardless of the challenge confronting her, Eileen beamed a generous smile that had acquired, thanks to Gina, a brilliant white sheen. Now that she was out of Gina DeMelia's shadow, the gum-chewing, pegged-pants peacocks also noted her chest had grown overnight to eye-pleasing proportions. Lastly, they eyed her auburn hair sculpted into a corona that gave added emphasis to her green eyes, black eyebrows, and high cheekbones.

Bobby made last minute adjustments to his shirt collar as Eileen approached. Under Galucci's instruction, he embraced Eileen. Soon the waltz music filled the gymnasium, now hushed, while those gathered in silence watched with anticipation as Bobby and Eileen whirled about the floor in increasingly graceful circles.

"Jeez, I didn't think dancing was that easy, did you?" Brian commented, looking on.

"Well, it might be harder than it looks," Wallace said.

"Nah, if those two can do it, anyone can," Brian added.

When the music stopped, Bobby looked Eileen in the eye. "That was great; I never knew I could dance."

"Thank you very much," she said with a coquettish smile.

Abruptly twirling around, Galucci clapped his hands. Moving nimbly to the center of the floor, he motioned gracefully for the boys and girls to join him. While the undisciplined migration ensued, Mrs. Merkel eyed the dance master with unabashed lust.

Chaotically, the groups of boys and girls merged around Galucci. Despite much pushing and shoving amongst the boys and pulling and posturing amongst the girls, the dance floor was at last awash with anxious couples. While this convergence was in progress, Mrs. Merkel and Mrs. O hovered nearby, ready to swoop down and defuse any malfeasance.

Clapping his hands for attention, Galucci once again demonstrated the one-two-three waltz step with agonizing slowness. Gliding to the record player, he dropped the needle on a 78-rpm record, initiating the music.

With awkwardness, fussing, and faces carved in stone, teen couples began moving in every conceivable dance variation except the one so recently demonstrated by Galucci: Foxtrot, Jitterbug, Lindy Hop—even an Indian rain dance—were executed to Viennese waltz music.

His smile deteriorating, Galucci pulled the needle from the record in despair. Pacing back and forth in front of his charges, he stopped to punctuate the air with an index finger, exclaiming loudly. "It's a one-two-three, one-two-three, not a two-three-one, not a one-one-two, not a one-two-two. It's a one and a two and a three. Capisce?" The shrill of his voice crackled through the air like a bolt of thunder, followed by the silence of a tomb.

When no one answered or even appeared to understand his outburst, he resorted to another three-step demonstration with Mrs. Merkel giving the boys and girls more time to fidget, chew gum, adjust shirt collars, or run a comb speedily through unruly hair.

The needle was again placed on the record, summoning music originally composed for and performed before Viennese royalty in the mid 1700's. Instead of ladies and gentlemen of breeding arrayed in silk and satin, the deflated Galucci looked over a dance floor populated with pimply pubescent teens in a garish assortment of clothes he wouldn't use to scrub his kitchen floor and who, apparently, could not distinguish left from right. With a toe tapping in time with the music, he fidgeted with his ponytail. Muttering, his eyes strayed to the statuesque Mrs. Merkel.

Moments before, Brian had worked his way through knots of comrades to come face-to-face with Gina DeMelia, who stopped abruptly in front of him. As their hands touched, he caught a hint of lavender wafting up from the depths of her angora sweater. A fragrance, until now, associated only with his mother. Not far from Gina's red lips was a small black mole the size of a pinhead. The music startled them into an embrace that filled his nostrils with the heady aroma of her body, now pressing close to his.

"This is the first time I ever danced with…," he began, but before he could finish, her cheek was resting close to his and the rest of the words dissolved in his mouth.

They moved slowly and gracefully, perhaps not up to the critical eye of Galucci, but they actually waltzed. All of the mechanics of technique were out the window when Brian felt Gina's hot breath on his neck. Soon his head throbbed with the intoxicating smell of her supple body. Her black hair occasionally brushed his cheek, teasing his nose with an exotic smell that made him think of palm trees, blue lagoons and deserted white sand beaches.

Who knows, maybe if I walk her home after the dance I'll get to kiss her again, maybe more than once, he thought.

Looking up from Gina's black, aromatic hair, he saw Bobby dancing with Eileen Hansen. A face of stone concealed the fact that Bobby was smitten by his dance partner.

Although the youngsters were forced to change partners at random intervals, Brian and Gina were paired up for the final waltz.

"Say, let me walk you home, but first we'll go to the Dipsy Doodle for a coke, okay?"

"That's fine with me, but I'll have to ask Eileen. We came together, so I just can't leave her," Gina said.

"Sure, sure, I'll bet Bobby will be glad to join us, what do you think?"

"Yes, I'm sure that will work."

That said, Gina's head once again found the comfort of Brian's shoulder.

Shortly after the dance ended, Brian convinced his friend, Bobby, that a brief outing to the soda shop was in order to cap off their evening, never mind the opportunity for him to get better acquainted with Eileen. Now that Bobby had been maneuvered around the dance floor most of the evening under the tutelage of Eileen, enjoying every minute, he was more than willing to go along.

Exiting the gymnasium, both couples watched as Mrs. O stalked Mickey Delaney to the exit. Spotting no roughhousing or rowdiness, she retired to the cloakroom downcast and disappointed.

~

Entering the door of the Dipsy Doodle was like opening a fire hydrant. Rock and roll music gushed from the *Seeburg* jukebox shattering the quiet of the evening twilight outside. Every counter stool was occupied, the booths along the wall overflowed with high school kids, and what little floor space remained was filled with mixed couples dancing the jitterbug to Elvis Presley singing *Heartbreak Hotel*.

Working their way in and around the dancing couples, Bobby spotted his big brother in a booth. Greg waved them over. He and his girlfriend, Angie, occupied one side of a booth, while on the other side Charlie Maguire chatted with his girlfriend, Kate. Both Greg and Charlie wore their blue and white satin varsity jackets, unequivocal evidence they were athletes.

As the boys approached, Greg called out, "Here's my toenail-scratching basketball players. Hey Charlie, you think they'll make it to state finals, like we did?"

Charlie the All star, CYO champ and MVP, looked over Brian and Bobby like they were insects, then turned to Greg with a smile of approval. "Sure, any of the kids on the block are great hoopsters. Listen, me and Kate were just leaving, so come on, make yourself homely," he quipped while pushing out of the booth and standing, uncoiling to his full height of six foot three inches. Reaching back, he took Kate's hand and helped her to her feet.

Both Gina and Eileen looked up at Charlie with wide eyes and mouths agape.

Sliding across the seat after Gina, Brian found himself once again staring at Angie's breasts now encased in a tight blue short-sleeved sweater.

"Hi again, Brian," she crooned with a gum-smacking smile.

Brian quickly averted his eyes and looked at Greg, whose left arm was draped over Angie's shoulder.

Bobby and Eileen managed to squeeze in next to Gina and Brian.

Greg looked over at his younger brother. "How's the arms doing?"

"Okay, just every once in awhile they ache a little," Bobby said.

"So, why don't you Romeos introduce me to your girlfriends."

At Greg's suggestion, introductions were made all around.

"The big dance tonight, huh? Don't tell me, Galucci was the dance instructor and Mrs. Merkel and Mrs. O were the chaperones, right?"

"Yeah, how'd you know?"

"The three musketeers. They've been doing the Friday night dances since I was in grade school."

Greg looked across at Eileen. "My brother step on your feet or what?"

"Just once, but that was to be expected from someone new to dancing," Eileen said.

"How about you, little cutie? Reilly here stomp on your dogs?"

Before Gina could answer, a waitress in a short skirt, apron, and soda jerk cap stopped at the booth and took their orders for cokes.

"Say," Greg began, looking at Brian, "I've got inside information you built a pigeon coop for your tumbler, that right?"

"Yeah, but I couldn't put it on the rooftop like I wanted 'cause Mr. Urtz put up a bunch of big antennas up there, so we had to build it on the garage roof."

"Hey, Ang, this guy has a pigeon that can do back flips."

"Yeah, it's a Birmingham Roller, a special kind of pigeon. The guy over at the Jews Home gave it to me that time I fell and broke my legs. Someday, Bobby and me will raise a flock and train 'em all to tumble," Brian said with an air of authority.

Looking across the room, they saw G. G. Wallace seated at the counter, his large body crowding out two adjacent stools.

Momentarily, the jukebox switched gears, finally dropping the needle on Nat King Cole's recording of *Mona Lisa*.

Greg looked across the table. "Well, let's see if you Romeos learned anything tonight. Get on out there and strut your stuff. Come on."

With added encouragement from Angie, the two couples moved onto the floor and soon were absorbed by the crush of boys and girls. Free from the scrutiny of Galucci, Merkel and O'Mera, both couples moved with more confidence and grace and were even a bit disappointed when the record ended.

Before they could escape to the security of the booth, a record by Little Richard started playing. Nearing the booth, Brian felt Gina's hand tugging at his. Soon he found himself in the middle of the floor surrounded by other gyrating, stomping kids as they interpreted the uninhibited bleeps and blasts of the jukebox. When this selection ended, Brian noticed small drops of perspiration glistening on Gina's forehead. To his surprise he felt small ribbons of sweat coursing down his sides.

Reclaiming their seat in the booth, they looked up to see Greg and Angie smiling.

"Don't think Fred Astaire has anything to worry about, but you two looked darn good," said Greg.

Brian, beaming with confidence, was surprised to see that his moist hand remained entangled in Gina's.

The foursome, curious as to the whereabouts of Bobby and Eileen, discovered the couple jitterbugging in the middle of a group of kids clapping to the beat of jukebox music. When the music finally ended, they returned to the booth, where they sipped the remains of their cokes.

Catching his breath, Bobby looked across at his brother. "Well, what do you think about that?"

"Not too shabby, not too shabby at all, little brother."

To Bobby this was the highest praise he could expect from Greg, whose motivational speeches ran to the negative.

Looking up, they watched G. G. Wallace approach their booth.

"Hey, I didn't know you could jitterbug?"

"Neither did I, but Eileen sure knew how."

"Say, did you finish off another Awful-Awful?" Brian asked with a smile.

All heads turned to Wallace, who appeared to be contemplating his ragged sneakers.

"Nah, they won't serve me any more Awful-Awfuls. They say they lose money on me, so I have to order ice cream sundaes instead. Darn, I really like those Awful-Awfuls. Well, I gotta go. Hey Eileen, thanks for dancing with me at the gym."

"You're quite welcome."

"Yeah, well, see ya later, alligator." Bobby piped up.

Watching Wallace depart, Eileen asked. "Why is he so fond of those Awful-Awfuls? They don't sound that appetizing to me. I say, two Awfuls must be twice as *awful* as one."

"Well, see, if you finish one without any help from friends, you don't have to pay for it. And you get a second one free."

"Well, that's a horse of a different color, isn't it? But how can it be *awful* if it's a chocolate milkshake? They're really quite scrumptious, aren't they?"

"Sure, sure, but they have twelve scoops of ice cream in them, and that's an *awful* lot of ice cream."

"Oh, how clever."

Bobby chirped in, "Yeah, and Brian here says he can finish one off all by himself, ain't that right?" Bobby said, dropping the verbal gauntlet.

"That a fact? The champ here can finish an Awful-Awful?" Greg inquired with raised eyebrows.

Brian, now the center of attention, looked down at his hand still entwined in Gina's.

"Well, maybe I did say something like that, but…"

"No buts, either put up or shut up," Greg challenged.

Brian felt a slight pressure from Gina's hand.

"Yeah, I bet a dollar, I can do it," he spat out.

With that, Greg withdrew a dollar bill from his wallet and placed it on the table.

Not long afterwards, Brian's eyes bulged slightly when the fountain girl placed a foot high glass topped with a swirl of whipped cream and a cherry on the table in front of him. With a sadistic smile, she also set down a silver container, half full, next to the glass.

"You gotta finish ALL of it," she said pointing to the glass and the metal container beside it, "and no help from your friends either."

"There a time limit?" Brian asked with a slight tremble in his voice.

"Gotta finish up before we close at ten o'clock," she said heading back to the counter, then stopped to stare at him. "I'll be watching, so don't try anything sneaky."

While Doris Day sang *Que Sera, Sera,* all eyes in the booth turned to Brian as he pulled the oversize goblet of ice cream milkshake in front of him and jammed the straw into the mound of whipped cream on top of the shake.

When the clock above the jukebox showed 9:30 p.m., couples and small groups of teens began to leave. Pouring the remainder of the shake from the metal container into his glass, Brian looked up to see Greg push out of the booth and reach for Angie's hand.

"We gotta go Brian, but keep at it, you've got it licked. See you kids later," he said with a mischievous grin.

With Greg and Angie out of the booth, Bobby and Eileen moved across to the other seat to give Brian more elbow room.

"Hey, maybe I could just sneak a sip or two," Bobby whispered.

Brian merely shook his head.

As the records played on, more kids drifted out the door, leaving only a handful of youths scattered about the soda shop. With increasing effort and decreasing enthusiasm, Brian continued his single-handed battle with the Awful-Awful. Putting the straw aside, he began taking quick gulps of the creamy concoction. In between labored swallows, he kept one eye on the dregs of the shake and the other on the clock.

Belching loudly, causing Gina to move away from him, just in case, he swore silently to himself that he would never, ever, drink another chocolate milkshake the rest of his life.

A mere four minutes before the hour, Joanie, the soda jerk, walked slowly to their booth, hands on hips. Brian slammed the empty glass on the tabletop. His eyes were as large as saucers, his stomach tight as a drum and filled to capacity.

Joanie, the soda jerk, crossed her arms over her chest.

"Just in time. That one's for free and you get another Awful-Awful at no charge. Like that now?" she sneered.

Brian looked her square in the eye.

"I never want to see, smell or taste another Awful-Awful ever again. Period."

Standing, Brian snatched the dollar bill wager from the tabletop, crumpled it in his fist and shoved it in his pants pocket. With that, the two couples headed for the door.

On the sidewalk, Brian held his stomach and announced to all, "I gotta get home. I think I'm gunna be sick."

Without even a parting wave to Gina, he bolted down the sidewalk toward Partridge Street, leaving Bobby to escort the girls home.

~

Later that night, when Brian was crawling into bed and praying his stomach would settle down, Jacob Blotnick backed his maroon Chevrolet sedan to the backdoor of his farm house. He had grown to manhood in this same house, originally built by his father, a German, who had tilled the soil and harvested crops of potatoes, rutabagas, corn, and melons. Also on the farm there had been pigs, chickens, and a few horses used to pull wagons and plows before a tractor was purchased. His mother, a silent, frail woman, had managed the stock until Jacob was old enough to assume those responsibilities. Though his parents had provided him with food, clothing and shelter, they had never displayed any affection to him or to one another. Mostly, they were uncommunicative, cold, and niggardly with both money and emotion. On his twelfth birthday, his father, Gunther, had taken him out of school to work in the fields and barns. No explanation or reason had ever been given, nor had Jacob expected one. That had been his life for many years, until his father had fallen sick and taken to his bed. Always a tightfisted tyrant, he had insisted his wife nurse and tend to him as best she could, instead of enlisting the help of neighbors or a doctor.

Jacob, in his late teens, had worked alongside a succession of hired hands. One of the itinerant workers, from the Balkans, barely able to speak English, had formed a reciprocal relationship with Jacob that had included the younger man's initiation to sex. Once he had acquired this knowledge, Jacob could not control his appetites. When his father died, he took over the management of the farm. Encouraged by the growth of the neighboring metropolis and his disillusionment with farming, he began selling off acreage to developers for industrial use. Most of the property was sold to a corporation that planned to build a plant that would provide cement for the construction of state office skyscrapers in the encroaching capitol city. The money allowed him to relocate his aging mother to a comfortable rest home. After many years of hard labor and drudgery, she welcomed the arrangement and died there in her sleep. His birthright plundered, his parents deceased, the sole Blotnick survivor indulged his perversions to the extreme, until financial circumstances had forced him to find employment in the new printing plant on the river south of the farm.

Not more than one hundred yards away from the farmhouse was the cement plant that, even at night, had numerous tentacle-like conveyor belts grinding away. Night lights, the incessant crashing and crushing, the constant roar and smoke of industrial machines created a macabre scene cobbled from childhood nightmares.

Blotnick shifted the transmission into neutral and set the emergency brake, letting the engine idle while hurrying into the farmhouse.

The absence of a moon amplified the lights of the industrial plant outlining the tall, ten-story central tower with all its thrashing belts reaching out in all directions like a giant octopus gone mad. A dark, brooding penumbra cast its malevolent silhouette across the empty fields surrounding it. Empty for good reason: the grinding and squealing issuing from the plant, twenty-four hours a day, six days a week, had made the area uninhabitable, except for Mr. Jacob Blotnick. Worst of all, the cement plant produced a fine gray dust that settled on everything within a five-mile radius, depending on which way and how strong the wind was blowing. Layer upon layer accumulated on tree foliage, the roofs of abandoned farm buildings, the weeds sprouting along the deteriorating two-lane road running past Blotnick's remote, isolated domicile and ending at the cement plant a half-mile farther north. Exacerbating the dust problem were monstrous trucks lurching by hour-after-hour, day-after-day, sometimes far into the night if a section of highway needed completion or a state skyscraper, under a tight deadline, required a few thousand yards of cement.

Great clouds of dust were churned up by the gigantic wheels, until the countryside appeared to be painted a drab gray. Respite from the dust came upon the arrival of the blessed spring rains or drenching summer thunderstorms that visited the area on a seasonal, albeit random, basis. Greens, browns, reds of fields and streams, leaf and petal resumed their natural state, if only for a few hours or days before the onslaught of gray dust once again silently, inexorably, reclaimed the countryside.

Thoughts of gray cement dust and spring rains were far from Jacob's mind that evening as he banged about his house, opening doors, slamming drawers closed, overturning a chair, tripping on a bag of trash standing sentinel for days inside the back door.

Tools—a shovel, a pick, a stained gunny sack, a monkey wrench— were carried up from the basement, hurriedly, with no regard for the chips of paint gouged in the walls and cellar door. This was done in the dark, as if he feared the prying eyes and ears of neighbors, the closest ones being at least five miles distant. Breathing erratically, he stopped to wipe a patina of gray dust from his eyeglasses. Shortly, a wooden match brought a flame to his cigarette, then was dropped to the cluttered kitchen floor to be stepped on by a thick-soled work boot. He inhaled lungfuls of smoke, exhaled quickly, and then inhaled again and again until he calmed down enough to look at his watch and at the suitcase. He rubbed a gloved hand across his forehead, removing a thin film of perspiration. With a sigh of resignation, he threw the cigarette butt into the kitchen sink and listened to it sizzle until it extinguished itself.

His only concession for personal comfort and safety was his work-worn leather gloves, especially the right-hand glove that in no small way protected the tender, sometimes swollen, stump of his pinky finger. To insure comfort, he packed the half empty digit space with cotton to minimize chafing and abrasion. A beige button-down sweater kept the evening chill at bay.

He closed his eyes and held his breath for ten seconds. Exhaling forcefully, he picked up the suitcase with both hands and carried it to the open trunk of the automobile. With the trunk closed, he got behind the steering wheel of the Chevrolet. He pulled the shifter into gear and drove out the rutted driveway to the road, gravel crunching under the tires. The only lights visible were the multitude of bulbs, many blinking like nocturnal predatory eyes, outlining the cement plant conveyor belts and machinery. He looked back reproachfully one last time at the house before turning onto the paved road. Only when he came abreast of the cement plant did he turn on his automobile's headlights. The dashboard lights cast a glow on a haggard face with pinched lips, perspiring brow.

Once he attained the legal speed, he pulled the right glove off. Soon, a small flask of liquor appeared his hand. He gulped a small, but satisfying quantity of spirits. In the process, droplets meandered drown his whiskered chin to settle, finally, on his ink-stained work shirt. Another cigarette was lighted. The thin fingers, with trimmed nails, flew to the dials of the radio, producing big band music that appeared to calm him.

An hour later, the Chevrolet passed the Six Mile Waterworks boathouse and snack bar, in darkness at this hour except for a small nightlight positioned over a register with the cash drawer pulled out revealing empty currency and coin slots—lifeless, too, save for a larcenous field mouse gnawing rabidly on a Snickers candy bar.

Headlights were extinguished as tires bit into the sandy track leading into the rolling hills surrounding the dump. The grinding of the differential increased as tires fought for traction in deep ruts divided by a strip of grass and weeds. The transmission was now in first gear. The Chevy was moving, according to the red speedometer needle, at three miles an hour.

He stopped at a dead-end and switched the ignition off. Except for the crackle and ping of the cooling muffler and tailpipe, an ominous silence enveloped the Chevrolet and its occupant. The automobile headlights illuminated mounds of trash, some rising to heights above the roof of the car. One such pile to his right still emitted ribbons of smoke. The smell of mildew, rot, and smoldering rubbish invaded the open driver's window. Hastily, Jacob pulled on his right glove.

Pushing his door open, Jacob stepped quickly to the rear of the car and stopped suddenly. He turned back toward the open door, stopped again and once more turned about. Now he was before the trunk lid and jerked it up. He reached for a shovel, grasping it with his left hand. Indecisively, he threw it back into the trunk. Suddenly, his chest began to heave, he choked on stifled moans. Clumsily yanking off his glasses with the gloved right hand, he pulled one side of his unbuttoned sweater to his eyes to staunch an unexpected flow of tears.

"Jesus, Jesus… this was never meant to be, never. I repent it," he stammered out loud, while looking down at the suitcase, the gloved hand now clamped over his mouth, stifling further self-recrimination.

His breath coming in short explosions, he grabbed the suitcase with both hands, pulling it to his stomach as he straightened up, and, in the process, striking his head on the trunk lid. Cursing, he moved toward a mound of trash. Gaining a foothold, he flung the suitcase with all his strength up onto the trash heap. By its own weight it came tumbling back down the steep incline, coming to a rest at his boot tips. In shock, he watched viscous matter leak from the bottom. Suddenly noticing a wet spot on the front of his sweater, he flinched. The syrupy substance matched, in color and texture, the liquid seeping from the bottom of the suitcase. A hand jerked to his mouth. He staggered back, falling down, and, in the process, inflicting sharp pain on the pinky stub.

"Clumsy, stupid fool. Filthy. Disgusting. I didn't intend to do it, I swear I didn't. No, no, NO. Out of my control. Absolutely," he yelled into the black night, his horrific profile displayed on the pile of trash by the two headlights at his back.

Again, his gloved hand clamped on his mouth. On his feet now, he trudged to the car, looking over his shoulder at the suitcase as though it might sprout legs and pursue him. The right glove was hastily pulled off to reveal fresh blood on the truncated digit. His eyes bulged at the sight and memory of the traumatic accident at the printing plant that had severed it. He cradled the damaged finger in his left hand until he reached the car. Finding a rag in the trunk, he wrapped it quickly and tightly on the bleeding finger. Jacob slammed the trunk and got behind the wheel. The engine purred to life as he pulled the car into gear and began backing out and around the trash heaps. Taking one last look at the suitcase, he bit his quivering, lower lip.

Driving past the boathouse, he pulled the knob that activated the radio. Now on a paved road, he shifted through the gears, speeding his way to the city whose lights appeared on the horizon.

16

Auntie

Still in pajamas and hunched over a bowl of Wheaties, Brian was listening to the scores of last night's basketball games. After emptying his stomach of that evil concoction on the way home the night before, he had promised himself never to mention it by name again, never mind imbibe it… ever again! Following that solemn promise, he had staggered home, holding his stomach with both hands. A brief explanation to his mother of his dubious accomplishment and its consequences when arriving home Friday evening had elicited her advice to drink a glass filled with Milk of Magnesia and water. Sure, enough, the chalky-tasting elixir had settled his stomach, allowing him a fitful night's sleep.

Brian felt a hand tousle his hair. Stopping suddenly, her hand began a slower, more thorough exploration of his scalp.

"Honey, your hair is almost grown out," Rita began. "Yes, it is. I'll bet you'll be able to put a part in it any day now."

Lethargically, Brian brought a spoonful of Wheaties to his mouth and spent an inordinate amount of time chewing the sodden flakes.

Seconds later, Rita placed two pieces of bread in the toaster.

"I want you to eat some toast, too; that always helps to keep my stomach settled."

"Ma, please."

"Well, I'm not the one who finished an *Awful-Awful*."

"Please don't mention *that* thing again, ever."

"Well, alright. Just trying to help."

"Is Dad at work?"

"Yes, he and McEvoy got a lead on that missing boy, the one who was fishing down on the river in North Albany."

"They never did find the kid, did they?"

"No. And, when you're finished with breakfast, please get dressed and go downstairs and wait on the stoop for Auntie. A taxi will drop her off. I want you to carry up her bag of goodies. She always brings so many things."

"When are you going away?"

"Soon."

"Why do you have to go all the way to a hospital in Buffalo?"

"Well, it's not that far. Dr. McCann said that's where the *specialists* are. Cape Cod was much farther. Remember the time we drove to Cape Cod?"

"Oh, sure. How long do you think you'll be gone?"

"A week, I guess. Now finish up and go down and wait for Auntie's cab."

"Ma, was Auntie ever married?"

"No, but she had a boyfriend once. Now he's a very powerful man in the Democratic Party. Back then, he worked on the Erie Canal; don't know what he did, exactly."

"She ever have any kids?"

"No. Why do you ask?"

"She's always hugging and kissing me."

Rita laughed.

"Well, she used to do the same to me when I was a little girl. Remember, we're the only family she's got. Now finish breakfast and get dressed."

Slathering his second piece of toast with butter and strawberry jam, he folded it in two before pushing away from the table and hurrying to his bedroom.

~

Dressed in dungarees, T-shirt, zipper jacket and sneakers, Brian climbed up onto the porch railing, where he tightrope-walked between two pillars supporting the second story porch. Jumping down from the banister, he seated himself on the top step. Looking down the street, he saw the red and black Freihoffer bread wagon stopped near the corner of Hudson, the aging chestnut horse with its blinders chewing contentedly from a bag of oats strapped to its head. Across the street, he watched one of the Gardner sisters sweep off her front porch. Setting the broom aside, she removed a bottle of milk from the small storage box, opened her front door and disappeared inside. Out of the corner of his eye, Brian caught sight of a window curtain settling in place.

Suddenly, he jumped to his feet and leaped down to the sidewalk. He watched a yellow taxi make its way down Partridge Street toward him. When it came to a stop at the curb, he pulled down on the handle, opening the rear door. Taking a large brown shopping bag crammed with an assortment of food, drink, medicines, and assorted items of clothing, he stepped back, both hands wrapped around the bag, waiting for Auntie to extricate herself from the rear seat.

"Hi, Auntie," he said as the octogenarian stepped out of the taxi with much effort, punctuated with several *Jasus, Mary, and Josephs* in various tones of voice and emotion ranging from exasperation to supplication. With Auntie at last on her feet, the taxi made its departure.

With arms securing her shopping bag, Brian had no option but to let his great aunt pull his freckled face to her wet lips and endure one of her slobbering kisses. To make matters worse, he couldn't run the back of his hand across his cheek to mitigate the lingering saliva.

"Now, ain't you the handsome lad with a fine mop'a hair, on the spot to help your old auntie," Margaret Duffy began, adjusting the black veiled hat on her gray head and smoothing the black coat, worn in all seasons, to match the hem of the black dress suspended mere inches above her lace-up black shoes.

At last presentable, she hooked the handle of her voluminous purse on her right forearm. The raven-colored attire accompanied her to weddings and funerals and every function in between. She cut a serious look at Brian.

"How's your Ma, the poor dear child," she said, a hanky rising to an eye.

"Mom's fine; come on, let's go upstairs." He was about to say, "Let's go upstairs before I drop this bag," but he'd thought better of it.

Taking one step at a time, with a hand on the railing, Auntie managed to finally achieve the front porch.

"Jasus, Mary, and Joseph! I'm just not as strong as I used to be, nor any younger. Now, hurry upstairs with the bag. I'll be right behind you."

Negotiating the steps as fast as he could, Brian knew she would be waiting for him at the bottom of the stairs after he put the shopping bag on the kitchen table and raced back to the stairwell. In no time at all, he completed the task and was at her side at the bottom of the staircase, supporting her left arm while she clasped the banister with her right hand.

Finally in the kitchen, she cinched the bulky pocketbook on the back of a chair, while Rita helped her out of the heavy coat. Brian placed it on a hook near the back door. To ward off the chill, two sweaters conserved what little heat Auntie's aged body produced. While the disrobing was in progress, Brian began a thorough investigation of the goodie bag. Setting aside a box of Fig Newtons, a canister of Nestle cocoa, two Hershey bars, and a quarter pound of bologna, he withdrew Auntie's flower-print apron and handed it to her. Even before removing her hat and veil, she slipped into the apron.

"Get the box of Lipton teabags; your mother and I are going to sit down and have our cup of tay, ain't we, my lovely?' she said, drawing Rita to her and delivering one of her sodden kisses.

"Let me get the tea, Auntie; you just sit and catch your breath," Rita suggested.

"Nay, nay, you sit and tell me all about yourself whilst I put the kettle on."

Brian continued extricating items from the brown paper bag and piling them on the kitchen table. While doing so, he managed to open the Fig Newtons and sample a handful in the process. He chewed on them while pulling a box of Lorna Doone cookies and two small applesauce cakes, wrapped in cellophane, from the bag and placing them on his growing pile of swag. Next came a quarter pound of Swiss cheese to complement the bologna.

The kettle warming over the gas burner, Margaret Duffy took a seat at the table. Opening her pocketbook, she searched its depths, removing sundry items: tissues, rosary, missal, the front section of the morning paper, a small leather change purse containing her carfare in case she decided to ride the trolley home instead of getting a ride with Chick or relying once again on a taxi. At last, she withdrew a case in which she stored her glasses. Before she closed the gaping jaws of the pocketbook, her eyes, with the help of the Five &Ten glasses, saw a gleam in its depths. With beaming face, she pulled a gold engraved watch with chain and athletic medal fit to adorn the vest pockets of any gentleman, high or low.

Rita smiled, knowing that beside the watch, was a pint bottle of Jameson Irish Whiskey, its seal most likely broken and the contents depleted by a few ounces. This was not the first time Margaret Duffy had displayed the watch and sworn that the elegant piece of jewelry would go to Rita upon her demise.

"T'was me father's, it was. Won in a foot race, the All Limerick Ten-Miler. The lads carried him off to the pub on their shoulders soon as his chest touched the ribbon. His name is engraved right there on the back," she said, pointing with pride at the engraved script, *Billy Duffy, First Place, County Limerick.* "And you'll have it when they cart me off to potters' field," she said.

While her soliloquy was in progress, Brian had filled his pockets with plunder before escaping to his pigeon coop on the garage roof, leaving the two women to their tete-a-tete. Hearing the back door close, Auntie spiked her tea with a dollop of Jameson—likewise, Rita's.

Born in County Limerick, Ireland, hard by the Shannon River, Margaret was first-born in a mixed lot of twelve boys and girls. Her father, William, a cobbler by trade, as well as an accomplished fiddler and sportsman, would race anyone for a pint of Guinness. Sadly, Billy Duffy had been carried home dead on a door one cold, rainy Limerick night after a grueling cross-country race that had won him his pint, as well as his grave. The already hard-pressed Duffy family had imploded. Shortly thereafter, Margaret and her younger sister Bridey had been taken in by the Sisters of Mercy, who had dispatched them to a convent in New York City, hard by the Hudson River. At the Limerick train station, Margaret's mother, at wits' end with travail, had pressed the gold watch into Maggie's hands and made her promise never to part with the one remaining artifact of her late father, not trusting herself to do the same. It hadn't taken young Margaret Duffy long to realize her role as an unpaid convent servant, a situation made even more unbearable by prolonged hours of prayer, never mind the occasional session of corporeal punishment.

Late one night, Margaret had taken Bridey by the hand and fled the convent, the gold watch concealed in a handkerchief stuffed in her coat pocket along with two sausages and the heel of a loaf of bread. A freight train had carried them north to Albany, where, with the help of a cousin, they had been assimilated into the burgeoning Irish-American community. Not long afterward, Margaret had met a young firebrand named Dan O'Conner, who had the gift-of-gab, an iron will, and a prolific talent for ward politics. Margaret had hooked her wagon to a rising star, or so she had thought. After years of dating and a formal, though brief, engagement with Margaret, Dan O'Conner's star had roared toward the heights of local machine politics. Shortly after he had assumed leadership of the Democratic machine, to Margaret's dismay, O'Conner's engagement to a young lady of breeding was announced in the newspapers. Distraught, Margaret became the spinster she would remain to the grave. Although the milk of human kindness rarely touched her lips, it flowed in abundance from her to a chosen few; principally to Rita, her only niece, and to her great nephew, Brian.

Thus began her Sunday visits to the Reilly home.

Following her usual protocol, Auntie would never refer directly to Rita's amputated arm or her forthcoming trip to the Buffalo hospital for a third operation. With the patience of Job, she would wait for Rita to come around to it by fits and starts. When the tears began, Auntie would ransack her pocketbook for the pint of Jameson.

Swallowing the liquor with difficulty, Rita followed the tot with a generous gulp of tea. Preoccupied, Auntie's hands strayed to the front section of the morning newspaper she'd saved to share with Rita. Unfolding it, she found herself looking at a black and white photo of two uniformed policemen pointing to an *X* drawn into a woodland scene beside a broad river. The news story explained that fourth grader Sam Pistone, still missing, had last been seen fishing at the spot marked with the *X*. Another picture showed Sammy's mother wringing her hands, the husband clasping her shoulders.

"Another reason not to let youngsters hitch rides with total strangers," Auntie advised, stabbing an index finger at the newspaper article.

~

McEvoy parked the squad car in a loading zone at the side of the hospital, a three-story red brick building operated by the County. It had been the first public county hospital established after the Depression: a great coup for the Democratic Party that had brokered the contracts that had enabled the brick structure to rise from what had once been a block of the city's oldest, least desirable tenements. That the hospital, one of many recent municipal construction projects, had been built in a Democratic ward was no coincidence, but then all the wards in the city were Democratic strongholds. It was only on the outskirts of the city proper that those *other* people, the ones who wielded considerable financial but only limited political power, lived. Somewhere behind the contracts, the political maneuvering, you were sure to find Dan O'Conner and the Irish-Democratic machine.

The two detectives walked through the side entrance of the hospital, turning immediately to their right and down a flight of stairs to a dim hallway that led them to the basement records department where patients' files were archived. At a long wooden counter just inside the doorway, McEvoy's palm smacked a silver bell, shattering the silence. Enjoying the sound and smiling with satisfaction, he whacked it again. His nose twitching, he sniffed the air redolent of stale tobacco smoke.

From long stacks of shelves on the other side of the counter came a voice.

"Okay, okay, I hear you already."

A middle-aged man, thin, a knee-length white smock covering his blue slacks, emerged from floor-to-ceiling shelving, his left arm clutching several folders, an empty coffee cup dangling from his right hand. A nametag was pinned to a breast pocket -Ed.

Chick looked up at a sign at the end of the counter, hand-lettered in red ink, that read *No Smoking*. The lights hanging down from the ceiling painted the clerk's bald head with a glossy spot that bounced about his pate like a tennis ball as he moved under the bare light bulbs. Placing the files on the counter, he raised the cup to his mouth. Frowning, he set it down empty beside the files, then looked at the two men while calculating how much work they were likely to inflict on him.

"Yeah," he said, two nicotine-stained fingers tapping the counter.

Both detectives, always cautious of ruffling the feathers of county workers who might be of assistance, either presently or in the future, produced gold shields and 24-carat smiles.

As usual, the display of badges produced an change in attitude. The man's bushy salt-and-pepper eyebrows snapped to attention; a begrudging smile cracked a face as gray and lifeless as a cement sidewalk.

I'm Detective Reilly; this is Detective McEvoy. I called yesterday about records of industrial accidents, Hudson Valley Press. This ring any bells?" he asked, sneaking a look at McEvoy.

"Sure, Officers. I dropped everything I was doing," the clerk said, waving a hand back at the stacks. "Ain't no small thing keeping these files up to date, yeah, and it's just me down here all day, every day."

"Whatta you got for us, pal?" McEvoy interjected.

"Hey, I'm not just whistling Dixie here, officers. Like I was saying, I dropped everything to dig through files. Jesus, there's a lot of industrial accidents, ya know. I mean, a guy sometimes wonders, like, are they really industrial accidents? A lug comes in with a broken nose, two front teeth missing, half-a-load on. Huh? I mean…what?"

Again, McEvoy's palm smashed the plunger activating the shrill bell.

Instantly, a box of files was placed on the counter in front of the detectives.

"Okay, here's your missing right pinky finger accidents. Knowing sometimes things get discombobulated on the phone, I threw in my missing left pinky fingers, too. No extra charge!" Ed slapped the counter, grinning from ear to ear.

McEvoy pulled the file box closer.

"Hey, fellas, that was a joke! Okay, so I'm not Uncle Milty, but, fer chrissake, a little humor, eh?"

Chick pushed back his fedora before counting the files in the box.

"I'll take the missing righties, you take the lefties, okay?"

"Sure," McEvoy agreed.

"Oh, and, fellas, you can't take the files out of the building, hospital policy, there's a nice little desk over there in the corner."

The files split between them, both men pulled notebooks from their coat pockets and got to work.

McEvoy looked up when the screech and rattle of a gurney passed the doorway. Shortly, a door across the hall opened, allowing a fetid odor to escape into the hallway, threatening to invade the records room.

Behind the counter, the clerk's gratuitous smile crumbled; his right hand automatically reached to a breast pocket for a cigarette.

166

Thumbing through the larger pile of folders, McEvoy commented that it seemed odd there were more lefties than righties.

"Think about it: righties outnumber lefties say, 10 to 1, right? So, is there something special about pressmen that most of them are left-handed?"

Not getting an answer, he continued.

"Maybe the guy that does the hiring is a southpaw, so he has a preference for lefties. Yeah, maybe that's the way it works?"

Still not eliciting a response, he rambled on, "Or, better yet, the guy that owns the place is a leftie, so he hires a Personnel guy who just happens to be a leftie, and so on down the line, like dominoes, bam, bam, bam."

"How you coming with those files?"

Grimacing, McEvoy opened a file and began copying the vitals.

A half hour later, McEvoy looked up. "Hey, listen to this: *Gerald Goldbricker*. I shit you not, Gerald Goldbricker, pressman, plate burner, etc., etc., yeah, here we go, good 'ole Gerald lives on Easy Street. Get it? A Goldbricker on Easy Street. Jesus. I mean, you can't make this stuff up."

Chick looked over the pages of his notebook. "Got three possibilities here. Narrowed it to five, but one is negro, the other is John Schermerhorn. Remember him? I was in the Navy with John, USS Savannah. He's a big deal in the VFW. Surprised I didn't think of him the first time Brian mentioned the guy with the missing pinky. Lost his loading a round during the Italy offensive. So, three possibilities. What kind of numbers you have with the lefties?"

"Six, including Gerald Goldbricker. I gotta see if this guy's for real. Hey, Chick, you know where Easy Street is?"

"I think it's across the river in Watervliet, one of those new subdivisions they built after the war. But we check out these three righties first. I don't think the boys were wrong about that."

When all the files were back in the box, McEvoy picked it up, walked a couple of steps and slid it onto the counter. With a gleam in his eye, he rang the little counter bell.

"Yeah, yeah, I hear ya, I hear ya," the clerk said, turning the corner of a stack and facing McEvoy. "Ya know, you oughta' get one of them. You're getting real good smackin' it."

McEvoy smiled as he reached for his cigarettes.

Ed moved to the counter, where he pushed the red-lettered *No Smoking* sign in the detective's direction.

"Sorry, officer, no smoking. Hospital policy."

"Policy, my arse! For chrissake, the place smells like a pool room."

"All the same, sorry."

"Come on, Mac, let's get going." Chick said.

McEvoy swiveled around, then stopped when the clerk called to him.

"Just across the way, that's the morgue, officer."

"Yeah, so what?"

"Well, they say people are dying to get in. Get it? *Dying to get in.*" The clerk slapped the counter, guffawing loudly, before lapsing into a cough that brought tears to his eyes.

McEvoy pulled his hat down as he hurried into the hallway, trying to catch up with Chick.

The clerk rested an elbow on the counter, catching his breath and shaking his head. "Cops! About as much personality as a cardboard box," he grumbled.

Lighting a cigarette, he grabbed the *No Smoking* sign and placed it on a shelf under the counter.

Moving alongside Chick on the stairwell, McEvoy pulled a cigarette from a pack in his suitcoat pocket.

"I ever catch that weasel on the street, I'm gunna hide my badge and kick his ass up around his ears."

"A piece 'a work, all right, but he's county," Chick said, chuckling.

"Waddaya say we get something to eat. I ain't had anything since last night. Corn beef on rye smothered in fried onions. Quart 'a beer."

"Poker game, or what?"

"Poker. Took a bath. That little weasel downstairs reminds me of someone, ya know?"

Walking toward the swinging back doors, they passed a time clock where men and women all in whites stood in line either punching in or out. A klunk-a-klunk erupted from the clock when a time card was inserted into the slot. Once punched with the date and time, the cards were returned to one of several racks fixed to the wall beside the clock.

Passing the time clock on his right, Chick noticed a small 3x5 index card thumbtacked to a bulletin board. Edward Montecristo in Records was looking for an efficiency apartment within walking distance. He stopped, directed a thumb at the index card.

"Your boy in the basement? Montecristo. Gotta ring to it, eh?"

McEvoy looked closely at it.

"Yeah, well, he got one thing right. Uncle Milty he ain't."

Leaving the antiseptic smell of the hospital hallways, the detectives emerged into sunlight. The air outside was filled with the smells of lunch being cooked in the hospital kitchen: coffee smells, soup smells, baking bread. Two men—one a skinny Filipino in whites, his T-shirt snugged tight on a lean frame, a stained apron tied at the waist, one foot up on a milk crate, smoking a small black cigar. The other, a tall man standing, the front of his T shirt soaking wet, smoking a cigarette. They watched the detectives get into the Buick with the chrome siren.

"Hermie's is just up the street next to the brewery, get some good chow there," McEvoy said.

"Yeah, let me call in these leads, see if they have any priors."

Pulling away from the loading dock, Chick steered the prowl car around an ambulance, the back door open. They could see two bare feet extending slightly over the end of a gurney. A yellow tag was tied to the big toe of the right foot.

Even with McEvoy filling the prowl car with his cigarette smoke, Chick could smell the heavy, hoppy odor of the Schafer brewery as they drove by. At close range, it smelled stronger than natural gas. He pulled up at the curb in front of the diner. A sign on a pole at one end of the Pullman car structure announced, with a flashing neon arrow pointing down at the entrance, *Breakfast, Lunch.* Chick thought back to the morning he and Brian had stopped there for breakfast with Benny before their fishing trip.

Pushing through the entrance door, they were greeted by the clatter of plates, the clink of glassware, the sizzle of meat frying, voices both subdued and boisterous, the sounds of laughter, and a gravelly male voice calling for a slice of lemon pie "and be quick about it!"

Chick nodded at Madge, behind the counter, over the backs of men seated on the swivel stools that obscured all but her head as she scribbled orders on her pad. She winked, even while her fingers scribed orders in arcane waitress shorthand decipherable only by her husband and cook, Hermie. His chunky body, back to the order window, was a whirl of white shirt, white apron, and white floppy hat above a smoky grille. His gyrating arms manipulated pots and pans, skillets and kettles. Though another white-liveried cook labored beside him, they never seemed to catch up with incoming orders.

In a booth, the detectives retrieved and scanned typewritten menus encased in clear plastic. Just as quickly, they pushed them aside, knowing the contents from years of patronage. Their hats were impaled on hooks on a pole attached to the side of the booth.

"Hell," McEvoy cursed, "I know what I want. I want that blonde waitress all dolled up in the pink uniform, little pink cap on her head. Hey, that's Genie, ain't it?"

"Yeah, but better think about something more substantial. We might be out late working these leads," Chick said, tapping the notebook on the table before him.

"Hey, look at the name on the menu, *Imperial Diner*. Hotsy-Totsy! Never noticed that." Looking up, McEvoy smiled. "Here she comes, my favorite waitress. How ya doing, Genie?" he said, reaching out to pat her on the buttocks.

"Anyone I can—the dumb ones twice," she said, her red lips pouty, her tongue moving gum to and fro.

"You're a panic, Genie, a real pistol."

"So they tell me. Whatta you have, hon?" she asked as she plucked a receipt book from her apron pocket with one hand and a -pencil from her hair with the other. She wetted the pencil tip on her tongue and held it poised over the order pad.

Getting no response from McEvoy, she looked at Chick. Now indecisive, McEvoy flipped open the menu.

"Let me have the club sandwich on some of that German rye. Iced Tea," Chick said.

"Potato salad or slaw?"

"Slaw. You behaving, Genie?"

She winked and looked down at McEvoy.

"You memorizing that thing, or what?"

"Okay, gimme ham and eggs and toast. Eggs over, not too hard, not too soft, just kind of runny, if you know what I mean," he said, taking in a generous view of her cleavage. "Plenty of java, too," he added with a wink, his hand again reaching for the buttocks.

"Ain't you the smart aleck," she said with a smile, turning and heading to the grille window, shouting the order as she went.

Shooting a look back at McEvoy, she ripped the order from the pad and affixed it to a revolving metal wheel hanging in the window. Before the wheel stopped spinning a hand snatched the order into the kitchen.

Chick pulled an ashtray toward him from an assortment of condiments at the side of the table.

McEvoy reached across with his Zippo to light Chick's cigarette, then lit one for himself.

Chick was looking down at his open notebook. The waitress whirled by, placed a large glass of iced tea in front of Chick and topped off McEvoy's coffee. Looking at her departing rear end, he muttered, to no one in particular, "Keep it coming, sister, keep it coming."

"Hey, listen, looks like the closest suspect lives in North Albany, just up the street, 128 Pearl, Marty LaFavre. Clean sheet."

Genie appeared at their table, multiple plates balanced on her arm. Distributing some of the food to the detectives, she warned McEvoy, "Keep them hands to yourself."

"I wouldn't think of taking advantage of a damsel in a dress."

"Chicky, get the shovel; it's gettin' deep."

With that, she scooted to the next booth. Looking over his shoulder, McEvoy called to her.

"Hey, what's with the coffee?"

"Just one minute, Buster."

Turning around, he plunged his fork into the eggs, filled his mouth, then brought the knife to the ham, dissecting it into four pieces. Suddenly, he looked up at Chick.

"Hey, now I remember who that weasel at the hospital reminds me of." McEvoy folded a piece of toast, brought it to his mouth, then stopped.

"Who's that?" Chick asked.

"Supply sergeant in our outfit, what a louse. Listen to this. My battalion takes eighty percent casualties at the Normandy. So after all the crap is over and we're back in England, this supply sergeant, the weasel, gigs me for losing an entrenching tool. For chrissake, an entrenching tool! Tells me it will come out of my pay. Huh? Nickel 'n dime prick. So my first sergeant, he gets with the supply sergeant and tells him he hears any more crapola like that, he'll arrange to get him transferred back to Germany, the nastiest part of Germany he can find." Pausing for breath and a gulp of coffee, the detective resumed his tirade, "Never a word from the louse from that day on. We're back in the States, we muster out. Me, I get a big check from Uncle Sam. I'm on Easy Street. Hey, Easy Street again?. Get this, that supply sergeant lost all his back pay in one of those nonstop crap games on the ship coming home. Asked me to loan him a double sawbuck. Can you believe that? The crumb."

Both men looked up to see Genie, coffee pot in hand, filling McEvoy's cup.

"Say, hon, what time you get off? Maybe we can get together later on?"

"Sorry, Charley, my dance card is full."

"Come on, if you're nice, I'll let you play with my gun."

"Gun? That's a little 'ole water pistol," Genie retorted, moving quickly on to the next booth, but not before jamming the bill into McEvoy's breast pocket.

"It's a cruel world, Chick. A cruel world," he said, hand over heart.

<u>17</u>

BB Guns

He was waiting for his cousins Ray and Mike. They would be turning the corner from Hudson onto Partridge any minute. Waiting. Running his hands into the pockets of his jacket he could feel the cache of Fig Newtons in one pocket and a Three Musketeers candy bar in the other—all booty claimed from Auntie's treasure chest of goodies.

The bottles of milk left in the insulated box early that morning had been taken upstairs, upon Auntie's request, before breakfast.

Today was the knife sharpener's day to make his rounds of the neighborhood, so "keep a weather eye out for him," Auntie had advised. That said, she set aside four kitchen knives and a pair of scissors whose blades, she conceded, were not really in need of sharpening, but Mr. Healy wouldn't be around again for another month. "So, keep an eye out for Healy. Mind now, keep on the watch. That's my boyo."

Dinny Healy, now in his mid-sixties, made the rounds of the city wards, knife-sharpener and self-appointed Democratic Party insider, constantly on the lookout for municipal imperfections: a pothole, a street light on the blink, a City Parks employee (no doubt recipient of a sinecure) snoozing on a park bench—this in full view of the electorate! A heinous infraction, grounds for immediate dismissal, per Mr. Healy. He would mentally collect and file these observations and report them, first hand, to Dan O'Conner himself, longtime Democratic machine boss, who would flash an avuncular smile, pat Dinny on the back and exclaim:

"You're my right-hand man, Dinny me boy, my man in the field, so to speak."

Or,

"Why, I couldn't keep abreast of the comings and goings without ya."

Or,

"Be Jasus, me eyes and ears, is what ya are."

Turning to one of his lieutenants, he would bark and wink, "Fitz, make a note of that—horse excrement uncollected at the corner of Jay and Myrtle, per me pal, Dinny."

More often than not, O'Conner would slip a quarter into Healy's eager palm. During holiday season, he was sure to appear before Dan O'Conner, hat in hand, full of boastful assurances of party line voting, to receive his *Christmas envelope*. The stipend, by fits and starts, would find its way into the coffers of various taverns and gin mills, wending its circuitous way, back into the party treasury from whence it came.

Brian saw him approach from a block away. Bowler hat swinging from side-to-side, whistling and singing out to the housewives to bring their knives down to Dinny Healy. Why, he'll put a sharp edge on'em. As sharp as me wife's tongue, he crooned and whistled.

A leather strap crossing his shoulder supported the weight of the small sharpening wheel that was quickly un-slung when he heard a "yoohoo" from an open window or front door.

In addition to his knife sharpening and intelligence gathering, Dinny considered himself a musician and a poet of the oral tradition, with a particular talent, when plied with the odd pint, for the recitation of limericks. The five-line poems provided youthful memories of his place of birth, a distinction he shared with Margaret Duffy. Often, he would slip a fiddle beneath his chin to accompany twin brother Eamon on the flute or penny whistle.

Healy would sit on the lower step of a front porch, push his derby back on his head and pump the sharpening stone up to speed with his right foot. While resurrecting a keen edge on a blade, he would recite a poem to a kibitzing housewife or a limerick for one or two of the neighborhood lads, thus insuring a few extra pennies for his entertainment kitty.

Auntie had furnished Brian with a nickel for Mr. Healy to grind a nice edge on the knives and scissors. An extra nickel was added for his recitation of a poem by Gerard Manley Hopkins titled, *Spring and Fall: To a Young Child*. With Auntie stationed at the railing of the second-story porch, Dinny would stand at attention, remove his derby, and looking up at Auntie, recite the poem in a lyrical, syncopated baritone.

"Margaret, are you grieving
Over Goldengrove unleaving?
Leaves, like things of man, you
With your fresh thoughts care for, can you…"

In closing, he would cover his heart with the derby and bow his head. Dabbing at her eyes, Auntie would return to the kitchen to savor another cup of tea.

Handing the sharpened knives to Brian, Healy advised, "Careful now, boyo, them blades will cut the hairs off a gnat's ass. Now look at that, will ya, that streetlight's been out for a month. Shot out with one of them air rifles, I wager. I'll raise a bit of hell about that downtown, I will. Now take them knives up to your Auntie and you tell her Dinny Healy will light a candle for her this Sunday."

Smiling affably, he pocketed his nickels.

While Brian climbed the porch steps carefully, the knives wrapped in a towel, Dinny shouldered his grinding wheel and continued on his route.

After returning the knives and scissors to Auntie, Brian resumed his watch for cousins Ray and Mike. Momentarily, the door of the McNally household across the street opened, deploying Bobby like a cannon ball directly across the street to Brian's porch.

"Want to come to the dump with us? Ray is going to bring his BB gun. We'll target practice on bottles and cans," Brian said.

"Sure. Ma was asking if your Mother went off to the hospital yet?"

"Not yet, I think they're waiting for the Doctor in Buffalo to call."

"How long will she be gone?"

"I don't know; my Dad says it *depends*."

"Depends on what?"

"Don't know that either. That's his favorite word."

"You going?"

"Nah, got to go to school. My father's going to borrow Benny's Chrysler for the trip, the one we went fishing in. I guess Buffalo is at least two or three hours away."

"Remember, next weekend we're playing Saint Joe's. We lose, we're out of the playoffs."

"It's them wops in the south end I'm worried about. Saint Vinny's, they've got that real tall kid playing center, Sal Gambrelli. He stayed back two times in eighth grade. Should really be a sophomore playing for the high school team."

"He's taller than Carmody, our center."

Looking up, Brian saw his cousin Ray approaching with his younger brother Mike. Ray had the barrel of the Red Ryder BB gun resting on his shoulder, his right hand supporting the stock. Brian's eyes took in the strip of rawhide dangling from the wooden stock and the lever action that pumped the BBs into the breech. Mike was entrusted with the cardboard cylinder of BBs, kept secure in a dungaree pocket.

After a brief discussion of the numerous merits of the BB gun, as well as a personal inspection by all, they began their walk to Partridge and Western to wait for the bus that would take them to the last stop on the bus line, Six Mile Waterworks. From there they would hike into the sand hills to the dump.

Along the way Ray announced there would be no hitchhiking under strict orders from his mother due to the notoriety of the missing Pistone boy. This edict was reinforced, according to Brian, by a similar warning issued by his father. To disregard those orders would be to invite all manner of disciplinary action. So they waited patiently at the corner of Partridge and Western for the bus.

At the dump they gathered around Ray, watching jealously as he filled the cylinder of the air rifle with BBs. When the chamber was full, he pulled back on the lever action to pressurize the firing mechanism. While he was accomplishing this task, Mike and Bobby scavenged an assortment of bottles and cans that were set up on the side of an abandoned icebox. Returning, they watched as Ray dropped to his right knee. With his left elbow propped on his left knee, he cradled the stock of the rifle in his left hand. Sighting down the peep sight on the barrel, he slowly pulled the trigger. The minuscule projectile struck and shattered a quart beer bottle. After a few more shots, he turned the rifle over to Brian.

Seated on the ground, he listened to Ray advise on the proper technique of aiming and firing the BB gun. But, still a bit gun-shy, he jerked the trigger, sending a BB on a flight into the mounds of refuse sheltering the improvised rifle range. As the air rifle passed from hand to hand, the targets rapidly diminished. Accordingly, a scavenger hunt for more targets was organized by Ray.

After another session, they had difficulty locating additional targets. Fanning out, Brian and Bobby found themselves drawn to an abandoned automobile. With doors flung wide, smashed headlights, the passenger side window missing, what remained was a treasure trove of target possibilities. A side view mirror was quickly appropriated, so, too, a taillight lens. In the trunk they found several empty wine bottles, assorted newspapers, a greasy sleeping bag, empty cans of pork and beans, a pair of battered leather shoes, and an empty Prince Albert tobacco container. Scattered about were several magazines, quickly scrutinized by the boys. The bodies of the men and women captured in black and white photographs looked sickly. Except for shoes and sox, the men were naked, some showing crude tattoos slashed on biceps or forearms. With legs spread wide, the women had sizeable growths of hair between their legs. Pointing this out to his friend, Bobby speculated that orifice so adorned was the site of urine evacuation. Perhaps, he conjectured further, it was also the location Greg had mentioned where human babies exited the womb, whatever that was. Could both functions be accomplished by the same orifice. Or might there be a third opening, they speculated? Perplexed, Bobby promised to interrogate brother Greg at the earliest opportunity regarding this cryptic anatomical feature.

Brian's eyes stared at the pictures of naked women and men caught in what appeared to be a wrestling match, perhaps an athletic contest as practiced by the early Greeks or Romans. Without a doubt, this was not the televised wrestling matches Auntie was so fond of. But, men and women wrestling each other? It was unheard of. He had a sneaking suspicion their behavior had something to do with the sex act he and Bobby had observed between a few of the neighborhood dogs.

"The hell you doing. Goddamn kids, that's my hidey-hole, now you git to hell outta here," someone yelled.

They jerked around to see an emaciated man in tattered coat and pants, a ragged salt-and-pepper beard concealing a sallow face. Thin lips opened to reveal a mouth missing several teeth. He hobbled toward them, one foot missing a shoe, a ragged sock afforded limited protection.

The boys backed away from the automobile trunk. The scarecrow of a man lurched forward, causing the boys to scatter around either side of the automobile, quickly outdistancing him. At the top of a nearby sand hill they stopped to see the man at the side the car, one hand crumpled into a threatening fist, the other hand holding a glass jug. From the hillock they could barely hear him shouting obscenities at them.

They ran the rest of the way to the improvised target range where Ray and Mike were waiting, seated on two overturned wooden milk cases. Alarmed at seeing their pals approaching in haste, they jumped to their feet.

Stopping in front of Ray, they bent over, resting their hands on their knees, gulping for air.

"A jakey-bum caught us taking empty wine bottles from the trunk of an old car. Chased us away," Brian spat, breathing hard.

"Yeah, looked like he was using the car as a hideout," added Bobby.

"Okay, okay, we stick together now, just in case. If I give the signal, we start running down the road toward the waterworks, like when we hitched a ride in that maroon Chevy. Got it?"

The boys nodded their understanding.

"Come on, we'll finish up the bottles and cans me and Mike gathered up, then we'll get out of here."

That said, Ray assumed a standing posture, took aim at a Nehi soda bottle and pulled the trigger. The pellet glanced off the round surface, merely rocking the bottle back and forth. A second BB shattered the bottle.

Next, Mike took the rifle. Pulling the small canister of BBs from his pocket, he filled the breech. Also in a standing position, he fired at a tin can, putting two punctures in it before passing the gun to Brian, who took aim with one-eyed concentration on a small jelly jar.

"I told you kids to git. Breaking all my bottles. All my wine money smashed to bits," the bum yelled advancing again toward the boys.

Facing about, they prepared to bolt.

"Gimme that gun. I'll shoot me some targets, yessir, I'll shoot some smart alecks punks. Gimme that damn gun," he yelled, lurching toward the boys.

The crack of a rifle shot shattered the afternoon quiet. Simultaneously, the jug of wine in the tramp's hand exploded in a balloon of red liquid and shattered glass.

Shocked, the boys looked around for the source of the gunfire. On a mound of trash the boys saw Joey Layton standing there with his .22 rifle pointed at the bum who, when he came to his addled senses jerked about and stumbled back down the dirt road.

Joey approached the boys with his .22 across his chest, the barrel pointed skyward, the bolt opened ready to receive the next bullet.

All smiles now, the boys watched Joey approach and stared enviously at his weapon. Someday, they told themselves, they'll have a rifle like Joey's.

"Sorry if I scared you. That jakey's been coming around bothering my mother for smokes and stuff."

"Thanks Joey," Brian managed.

Layton nodded his head at the other boys, noting the BB gun now cradled in Ray's arms.

"Come over to my place. You can shoot that air rifle down at the river. I'll throw some cans in the water and you can fire at them as they go by. That's how I practice. Harder to hit a moving target."

The boys followed Joey down the same trail they'd used to escape from the man who gave them a ride in his Chevrolet. He led them down a dirt path through sumac trees, waist high weeds and berry vines. Two hundred yards farther, the trail opened up on the clearing and the Layton trailer. There at her table, folding assorted castoff clothes, was Joey's mother, a cigarette hanging from the corner of her mouth. Seeing her son and his friends approach, she looked up and waved.

The boys gathered around a water crock at the end of the table. Handing Brian a tin cup, Joey went to the trailer, opened the screen door and set his rifle inside the doorway. He stopped at his mother's side. She reached up to pat his cheek.

"My man child, give your Ma a kiss, hon."

Joey bent over and, with no hesitation or embarrassment, pecked his mother's cheek while the boys looked on. After a puff on the cigarette, she resumed her chore of straightening and folding articles of clothing gleaned from the dump.

"They ran into that jakey-bum who came around pestering you the other day," Joey explained.

"Do tell. That's the kind of company we can do without."

"Had to fire my rifle and run him off. Looked to me like he had his eye on Ray's BB gun."

While Joey told his mother of the confrontation, Brian walked to the side of the trailer and sat on a back seat scavenged from an abandoned car.

"I know you don't waste yer bullets. Just mind what your father told you about when to use your rifle and when not to," she cautioned, then announced, "Can I get you fellas something to eat?"

"Thanks, but we'd better be getting back to the waterworks to catch the bus for home," Ray answered for the boys.

Brian looked up at Mrs. Layton, who was frowning at something before her on the table.

'Wouldn't you know it," she turned to Joey, "you just found one of these nice leather gloves?" she said holding it up for his inspection.

"Yup, just one."

"Durn, a pair would have brought maybe twenty five cents."

Brian, now standing before Mrs. Layton, looked suspiciously at the black glove.

"Hey Ray, take a look at this. Don't it look like the glove that guy in the Chevy had on?"

Ray handed the BB gun to Mike and moved to Brian's side.

"Here, go ahead take a close look," Mrs. Layton said handing him the glove.

He turned the glove inside out, discovering a small wad of cotton in the pinky. Picking it out with the tip of his penknife he could see a bloodstain on the cotton.

"Yeah, I'll bet it belonged to that guy, alright. When he took his right glove off to light a cigarette I could see most of his pinky finger was missing. And this is a right hand glove. We better get home and call your father," Ray said to Brian.

Before another word was said, Mrs. Layton encouraged the boys to take the glove with them if it would help in any way.

Ray looked at Joey. "Where'd you find this?"

"It was in the road, the other end of the dump near the Waterworks. Cars get stuck there 'cause of the sand, so it don't get much use. Found it coming home from the snack bar at the reservoir. Almost stepped on it."

With that the boys thanked Joey again for running the bum off. Saying goodbye to Mrs. Layton, the four boys hurried down the road to the Waterworks, where they would get the Western Avenue bus back to the city.

They listened to the prowl car siren wind down as it pulled beside the house. Seated in the living room in silence they would occasionally look over at Ray, who had the black glove spread out on his right knee.

At the kitchen table, Rita and Auntie nodded to Chick and his partner, McEvoy, as they hurried past on their way to interview the boys.

Immediately, Ray handed the glove to his uncle. He explained that it was found by Joey Layton at the dump near Six Mile Waterworks. He showed Chick the cotton wad still wedged in the pinky finger of the glove. Chick looked at McEvoy.

"Mac, get on the prowl car radio to headquarters; tell them what we have. Get out a couple of cars to the dump…and have one of them pick up the Layton boy so he can show them exactly where he found the glove."

Nodding in agreement, McEvoy turned to leave.

"And tell'em we're headed to our number three suspect, Jacob Blotnick, to bring him in for questioning."

~

It was twilight when the prowl car pulled into the gravel drive beside a nondescript one-story farmhouse. Chick observed the empty driveway, the dark windows. The radio in the dash came alive. McEvoy cradled the microphone in his hand.

"Twenty one, go ahead."

"Two uniform officers found a suitcase at the dump."

"Yeah?"

"Body of a small boy inside, chopped up."

"Was it the Pistone kid?"

"Don't know. Coroner's doing an autopsy now."

"Ten four. We're at the suspect's house, over."

"Roger that. Out."

McEvoy looked over at Chick with raised eyebrows.

Neither spoke as Chick stared at the house.

The two detectives emerged from the squad car and made their way cautiously to the front door.

Pulling open a torn screen door, they walked onto the enclosed porch. A lone metal chair was turned on its side, leaves and scraps of paper scattered nearby.

"Police. Got a few questions for you, Mr. Blotnick," Chick shouted, knocking loudly on the front door.

Waiting impatiently, McEvoy eyed Chick with an inquisitive look.

Except for the grinding noises issuing from the nearby cement plant, the house and surroundings were quiet.

With a jerk of the head, Chick signaled they would go to the rear of the house. They noted the absence of vehicles in the driveway or in back of the house. Cautiously, the detectives searched an abandoned chicken coop and one-car detached garage filled with rusting farm machinery. The maroon Chevrolet was nowhere to be found. At the top of a three-step staircase, Chick knocked loudly on the back door. Again, his attempts at summoning someone, anyone, went unrewarded. He turned to McEvoy.

"What do you think?"

"No warrant, nothing fishy," McEvoy began. "But let's see what we can do."

He walked a few steps to a metal trashcan and gave it a good kick. The lid popped off, and the container spilled an assortment of items in the weeds cropping up along the brick foundation. Another well-placed kick sent an assortment of rubbish onto the ground. Spreading and scattering the items about with a bent curtain rod, McEvoy pinned down a pair of bloodstained Jockey shorts. Dangling them from the end of the curtain rod he held them up for Chick to see.

"Your call, pard. And lookee here, rubber gloves, empty food cartons, bloodstained rags. Not good, not good at all."

"We better get a search warrant," Chick said.

Turning over another clot of trash, McEvoy hooked something on the end of the curtain rod. He held it up, calling to Chick.

"Bingo."

A used prophylactic dangled from the curtain rod.

"Okay, that's enough to keep us out of hot water. Go around to the front, just in case Blotnick's playing games with us," Chick said, as his right hand pulled the .38 from his holster. His left hand grasped the doorknob that gave way to a slight twist.

Not locked.

Nodding his head, McEvoy pulled a .25 automatic from a holster on his belt and made his way speedily to the front of the house.

Now at the top step of the small stairway at the backdoor, Chick was able to look through a pane of glass clear to the front door. Seeing McEvoy enter, he twisted the doorknob and shouldered his way into the kitchen, noticing at once the rubbish and cigarette butts scattered on the peeling linoleum floor.

Bracing his shoulder against the door jam, his pistol raised in front of him, Chick waited until McEvoy emerged from a bedroom off the living room. There he glimpsed a large easy chair, a footstool, an overflowing pedestal ashtray, and a three-bulb floor lamp. The floor beside the chair was covered with discarded newspapers. Moving closer, he noted an overturned glass had spilled its contents onto the frontpage picture of two uniformed policemen pointing at the site where the Pistone boy had been fishing.

Turning around facing Chick, McEvoy pointed his pistol at the floor. Acknowledging with a nod, Chick turned back into the kitchen. Pulling a hall door open, he was confronted by a dark stairwell leading down into the basement. Holding his freehand up to signal his partner to stop where he was, Chick listened at the top of the stairs and heard what he thought was the wind invading a weathered window frame, or, possibly, a moan. The susurration was overridden by grinding noises issuing from the cement plant. McEvoy was now at his back surveying the kitchen. Scattered and overturned on the counters were bottles, empty soup cans, more food cartons with chopsticks protruding from them, several cartons discarded on the floor.

Stepping down the staircase, Chick paused. He was now sure he heard a low choking, perhaps a cough. Though it seemed he was descending into a black bottomless pit, he kept edging his way carefully down the stairs, his hand searching the wall, fruitlessly, for a light switch. His foot at last found purchase on a dirt floor. His hat brushed the floor joists as he moved into darkness. He was certain moaning was coming from somewhere in the pitch black surrounding him.

Miraculously, the basement was filled with light, startling and blinding Chick and forcing him to cover his eyes, in the process of which, he banged his head on an exposed beam.

McEvoy appeared at the top of the stairway. "How's that, Chicky?"

Scanning the area, his eyes adjusted to the light of a cluster of high-wattage bulbs dangling from green metal fixtures on a beam a foot from his head. The basement was a complete contrast to the rooms above. Here, things were in order, no overflowing trashcans, no piles of refuse, no overturned bottles, no empty food cartons. A workbench contained rows of hand tools, glass jars containing nuts, bolts, nails of all sizes. Not five feet in front of him was the rounded structure of a coal furnace with its unmistakable smell of soot, now cold to the touch. Next to the furnace was a cot with a bare mattress. In deep shadow nearby was the coal bin, from which came a whimpering that grew in intensity as he approached. In back of a chest-high mound of hard coal he could see the outlines of what looked like a cage fabricated from steel rebar.

Holstering his weapon, he squatted down on his heels.

"Jesus H."

Inside the cage was a naked boy about four feet two and weighing, he guessed, maybe 90 lbs. The cage was so constructed that its captive could not stand up, forcing him to lie prone or sit in a cramped position.

The naked youngster, his flesh blue with cold, was curled up in a fetal position, chin pressed to his chest, his body quivering with fear, evidently expecting whatever maniacal demon was responsible for his captivity to initiate a session of torture or sadism.

"Son, listen we'll get you out of here. I'm a cop, you understand. No one will hurt you anymore." He looked over his shoulder and yelled up to McEvoy, "Get an ambulance."

After he called in for the ambulance, McEvoy hurried back down the steps into the basement where Chick had broken a padlock on the cage door to free the youngster. With his coat covering the boy's nakedness, he held him bundled in his arms.

When asked if his name was Sammy Pistone, the boy acknowledged with a nod of the head and choking sobs. Chick moved the boy to the prowl car's back seat.

The child pulled Chick's suit coat tighter around him. While lighting a cigarette, McEvoy called headquarters again to demand the ambulance hurry up. The dispatcher assured him, in a laconic tone of voice, that it was on its way with all possible speed.

Chick looked at the Pistone lad cowering in the depths of his suit coat. He turned to McEvoy.

"Better keep an eye on me if we catch up with this Blotnick character. I'm on the ragged edge with this one."

"Yeah, yeah, the whole thing is kinda wacko."

At last the two detectives breathed a sigh of relief at the wail of the approaching ambulance.

"About time," snapped McEvoy.

Breaking the tense silence, the squad car radio crackled to life.

"Twenty one, car twenty one."

"Twenty one," McEvoy spat into the microphone.

"Be advised your suspect, Jacob Blotnick, was found at the Ten Eyck Hotel."

McEvoy turned to Chick.

"Roger that, we're en route to the Ten Eyck. Make sure Pistone's parents are informed of his whereabouts ASAP."

"Ten four."

~

The squad car pulled to the curb in front of the hotel entrance canopy. The street in front of the hotel, normally deserted at this late hour, was jammed with a half-dozen police cars, an ambulance, and the coroner's wagon. The revolving red lights on the vehicles reflected off the plate glass windows of the hotel and the pavement slick from a recent scouring by a city street sweeper. Two uniformed policemen, dressed in their full length blue overcoats with polished brass and silver shields gleaming on their chests, nodded at the familiar faces of the detectives as they hurried into the lobby. They were met by the night manager, who briefed them on what he referred to as an *incident*, also assuring the detectives that *incidents* like this were not in character for the *establishment*. McEvoy winked at Chick as the manager rambled on about the *impeccable* reputation of the *establishment*. When the doors of the elevator closed on the three men, the manager continued his impassioned defense of the hotel's *unimpeachable* reputation. Chick watched the panel of lights with ascending numbers blink on and off as the elevator moved steadily upwards.

"Yowza, yowza, the *establishment*, hey-hey," crooned the grinning McEvoy, silencing the manager forthwith.

The elevator doors opened to an explosion of white light from the bulb of Times Union photographer Artie Zeller's speed graphic.

"Jesus, Artie, you ever do that again I'm going to kick your ass up around your ears," McEvoy cursed, rubbing his eyes.

"Come on, fellas, I need a picture for the morning paper," Artie pleaded.

Chick looked down at the diminutive photographer as he approached the open door of a room flanked by a heavyset uniformed police sergeant, who pointed a thumb into the room at his back, crowded with additional policemen. Two ambulance attendants waited beside a gurney while the coroner examined a body on the bed. Three men dressed in suits and hats looked over at Chick when he entered the hotel room.

One of the suited men, a reporter, grabbed Chick's coat sleeve and fired a barrage of questions at him as he approached Phil Bogart, the coroner. Looking around the room, Chick signaled to a police officer with a gold badge on his blue uniform coat and hat.

"Johnny, clear some of these people out of here, will ya?" he said, stopping beside the coroner.

A tap on his shoulder prompted him to look into the face of the uniformed policeman with the gold shield, who was thrusting a piece of paper into Chick's hand.

"Suicide note, Chick."

"Thanks, Johnny," he said, turning to the coroner. "Okay, talk to me, Phil, what's with Mr. Jacob Blotnick?"

"This is a first. Blotnick, the deceased, apparently swallowed over half a can of Drano, chasing it with a tumbler of water, at least most of it, before the chemical reaction started and he dropped the glass on the tile floor, bam. Some cocktail, huh?" He pointed to the bathroom, "the Drano, what's left of it, and… you got the suicide note, doncha?"

"Yeah," Chick said holding it up.

"Now, this is interesting. How do I describe the cause of death? Maybe, death by chemical reaction? Death by asphyxiation caused by a lack of oxygen…"

"I don't care what you call it, so long as he's dead and stays that way."

"Yeah, a real sicko," McEvoy added.

Both Chick and the coroner turned and looked at McEvoy.

McEvoy jerked his head at the bathroom.

"Take a look when you get a sec. Not much to see, just so's you know what was where, you know, the et cetera stuff that goes in the report," McEvoy said, holding up his notebook.

"Do me a favor?" said Chick.

"Sure."

"Go outside and brief what's-his-name from the Times-Union on the et ceteras."

"Yeah, consider it done," McEvoy said still looking at the dead body.

"If we're finished here, I'll have the body taken to the morgue for an autopsy. No hurry, mind you, but it's way past my bedtime," the coroner said.

"Yeah, go ahead."

"Ever wonder why people go to a hotel to commit suicide?" the coroner began, "Probably not. They usually throw themselves out a window or put a gun to their head. Drano? Like I said, a new one on me." The coroner yawned while shrugging his shoulders.

"Well, I know why he didn't blow his brains out at home," McEvoy chimed in.

"Why's that?"

"It was like his own private morgue. A real creep. Good riddance."

"You going to get with the reporter?" Chick snapped.

"Yeah, yeah."

The gurney with a sheet covering the dead body of Jacob P. Blotnick rolled out the door and down the hall to the elevator. Chick went to the telephone on the nightstand beside the double bed. He called headquarters to report his findings at the scene. He asked about the Pistone boy, who he learned was at the hospital with his parents and would remain there overnight, possibly longer. His mother had been assured that she could stay in the same room with her son. He also called home just to hear Rita's voice and learn that Brian was sleeping, safe in his bed.

Placing the phone receiver back in its cradle, his hand went into his side pocket to discover Blotnick's suicide note, still unread. He looked it over carefully. The ink scrawl was penned raggedly on hotel stationery.

I regret my actions fully. If I could undo my perversions I would do so. It was out of my control, I am sick. At last, it comes to an end.

Stifling the urge to crumple the note in his hand, he folded it along an existing crease and placed it back in his suit coat pocket.

18

Departure

From his bedroom window, Brian stared down at Benny's Chrysler. With its profusion of chrome strips, bumpers, hubcaps and ornamentation, all glittering in the morning sunlight, it looked like a diamond-encrusted chariot. Minutes before, when Rita had embraced him, he felt his body tense while she pressed her lips to his cheek for what seemed like hours. Out of his left eye he could see the brown and black pheasant feather dangling from her new hat. When her arm slipped from his shoulder, he noticed quivering red lips. Abruptly turning away, she moved swiftly out his bedroom, stopping briefly to hug Auntie, standing at the kitchen table, before hurrying down the backstairs.

Her bags were already secured in the trunk of the car, enough clothes for a week or more at the special Buffalo hospital. Looking down at the Chrysler, Brian watched his father close the passenger door once his mother was settled in the front seat. Minutes passed while he stared at her obscured profile through the window glass.

Wheeling around, he was surprised to see his father framed in the doorway. Chick had on a blue pinstripe suit with a matching tie. A gray fedora sat at a slight angle on his head. He stepped into the bedroom and looked at his son.

"You know, I believe this is the first time your mother and I have ever been away from you. Say, you'll be the man of the house, so I want you to take good care of Auntie. And don't eat too many Fig Newtons," he jested.

He walked up to his son and clasped him in his arms. Both felt slightly awkward embracing.

"Take care now. I'll be back as soon as I can." While saying this, he pressed two one-dollar bills into Brian's hand.

The doorway appeared to fill with blue pinstripes as his father crossed the bedroom threshold. Then he heard the purr of the Chrysler engine. He watched the blackness and chrome flash by as his father turned the car around in the driveway. It made a left at the end of the drive and disappeared on Partridge Street. Looking down from the bedroom window at the empty driveway for many minutes, he wondered why his mother had to go all the way to Buffalo for an operation when there were three hospitals in Albany and dozens of doctors. He suspected that, once again, he was not privy to all pertinent information.

Walking listlessly into the kitchen, he was overwhelmed by the silence pervading the house. Auntie was sitting at the table in her flower print apron and black dress, black stockings rolled down, black lace-up shoes crossed at the ankles. Her teacup was covered with a saucer, the teabag imprisoned in the cup beneath. Watching her lips move slowly, he guessed, correctly, that she was saying the rosary.

Brian slid into the chair across the table from her. She was looking away from him as her gnarled fingers withdrew the rosary from her lap and restored it to its place in her black pocketbook. Only then did she look over at Brian.

"Let me make you a cup of hot cocoa. Warm your insides, it will."

He shook his head as he reached for the radio dial. Switching stations aimlessly, the speaker belched a few seconds of a news report, a partial weather forecast, the end of a soap commercial jingle. At last, the dial stopped on a station playing the Lucky Strike Hit Parade. While Nat King Cole lamented the enigmatic Mona Lisa, Brian watched Auntie remove the saucer from the top of her cup, pour a tad of steaming tea onto the saucer, then slurp it until satisfied it was steeped to perfection. Squeezing the liquid contents from the teabag, she sipped her tea thoughtfully.

Pushing away from the table, Brian announced, "I'm going take my tumbler pigeon over to the Jews yard. The caretaker is going to show me some training secrets."

"Be careful climbing onto the garage roof. If you break a bone I wouldn't know what to do," she said.

Her hand was already retrieving the rosary beads from her pocketbook when the backdoor slammed shut. Her eyes clouded over as she mumbled, "Jasus, Jasus, my poor, sweet precious."

~

The McNally twins, Dylan and Dermot, and brother Sean, looked down from the back porch as their brother Bobby marched shoulder-to-shoulder with Brian to the back fence. The highlight of their afternoon had been a close-up inspection of Brian's sleek blue and white-feathered Birmingham Roller, cooing and strutting regally in the confines of its portable wire cage. Connor blubbered incomprehensible accolades from his highchair, even launched a saliva-soaked piece of buttered toast at the cage to show his appreciation. With that outburst, he was dispatched by Mrs. McNally to his crib for a nap he vehemently objected to, but swiftly embraced.

The two comrades halted momentarily beside the chestnut tree next to the back fence. Bobby pried back a nail that secured a fence board, freeing it enough to be pulled aside and admit them into the Jews yard, a safe haven for unlimited exploration now that Johnny Russian had inexplicably shed the dubious honor of being the neighborhood's reigning ogre. The pivoting fence slat had been mandated to accommodate Brian and his caged tumbler, whose safety, the boys had concluded, would be jeopardized if they climbed over the fence. A lace curtain in the second story bedroom of the Gardner house fell in place when the boys were out of sight.

High up in the pigeon loft, Johnny Russian was tending to newly hatched squabs and their mothers, careful to separate them from the male pigeons that sometimes attacked their offspring. He paused occasionally to scribble in his tattered notebook, kept handy in the chest pocket of his overalls. Following this, he measured out precise quantities of feed for the stabilized kit, giving more to those birds whose performance exceeded his standards and restricting feed to those that underperformed. Although he tried not to show favoritism, he always took a few minutes to inspect and admire his Galati Roller. Proudly, he would stroke the pigeon's blue-black wings and the snow white feathers of its neck and breast. Holding it, he smoothed its tail feathers. He looked with pleasure into its pinkish eye, admiring the way it held its head high, thrusting its white chest forward. Feeling the bird's body heat seep slowly into his hands, he listened attentively to its measured cooing.

Observing this denim clad beast of a man with all of his physical imperfections, one would hardly conceive that he was capable of expressing any of the numerous emotions that we take for granted, as though we were chosen by some God or Goddess to be exclusive recipients of those complex feelings. How could this hideous example of humanity incorporate anything but the most elementary ingredients of life, like the oak tree that graced the center of the rest home driveway? Is he not also a piece of wood, a mere husk of a man—certainly, far below our exalted status?

Yet, look how the diminutive feathered creature responds with reciprocal affection to those callused, scarred hands that hold its very life in the balance. Does it not coo, its miniscule heart beating with increased rapidity as the man presses the purplish-black feathered wing to his scarred cheek?

A shrill whistle from below made Johnny's ear twitch. With care he restored the Galati Roller to its place in the coop. Opening one of the entry portals of the loft, he peered down to see the two boys. Brian waited with his caged Birmingham Roller, the bird grown sleek and strong while in his care. For the remainder of his life Johnny would never forget the boy plummeting from that beam onto the bales of hay. Instantaneously, his mind resurrected a memory of the shallow grave in Berlin and the American soldiers who rescued him.

Below, with the boy is his best friend.

Another fragment of memory finds its way to the surface. Did he not have a best friend in that small village in rural Russia? Did he and his friend keep a kit of tumblers, train them, exhibit them at fairs and the weekly market? Vaguely, he remembers being awarded a blue ribbon. What was his friend's name? Surely, he had a best friend.

His answering whistle alerted the boys and his tumblers. Immediately, the cooped birds beside him began strutting and flexing their wings in anticipation.

Shortly, Johnny Russian emerged from the barn with his caged kit of tumblers. He spied the boys at the back porch where Sol Horowitz, in his wheelchair, was admiring Brian's roller.

"Such a beauty. You're a lucky boy to have such a *boid*," Sol shrilled, while cigar smoke escaped his hairy nostrils. Pulling his spectacles off, for a quick cleansing, he readjusted the glasses on his ears before taking another look at the Birmingham Roller.

"Brian, my young friend, this *boid* was such a favorite of Johnny's. And here comes himself," Sol whispered with a smile.

Setting the portable coop of tumblers down in the middle of the driveway, Johnny approached the two youngsters and Sol. Though the denim-clad giant had rescued him, Brian still harbors a jot of fear in his presence. All three persons followed Johnny's progress to where they congregate at the porch railing. Stopping in front of them, Johnny's callused fist searches a back pocket for a tattered red bandana. He removed the army forage cap and mopped his bald head with the red cloth. The boys stared at the surgical scar perforating his scalp as though it had been split open by a meat cleaver. A sigh of relief nearly escaped Brian's throat as Johnny placed the cap back on his head.

Silently, he observed Brian's caged tumbler. He nodded, a wisp of a smile slashing his lopsided mouth.

"Wanna see her fly?" Brian asked.

"Give us a show, why not?" Sol encouraged, puffing his cigar.

Sol watched the boys troop behind Johnny as he made his way to the kit box. Brian quickly and carefully freed his tumbler from its cage. Gently holding it in his hands, he fed it kernels of corn from a dungaree pocket.

Looking closely at the tumbler, Johnny Russian pulled his notebook from an overall pocket. Flipping through the pages, he stopped, inspected the bird again, and finally asked Brian in a heavy Russian accent, "Name?"

Not understanding the boy's response, he handed his pad and pencil to Brian, who quickly printed the bird's name – Citation.

That accomplished, Johnny returned the notebook and pencil stub to a chest pocket. Brian held the bird out to him. With seeds to encourage it, the tumbler jumped to Johnny's open palm.

While Johnny petted the tumbler, a loud crashing noise was heard at the side of the rest home, causing all to look up with expectation and alarm. Around the corner of the building rolled a gasoline-powered truck driven by the iceman, Mario, who sat stiff and straight, grasping the steering wheel tightly in both hands. Johnny and the boys stood aside to let the truck, laden with its cargo of ice, pass and come to a halt opposite the backdoor.

When the motor was silenced, Mario jumped down from the driver's seat, closed the door carefully, then made his way to the back of the vehicle, where he greeted Johnny and the boys, as well as acknowledging the presence of Mr. Horowitz. Pushing back the cap on his black curly hair, face beaming, teeth gleaming in the sunlight, Mario enthusiastically greeted all with a hearty, *buon giorno*, accompanied with a slap on the back or firm handshake. Lapsing into Italian, he tried to explain the difficulty of navigating the new motor vehicle, as opposed to his tried and true pair of horses, now relegated to a farmer's plow on the outskirts of the city.

Unexpectedly, Mario grabbed Johnny by the shirtsleeve, dragging him to the truck, where he struck the side with a muscular hand and pointed to the sign that declared to the world that here was a Union Ice truck, Serving the Capitol District since 1923.

His roving eye catching sight of Sol Horowitz, he slapped his forehead as he advanced toward the porch. Drawing close to the railing, he pulled one of his black, twisted cigars from a shirt pocket and presented it to Sol as though it were a gold ingot. Sol passed it under his nose for a few seconds. Before he could clamp it in his dentures, the back door burst open. A nurse's aide made her formidable entrance.

"No you don't, Mr. Sol, you had you cigar for the day; now it time for yo' pills," the muscular black woman in a crinkly white uniform announced.

Even before she finished her declaration, Sol stashed the cigar away in an inside coat pocket.

"For this I pay good money?" he wheezed, hands raised, shoulders shrugged, as if addressing an audience of victimized seniors.

Still smiling and tipping his cap to the nurse, Mario retreated to the ice truck where he watched Johnny Russian open the portable coop, allowing the birds to exit. A clap and sharp whistle from Johnny sent the birds into the air. All watched as they wheeled high above the rest home.

"Just one minute, my little shiksa," Sol pleaded with the nurse.

Relenting, the nurse's aide also captivated by the aerial performance, commented, "I ain't never seen no pigeons do them tricks, nossir."

Flying in near perfect formation, the pigeons embarked on a series of backward somersaults, then reformed, and circled high above the yard before engaging in another series of tumbles.

When at last Johnny raised a pole with a bright yellow cloth attached and waved it back and forth, his kit broke formation and swooped down to the coop entrance portals high on the front of the barn.

Realizing the avian performance had ended, the aide grasped the sides of Sol's wooden wheelchair with strong hands. "Don't sass me no mo', Mr. Sol, or I'll take that cigar you put in yo' hidey pocket and smoke it myself. I ain't foolin' now," she cajoled.

"Persecution! I could get it wholesale from my dear departed wife."

The protesting cigar connoisseur was finally pushed over the back-door threshold, with Mario not far behind with a cake of ice on his leather-padded right shoulder. Minutes later, he hurried to Johnny Russian's side. In a flurry of gyrating hands, accompanied with a machine-gun burst of Italian, he heaped praise on Johnny and his kit of feathered gymnasts.

When Mario paused to catch his breath, Johnny turned to Brian, pointing at the Birmingham Roller. Brian freed the bird and held it up proudly to Johnny before gently tossing it into the air from cupped palms. The pigeon rose to the heights above the yard with uncommon speed. After making a few passes overhead, Citation began a series of several somersaults. Concluding the exhibition, the roller stopped high above the barn before tumbling down with increasing velocity, breaking its fall with outstretched wings at the last possible second before landing at their feet. Brian proudly scooped it up and rewarded the roller with seeds.

For the first time, Brian intuited by the shine of Johnny's eye and cut of his mouth that Johnny was experiencing happiness, an emotion never, until now, associated with the scruffy, denim-clad handyman. Usually, Johnny Russian's face was a blank slate. Today, however, something had bubbled to the surface.

The display of aerial prowess concluded, Brian placed his thoroughly exhausted tumbler back in its cage and said goodbye to Johnny Russian. He and Bobby made their way out of the Jews yard. A *shave 'n a haircut* melody, coaxed from the ice truck's horn, had the two boys turning and waving at Mario as he drove the new truck down the gravel drive circling the rest home and onto Western Avenue.

Johnny Russian stood there watching the exodus. With late after-noon sunlight illuminating him, a smile breached his twisted mouth. Indeed, he remembered, once upon a time, he did have a best friend.

~

Chores completed, pigeons fed and watered, Johnny made his way to his windowless cellar quarters. He switched on the bare light bulb sus-pended from a wire dangling from an exposed beam.

In one corner of his Spartan cell was a metal cot made up with a brown army surplus blanket. Close by was an armoire, passed on to Johnny from a deceased resident, containing an assortment of overalls, long sleeve shirts, a wool sweater with leather patches at the elbows, and a sheepskin winter coat. A drawer held a collection of frayed un-dergarments, bandanas, and pairs of work gloves frozen in the shape of the hands that formed them. At the base of the wardrobe, nearly hidden under a row of shirts, coats and overalls on hangers, was a pair of shiny, brown leather shoes, of the highest quality and latest style, footwear incongruous with their surroundings and doubly incongruous with their current owner. They were treated with great care, nonetheless, as were all of his meager possessions, a habit nurtured in childhood and refined during service in the Russian army.

He stood, immobile, before the tumblers' genealogical chart pen-ciled on the plaster wall before him. His brown eye followed the mating progress of members of his current prized kit. Notebook in hand, he sat at a narrow desk cobbled together from the planks of wooden crates long ago emptied and abandoned in a corner of the barn. On the desk was a cigar box where he stored small stubs of pencils discarded to trash cans in the upper rooms and coins of various denominations, along with paper currency amounting to a few hundred dollars, a combination of his wages for ten years' service, as well as gratuities from the likes of Sol Horowitz, who, in addition to the goat's milk, commissioned him to clandestinely purchase cigars for him. Occasionally, Johnny would prepare a bouquet of his flowers for the bedridden Mrs. Klein, a dowa-ger on the third floor—a good deed that would merit a ten cent reward.

From the metal trash cans located throughout the rest home he would glean a bright ribbon, a piece of hard candy, perhaps a colorful stamp from a discarded envelope. Acquired during the performance of one of his many chores, these prizes, valuable only to Johnny, would be stored in the cigar box.

When the aged itinerant vendor of used magazines and comic books would make his rounds, Johnny would purchase three or four *Life* or *Colliers* magazines for the retired librarian, Miss Goldberg, who forced him to accept a penny or two for his thoughtfulness.

Finalizing the pigeons' genealogical updates, Johnny restored the notebook to its customary pocket. Pausing for a minute, his hand migrated to the cigar box, where his fingers rooted through the collection until they came in contact with a small round mirror, the size of a silver dollar, also a consignment to one of the hallway trash baskets. The looking glass was gently extracted and held before his face with a quivering hand. Working up the nerve, he looked into the mirror and noticed, with surprise, wrinkles around his eyes, the corners of his mouth slightly pinched upwards, forming the genesis of a smile. Scrutinizing this new development provoked a corresponding feeling of self-consciousness. The more he studied his image in the glass, the more pronounced the incipient smile became. The same mystical feeling that suffused his body when tending to his pigeons coursed through his veins like an open electrical circuit. Reluctantly, he returned the mirror to the cigar box.

~

Friday night. Bobby was seated at the kitchen table, listening to music on the radio while Brian completed his time-consuming toilette. Across from Bobby sat Auntie with her teacup covered with the saucer while the teabag steeped. Extracting a box of Luden cough drops from her pocketbook, she held them out to Bobby.

"Take one, boyo. Good for ya. Can I get you a Lorna Doone, maybe a wee bit of applesauce cake?"

He shook his head. "No, thanks. I just ate a little while ago."

Turning in his chair, he yelled toward the bathroom.

"Come on, we can't be late."

Brian was putting the finishing touches on the part in his fully sprouted head of hair. Carefully, he ran the comb through the brown hair ending with a wave above his right eye. Not quite satisfied, he reached for his father's tube of Brylcreem. As a precautionary measure, he massaged an overly generous handful of the dressing into his hair. Following another combing, he stood back to admire the carapace he'd constructed on his head. Satisfied, he slipped the comb into a back pocket. Running his hand over his cheeks and chin with concern, he reached up to a nearby shelf to grasp his father's Gillette razor with its days old blade. Pulling it slowly across his upper lip, he assured himself the minuscule hairs he had seen growing there were now eradicated.

Once again, he heard the impatient request from his friend to hurry.

Lastly, he propped his right foot on the edge of the claw foot tub to buff his cordovan shoes to a glossy shine. Discarding the washcloth to a nearby clothes hamper, he made his entrance into the kitchen.

Bobby jumped to his feet, while Auntie inspected her great nephew with a mixture of surprise and pride.

"Aren't you the handsome lad," Auntie exclaimed. "Where are you lads off to?"

"To the Dipsy Doodle over on Madison for a coke."

"When the street lights come on, I want you on your way home."

"Okay. What are you going to do tonight," Brian asked.

"Going downstairs to visit with Mrs. Urtz. She invited me to watch their television. I ain't never seen one in person."

Brian shrugged. "I just hope you get to watch something besides test patterns and Howdy Doody."

"Well now, the missus says there'll be a wrestling match with Pat Kelly and a variety show with Milton Berle—that'll be something. Now off with yuz and, mind, get home on time."

Trying to ignore her final appeal to behave and get home on time, the boys hurried down the staircase to the front porch where Mr. Urtz was seated in a metal lawn chair reading a newspaper and smoking his pipe. He lowered the paper just enough to observe them scurry to the sidewalk and turn toward Madison Avenue.

"Gotta hurry, I told Eileen we'd meet them at the Dipsy Doodle at 6:30 p.m. Don't want to be late," Bobby said.

"Okay, okay, but we don't have to run. I don't want to be all sweaty when we get there."

"Yeah, you're right, we better walk quickly."

Regardless, it would have required a great expenditure of energy by a mere mortal to keep up with the boys as they hastened to the soda shop.

Standing outside the Dipsy Doodle, they looked up and down the street searching for Gina and Eileen. Brian turned to his friend.

"You sure they were supposed to be here at 6:30 p.m.? It's already 6:33 p.m."

"I said half past six. Maybe they thought I said half past seven. Nah, that don't make sense," Bobby said.

"Maybe Gina's mother wouldn't let her out?"

"Let's go inside and look around. They could have got here before us."

With that, the boys entered the soda shop to the blare of rock and roll music issuing from the Seeburg jukebox. At the counter was their teammate, G. G. Wallace, pleading with Joanie the soda jerk for an Awful-Awful. They spied Bobby's brother Greg in the back booth with his girl and some other friends. Among them was the high school sports hero Charlie Maguire. Rumor had it he'd been offered a contract to play for the Boston Red Sox farm team.

Not seeing either girl, Brian's face became a pool of doubt.

"Heck, let's just sit in a booth and wait. They're only forty minutes late."

"Well, maybe they don't walk as fast as us, ya know."

"Probably not."

Looking up from his second glass of Coke, Brian watched as the big hand on the neon-framed clock behind the counter clicked on the seven. He looked up to see Greg standing beside the booth with an arm draped over his girlfriend's shoulder.

"What's up, sports fans?"

"The girls we were supposed to meet here never showed up," Bobby said.

Greg smiled. "What time were they supposed to be here?"

"Six thirty," the boys replied simultaneously.

Greg's glance at Angie provoked a smile and a stifled laugh.

"Silly boys, you've got a lot to learn," Angie began, "no girl is going to show up on time for a date. It just isn't done," she announced, looking sternly at Greg. "Isn't that right?"

His right hand raised as if he was swearing on a bible, Greg replied, "God's honest truth guys: never expect any self-respecting girl to arrive at the appointed hour."

With that, he squeezed Angie in the crook of his arm. Giggling, she half-heartedly attempted to push him away.

The door opened, and in came Gina and Eileen. Brian waved to get their attention. Sizing up the situation, Greg and Angie made their exit.

All smiles and perkiness, Gina slid into the booth next to Brian and patted his hand. Glossy red lips and the small mole on her cheek caught his eye. She was wearing a red angora short-sleeved sweater. Her long, black hair, tied in a ponytail, fell down her back. The outline of a Poodle was stitched on her gray knee-length skirt.

"I thought maybe you couldn't get out or something," Brian began awkwardly. Looking across the table he couldn't help but notice Eileen's dour appearance. She was dressed in an identical outfit, but her unpainted lips were clamped tight.

"Sorry," Gina began, "Eileen had second thoughts just minutes before we were about to leave."

A pained look appeared on Bobby's face, as though he might in some way be the source of Eileen's reluctance.

"Go ahead, show them. You have to sooner or later," Gina encouraged.

With that, Eileen opened her mouth in a mock smile displaying a grid of wires on her teeth.

"My aunt insisted these… these devices be installed. I just loathe the whole idea of braces," Eileen said, attempting a smile that dissolved quickly to a frown.

With that announcement, Bobby's fantasy of kissing her on the porch that night when he walked her home exploded like a clay pigeon struck by a shotgun blast. Regardless, he soon warmed to the idea of her company, braces or no, when Eileen's hand found his below the table and squeezed it energetically.

Rubbing shoulders with Gina, Brian became aware, for the first time, of the signature aroma wafting from her neck and exposed arms. His roving eyes also noted her glossy and meticulously shaped fingernails. Though not painted with any colored polish, they seemed to glow with some type of wet enamel. Pressing close to him as he sipped coke from the straw in his glass, he felt the side of her breast brush against his arm. All the while, he kept glancing at the clock over the counter that kept reminding him they would soon have to leave.

Later, on the way to her house, Brian helped slip a lightweight jacket on her shoulders. The task completed, his right hand remained there. Shortly, he felt her left arm encircle his waist.

Bobby and Eileen stopped in front of Eileen's house a half-block away, while Brian and Gina continued their walk.

It was nearly dark when they stood in front of Gina's door on the first floor of the two-story duplex. Both her arms moved around his waist and pulled him closer. Again he was aware of the intoxicating aroma wafting from her body. His lips brushed her cheek. Soon, her lips pressed up against his, then her tongue made a slow exploration of his mouth. Suddenly, the porch light blinked on, making Brian feel like thieves caught in a searchlight. Gina backed away reluctantly.

"My mother! I have to go in. I hate to, but if I don't she'll come downstairs."

Catching his breath, Brian nodded his head.

Gina pulled him to her for one last lingering tongue-probing kiss. Suddenly, the porch light began blinking spasmodically. Gina pushed away. She caressed his cheek with a hand before opening the door and hurrying up the stairs. In her wake, Brian stood bewildered looking at the stairway leading up to the DeMelia household. Just as suddenly as it had come on, the porch light was extinguished. He realized he had to hurry home.

A half block away, he found Bobby sitting alone on the front porch steps of Eileen's house.

"What took you so long?" Bobby asked, getting to his feet and walking rapidly beside Brian.

"I kissed Gina and some other things."

"Yeah, well, lucky you. Take it from me—don't ever try kissing a girl with braces."

"I lost all track of time. We better get home, or else," Brian said.

"So, you and Gina kissed, huh?"

"Sure, but I never knew girls kissed with their tongue."

Bobby made a face. "What do you mean?"

"She actually pushed her tongue in my mouth, and I did the same to her. Tasted kinda good."

"Oh boy, that might get her pregnant."

"You think so?" Brian said with alarm.

"What if she swallows your spit; you ever think of that?" said Bobby.

"No. Jesus, we'd better talk to Greg. He'll know all about that stuff from Biology."

Turning the corner onto Partridge, Bobby cut across the deserted street to his house, while Brian climbed the stairs to his. Opening the door at the top of the staircase, Brian walked quietly through the living room. Auntie was in the front parlor, glasses perched on her head, newspaper spread on her lap, a section or two cascading onto the floor. She was fast asleep and snoring in his father's easy chair. Reluctantly, he went to her side and shook her awake.

<u>19</u>

Homecoming

Brian jumped down to the sidewalk and raced around to the side of the house when the Chrysler pulled into the driveway. His father was quickly out of the driver's side to the back of the car greeting him with a hug and a look of caution—a look Brian remembered his father displaying, weeks ago, when he had asked why his mother had to go to the Buffalo hospital.

While his father opened the trunk, Brian hurried to the passenger door and pulled it open. He blinked his eyes. He barely recognized the woman in the front seat. Was this his mother or an inferior substitute? Rita sat staring straight-ahead, smoking a cigarette. Large red marks were blotted on the tip of the cigarette. A tiny piece of tobacco hung from the corner of her lower lip. Ashes had dropped onto her lavender dress. The new hat with the pheasant feather sat awkwardly on her head, the veil pulled down shielding her eyes. Brian waited. Words failed him. He bit his lip. She turned and threw the smoking cigarette onto the gravel at his feet forcing him to back away. At last, her erratic gaze fixed on him as though he had magically appeared before her. Poof!

Her right arm reached out, pulled Brian to her side, filling his nostrils with the rank odors of cigarette smoke, powder, and the smell he remembered from that morning when he had opened the car door to see his father curled up asleep on the front seat of the Ford.

"Mom, I'm… I'm glad you're home."

He helped her out of the car. Her hand thrust out to his shoulder to steady herself. Brian stared at her. He couldn't help it. His eyes widened when seeing the slackness, the emptiness of her left side. He was about to ask her about the operation when his father was at his side suggesting Brian take one of the suitcases while he helped Rita up the backstairs. Following behind his mother and father, he watched as she stumbled slightly on the porch stairs, chuckling as she did so. His father's arm was holding her protectively.

Sure, sure, welcome home.

They walked in the back door to the kitchen, where Auntie was waiting, rosary beads in hand. One hundred and thirty-six rounds of it completed since Rita had departed for Buffalo.

Jasus, Mary and Joseph, she thought while taking Rita by the hand and leading her to the bedroom, where the door was quietly closed behind them.

Brian watched all this in a daze, expecting everyone to be happy now that his mother was home. Homecomings were supposed to be happy, weren't they? Weren't they? Why couldn't there be happiness?

When his father came home from the Navy, the whole city, the whole country, was happy. Something was wrong here, and, as usual, the adults knew something he didn't.

Please, where is the happiness?

His father was coming up the staircase with more luggage. Setting the bags beside the back door, he removed his hat. Hanging it on the coat tree in the corner where Arrow's bed and bowl used to be, he turned to Brian.

"Hey, sport, sit down, take a load off," his father encouraged with a forced smile. Brian pulled a chair out and watched his father light a cigarette. He sat down across from his father, who was looking out the window over the sink. Staring out the window. He turned to Brian.

"Listen," he began, then stopped to take a deep breath, "the operation was real hard on your mother, they took…they amputated her left shoulder. All of it. Some of the chest, too."

Brian winced.

Chick stopped, took a drag on his cigarette, letting smoke slowly escape his nostrils.

"Listen, what can I say, there's a lot of medicine. Medications for the pain. So's you know, your mother won't be quite herself. You've got to be on your best behavior'n all. Jesus, son, I don't know how to explain it all. I just don't."

"Can I see her?"

"Sure, but let Auntie and her have a little time together."

Brian absorbed the information slowly. "Can I go feed my tumbler?"

"Sure, sure. Don't stray too far, just in case she wants you. Okay?"

"I'll be on the garage roof."

After feeding Citation, he let the bird launch itself eagerly into flight. He watched it perform series after series of avian acrobatics before signaling it to return to the coop. The sleek roller landed on his hand displaying a ration of seed. Closing the cage door, he wondered if Citation needed a mate. Being alone in a cage can't be any fun, he thought. Then too, she should have a companion to fly with, to pass on her superior tumbling skills.

He heard the Chrysler start up. Looking down from the garage roof, he watched it make a U-turn in the drive. He raced down from the roof as fast as he could, but as he turned the corner of the house, all he saw were flashes of chrome and black paint turning onto Partridge Street. Returning Benny's automobile, he guessed.

Mrs. Urtz, on her way out, passed him as he entered the kitchen door. A little visit to say hello, she said, patting his arm, encouraging him to come downstairs any time to watch the television. Promising to do that, he closed the door quietly behind him. There at the table sat his mother and Auntie. Walking to his mother's side, he watched Auntie finish pouring a nip of whiskey into their teacups. She returned it to the black pocketbook hanging on her chair. Rita pulled Brian closer with her right arm, looking up into his face with curiosity as though he were an urchin off a street corner. She was dressed in a loose-fitting sleeveless nightgown that gave much exposure to her diminished left side. The procedure had been so extreme she looked off-kilter, he thought. Brian gritted his teeth as he stared down at a surgical scar where her arm and shoulder had been.

Across the table, Auntie slurped tea from her saucer, eyes roving from mother to son.

"You'll have to sit down and get me caught up on school and sports. It seems like I've been gone months, oooh, how do they say it in the movies, *I've been gone eons and eons, daaarling*. Does that sound better? I'm blabbering now, blabbering and babbling… it's the medicine, honey. How does my hair look? I just can't brush it out like I used to. Auntie will do it for me, won't you? I remember when I was a little girl she did it every Sunday, didn't you, yes… *ring around the rosy, a pocketful of posies, ashes, ashes, All… Fall… Down*! Remember that? God, you were the best Auntie."

Rita's monologue stopped. She reached for a cigarette and lit it. Exhaling, she looked up at Brian, at her side. She eyed him curiously.

'Hi there, sonny boooy. Who dat, sonny boy?" she crooned, her index finger tapping his chest. A spasm of giggles made her choke on cigarette smoke. Recovering, she looked closely at him again.

"You'll have to sit down and get me caught up on school and sports and your pigeon. Can't forget the pigeon, can we?"

Suddenly, she lapsed into silence. Her right hand slipped from his waist to take up the smoking cigarette from the ashtray.

He looked over at Auntie, whose lips formed the words *Jasus, Mary, and Joseph.*

"Where did Dad go?" Brian asked.

"He returned Mr. Mizzeli's automobile," Auntie piped up. "He had to go into work right away. Mr. McEvoy called."

"Jeez, I wanted to go with him in the Chrysler."

"Gawd love ya, boyo, you can spend a bit of time with your mother," Auntie snapped. "Come now, I'll fix you a bologna sandwich."

"No thanks, I, I have to study for a history test."

Rita was staring down at the smoking cigarette in the ashtray.

"Okay, Ma?"

A crooked smile distorted her lips as he backed away.

The history exam had been a jumbled blur of dates, names, medieval battles, kings signing parchment treaties, naked Indians hurling spears at Henry Hudson. Climbing the backstairs, books clutched tightly in his arm, his mind was in turmoil.

In disguise, his mother had stepped out of a foreign movie, speaking a strange language. That's the only explanation that made sense to him. All during the test his eyes inadvertently strayed to Gina's profile in the row next to him. His eyes kept staring at her left breast as she wrote out test answers. All he could think about was Frenching and her caressing hand. He would suddenly look up and see Sister Eugene staring at him with those nun's x-ray vision eyes that said she knew exactly what he was thinking, each and every sinful thought, guarantying him an express ride to the all-consuming flames of hell.

He just couldn't seem to concentrate on schoolwork anymore, except maybe for the music class they had once a week when one of the student teachers from Saint Rose College came in to teach the class. It was always the same beautiful girl, about his height, and she wore lipstick. Long brown hair fell to her shoulders. She smiled a lot, making learning about music fun. Why couldn't she teach them history and geography? Her congenial smile reminded him of his mother's smile, the way she used to smile. It was a different smile now, an alien, freakish smile that accompanied her new language. Her eyes, more often than not, were dilated by medicine or alcohol. Or both. It was a new smile and he didn't like it. He wanted the old smile back.

Entering the kitchen with those thoughts running through his mind, Brian looked up to see his mother at the table with Monsignor McGinty. Clad in her flower print apron, Auntie was at the sink filling a kettle with water.

"Here's our young hero, our baseball star, home from the halls of academia," McGinty crooned.

A tall, solid man, his voluminous black cassock with red trim, did nothing but emphasize broad shoulders, a thick frame. The red beanie perched on his white head gave added emphasis to a swarthy face. When Brian had served mass for him when he was still a parish priest, he remembered staring at his feet encased in what must have been size 15 boots, big leather boots with rawhide laces worn by lumberjacks in the north woods. An older altar boy had told him that before Father McGinty got the *calling*, he had, in fact, been a lumberjack in Maine, where he'd been born and raised.

McGinty, it was said, was expert with a double-bladed ax, a chainsaw, a knife, and a gun. With spiked irons fastened to his boots, he could climb trees like a squirrel to heights of seventy and eighty feet.

His epiphany had come one day while working a particularly lofty grove of old-growth spruce high in the northern Adirondacks. Standing in a clearing lighting a smoke after a lunch break, he heard the paralyzing cracking and snapping of a falling tree. Out of curiosity, he looked up to see the green colossus come crashing down from the heavens and land mere feet and inches from him, spraying him with dirt and bark where he stood frozen like a statue. When the cigarette, still clamped in his index and second fingers, burned down to a searing red tip burning his skin, he snapped out of his paralytic trance. Turning about, he grabbed his black and red mackinaw, his lunch pail and thermos and walked out of the woods. Twenty-seven miles to the village where he lived. There, he'd entered the small clapboard Catholic Church, marched straight to the altar rail and got down on his knees. Calling out in his gruff voice, he asked God what he wanted him to do. The black sheep had returned to the flock, begging the shepherd for guidance and forgiveness.

A raspy, gravelly voice had called back that the first thing he could do was close the front door so the heat wouldn't escape. Next thing on the list was to come into the sacristy and help fix a malfunctioning light switch and, with God's help, the rest would follow.

"Hi Monsignor," Brian said as he went to his mother's side and cautiously kissed her cheek. Her black hair smelling of lavender, he surmised Auntie had recently washed and combed it for her, as well as assisting her into the pink robe that shielded her left side.

"How's the lad? Been a good soldier of Christ, eh? Come here and let me take a look at ya," McGinty said.

Setting his books on the table, Brian moved slowly to McGinty's side of the table.

His upper arm was clamped in the monsignor's bear trap of a hand.

"Tell me the truth now, you been minding your P's and Q's?" McGinty asked slyly winking across the table at Rita.

Bewildered as to what P's and Q's were, Brian stood there silently chewing a mental cud.

"What's this, cat got the tongue?" Another wink across the table. "Now, be honest with me, no prevarication, no lasciviousness, no lechery? Come, come, spill the beans laddy. How many girls are chasing after you? Come now, out with it."

Coloring slightly at the mere suggestion of girls chasing him, Brian tottered on the brink, then burst out.

"I've been too busy with my schoolwork and ah… basketball to notice girls. In fact, I better get to my homework…"

"Sure now, homework can wait a wee bit." McGinty's hand clamped down tighter. "Well, well, well, you'll soon be goin' to dances and parties with the *opposite sex*, eh? You'll have to guard against the devil's temptations. Mind now, always on the watch against sins of the flesh, impure thoughts and actions, eh… good Catholic altar fella that you are."

Brian's mind experienced minor temblors at the sound of the word— *sex*. Somebody must have squealed on him, maybe one of the other altar boys. God forbid his mother or Auntie had somehow intuited what lay behind his frequent trips to the Dipsy Doodle.

"Remember, jocko, you're a soldier of Christ, thy sword and buckler shall protect thee. Smite the devil in his insidious quest for your pure sinless soul." With that, the muscular hand pulled him closer. "No patty cake with the watchamacallit, eh?" he whispered in Brian's ear.

At last, the hand dropped from his arm. Brian massaged his shoulder while eyeing the monsignor.

He breathed a little easier when Auntie set the steeping pot of tea on the table and asked him to bring in an extra chair from the dining room, knowing full well that McGinty's interrogations could be wearisome. With the three adults busy with their tea, Brian slipped off quietly to his bedroom. There he changed quickly into his dungarees, sweatshirt and high-top sneakers. Just as quickly, he slipped down the front stairs, leaped down from the porch steps to the sidewalk and raced across the street to Bobby's house.

Bounding up the steps, he was met by Mrs. McNally exiting the door with a pound cake clutched in her sinewy arms. After a greeting and assurance that his mother was receiving visitors, he turned to the staircase, taking the steps two at a time. He found Bobby in his bedroom sprawled in the middle of the floor, flanked by two sets of bunk beds, reading a comic book.

"Come on, let's go down and feed the Freihofer bakery horse. Mr. Early should be coming up the block real soon. We can shoot some marbles while we wait," Brian said.

Discarding the comic book, Bobby rummaged in an open dresser drawer overflowing with sweat socks, T shirts, a brown paper bag containing the uneaten half of a peanut butter and jelly sandwich, a Boy

Scout sash with several merit badges attached, a blue and white basketball jersey with number ten on the back, a pair of Jockey shorts, a
picture torn from a magazine of Bob Cousy accepting his NBA championship ring with the Boston Celtics. From the jumble, Bobby pulled
his bag of marbles.

Noticing how quiet the McNally residence was, Brian turned to his
friend. "Say, where is everybody?"

"Ah, twins have tap dancing lessons, Greg is refereeing a basketball
game at the CYO, and I think Sean's raking leaves for the Gardner sisters."

"Yeah, but I don't hear the baby yelling or crying."

"He's downstairs. Colleen is babysitting him while my mother is
visiting at your house."

They sprinted to the grassy side alley between the McNally house and
the Schermerhorn house, the matching two-story home next to it. Bobby
dumped his collection of glassies and steelies on the ground. From this
mixture of marbles he selected several multi-colored peewees, leaving
the large glass and steel marbles for another time. Pulling his favorite
shooter from a watch pocket of his dungarees, Brian prepared to knuckle down against Partridge Street's acknowledged master of the game.

But first, the boys lagged to see who would go first. Brian stepped
to the edge of the roughed-out circle and tossed his peewee marble as
close to the opposite edge as he could get it. The marble rolled a few
inches and came to a stop three feet shy of the line. After surveying the
situation, Bobby tossed his marble at a lower angle and watched it roll
past Brian's by a mere inch or two, but enough for him to win first shot.
He arranged 13 marbles in the center of the circle, roughly in a cross
pattern, and then moved outside the circle. He dropped to one knee,
lowered his right arm with a marble fixed between thumb and index
finger, prepared to shoot. Closing his left eye, he sighted on the marbles
in the center. Propelling his marble with his thumb, he watched it strike
the arrangement of marbles, hitting one directly and knocking it outside
the ring.

"Lucky dog," Brian muttered, knowing he was in for a drubbing.

Whistling to himself, Bobby picked up the marble he had knocked outside, then proceeded with his next shot, which succeeded in hitting another marble but did not knock it out of the circle, nor did his shooter go out of the circle, so he had to let it stay where it stopped.

Now it was Brian's turn. Seeing Bobby's shooter a foot or two from the edge of the circle, he got as close as he could, but remained outside the circle, before knuckling down.

"Fairsies," Bobby called out, seeing in advance Brian's strategy.

Nodding his head, Brian knuckled down as close as he could to Bobby's shooter before sending his own shooter colliding into it, succeeding in knocking the shooter outside the circle and winning all the marbles.

"You the lucky dog," Bobby called out.

"Come on, let's play another game."

In the midst of the setup, they looked up to see a motorized van pull to the curb beside the chestnut tree. It was painted the same red and yellow as the horse-drawn bread wagon that had made neighborhood deliveries since they could remember. But this shiny new van had no brown horse pulling it. Fearing something had happened to the horse, they abandoned the game of marbles. But seeing Mr. Early filling his basket with orders, they were reassured.

Getting closer, they confirmed that indeed the man had the familiar white uniform shirt, white pants and black bow tie.

"What's up, Doc?" Early said with a wink.

"Where's Brownie, Mr. Early? Is he sick or something?"

"Ain't going to be no more Brownie. This is my new mode of transportation, fellas. Got me a little old Ford four-cylinder motor instead of an oat-eating, manure machine."

Flabbergasted, the boys looked at each other with concern.

"What'd you do with Brownie? Are you going to sell him?"

"Sell *her*, not *him*. 'Sides it wasn't up to me to get rid of all the horses, it was the high mucky-mucks that run the bakery. I guess they figure they'll save money in the long run. You don't have to house, shoe, or feed a gasoline engine. So help me Hannah, it's happening all over, even down at the plant. You know, they've got a newfangled machine that fills the jelly donuts with jelly. Replaced a half-dozen women who used to fill them by hand. Why, heck, there won't be any horses anywhere in the city in a few years. Everything will be motorized: the milkman, the iceman, the coalman, everyone, just like yours truly. Take my advice, start studying up on these gasoline engines, get in on the ground floor," he rattled on, stopping to pluck something from his delivery basket. Turning, he tossed a jelly donut to each boy.

"Stick to your studies fellas so's they don't replace you with a machine."

"Thanks, Mr. Early," Bobby said biting into the powder-coated donut that left a gob of red jelly at the corner of his mouth.

"But what will happen to the horses if nobody wants them anymore?" Brian asked, the jelly donut poised at his lips.

Mr. Early screwed up his face. After a few moments of contemplation, he blurted out, "Sent 'em all out West to a Dude ranch where they can eat all they want. The only work they'll do is haul tourists around a corral for a few minutes, then back to the barn for more oats, drink of water and a nap."

With that, he stepped down from the van with his delivery basket filled with loaves of bread, boxes of donuts and cookies for his house-to-house deliveries.

In his wake, he left the boys to ponder the loss of their aged friend Brownie and the future of jelly donuts in the age of modernization.

Later that day, they hiked many blocks past the Saint John's high school, past Stackie's, even past the public school, at last arriving footsore at the sprawling site of the Freihoffer Bakery where Brownie had been stabled. Even at that late hour, the neighborhood surrounding the bakery was redolent with the aromas of fresh bread and donuts just out of the ovens. They felt obligated to investigate the malicious rumor of horses banished to the western frontier.

Climbing up onto the back fence that enclosed the yard where the horse vans were parked and the horses stabled, the two boys peered down at the empty bread wagons jammed unused, side-by-side, their shafts resting in the dirt. At the far end of the yard they could see the horse stables, now empty, that had at one time housed as many as two-dozen horses. On many a summer day, they would hike to the bakery to watch as the horses were fed, washed and curried. The old man who tended the animals would let the boys feed their favorite horses lumps of sugar or a carrot purloined from home.

At the end of summer, when apples garnished the branches of the Jews yard trees, they would stuff their pockets with the fruit and race to the horse stalls at the bakery to feed the tart, juicy apples to the chomping white teeth of the horses. The old fellow, in soiled work pants held up by suspenders that looped over his bony shoulders, would let the boys run a currycomb over the horse's thick hide. The old-timer with his gray, balding head would grasp the halter while Brian or Bobby reached up on the horse's flank with the currycomb and pull it down awkwardly. All the while the overpowering smells of horseflesh, manure, urine-soaked hay would flood their nostrils, purging the sweet smells wafting from the bakery.

The aged fellow, whose name they never knew, was always outfitted in the same suspendered work pants, feet plunged into calf-high rubber boots, and a sleeveless undershirt. His lined and whiskered face resembled a giant walnut. After a horse was curried, he would slip a feedbag of oats over the animal's head and lead it back to its stall. Shortly, another horse would be led into the paddock.

Shocked by the somber mood of the yard, the boys climbed down from the fence to inspect the abandoned bread wagons, already beginning to accumulate layers of dirt and soot from the bakery smoke stacks. A few of the spokes on the high wooden wheels were beginning to warp and crack. More than one wagon showed evidence of rodents taking up residence inside.

Investigating further, they heard the sounds of activity in a shed attached to the horse stalls. Inside the cramped, dim interior the boys saw the old man, who was still clothed in the soiled pants, but now a leather jacket covered his torso. Startled, he looked up from an open valise into which he was pitching various articles of clothing and toiletries. The boys backed into the paddock as he approached.

"Well, look around, lads, take one last look, 'cause real soon the place will be filled with motor vans and their stinking exhaust and no end of noise and filth. Nope, no more horses and no more Shorty Johnson to look after'em. What the devil is the world coming to, I ask ya?" he grumbled, looking out at the empty horse stalls and the abandoned bread wagons.

"Where's Brownie and all the other horses? What happened to them?"

"Well now, they got a one-way ticket to the glue factory, that's what. With any luck, I'll be joining them."

"Glue factory? Mr. Early told us they were shipped out West to a dude ranch," Brian said.

"Hah, dude ranch is it! Every damn one of 'em off to the glue factory."

"Where's the glue factory? Maybe we can go there and feed them apples and carrots?" Bobby suggested.

"Apples and carrots is it? You'll not be feedin' anything there, lads. They'll boil up the horses in big vats, everything gets cooked up: hides, bones, the insides, the outsides, all boiled down into a big tub 'a glue."

The boys looked at each other in disbelief, eyes wide, lips trembling.

"But they were supposed to go out West to a dude ranch, they were supposed to," Bobby insisted, tears welling in his eyes.

"Dude ranch, huh. Maybe that's where old Shorty will go. Play patty cake with the tourists and the movie stars and eat chocolates and sugar plums. Ah, away with ya, get away before they send yuz to the glue factory," he said, spittle spraying from his lips.

Eyes staring straight ahead at the empty horse stalls, the boys began backing up, then turned and ran, climbing up and over the fence and leaving the old man to finish packing his kit before reluctantly leaving what had been his home for twenty years.

<u>20</u>

Downtown

After inspecting the crease he'd just ironed in his dungarees, Brian finished buttoning his shirt, completing his date preparations with a quick buff of his cordovan shoes. Looking up, he saw Auntie standing in the bedroom doorway, wiping her hands on a towel.

"Now look at you, and a part in the hair. Gawd love ya. Where are you off to?"

"Just a movie."

"On a Friday night is it? Why, you and your pal always go to a Saturday matinee."

"We won't be out late," Brian said with a trace of irritation in his voice.

"Well now, before you go, you'll please to help your mother from her bath. Me old bones ain't strong enough to lift her out of the tub."

Proud of the strength and masculinity of his growing body, Brian began a march to the bathroom where his mother was bathing in the claw foot tub. Opening the bathroom door and stepping into the steamy interior, he came up short. It was the first time he could remember seeing his mother naked. Before him were all the heinous effects of the surgeries staring him in the face. It shocked him. He clenched his teeth.

Auntie moved to his side to assist in any way possible.

Modestly, Rita attempted to cover what remained of her chest with her right arm. Moving closer, Brian could see the red surgical scars, enhanced by the bathwater, running up her left side where the arm and shoulder had been amputated. With half her torso cut away, she was diminished.

Moving closer, he could see that her left breast had also been removed. A small pink nipple of her right breast peaked out from the crook of her arm. She looked away as Brian stopped at the side of the tub. As he stood there dumfounded, Auntie handed Rita a bath towel.

"I can't find my balance. I'm clumsy," she mumbled apologetically.

With Auntie's assistance, Rita attempted to cover her nakedness. Carefully, Brian reached down securing his arm under her right armpit, he could feel her breath tickle his ear, could smell the odor of whisky. He lifted her up, surprised at how light she was. He placed her carefully on the bathmat, half expecting her to fall down if he withdrew his arm. Auntie moved closer to support her. When she was standing and covered with the towel, he turned to leave.

"Will you kiss me?" Rita whispered.

Turning slowly to his mother, he pressed his lips hesitantly to her cheek, then hurried from the bathroom leaving Auntie to fuss and fret over her.

"I'm off to the movies," he called, while pulling on a blue suede jacket and heading to the front stairwell.

On the sidewalk, he was stopped by Dinny Healy dressed in a blue suit and black bowler hat and clutching a small bouquet of flowers.

"Well ain't you the spiffy fella, eh? Would the missus be receiving visitors? I've got a bit of a nosegay for her."

"She's just out of her bath; maybe you'd better give the flowers to Auntie."

"Now, Maggie's still here, is she? I'll just say hello to me old pal."

Before Brian could resume his flight across to Bobby's house, Dinny grabbed him by the arm drawing him near in a conspiratorial embrace.

"Now, listen, boyo, here now, what's yer hurry? Have ya heard this one? There once was a fellow named O'Doole, who found red spots on his tool, his doctor a cynic, said get out of me clinic, and wipe off that lipstick, you fool."

Healy released his grip on Brian's arm and doubled over in silent laughter while Brian stood there, his face expressionless. Gasping and sputtering, Healy straightened up, saliva garnishing his lips.

"…and wipe off that lipstick you fool. I, be Jasus, be Jasus, ain't that the damnedest, by golly?"

Observing his young friend standing beside him impassive, Healy's smile evaporated.

"You do get it, don't ya laddy?…wipe off that lipstick… I mean it's as plain as the nose on yer gob! For Christ's SAKE!"

"Gotta run, Mr. Healy, thanks for the joke," Brian said backpedaling from Healy, ready to turn and sprint across the street.

"Joke? It's a Limerick!" he yelled, watching Brian's retreat. "A *joke* he sez. What the devil, they just let you out of the monastery? By Christ, I don't know what's got into these youngsters. Well, well, well, now Maggie's the girl for a good limerick, fair or foul, now, now… there once was a young maiden named Molly…" he muttered, ascending the steps to the Reilly abode.

Brian reached the top steps of the front porch just as Bobby exited the staircase. They looked at each other and smiled. Except for the color of their long sleeve shirts, they were dressed identically, right down to the blue suede jackets and buffed cordovan shoes. Bobby's pomaded hair may have been a shade darker, but the new part on the left was the same.

They continued down the front steps to the sidewalk.

"You got enough money?"

"Plenty, I've been saving all my paper route tips," Bobby said.

"And I've got two dollars of my birthday money, plus twenty five cents Auntie gave me for going to Franco's grocery for her."

"We should have enough for sodas after the movie."

"You tell your mother where we're going?" Brian said.

"Heck no, told her we're just going up to the Madison."

"Same here. This is the first time I've been downtown to a movie on my own."

"Me, too."

"Don't tell the girls that," Brian cautioned. "Pretend like we do it all the time. We'll catch the Madison Ave. bus down to Pearl and walk over to the Palace Theatre. That's the biggest movie house I've ever seen. My father took me there once. We got in free 'cause he showed his badge," Brian said.

"I've never been inside."

"It's got balconies and loges and red velvet curtains all over the walls, even the stage has these big red curtains that open up when the movie starts."

"What's playing?" Bobby said.

"A movie called *On The Waterfront*, it's all about longshoremen and boxing, plus a newsreel."

"Doesn't matter much what's playing, 'cause Eileen finally got her braces off and said I could kiss her if I wanted to."

"Yeah, maybe even some of that Frenching," Brian said.

"Think so?"

"Sure. We'll get seats up in the balcony so we can have a some privacy. If we went to the Madison, there's always a bunch of kids running up and down the aisles and making noise."

Walking past the Dipsy Doodle, they looked in the window to see the high school kids crowded in all the booths and counter stools, even some girls dancing near the jukebox.

Two blocks farther, Bobby stopped in front of Eileen's house.

"We'll wait for you here," he called to Brian as he mounted the porch steps.

The two couples stood at the corner of Madison and Ontario waiting for the bus. Bobby noted that Eileen displayed her newly straightened white teeth with an uninhibited smile. A bit of posturing and petting just might lead to some healthy frolicking up in the balcony, he conjectured.

"Oooh, I can't wait to see Marlon Brando; he's so, so sexy," Gina announced.

"Well, what's so great about him? It's not like he's anything close to Mickey Mantle or Yogi Berra," Brian retorted.

"He's way, way better and different. Eileen and I saw him at the Palace in *The Wild One*. We snuck down on a Saturday for the matinee."

"I think James Dean is even cuter," Eileen added.

"You've been to the Palace already?" Brian asked.

"Sure, haven't you?"

"Yeah, well me and Bobby go to the Palace all the time."

"Hey, here comes the bus," Bobby called, his hand clutched tightly in Eileen's.

They got off the bus at State and Pearl where they began their walk to the movie theatre. Along the way they passed brightly lighted department stores with display windows showing the latest styles in men and women's fashions. The five and ten store had a cart out front with a man selling popcorn to the crowds of people moving back and forth on the sidewalk and entering and exiting the various stores.

Passing another movie theatre on their trek to the Palace, they noticed a 3-D horror movie was playing. Excited by the possibility of seeing axes and long, sharp butcher knives come hurtling out of the screen, all possible because of some funny little paper glasses you wore, they vowed that would be the next movie they would attend.

The girls pulled their boyfriends to a stop in front of a women's dress shop whose plate glass window displayed the latest New York fashions on thin-limbed, faceless mannequins. Though the boys grumbled, both used the opportunity to inspect their pomaded hair reflected in the window glass. Assured that not a single hair was out of place, they gently tugged at the girls' hands to get them moving again.

At the intersection where the Palace Theatre occupied an entire wedge-shaped city block, they paused to admire the soaring stone and brick edifice. The marquee ablaze with neon lights and colorful signage informed the passing public that the latest Hollywood film, *On the Waterfront*, from "the world's most accomplished director," was now playing.

In the twilight, they watched as hundreds of light bulbs snapped on, adding even more brilliance to the theatre marquee. Crossing through traffic, they headed directly to the little box office kiosk centered below the flashing neon marquee. Inside the ticket booth, an overhead light outlined the uniformed vendor in her white blouse and red and white pillbox cap with gold trim. The hat perched jauntily on a head of raven-colored hair; she looked up from a movie magazine at the two approaching couples stepping onto the curb. Out of nowhere, a one-armed man in a ragged Army trench coat, with the gold stripes of a sergeant, approached the couples with his overseas cap turned up. She watched the taller of the two boys push past the war veteran while the two girls hurriedly pulled coins from their purses to drop into the cap.

The girl in the box office could see quite clearly the tall boy's face; his jaw clamped shut, his eyes narrow slits, as though he had seen a ghost. Then the girl with the long black hair was at his side, her hand massaging his shoulder, then going to his face, caressing it. Pulling his head down, she kissed his cheek. All the time that she was talking to him, he stared ahead at something in the distance. At last, he looked down at the girl's face and he, too, smiled.

The shorter boy was at the window with its small opening in the glass panel. A dollar bill was placed in the scooped out bowl of the marble countertop. Taking the money, she pressed a red button on a chrome-plated panel in front of her. Two red tickets popped up. She tore them away and passed them through the small opening in the window. Next, the tall boy, his suede jacket zipped to the neck, stepped up and placed his money in the small bowl.

Watching the two couples move through the theatre entrance doors, the cashier pulled a small compact, along with a tube of lipstick, from her purse. Opening the compact, she puckered her lips while looking into the round mirror. Quickly, she swiped the tube across her lips. Putting the compact and tube of lipstick back into her purse, she undid the top button of her blouse. Jerking her head from side-to-side and seeing no one approaching the kiosk, she cupped her hands under her breasts. Her red lips pouting slightly, she went back to thumbing through the movie magazine.

At the entrance door, an usher in a navy blue uniform with gold piping silently ripped the tickets in half, allowing the two couples to enter the theatre lobby.

In front of them was a long counter where candy, popcorn and soft drinks were sold to an eager gathering of moviegoers. Both Gina and Eileen worked their way up to the glass counter, while Brian and Bobby stood back.

Bobby jerked his head toward the wide stairways carpeted in red on both sides of the snack counter. The stairways tapered as they rose to the balcony entrance on the second floor.

"Let's take the girls upstairs to the balcony. I think it's darker up there," Bobby suggested.

"Sure, I've never been in a balcony. The Madison sure is dinky compared to this place, huh?" Brian said.

"Yeah and look at all the fancy statues in the walls and the red curtains all the way up to the ceiling. Must be a hundred feet to the roof.

Finding back row seats in the center of the narrow balcony, they were assured there would be only one row in front of them and no one in back. All but two seats were currently empty. A brass rail topping the balcony's short wall separated them from a precipitous drop to the first level. In the subdued lighting it appeared to be a bottomless pit. As soon as Brian put his arm around Gina's shoulder, he could feel her snuggle up closer to him. He shook his head when she held the box of popcorn up to him, reasoning that, if he ate popcorn, the little kernels would get stuck in his teeth, possibly compromising his newly acquired kissing technique. Teeth he had spent at least ten minutes cleaning. When the house lights dimmed, Brian was pleased to see that most of the seats in front them were not occupied, but for a few scattered couples.

What a relief it was, Brian thought, not to have to listen to all those kids at the Madison, yelling and running up and down the aisles. Here at the Palace you could enjoy the movie in silence and semi-darkness and *make out* without the constant interruptions from inconsiderate juveniles. Thankfully, the Palace catered to an adult audience, he reflected.

The towering red velvet curtains on the stage began to slide silently to the wings as music started playing. Suddenly, the huge screen was filled with black and white images.

He felt Gina's hand brush his leg. Gleefully anticipating a solid hour of necking and petting, he looked up to see a man and woman enter the aisle in front of them. And watched with added annoyance as they settled into seats directly in front of him and Gina. Seeing the red bow tie and pipe clenched in the man's teeth, it dawned on Brian that the couple was none other than Mr. and Mrs. Urtz, his downstairs neighbors. Momentarily, the credits rolled for the feature presentation.

Reaching over, Brian tapped Bobby on the shoulder, indicating with a tilt of his head the presence of the Urtzes. A reaction not forthcoming, he glanced over to see Bobby and Eileen entangled in a passionate embrace.

He whispered in Gina's ear that perhaps if they were quiet and watched the movie, his neighbors wouldn't recognize him. If they did see him, he knew that information would be transmitted to his parents, sooner than later, and he would be in *Dutch* for lying about going to the Madison theatre. He attempted once more to pass on the Urtz information to Bobby, but was appalled at seeing his friend so involved in kissing Eileen, he was unapproachable. And too, Brian was somewhat titillated by the aggressive response Eileen was making to Bobby's clumsy foreplay.

When Gina finally poked him in the ribs, he turned to the screen to see Marlon Brando, battered and bruised, walking down a gangplank with a crowd of angry men at his back. To add insult to injury, Gina whispered a bit too loudly how *yummy* Marlon was, causing Mrs. Urtz to turn in her seat and shush her with an index finger to her lips. With his face concealed in the folds of Gina's tresses, his lips caressing her neck, Brian escaped detection. Dividing his time between the escapades of Marlon and the sexual heat being generated by his best friend and Eileen, Brian lost interest in the movie, but kept a guarded eye on the Urtzes.

Occasionally, after looking over at Bobby and Eileen, he thought it might be a good idea if he cautioned them not to get too enthusiastic in their lovemaking or they might just attract the attention of the Urtzes. Even this thought was squelched when, midway through the film, Mr. Urtz began caressing his wife's shoulder and kissing her neck and ear. Brian's hands kept tightening into fists at the sight. While he was preoccupied with the Urtzes, Gina was completely captivated by the posturing, petulant movie star who, at that moment in the film, was attempting to seduce an innocent young woman.

When next he looked up at the screen, the movie was ending. Quickly, the Urtzes got to their feet and hurried to the exit with coats on their arms. Breathing a sigh of relief mixed with a measure of disgust, Brian looked over at Bobby and Eileen still intertwined and oblivious.

After the screen went dark and the house lights came up, Brian reached over to tap his friend's shoulder in a unsuccessful attempt to get his attention. Finally, he punched Bobby's arm.

"Come on, the movie's over."

As the other moviegoers trooped to the exits, Bobby and Eileen looked about bewildered.

"Boy, that was some movie," Bobby exclaimed, with a sheepish smile.

"Yeah well, we better hurry or we'll miss our bus."

With that, Brian and company fled the theatre into a night sparkling with neon lights and store windows ablaze to the nearby bus stop.

At her front door, Gina slowly unzipped Brian's blue suede jacket, allowing her to slip her hands inside and encircle his waist. She looked up into his blue eyes before pressing her lips to his. Drawing back, she surveyed his face.

"You're all tense, I can feel it in your back and see it in your face."

"Well, we narrowly escaped the Urtzes and now I've got a feeling that porch light is going to come on any minute. Maybe we better not get started."

Gina smiled. "Didn't I tell you my parents went to the dinner dance at the VFW post and they won't be home until midnight or later?"

"Hey, that's right. I think my father's taking my mother there, too. It will be her first time out since coming home from the hospital."

Withdrawing a house key from her purse, Gina inserted it in the front door lock. Brian's heart raced. He could feel blood pumping in his eardrums as they mounted the stairs. After checking to insure her parents were indeed gone, she took Brian's hand and led him to her bedroom. Flinging their coats onto a nearby chair, they came together and held each other tight. Gina's tongue pushed its way past his lips and teeth deep into his mouth. He removed the red neckerchief encircling her throat, letting it drop to the floor. Reaching for the chain at her neck that held a small ring signifying they were going steady, her hand caught his midway to her neck and pulled it down under her angora sweater. Her tongue made its way into his mouth again, triggering an eager response. Embracing on top of her bed, they continued their mutual exploration.

~

Climbing the back stairs as quietly as possible, Brian opened the kitchen door with stealth. Upon seeing Auntie sitting at the kitchen table, empty teacup before her, a rosary twisted around her arthritic hands, eyes closed in what appeared to be a peaceful sleep, he smiled. Wrapped in her ancient bathrobe, she snored fitfully.

The linoleum floor squeaking at Brian's every step, her eyes popped open.

"…and forgive them their trespasses forever, amen," she muttered untangling the rosary and depositing it in the cavernous pocket of her robe. Sniffing and pulling a Kleenex from another pocket, she wiped her nose and looked up to see Brian frozen in mid-stride.

"Well now, it's himself slipping in the back door. Come sit and talk to your old Auntie for a minute. Mind, I have no idea what time you came in, hair all tumbled about, eh? Come now, sit, and I'll make us a bit of tea."

With some reluctance, he did her bidding. Pulling out a chair, he draped his suede jacket over the back. Sprawling in the chair, he noticed the light on the radio illuminating the dials. Bending closer, he could barely hear *The Hit Parade* music coming from the speaker.

The kettle, always kept full, soon spouted steam accompanied by a high-pitched whistle that was squelched by Auntie. She pulled it from the gas burner and filled the cups.

"My mother and father back from the VFW yet?" he asked guardedly.

"No. I'm surprised. Rita shouldn't be out this late what with, ah, her condition."

"Heck, this is the first time they've been out since she came home."

"Sure and that's the truth of it. All's I'm sayin' is she might be better off getting her rest. That was a terrible thing they done to her, I don't mind telling you. Terrible."

Auntie placed the kettle back on the stove with a little too much force. "It ain't none of me business, but you wouldn't be doin' that to me. And way out there in Buffalo, for gawd sake. Might as well have been to the moon."

Brian sipped his tea trying to conceal a grin sparked to life by the diatribe he knew was coming.

Auntie poured a few ounces of tea onto her saucer and gave it a cooling puff before slurping it noisily. "She was always so particular about what she wore. Everything had to be perfect. A bit of a stain on a dress and off it came, a clean one in its place. Mind you, she was a fussy little girl. And look what they done to her, eh? Jasus, I never in me life."

"Jasus, Mary and Joseph," Brian mimicked.

"Don't go sassing your Auntie. You ain't that big I can't take you over me knee," she began with a raised eyebrow. Then added, "Well, maybe not over the knee, but I'll get youse in a head lock like that wrestler fella Pat Kelly. Then we'll see who has the last laugh, eh?"

Brian guffawed, choking on the mouthful of tea he was in the process of swallowing. Catching his breath, he looked over at his great Aunt.

"So, you've been watching more wrestling matches on television, down at the Urtzes'?"

"Well, they was wanting to go to the movies and asked if I'd sit with Terry whilst they was gone."

"Isn't watching wrestling matches a sin?"

Again, the eyebrow shot up. "Hush now with your sins. Why…why wrestling's just like watching a baseball game. An athletic contest is what it is."

Looking closely at Brian, realizing that he was baiting her, she pointed an index finger at him. "Oh, you're a bold one you are, bold as brass. Why I just might have to take you over me knee after all."

Laughing now with her, he stood up, grabbed his jacket from the chair. "Time for bed. I'll see you in the morning."

"I'll sit up for a bit. Now mind, don't forget your prayers'n say one for your old Auntie. And your dear mother, eh?"

With that he closed the door to his bedroom. Piling all his clothes on his desk chair he climbed into bed in his underwear. Sleep came quickly. And with it seductive thoughts of Gina.

~

Something, some noise close by, woke him up. Rolling over close to the wall that separated his bedroom from his parents' room, he heard glass shatter. Glass breaking? Wide-awake now, he propped himself up on an elbow.

Rita stood facing her makeup table; the shattered glass from the broken mirror littered the tabletop. Stumbling backward, she came to rest on the edge of the bed. She watched as Chick carefully removed shards of broken glass and placed them in a nearby wastebasket. He returned the multitude of vials containing her medications, scattered on the floor, to the bureau top.

Cleaning the vanity table as best he could, he rose from his knee and began removing his suit coat, then a blue striped tie. Lastly, he slipped the suspenders from his shoulders.

"I can't stand to look at myself anymore. Who would?" Rita shrilled, her eyes blazing.

Chick continued undressing in silence.

"Are you listening?"

He turned from the closet where he had hung his suit. Now in pajama bottoms, he came to the bed and sat beside his wife.

"Better keep your voice down," he said, nodding his head at the wall. "I saw that woman cozying up to you at the bar."

"One of McEvoy's girlfriends is all," he said, a little too quickly.

Rita's right hand formed a fist that pounded her knee.

"You didn't have to throw your martini in her face," Chick added.

"She was flaunting her sex, rubbing your nose in it. Did you expect me to just stand there, the cripple wife?"

"Listen, let's get some sleep, huh?"

Rita's shattered body began quaking with pent up rage and anger. Her right hand went to her mouth. Her teeth came down on her index finger. Clamped on it. Tears flowed down her face as she sobbed, her head rocking back and forth.

When Chick tried to put his arm around her shoulder, she pushed away from him and got to her feet.

"You haven't touched me since I came home. Please take me one more time… just once. Please."

Chick got up from the bed. "Let me help you undress."

"I'm still a woman down here," she screamed, the hand on her crotch. "They didn't cut that away, those damn lying doctors."

Fully dressed, Rita climbed into bed. She pulled the sheet over her, pressing her face into the pillow while her body convulsed.

Brian continued staring into the darkness. When at last the room next door was silent, he closed his eyes, but sleep evaded him for the remainder of the night. Only when the light of dawn illuminated his room was he able to turn on his side and leave the troubled world behind.

<u>21</u>

Farewell, My Lovely

And then the cold weather came and with it snow, ice, and slush. Brian was forced to spend more and more time in the house. With Bobby's help, they constructed a small pigeon coop on the back porch against the wall, shielded on the east side by the enclosed stairwell. This provided added security and comfort for the tumbler, but when the temperatures dropped below zero for days at a time, he watched with concern as the pigeon shivered alone in its cage. As a last resort, he brought Citation down to the cellar relocating it to a wire cage near the coal furnace. It may be cramped he told himself, but it would be warm, it would not freeze to death. Not far away was Mr. Urtz's workbench with its jumble of vacuum tubes, meters, screwdrivers, drills and a large oscilloscope. Though the shivering stopped, the pigeon's feeding regimen diminished. He promised to seek the advice of Johnny Russian, but that never came to pass. He knew what the tumbler needed and wanted, but it was just too cold out to let it perform its aerial acrobatics. At the first sign of sun and warmth, he would bring the pigeon outside for much needed air and exercise.

Above all else, the thing that worried him most was his mother's deteriorating health.

Brian began falling asleep in class. The nuns were lenient at first, but, after many warnings, he was sent home with a note he crumpled in a fist and dispatched to a gutter. For some inexplicable reason, he stopped seeing Gina outside of school. When she confronted him, he told her to stay away from him, to mind her own business. He even stopped helping Bobby with his paper route, this at a time when Bobby needed him most. He invented elaborate excuses for avoiding friends.

Sleepless night after sleepless night passed while he stationed himself as close to the bedroom wall as possible, listening for the slightest noise or bit of conversation. His mother was now the sole occupant of that bedroom. The alcove off the parlor had been converted to his father's makeshift billet.

Auntie was now bringing meals and tea to Rita at all hours of the day and night. Fighting sleep, Brian was on the alert for the click of a doorknob, the squeak of a hinge, a single spoken word. Nocturnal noises would generate images in his head: Auntie setting a tea tray on the nightstand beside Rita's bed. His mother sprinkling pills into the palm of her hand then washing them down with a tumbler of Jameson. His father moving in and out of the bedroom as quietly as he could, trying to escape her stinging recriminations, mere fictions of a failing body and mind.

Sleep avoided Brian on nights like that.

The management of the house—cleaning, preparing meals, attending to his mother like a private nurse, became Auntie's domain. Brian was also included in her purview. She would make his school lunch, iron his clothes, try to cheer him up with fantasies of miraculous recoveries. Saints surviving unscathed in the lion's den, the snake pit, the dungeon. A bit of prayer to St. Jude, a couple decades of the rosary would suffice, she believed. When these fictions failed to bolster his spirits, she regaled him with scenarios of the family packed in the old Ford, overloaded with camping and fishing gear, headed to a rented cottage on the shore of an Adirondack lake. The little blue coupe bounced and swayed down the highway as they all sang along to a tune blaring on the radio. Word games. Limericks. He was squeezed between his mother and father in the front seat. The trio quaked with laughter. Endless joking, horseplay and silliness to the point of embarrassment. The three musketeers, one for all and all for one. Hi ho, Silver!

These chimeras would always evaporate instantly when Rita screamed for Auntie's immediate attention. Or at the noise created when she sent the array of medications (sometimes by accident, sometimes on purpose) on the dresser top crashing to the floor.

His ear next to the opening in his side of the bedroom wall, the plaster gouged out by his hand. Alert to every sigh, sob, or profanity.

Finally, there was nothing left to believe in.

He turned away to stare into darkness.

Sleepless, around midnight, he heard his father park the Ford below his bedroom window. Minutes later, he listened as his parents' bedroom door opened.

"Ah, the detective returns," Rita began in a groggy voice. "The city safe from criminals, my dear? All the gangsters and their molls gone to bed?"

Chick continued undressing in silence, putting his wallet, keys, badge and change on the dresser top. Hanging his sport coat on a hanger in the closet, he turned to face his wife.

"I think I'll sleep in the alcove."

"Sleep wherever thee wishes. Hand me… hand me that glass of water before you depart. I'm so thirsty with all these pain pills. Go ahead, check it, Dick Tracy. It is, in fact, mere tap water devoid of any distilled spirits."

Chick turned from the dresser with the glass. He sat on the side of the bed holding the water glass to her lips. She gulped at it eagerly, spilling some on her neck.

After wiping her mouth with the back of her hand, she laid her head back on the pillow. Her eyes closed.

"I notice you don't leave your pistol on the dresser any more. Afraid mother will do something drastic?"

"Nah, it's safer for all concerned in the gun closet."

"Under lock and key…lock and key."

Her head slumped down sideways on the pillow. Chick got up, switched the light off and walked down the hall to his cot in the alcove.

It was odd, Brian thought, the only person who visited Rita was Bobby's mother and Mrs. Urtz. Of course, Auntie was there all the time, so she didn't count. That was funny, too. How could she not count?

One night after his father came home from his shift, long after he had undressed and gone to the alcove cot, Brian heard his mother moaning, real low. He got out of bed and walked barefoot to her bedroom. He opened the door as quietly as he could and padded noiselessly into the dark room. The bed was empty. His foot touched something. His mother was sprawled on the floor; an empty bottle of pills lay nearby. He raced down the hall to get his father.

The next thing he knew, his father was carrying Rita down the back stairs to the car, telling him to take care of Auntie, then changing his mind and saying "YES, YES, you can come, get your shoes on." And he did. Arriving at the emergency room at St. Peter's Hospital, he followed his father inside. His father was yelling at the intern that she needed to have her stomach pumped, right away. A white uniformed nurse took Brian by the hand and led him into a deserted waiting room, where he watched a janitor mop the silent, empty corridor.

His father had to shake him several times before he woke up, blinking and looking around at the strange place he was in. Where was his desk, his trophies? For a minute he thought he was dreaming. Dreaming, yes that's what he wanted to do all along. Just dream. Walking to the car in the cold and dark brought him quickly awake. He realized then he was dressed only in his pajamas and rubber boots. When he finally did crawl into bed, Auntie stood over him in a flannel bathrobe, her gray hair trapped in a hairnet. Instantly, he fell asleep.

He didn't go to school that day or the next. On the third day his father brought Rita home from the hospital. Auntie met them at the top of the stairwell and escorted her to the bedroom. Under Auntie's prodding, Brian went in to see her, but she turned away to face the wall pretending to sleep. Reluctantly, he returned to his room to sit at his desk staring down at the page of a textbook. Rubbing his eyes, he was suddenly aware that he was staring down at a color illustration of a cherub with elaborate white wings sprouting from its shoulders. Immediately, he envisioned himself flying alongside Citation, feathered wings beating the air, both performing mid-air somersaults, soaring and gliding above the rest home where Johnny Russian stood, clapping and staring up at the spectacle. A knock at his door and call from Auntie shattered the dream.

Gradually, Rita imprisoned herself in the bedroom, allowing only Auntie to enter it. Auntie became her nurse and body servant, at her beck and call, always glad to serve, to prostrate herself if need be before her precious niece. Rita's main preoccupation in her self-imposed exile was rummaging through old albums, yearbooks, and trunks, bursting shoeboxes tied with string. Brian helped his father bring up a dust-covered steamer trunk from the cellar. They scrubbed it clean on the back porch before depositing it at the foot of her bed.

Occasionally, Auntie would enlist him to carry a bulging paper bag down to the cellar to be burned in the coal furnace. Investigations of these brown packages revealed curios: black and white snapshots of his mother and father dressed for a costume party; he in a dress, a lampshade for a hat; she in a white Navy uniform with sleeves rolled up revealing nautical tattoos. A clay pipe was clenched in her teeth, a white sailor hat perched rakishly on her head. A large sepia photograph of a wedding party banquet. Looking closely, he recognized a much younger Uncle Joe and Uncle Marty. There was Auntie, Margaret Duffy, seated next to the bride, attractive and smiling, but doomed to live out her life as a spinster. His father in a pinstripe suit and tie, his black hair combed straight back. Into the coal fire they went.

A black and white of Chick sitting at the end of a dock, casting his fishing rod with one hand, the other holding a toddler encased in an orange life jacket. A 5x7 colorized picture of a little girl, maybe seven or eight, seated on a brown and white pony, her cowgirl boots in the stirrups of an elaborate western saddle with an abundance of silver ornamentation, even a small lariat attached to the pommel. On her head, a cowboy hat tilted back revealing brown spit curls, wide brown eyes. A reluctant smile exposed a missing front tooth. On the back of the photograph a name: Rita, a date: 1936. In her late teens, a newspaper clipping with a photo of Rita in a bathing suit sitting on a block of ice. The caption: *Local bathing beauty knows how to keep cool*!

It dawned on him that his parents had experienced all the joys and sorrows of the aging process, too. Their secret lives exposed! Inconceivable as it seemed, they had once been young and carefree. They had not appeared on earth as mature adult parents, after all. Why hadn't he discovered this earlier, been taught this in school or read about it in a magazine? He stored the cowgirl picture in a back pocket, unwilling to consign it to the flames. Soon, he resorted to filling an empty grocery bag when his pockets overflowed. Later, another bag was requisitioned.

All else turned to ashes before his eyes.

Post cards: a hula girl, palm trees, ocean surf, Hawaii. 1941. Cryptic messages from cryptic times, *Don't believe what you read in the papers; our ship survived the sneak attack. Or, Can't tell you where we're headed but weigh anchor in X days. XXX OOO.* Letters postmarked with a Navy APO. Inside a picture of three sailors at an outdoor café, drinking wine and smoking cigarettes. A portly waiter, white apron dropping to his shoe tops, smiling in the background. Another letter, the envelope with red lips pressed on the outside. Inside, a long narrative whose principal topic was *missing you, P.S. – Brian goes to a day care center while I'm at work. He misses his father too.* Numerous X's and O's.

A snapshot of his father in full police uniform saluting another policemen, but one of rank, judging from the medals and ribbons on his chest.

He set these aside, as well. His hand could not consign them to the furnace. Soon he had two overflowing bags of culled mementos saved from the flaming maw. He concealed these in the storage area next to the coal bin.

The discards kept coming. School papers: a book report by Miss Rita Stephens on *Silas Marner*. Grade B+. A handwritten poem by Rita Stephens to her best friend, Maureen Fitzpatrick. A photo album of girls playing badminton, a sleep-over, a nun at her desk in front of a blackboard. A drawing of a small boy with a poem underneath – *I'm going into the garden to pick worms. Yesterday I picked two wooly ones and one slimy one.*

All her memories, keepsakes, curios, souvenirs, gathered over a lifetime to be incinerated in a matter of minutes? No, he could not, would not allow this.

Also in the trunk was a velvet-covered box containing the ersatz diamond necklace he had given his mother for Christmas three years ago. He opened the hinged box; there inside, on a layer of blue satin, was the multi-string necklace of fake diamonds, glistening like the lights on a Christmas tree. At the time, he hadn't known the difference between real diamonds and costume jewelry. Why would he? They glistened, they sparkled, they pleased the eye. His mother wore them all that day in her bathrobe and that evening dressed for Christmas dinner. They sparkled. They sparkled still.

He put the necklace aside with the other booty.

Purging by fire went on for a week, perhaps longer, then stopped. He helped his father store the empty trunk and boxes she had plundered in her bedroom in their corner of the cellar. Later that evening, he descended alone to the cellar storage space to transfer the commandeered bags of his mother's memorabilia into the empty steamer trunk from whence they had come. Ashes to ashes, dust to dust.

Avast mateys, Long John Silver's treasure chest.

~

Bobby talked him into to playing hockey at Washington Park Lake. Get out of the house, get some air, will ya, Auntie encouraged. The snow had been cleared off the frozen ice by a small army of city parks employees who had little to do in the winter but shovel sidewalks and sprinkle rock salt on patches of ice. Wobbly at first, Brian's ankles slowly strengthened and soon he was swatting a puck across the ice to Bobby, who trapped it, did a backspin and sent it far ahead of Brian, who chased after it with his hockey stick waving back and forth in his hands.

Into the reeds and frozen cat'o nine tails the puck disappeared with Brian in hot pursuit. He felt the ice beneath his blades buckling. He stopped and heard the sickening sound of ice cracking. In a second, he was up to his waist in the water, his skates sinking in the muddy lake bottom, icy water up to his chest. He heard Bobby calling to him. Turning, he saw him lying on the ice nearby.

"Take the end of my hockey stick, come on, I'll pull you out."

He couldn't feel anything below his waist. His hand secured itself to the proffered hockey stick like a vice. Bobby began pulling slowly. Rising up onto the edge of the ice, his chest cleared the frigid water, but the ice once again gave way. He was back in up to his shoulders. He was too cold to be scared. He would just have to do what Bobby was yelling at him to do. Other skaters came close, but were warned to stay back for fear their added weight would send them all through the ice.

Again, he held onto the hockey stick with both gloved hands. And again, Bobby was able to pull him up onto the lip of the ice. Once he was out and into the safety zone, it was a slow process of inching him closer and closer to the thicker, solid ice. Finally, Bobby and two other skaters helped Brian to the opposite shoreline, where a wood fire was burning.

Brian stood there half frozen, rubbing his stiff gloves together. Bobby forced him to sit on a log. Tearing the skates off, he forced Brian's dry boots over ice encrusted wool socks. Brian stood over the flames shivering uncontrollably and wheezing. His fingers hurting terribly.

Seeing him hobble through the back door, Auntie blurted out her short prayer to the holy trinity, then began pulling the wet steaming wool coat and pants from his blue-tinged body. There he sat at the kitchen table wrapped in blankets, a hot water bottle in his lap, his feet submerged in a basin of water. Auntie put the teakettle on, talking to herself while doing so.

With his cup of tea steeping, she pulled the pint bottle of Jameson from her pocketbook. Filling a juice glass with whiskey, she placed it in front of Brian. Lifting the glass of spirits to his lips, Rita appeared in the kitchen doorway, dressed in nightgown and bathrobe, her hair uncombed.

She cut an evil look at Auntie.

"Don't you ever let him drink that filth again," she scolded.

That said, she hurried back to her bedroom. Both Auntie and Brian shuddered when the door slammed shut.

Stunned and confused, Auntie lifted the corner of her apron to her eyes and dabbed at the tears appearing there. Brian stared down into his cup of tea.

~

He was awakened by the wail of a prowl car, siren blaring, stopping abruptly in the driveway. Running from the bedroom, he saw Auntie fling open the kitchen door admitting his father and Monsignor Mc-Ginty. They hurried past Brian down the hallway to his mother's sanctuary. Moments later, Auntie emerged to take his hand and lead him into the bedroom. The monsignor was bending over Rita, his torso clad in black blocked her diminished, inert body. What was left of it. Brian watched terrified as the monsignor repeatedly made the sign of the cross over her head, anointing the lips, the eyelids, the forehead with holy oil, all the while mumbling Latin prayers. He removed a rosary from a pocket in his black ankle-length garment. Turning, he encouraged those kneeling behind him to join in the recitation of the rosary.

Auntie pressed a delicate, ornate, ivory rosary into Brian's hands. Much later, he learned she had presented the rosary to Rita on her First Communion—evidence that another scavenger had been at work rescuing memories from the conflagration.

His eyes closed, head bowed, Brian suddenly realized the prayers had stopped, the sound replaced by Rita's rasping, labored breathing.

Suddenly, the breathing stopped. Forever.

The room was frozen in silence. McGinty closed the eyelids, pulled the sheet over her face while Brian looked on, hoping someone would explain things. Surely, she would start breathing again after this elegant ecclesiastical ritual. The school religion books were full of miracles of people coming back to life. Why, even Jesus himself rose from the dead. Rita had been baptized, received her first communion, been confirmed. She and his father had been married in the Catholic Church; he had pictures hidden away to prove it. Surely, she would start breathing again.

But she didn't.

Auntie struggled to her feet, grabbed Brian's hand and pulled him from the bedroom. Seated at the kitchen table with her, he noticed her black hat with a veil contrasted sharply with her floral print apron. There was a knock at the back door. Out of nowhere, his father appeared and opened the door, admitting Doctor McCann, who had been summoned to fill out the death certificate.

Again, Brian questioned the wisdom of this. A misguided action, such as this, might otherwise invalidate the miracle in progress. Why not wait a day or two, let things settle down, give the miracle time to work, to gel?

Her tea steeping before her, Auntie sat rigidly at the table, a rosary entangled in her fingers, the colorful apron covering multiple sweaters, the round black hat and veil still perched on her gray head. Putting the rosary aside, her hands began an investigation of the pocketbook, her cornucopia. Out came a box of Vick's cough drops, a black change purse, an eyeglass case, a magnifying glass and, finally, a pint of whisky, the contents greatly diminished. She poured a bit into her tea and hesitated a split second before pouring a second generous measure.

On a gunmetal gray, blustery February morning, he heard the black Cadillac from the funeral home pull into the alley and wait with engine idling. Brian called out to his father and Auntie, while pulling on a heavy blue overcoat. In the kitchen, he sat in one of the chairs at the table. He fiddled with the dial on the radio, turning it back and forth, back and forth, finally turning it off.

Auntie stood at his side, dressed in black, head to toe; even her pocketbook was ebony. The veil was pulled down on the pillbox hat covering red eyes and nose.

"Come on, let's go; the limousine's here," his father called from the hallway.

Auntie turned and started walking toward the front stairwell.

Brian remained seated, his hands deep in his overcoat pockets.

"Brian?"

He sat there immobile, his chin tucked into his chest.

Losing patience, Chick walked into the kitchen.

"Didn't you hear, come on; we have to go to the church for the requiem mass."

"I'm not going," Brian muttered.

"You're not…what do you mean NOT GOING. You have to go."

"None of this should have happened. A couple of years ago we were swimming at Midcity Pool. We were at that camp on Crooked Lake; we were all trolling in that row boat. The church screwed up."

"Jesus Christ. What the, listen to me, there's a lot of things you're going to have to do in your life that's gotta get done whether you like it or not. Forget the church, that's up to you, but honor your mother, your family; that's what this is all about."

Brian looked up at his father. Chick put his hand on Brian's shoulder and squeezed it.

"I know how you feel, it's a lot of crapola is all I can say. Her chances were slim even without the operations. Come on, okay? I need your help."

Brian got to his feet, his father's hand still on his shoulder. They walked silently down the front stairs and around the corner of the house to the limousine. Auntie was in the back seat, her pocketbook resting on her lap, her rosary bridging crooked, gnarled hands.

The Cadillac limousine splashed through narrow streets, gutters clogged with the dregs of winter storms. At the church, relatives, family friends, even some of Brian's classmates were waiting on the church steps, many shielded with umbrellas. McEvoy and two other night squad detectives were standing off to the side of the church steps smoking cigarettes, talking.

The funeral mass, performed by Monsignor McGinty, was a brief rambling memorial that touched on such disparate subjects as omnipotence and eating meat on Friday. McGinty extolled Christ's limitless mercy and forgiveness, provoking a snort from Brian, causing Auntie to cut an icy look in his direction.

At the cemetery a cold, raw wind toppled the largest floral wreath standing precariously beside the grave on a tripod of thin metal legs. Ironically, the floral arrangement was from Benny Mizzeli, a man whom Rita had disparaged all of her married life.

The graveside ceremony finished, Brian hooked his arm through Auntie's and helped her back to the limousine that would return them to Partridge Street.

~

That Night. His feet were cold and sodden. The thin-soled cordovan shoes did him no good. Brian lighted a cigarette snitched from his father's pack of Chesterfields. He would wait in the black night as long as necessary. He knelt down beside the gravestone: *Devoted wife and mother*.

He would wait, goddamnit, until something changed.

The wind whipped about his head, turning his ears red. Icy.

"Come on, come on, where are the miracles now?"

Sure, the boulder somehow rolled aside magically allowing a globe of fire to ascend to the heavens. Well, he didn't see any ball of fire now or hear any fancy music. What he heard was an automobile engine. He watched headlights cut through the black. Caught in the twin beams of light, he winced and flipped the cigarette away.

A car door opened. Chick shuffled through the frozen grass and mud to Brian's side. The blue wool overcoat, the gray fedora caught in the headlights warped his shadow into a villainous caricature.

Chick knelt down beside Brian in front of her gravestone.

"I wish I could tell you something, but I can't. Here, she wanted you to have this."

It was a candid picture taken of him at bat in a Little League baseball game. On the back she had scrawled, *My Sonny Boy*.

The blue Ford cautiously negotiated the frozen track to the grave-yard exit.

22

The Wake

Relatives, neighbors and friends seen only at Thanksgiving and Christmas filled the living room. The men shed their suit coats, exposing suspenders, starched white shirts with ties, vests, even a gold watch chain, here and there, strained against a bulging stomach. Uncle Harry, sitting in his father's easy chair, with a leg crossed over a knee, revealed a black silk sock held up by a garter. He was reciting a colorful joke to his sister and sister-in-law, attempting to buoy their spirits. A mixture of relatives, neighbors and friends of his father and mother, a few Brian had never seen before, filled every available chair and sofa in the house, with many standing in small groups of three and four, drinks in one hand, a smoking cigar or cigarette in the other.

Dressed in a lavender shirt with French cuffs, narrow silk tie, brown pegged pants from the Snappy Men's Shop and buffed Scotch grain wingtips, Brian wandered from room to room.

Stopping by his Uncle Harry's chair, he listened to Mr. Urtz, a Scotch plaid bow tie bobbing up and down at his Adam's apple, pontificate on the future of television, spaceships, and flying saucers to an unenthusiastic audience.

"My point being," he lectured, "that in the not-too-distant future the inhabitants of far flung planets in our solar system will also be listening to *Howdy Doody, Kukla, Fran and Ollie* and numerous other educational presentations on their television sets. Oh yes indeed, every man, woman and child will have a television. Why, youngsters will scamper about the playgrounds with miniature televisions strapped to their wrists, just like

Dick Tracy." At his side, Mrs. Urtz patted his hand, smiling, proud of her *man of science*, her *visionary*.

"Indeed, space ships will shuttle back and forth to distant planets with all manner of electrical appliances: TVs, toasters, vacuum cleaners, refrigerators, all invented and manufactured by my company, not twenty miles from where we sit," Urtz said.

After a bit of throat clearing, a tug at his shirt collar, he waved his pipe like a baton, "And what every owner of every television set will need to enhance television broadcasts is a rooftop *antenna*," he said with arched eyebrows and a quick puff on his pipe. "And you, my friends and neighbors, will be pleased, no… elated to know that I have invented a technologically superior antenna with a remote control slated for production as soon as funding is consummated. A prototype of the Urtz Genie antenna is affixed to the roof of this very house.

"For a minimum investment, of $1,000, you and your loved ones can get in on the ground floor of the *Urtz Genie Antenna Company*. This paltry investment secures 100 shares of preferred stock at $10.00 par value."

Fingernails were inspected, cigarettes lighted, ties loosened, but not a soul stirred, or question asked.

Uncle Harry looked up at Brian, rolled his eyes and winked. On his Uncle's lips Brian deciphered the words – *Nut Boy*.

The dining room table was overflowing with bottles of liquor, quarts of beer, platters of cold cuts, sliced bread, covered bowls, salads, pans of cornbread, baked beans, pies, muffins, all prepared by the women. Early that morning, to Brian's surprise, a beer truck had pulled into the driveway. Two uniformed men began carrying cases of quart beer from the local brewery, owned by the O'Conner family, up the front stairs to be stacked against the dining room wall. As quickly and anonymously as the men appeared they vanished with equal discretion.

Making his way into the kitchen he saw Dinny Healy serenading Auntie, at the kitchen table, with a Celtic dirge on his fiddle, while brother Eamon accompanied on flute. The elder members of the conclave sang the refrain to Healy's rendition of *Sliabh Gallion Braes*. Ending the piece with a flourish, Dinny smiled, bowed at the waist and shot his cuffs to encourage more applause and laughter from his appreciative, albeit, captive audience. Speedily, the Healys soft-shoed into the dining room to "wet their whistles."

Even here in the kitchen, men and women stood shoulder-to-shoulder or perched on the folding chairs Brian had stacked earlier near the back door. Looking around, he wondered where all these people had come from.

Standing near the kitchen table he watched as Eamon Healy placed a paper plate containing a small mountain of a sandwich garnished with potato and macaroni salad in front of Auntie. His task completed, he pulled an equally generous sandwich from his coat pocket and pushed it into his cavernous mouth. An arm quickly encircled his waist when Brian stopped beside Auntie.

"How's me boyo?"

"Okay, but I don't know a lot of these people."

"Well now, many are from the old neighborhood, back when our people was downtown. You don't remember 'cause you was born in a hospital. Back then the women gave birth at home with the help of a midwife. Why, most of the folks couldn't afford a hospital, unless Uncle Dan sent the ward healer by with an envelope. When complications arose, Doctors would come to the house with their black bags to check on mother and child. Now it's all turned around. And many a *ceili* I enjoyed back in the old neighborhood. Why you should a seen the Healys back then. A lively pair they was, singin', dancin', playin' music all night. Give'em a sandwich and a pint, they'd go 'til the rooster crowed. Gad, they was a clever pair as you'd ever see."

He watched Auntie toy with her food, calling forth ghosts from the past. Her loquacity stimulated by whisky.

"And your mother's father, John, he married me sister, Bridey. He was at the funeral, but you ain't going to see him here. A German fella, he started running around with a waitress from the diner down the block from his boiler shop. Next thing ya know, Bridey's in a nursing home and he's living with the hussy. Shameless hussy she was. Your mother, grown up and out of the house, never spoke a word to her Pa again. Pity, a daughter should love her father, eh? Me poor Bridey, why she wasted away and died in that place."

Suddenly, a hand patted Brian's shoulder.

"How's the fisherman these days?" Benny growled. Turning to the men at his side, he announced loudly, "This kid caught the biggest goddamn bass I ever saw. Didn't ya?"

Turning, he looked at Benny, surprised to see he was at eye level with him. Benny was attired in a cashmere overcoat, a blue silk scarf draped around his neck, partially covering a French shirt collar with gold collar pin securing a blue tie with tiny red polka dots. His upper lip sported a pencil thin black mustache. Black curly hair streaked with gray was combed straight back. Benny pulled a fat cigar from his mouth.

"You and me and the old man, we'll go fishing this spring." Pausing, he whispered, "Down Below."

"Sure."

"And fer chrissake, don't listen to me about the shiners. Hey, whadda I know? You're the one caught the monster. Okay, I gotta get outta here. Go open the joint. Good dinner crowd tonight. See yuz," Benny called to his old pals.

He disappeared into the dining room to pay his condolences to Chick, who thanked Benny profusely, again, for the loan of his Chrysler.

Benny waved him off. "Hey, Chicky, what're friends for, huh. Listen, you get squared away, you and the kiddo come down to the joint for dinner."

Buttoning his cashmere coat, he poked the cigar in his teeth and turned to the front stairs.

The door to the stairwell opened as he approached. Stepping in, gray fedora casting a shadow on a swarthy face, was none other than Dan O'Conner himself. He stopped briefly to shake Benny's hand and say a few words to him.

"Surprised to see yuz here," Benny quipped.

O'Conner's eyes surveyed the room; momentarily he looked back at the dapper restaurateur and gambler.

"I never miss a wake or a clambake."

O'Conner caught sight of Chick and began moving toward him through a coterie of cronies and ward chums, eventually reaching him at the dining room table. Along the way he took note of the stack of beer cases against the wall.

Drawing Chick aside he accepted a highball from Chick's sister Peg, a grade school classmate of O'Conner.

"I was saddened to learn of Rita's demise. Never realized the seriousness, nor the severity of the operations. Gawd bless us and forgive us, I hope we never have to endure that indignity."

"It was hell watching her break down the last few years. She wasn't herself," Chick commented.

"You want time off? Go see the Police Chief. I'll put in a good word for you," O'Conner said with a wink. "Now, you'll have to excuse me while I do some mingling."

Before taking two steps toward the kitchen, his favorite political venue, he found himself surrounded by old friends, even a brazen partisan with his hand out, a tale of woe tumbling from his lips. Sipping his high ball, Chick watched O'Conner being inundated.

Momentarily, the hulking black and red clad figure of Monsignor McGinty, with a broad smile and unruly shock of white hair sweeping his forehead, came bounding into the dining room from the stairwell, his boots hammering the hardwood floor. Heads immediately turned in his direction. Chick greeted him before he could take a dozen steps, thanking him for all the courtesies and obsequies at the requiem mass and graveside service, never mind his presence at Rita's deathbed.

Shaking one hand, McGinty clasped Chick on the shoulder with the other. "Why twas an honor, a privilege and honor. Say no more, say no more. How's the young basketball star taking it? None too well I'd wager."

"He's a hard read, Monsignor, he gets so quiet at times. Just never know what he's thinking."

"Losing a mother is as tough as they come. What am I talking about? It wasn't that many years ago your own sweet mother passed on. A saint if ever there was one."

"Let me fix you a drink, Monsignor."

"A wee dram would be appreciated."

Across the room Dan O'Conner saw the gleaming white pate of the Monsignor sticking up above all those surrounding him and began a circuitous path in his direction.

"For crying-out-loud, if it ain't me old friend the lumberjack. How are ya, Monsignor?"

"Hunky Dory. And you?"

"Tip top. In the pink, as they say."

The two men touched their glasses and sipped their drinks.

"Mud in your eye," McGinty said sipping his whiskey and water.

"No offense intended, your eminence, but I thought you looked a bit peaked at the cemetery," O'Conner quipped with a sly grin.

"Dano, me pal. If you're that concerned with me health and welfare stop by Saint James at six a.m., Monday through Friday, and you'll see living proof of what a life of solitude, celibacy and prayer can do for a man's constitution," McGinty said.

"I'll do just that, I will, if you don't give me the stink eye if I'm a wee bit late. Better yet, why don't you come down to the Elks Club some Thursday night and be my dinner guest? It's always a pleasure to see a man like yourself shovel down the meat and potatoes like you was still chopping down trees in the Northwoods."

Seizing the opportunity, McGinty made a fist and flexed his right bicep. "Feel that muscle, if you will, Danny. Strong as a man half me age. Why, come now, let's arm wrestle. We'll see who's in tiptop shape."

Smiling, O'Conner held up a cautionary hand. "Now your eminence, it wouldn't do to put a strain on the old ticker, would it?"

"Now yer talkin' Danny boy, now your talkin' turkey. Wouldn't want to see an old fella, *like yerself*, overdo it. But think about it, Dano, your old pal the Monsignor, Johnny-on-the-spot with the last rites and prayers for the repose of the soul."

As they bantered back and forth, pausing occasionally to quaff their drinks, the lively sound of fiddle and flute issued from the kitchen.

"Now then, what's this I hear you've been after the Bishop to have Irish taught in the Catholic schools?" McGinty inquired.

"That I have. It's long overdue, long overdue. Here's the way I doped it out to his holiness. For one thing, most of the nuns teaching in the schools were born and bred in Ireland, and many's the one who got birched for speakin' their native tongue. Twas the English outlawed it, ya know. It ain't no crime to speak your own language, is it? Now *that* was a sin, my friend. Just look about the room, why there's but a handful of us who can sing an Irish ditty, say hello, thank the good Lord in our own language. It's a shame is what it is," O'Conner said.

"Easy now, Danny, easy does it, fella. I know for fact it was debated at a recent College of Cardinals in Rome. Heard it from Spellman himself, him with his own television show. And a hot potato it was, is what

I heard. The Eyetalians wanting their language taught and the Polacks wanting theirs, even the Swedes piped up. Well, Danny, can ya see the way it is? Everybody wants their native tongue taught in the catholic schools. Mind you Dan, what we've got is a Heinz 57 mix of kids. The hell of it is the kids could care less. All they want to do is jitterbug, go to the movies, run wild."

"Years ago is when we should a done it, by Gawd," O'Conner spat.

"That's the truth of it. Now, here's what I'm tinkin' Danny boy, we get the Jesuits in the colleges to offer it was an elective, eh? Why you wouldn't believe what they teach the kids in college these days: finger painting, hieroglyphics, makin' pots and pans, for God's sake. I hear by way of the grapevine they're going to teach the kids to talk to gorillas or monkeys using sign language no less. God as my witness. Now, don't go frowning Danny, think about it. Wasn't it Saint Francis himself hobnobbed with the birds and bees? Sure it was. Why next thing ya know, you'll see good Catholic boys and girls speaking Hebrew, eatin' kosher. For Gawd sake! It comes to that, I'm heading back to the woods, up at dawn, a plate of bacon and eggs, a gallon'a coffee and turn me loose in the forest with an axe."

"Yeah, yeah, yeah…," O'Conner muttered, his free hand brushing across his mouth. "It ain't like the old neighborhoods downtown. Years ago, like Maggie Duffy sez, the Irish had their place, the Italians had theirs, the Polacks theirs, the Jews theirs. You hit the nail on the head Billy, today why it's all Heinz 57. Sure, and next month I'll see you celebrating mass in a synagogue," O'Conner chuckled.

"Well now, I'll wager the collection baskets would be a lot heavier than down at Saint James," McGinty said with a nod of the head and raised eyebrows.

While O'Conner quibbled, Monsignor McGinty's firm hand patted his shoulder. Dan looked him in the eye.

"Billy, Billy, was it that long ago me own ma and pa come over to Canada on a coffin ship with the spoiled food, disease, no fresh water, packed in the hold without facilities? The sick and the dying entombed in their own filth? Oh, the stench of it, the wickedness. Why I'll wager there's more Irish bones at the bottom of the Saint Lawrence than in Calvary Cemetery, but I'll not venture farther down that path. For cripes sake, Pa diggin' the Erie canal, Ma cookin' and cleanin' for them that had. I, Billy me pal, coffin ships, the Irish language, all but forgotten. Why not talk to the monkeys and apes is what I'm thinkin'? Maybe they'll listen. The devil of it is, will they vote democratic, I ask ya?" He concluded with a smile.

O'Conner swallowed the rest of his drink and lighted another Camel. He fixed his eye on the Monsignor.

"Yer onto somethin' Billy, yup, always one step ahead of the hoi polloi."

"The next thing ya know, I'll be sayin' the mass in English and Latin will be a thing of the past," added McGinty.

"And good riddance, too."

"Hold yer tongue, Dano, that's blasphemy. Heresy is what it is. Why, we used to flay old sinners like yourself for less."

The music from the kitchen getting louder, Dan O'Conner cocked his ear. "Excuse me, Monsignor, but I've got to shake a few hands, pat a few backs."

With that he began a steady, though oblique meander toward the wellspring of the music.

The sleeves of his white shirt rolled up, tie loose at the neck, suspenders supporting baggy gabardine pants, O'Conner looked into the kitchen from the hallway. Dinny Healy, sawing away on his fiddle, jigged in place while his twin filled the room with a raucous ballad on the flute, all to the toe-tapping, handclapping of the men and women crowded in the kitchen.

Venturing into the din of the smoke-filled kitchen, O'Conner saw his old girlfriend and spurned fiancée, Margaret Duffy, seated at the table awash with half-full glasses of beer, jiggers of whisky and overflowing ashtrays. Auntie was smiling and clapping her hands to the music, the black pillbox hat cocked to one side of her head. Looking up and seeing O'Conner blocking the doorway, her hands clasped together and fell to her lap.

O'Conner stood there for a minute drawing deeply on his cigarette. Men and women opened a path as he made his way toward Auntie. A chair was vacated at his approach, allowing him to take a seat beside her. Auntie's eyes clung tenuously to the Healy twins.

O'Conner stubbed out his cigarette in an ashtray.

"Well now, Maggie, it's been a long, long time ain't it? They taking care of you down at City Hall are they?"

"They are and I thank ya for it."

"Don't mention it."

A strained silence was filled with the fiddle and flute, the clapping of hands.

Dan exhaled with a bit of a sigh.

"Can ya ever forgive and forget?"

"I don't think so, Dan. It just ain't in me."

"Would ya do me a favor then, Maggie, for old times sake?"

Auntie looked into his lined face.

"And what would that be?"

"Would ya do a bit of a dance with me while the boys are capering so?"

Without hesitation, she got to her feet, the colorful apron still covering a black dress. They stood facing each other, hands on hips, feet moving slowly, then gradually keeping pace with the music and clapping. Soon enough, they were in the center of the floor, everyone encircling them as they did their jig, smiling and laughing.

Brian, watching from the hallway, turned around and walked to his bedroom. Opening the door, he saw his Uncle Marty, VFW commander's hat still on, doing card tricks for his cousins Ray and Mike and his friend Bobby. Mike was in the act of pulling a card from the deck, looking at it, then replacing it. Ray was seated at Brian's desk thumbing through an old *Field and Stream* magazine. Brian took a seat on the bed between Mike and Bobby and watched his uncle shuffle the deck several times. Passing his hand slowly over the top of the deck he uttered some mumbo-jumbo then flipping over the top card, showed it to Mike, whose eyes widened in wonder at seeing the same card he had so recently pulled from the deck. Losing interest, Brian stood and ambled to the door while his Uncle ran the deck of cards up and down his outstretched arm.

Opening the door to his parents' bedroom, he was met with the indignant eyes of several women seated on folding chairs and on the bed, smoking and holding ashtrays or drinks on their knees. Suddenly, he realized his impertinence at disturbing the female gathering and withdrew, closing the door behind him.

Wandering into the living room again, he was stopped by the vice-like hand of Monsignor McGinty.

"How's the lad doing? Tell me now, its been rough sledding hasn't it?"

Relieved the hand had released its grip on his shoulder, Brian looked up at the Monsignor knowing he was obligated to tell the truth.

"Yessir, Monsignor."

"To be expected, you wouldn't be much of a man if it didn't bother you. I understand yer havin' a bit a trouble in school. *Obstreperous* is how one individual put it. Don't deny it. The nuns let me in on these things ya know. You'll be snapping out of it soon enough, won't ya?"

"Yes, Monsignor."

"That's the lad. Now about serving the mass, you can't get sloppy there. And if ya have anything, anything a'tall on yer mind, come to Mc-Ginty, we'll have a bit of a talk and things will be right as rain. Clear the air, get it off yer chest, eh? Mind now, keep yer hands to yerself when it comes to the girls. I remember the temptations, don't think I don't. Why when the vapors came over me, I'd grab me axe and chop down a few trees. That'll clear out the system, sure enough. No patty cake with the privates, now. Self denial, that's the ticket."

"Yessir."

"There ya go, keep the chin up, maybe an apology to Sister Monica for throwing her hydrangea out the window?"

"I will, Monsignor."

"Let bygones be bygones, I always say. Sure, a bit of a chat helps a fella calm his soul and mind. Come to the Monsignor any time."

"Yessir, I will."

"Now, a few words to your father and its back to the rectory, back to business. Mind what I told ya."

As the big man went off to find Chick, Brian breathed a sigh of relief. Out of nowhere his Uncle Marty was at his side, tapping his shoulder.

"Someone to see you down on the front porch."

Fearing the Monsignor had another lecture to share before departing, he shrugged and made his way haltingly down the stairs. Opening the front door he was both surprised and pleased to see Gina waiting there wrapped in a thick winter coat. Holding the door open, she joined him inside.

"I had to see you. I hope you're not mad."

"Listen, I'm sorry for the way I've been acting…"

"Don't apologize, I know it must be hard. Its just that I don't want you to be mad at me."

"Well, I guess I was mad at everyone. I can't explain it. None of this made any sense. Still doesn't."

Gina moved close to him. Her hand went up to his cheek. He could feel the heat from her breath on his neck as she laid her head on his shoulder.

He kissed her forehead.

With her lips pressed against his, the door at the top of the stairs was flung open. The clomp of heavy boots was heard descending.

They stepped out onto the porch to let the Monsignor pass.

"Well, there's the lad and it's the DeMelia girl, isn't it?"

"Yes, Monsignor."

"Remember Brian, if it's a talk ya want, I'm yer man."

"I will and thanks."

They watched McGinty march to his car.

"I've got to get home, but call me, please," Gina said, then pointed an index finger at him. "If you don't, I'm coming over to see you."

Brian walked her to the bottom on the front steps and said good night. At the end of the block, she turned and waved.

Mounting the steps again, he moved aside to let Dan O'Conner pass. Minutes later numerous men and women began drifting away.

~

"Get a load of that." McEvoy said when opening the backdoor.

Standing there motionless in his workman's garb, hands plunged in the pockets of his sheepskin coat, stood Johnny Russian.

The men and women in the kitchen, just seconds ago singing and clapping their hands in time to the Healy brothers' music, were now mute. As was the fiddle and flute.

Auntie approached the silent figure.

Brian was summoned to the back door. Johnny declined the invitation to enter the warmth and camaraderie of the kitchen, so Brian stepped onto the back porch, pulling the door closed behind him. Opening his sheepskin overcoat, Johnny produced his favorite tumbler, the Galati roller. He held it out to Brian.

His hands clasping the feathery, nervous pigeon, he looked with great admiration at the man whose face remained half in the shadow of the porch light.

Brian stammered, "Are you sure you want me to have him?"

The giant nodded, yes.

"I'll put him in the coop with the Birmingham tumbler. Follow me."

With care and thoughtfulness, the gifted tumbler was secured in the coop with the Birmingham roller, who puffed out its chest and moved about the cage with new energy, something lacking during its months of solitude. Both tumblers strutted about their confined space eyeing each other with interest. Satisfied and getting to his feet, Brian was already making plans to improve the coop on the garage roof. Turning around, he was disappointed at not seeing Johnny Russian. Quickly looking over the porch railing, he saw a shadow pass below and turn into the driveway headed for the street.

After a thorough inspection of the mated pair of tumblers, he walked slowly to the back door. Opening it, he was greeted with the sounds of music, song, and laughter.

23

The Egg

Finally, the cold and chill relented. A temperate breeze brought warm, mild weather, signaling the approach of spring. Encouraged and energized, Brian relocated the tumblers to the coop on the garage roof. At last, released from the cramped cage on the back porch, the birds appeared to fill their lungs with great draughts of fragrant air, to move with revitalized strength. Encouraged, they began to fly again, to soar above the earth and perform their magnificent acrobatics. While the Birmingham Roller nested, the Galati tumbler strutted about, preening and flexing its wings. One morning, while performing the feeding, watering and cleaning chores, Brian was dumbfounded to discover an egg in the nest of the Birmingham hen, the first he'd ever seen. Immediately, visions of a long and prolific line of tumblers, perhaps a dynasty, issuing from the mated pair blossomed in his head. He would relay this information posthaste to Johnny Russian and enlist his advice, possibly his help, in caring for the squab when it hatched. Yes, yes, he scolded himself, there were a hundred details regarding the fledging of the squab needing Johnny's immediate attention. Why, Johnny had nurtured and trained these two rollers. Of course, his assistance would be invaluable. No time to waste. How he would carry out a successful dialogue with Johnny regarding the urgency of the matter remained to be seen. With no one to help resolve the dilemma, he decided to bolt to the rest home, where, in some manner, he would persuade Johnny to return with him to his garage coop. Once there, he felt sure Johnny would instantly see into the heart of the matter. Sizing up the situation, he would in some way communicate to Brian the most prudent course of action. His plan decided, Brian climbed down from the rooftop and made his way speedily to the Jews yard in search of Johnny.

Breathless, he stopped at the back porch of the rest home. Sol Horowitz was slumped in his wheelchair, a cigar clutched in the fingers of one hand, the free hand massaging his balding head. Mr. Horowitz would know Johnny's whereabouts, Brian guessed. On the steps of the porch, Brian stopped. Horowitz stared down, trance-like, at the tips of his battered slippers, the cigar going cold in his hand.

Excitedly, Brian burst out, "Where's Johnny, Mr. Horowitz? Where's he at? I've got great news."

Downcast and mute, Sol Horowitz flung his free hand out in the direction of the barn. With eyes narrowing, Brian's head snapped around to see a pickup truck, it's tailgate down, a half-dozen cardboard boxes arranged in the bed. Next to one of the boxes were Johnny's battered work boots. Brian looked back at Sol, his face screwed up, uncomprehending.

Brian moved closer to the man in the wheelchair. "Is he going someplace, or what?"

Horowitz looked at the unlighted cigar in his hand. With a growl, he flung it into the driveway. "He's gone, my boy." Shrugging his narrow shoulders, he repeated, "He's gone."

The screen door opened, allowing Mr. Rubenstein to exit with a large box in his hands. He stopped short when seeing Brian on the porch. Setting the box aside, he approached the boy. Together, they walked down the steps onto the gravel drive.

"Harriet, my darlink, come get me, already," Sol wailed.

Momentarily, Mr. Rubenstein informed Brian that Johnny Russian had died in his sleep. Bereft and bewildered, Brian began backing away from the man, then spun around and broke into a run that ended at his rooftop pigeon coop. Ringing his hands, he stared first at the strutting Galati roller, then his eyes came to rest on the nesting hen.

His shoulders sagged; his hands went limp. Yes, there would be a long line of superior tumblers. Johnny Russian had planned it. These were his two finest tumblers and they would produce champion offspring. Smiling, Brian entered the coop to do his chores.

24

Epilogue

Fourteen years later, Brian and his father stood beside Margaret Duffy's open grave in Calvary Cemetery. His cousins Mike and Ray and his longtime friend Bobby McNally stood silently beside him, as did aunts and uncles. Only a few feet away was the small marble stone marking his mother's gravesite. The chill damp February weather reminded him of the day they'd lowered his mother's casket into the ground. Back then, he'd fully expected a miracle; a priest would leap from a speeding automobile to announce that a mistake had been made. Rita Reilly was not to join her heavenly host, after all. With that, she would appear at his side, smiling, a healthy, happy woman. It had taken him many years of anguish, guilt, and self-recrimination before he'd reached a tenuous acceptance of her passing.

Auntie's only known surviving kin, Brian and his father, looked at the handful of mourners, two of whom were nuns from the nursing home where she had lived out the final years of her life.

A white-haired priest, an inferior substitute for the gregarious Mc-Ginty, also deceased, recited obsequies by rote and none too slowly.

Hearing his cousin Ray whispering, Brian turned to see a long black Buick pull up and stop behind the empty hearse. A rear door was flung open. Emerging slowly from within was a man perhaps eighty years old. He adjusted the collar of a heavy topcoat and pulled the brim of a fedora low on his forehead. With the assistance of his driver, he moved forward slowly, flowers cradled in his right arm.

Brian looked at his father.

"That's Dan O'Conner," Chick whispered. "Auntie's old boyfriend.

Ah, yes, Brian's mind's eye pictured the white-haired man joshing with Monsignor McGinty at Rita's wake.

The prayers ended. The mourners began their exodus, some tipping their hats to the priest or to Dan O'Conner, a few making quick, awkward salutes to Chick.

While walking back to the car, Brian glanced over his shoulder to see O'Conner press an envelope into the hand of the priest, who nodded submissively before slipping it into a coat pocket.